Will's War

About the Author

For Lynn, the Civil War began in Franklin, Tennessee, where an exhibit of letters from Union and Confederate soldiers covered a wall of the small battlefield museum. After reading the letters, she realized how similar they all were. And why wouldn't they be? These soldiers had once been part of the same country, sharing history, language and culture.

Why did this war have to happen? This question haunted Lynn and led her to spend nine years studying the Civil War. It also led her to write *Will's War*.

Lynn lives in New York, but part of her heart lives in Virginia.

Will's War

Lynn Lowin

The author may be contacted at lynnlowinwrites@gmail.com.

Front cover image adapted from Library of Congress, Prints & Photographs Division, photograph by Carol M. Highsmith, LC-DIG-highsm-14288. Back cover adapted from "Map of Route of The Army of the Valley from Franklin, Pendleton Co., Va., May 15th, 1862, to the Battle of Winchester, May 25th, 1862, and the Pursuit of the Enemy, by Jed. Hotchkiss, Act. Top. Eng. V.D., 1863," in Clement A. Evans, editor, *Confederate Military History*, Volume 3, Confederate Publishing Company, Atlanta, Georgia, 1899, p. 240.

Cover and book editing and design by Sarah E. Mitchell, VintageDesigns.com.

Acknowledgments

To my husband who was always there for me . . .

To my dear children who endured an obsessed mother . . .

To my sister, cousins and friends who fed, housed and generally nurtured me . . .

To the scholars, professors and librarians who answered question after question . . .

To the rangers in our national parks who shared their information . . .

To my editor who was always there to help . . .

And to so many Virginians who willingly gave their expertise, guidance and, most of all, their stories.

Thank you all.

Prologue

I was in a war.
You call it the Civil War.
I call it My War.
I was 13 when I traveled back to 1861.
I'm 17 now and the War is over.
It ended for you years ago.
It ended for me in the 21st century.
I'm Will.
This is my story.

Chapter 1

Will kicked a faded blue textbook and grumbled out loud. He grumbled a lot these days. His school. The new school as he still called it. And if school wasn't enough, here he was dragging books down from the attic, the very same books he dragged up to the attic when they moved here last year.

He told his mother that nobody bought books anymore, especially not from a library sale. She said that people did still read. "But they read online," Will tried to explain, knowing it was futile. No one under eighteen can convince old people of anything.

Will lifted a huge book, thinking it was big enough to be a weapon. He turned to the first page where rows of bayonets were pointing straight to the sky. "For all I know, maybe it is a weapon," he thought. "Or was. Maybe that's what I need to survive at school . . . a bayonet!"

He put the book on top of a pile of books, picked them all up, and began to climb down the stairs. Suddenly, he tripped. As he tumbled, he felt as if he was watching himself fall, but couldn't figure out how to stop.

He landed with a thud.

"What you doing here?"

"Are you talking to me?" Will looked at the strange-looking man standing in front of him.

"No one else but you right here, 'cept for them." He pointed to a group of African-Americans working in the fields nearby. "What you doing in the middle of the wheat field?"

Will stood up a bit shakily. "Oh, so that's what this fuzzy yellowish stuff is . . . wheat. I never saw wheat growing before. You know how it is. You take out a loaf of bread and it's all wrapped up in a cellophane bag."

"What you talking about? Did you hit your head? You seem a little confused and you talk funny. Where are your people?"

"That's a good question." Will thought for a moment. He remembered falling down the attic stairs and a big book and bayonets. Somehow, he didn't think the man in front of him would be sympathetic.

"Well? Think harder, boy."

Will thought harder. "I remember the book now. It was *The American Heritage Picture History of The Civil War* by a man named Bruce Catton. The first page had bayonets pointing up to the sky."

2

"Never heard of a civil war. Where is your home?"

Another good question.

Will stared at the man.

"Maybe you better go on up to the house," the man suggested in a nicer tone.

"What house?"

"That house over there. Willows."

Will looked and saw more fields and a mountain range in the distance. The man pointed and Will turned his head slightly to see a house made of some kind of stone with steps leading up to a porch that was surrounded by tall white columns. There seemed to be a circular driveway in front of it, only it didn't look like any driveway he had ever seen. Actually, the house looked very old, like something he'd seen before in a picture book or a movie.

"Where are the cars parked? Are they out back?"

"What you talking about?"

"What did they do with the cars?"

"The cars? There ain't no railroad here. You want to ride them railroad cars, go on over to Strasburg."

Will looked around and pointed. "Why is smoke coming out of that building over there? Is there a fire?"

The man shook his head. "That's the smokehouse. In a smokehouse, there is smoke."

"What's it for?"

"What do you mean, what's it for? The smokehouse is where we preserve meat. And if you're gonna ask, the ice house stores ice and the springhouse keeps food cool. What kind of place do you live in? How you do you preserve your meat? How do you get ice and water?"

Will decided that a discussion of refrigeration and freezers would not be productive. "Only kidding."

"You are a strange one," said the man, "and I ain't got time for you."

Maybe this is a dream, Will thought, pinching himself. It hurt. "I guess it's not a dream," he said aloud.

"No, this ain't a dream. War's about to happen here and I'll be off fighting soon. Them slaves will be gone whatever Mr. and Mrs. Mitchell think. 'Specially, Mrs. Mitchell. She thinks them all love the Mitchells but what can you expect from a tender-hearted lady like that. Ladies are too gentle for this world, sometimes I think."

Remembering the girls in his class and his sister, Rebecca, not to mention his Mother, Will shook his head. "That's not been my experience."

4

"Well, boy, you ain't had muc. experience now, have you? How old are you anyways?"

"Thirteen."

"So you're Edward's friend?"

"No."

"You're too young for Joseph and too old for Benjamin, so who are you here to visit?"

"Actually, I'm not here to visit."

"So, why are you here?"

"That's a good question."

"I don't have time for this; I've got to get back to work and they," he said, pointing to the field hands, "work better when I am with them."

"Just one question before I meet the family. Where are we?"

"You don't know where you are, boy? Where do you think you are? In New York City?" The man laughed uproariously, although Will couldn't imagine what was so funny.

"No, not New York. Connecticut. I think that's where I live."

"Connecticut? You're a right one for making jokes. Well, we have no Yankees here anymore and soon we'll all be off fighting in the war."

"What war?"

"The War of Independence, of course."

"Is this 1775?"

5

ıre scaring me. Is you touched

ıink so."

as the Revolution. Ain't you had
α.   ıg? And now, 1861 will be the new
Revoluɪᴄ n, 'cause our Confederate States of
America will fight for the same reasons we
fought back in 1775."

"What reasons are those?"

"To stay true to the Constitution. To let
each state make its own decisions. To
preserve our way of life which them
Northerners want to destroy."

Will felt the earth shift underneath him.
"Umm . . . where exactly am I?"

"You're in the Shenandoah Valley of
Virginia, the best place on earth for growing
food. Why, we can feed all of Virginia with
what we grow!"

"And, uh, what year is this exactly?"

"It is the year of our Lord, 1861. And it's
April 16th and it's a Tuesday. Anything else?
And now," he added more kindly, "maybe
you better get on up to the house. They'll
help you. Mrs. Mitchell helps everyone and
Mr. Tom's wife, Mary, is a good lady, too."

"Who are these Mitchells?"

"If you don't know that, what are you
doing here? This is their plantation."

"Plantation?"

"Not big like them tobacco ones along the James River, but big enough for here. Now go on and git. I've got to get back to work or I'll be in a heap of trouble."

Will thought about his options. Basically, there were none. The man was watching him, so he headed toward the house. Besides, where else could he go? He had no idea how to get back to Connecticut.

The sun was high in the sky so he figured it must be around noon. As he climbed the stairs, he took a deep breath. "I can do this." He looked for a bell to ring and, finding none, knocked on the door.

A dark-skinned woman answered and invited him in. "The family is having their dinner. I'll take you in to join them."

"Well, wait a minute. I can't just crash a meal with complete strangers."

"Is you hungry?"

"Yes, I am."

"Then that's all right. The missus is used to feeding all sorts of family."

"I'm not . . . " he began, but it was too late. She had ushered him inside the dining room.

"Well, hello and welcome."

He looked up at the voice and smiled tentatively. "I'm William Bradford, but everyone calls me Will. I, ah, am sorry to bother all of you at this time. I was just a bit

7

lost and I thought, or rather the man in the field thought, you could help me."

"You must mean Jim, our overseer. I'm Mrs. Mitchell and this is my family," a pleasant looking woman smiled at him as she gestured to everyone around the table. "Please join us for dinner, but, Edward, first show our guest to the water pump so he can wash."

Will looked down at his clothes. To his surprise, he saw that he was no longer wearing his usual jeans and t-shirt.

Edward, a tall boy with dark hair, got up from his seat and said, "Follow me." Will guessed that Edward was probably close to him in age, maybe a little younger. "I am kind of dirty," admitted Will. "I'm not usually this way. It must be from my travels."

Edward gave him a curious look, but Will said nothing further.

They walked over to the kitchen, which was located in a separate small building behind the house. As they approached the kitchen's door, Will saw the water pump. He hoped he could figure out how to use it.

He began to pump and, to his surprise, water flowed out easily. "Wow! This is cool."

"Cool? What did you expect? Water that's hot?" Edward laughed and Will joined in uncertainly as he washed his hands and face.

"Here you are, tired and hungry, but can you just sit down and eat? No, not with my Mamma," Edward went on. "No matter what, you have to wash yourself. Always washing; that's my Mother. What about yours?"

"Uh, yes, she believes in hygiene."

"So, where are you from," Edward asked as they walked back to the house.

Remembering the overseer's response, Will decided to try another answer. "Outside of the Valley," he said firmly, which was strictly true, of course, since Connecticut was definitely not in the Shenandoah Valley.

Edward just nodded. This, apparently, was a more satisfactory answer. He must remember it for the future, although it was unclear what the future might bring. "I must remember to think before I speak," he thought to himself, then asked, "What's going on around here?"

"Besides all the states seceding? All except us here in Virginia, that is, but I know that's going to change. It has to."

"Why?"

"We can't just sit around and watch, can we? What kind of men would we be to let other states fight for us?"

"Fight?"

"Well, there's going to be war, isn't there?"

"When," Will asked before he remembered that this was April of 1861.

"We're not sure. Tom joined a militia company and so did Joseph, but Robs says all these companies will end up in the regular Army. Robs went to West Point so he knows a lot about these things. So does our President, doesn't he?"

Will didn't know how to respond. As far as he knew, there were no militia companies anymore; at least, none that he knew about. But Edward seemed to be expecting an answer. "The President knows a lot of things."

"You're so right. President Jefferson Davis surely sounds a lot better than President Abraham Lincoln."

Will was surprised. He had always liked Abraham Lincoln, when he thought about him, that is. However, Edward didn't seem to expect an answer and the boys just continued walking.

"Please sit," Mrs. Mitchell said with a smile as they came back into the dining room. "Nellie, get this young man a plate. I'm sure he's hungry."

"Where are you from?"

"Who are you visiting?"

"Have the men in your family enlisted yet?"

"Children, please. Enough. Where are your manners? Leave Will alone and let us introduce him to the family," said Mr. Mitchell firmly. "Tom is our eldest and a great help to me here at Willows. Of course he wasn't always so helpful. Why, when he first came home from the University of Virginia, he . . ."

"Father, please. That was a long time ago."

"Almost two years. Well, anyway, now he is my right-hand man. Next to him is his wife, Mary."

"Hello," said a young woman with light brown hair and a sweet smile.

"And I'm Jane," interrupted a dark - haired girl with a decidedly determined look on her face. "I am going to the Comstock Female Academy one day and I will study French and music and mathematics."

Edward hooted, "Mathematics? You?"

Benjamin immediately stood up and chanted:

"Boys go to school to learn how to rule
Girls go to Jupiter to get more stupider."

11

Jane stood up trembling, her dark eyes flashing, and her face red with anger. "Benjamin, I am going to . . . ."

"Enough. We are at dinner and we have a guest. I want peace and quiet here and now," Mr. Mitchell said sternly.

Jane sat down, muttering to herself. Will looked at her face and decided he wouldn't like to have her for an enemy.

"Do girls usually go away to school," he asked Jane.

"Yes, but I have to be older before I can go," she explained sadly. "Before Mary married Tom, she studied at the Comstock Female Academy and she told me all about it."

"Before you are old enough to go away to school, Jane," Mrs. Mitchell reminded her daughter, "you need to learn more. Be sure to remember to study your geography today. Miss Agnes will be coming and she said your geography is weak."

Jane turned to Will and said, "Miss Agnes teaches us here at home. Edward used to go to the village to the schoolhouse, but the schoolmaster quit because he was a Northerner and he had to go back home. Now Edward is learning Latin from Miss Agnes and Benjamin is learning to read. Tom and Mary have a new baby, and they live here with us. Baby Tommy is upstairs with Betsy. Father was going to build them a house, but what with war coming, he says . . . ."

"Jane," her mother interrupted. "I am sure Will does not want to hear all this."

"Is Betsy your sister," asked Will quickly, in the hope of averting another argument.

"No. She's one of the servants. Actually," Jane went on, "she's just a little older than me . . . "

"Than I," corrected her mother.

"Than I, but Mary says she's very good with Baby Tommy."

"Enough," called out Edward. "Next in line would have been Robs if Jane hadn't interrupted. She always interrupts everyone."

"Do not."

"Do too."

Jane glared at her brother.

"Anyway, to continue before we are interrupted again," Edward went on, "Robs goes after Tom, but he's up at the Ferry now and after him comes Joseph, but he's at the University of Virginia."

"The Ferry?"

"That's Harpers Ferry where Robs went to join Colonel Thomas Jackson. Robs is helping to train the volunteers there."

Will remembered learning about Harpers Ferry and an abolitionist named John Brown who attacked the arsenal because he wanted to free all the slaves. That had to have been before this year, though. He wished he had paid a little more attention in history class. Of course, he never imagined that history would become so important to him, but, actually, right now it wasn't history anymore. It seemed to be real life.

"Then there's me. I'm after Joseph but obviously before Jane."

Again Jane glared at her brother.

"Next is Jane and, after her, Benjamin. Sarah and Henry are the youngest and they have their meals in the nursery."

Will stopped struggling to remember the story of Harpers Ferry and focused on what Edward was saying. Benjamin looked like he was around six or seven years old and Jane was somewhere between him and Edward. Maybe ten or eleven; it was hard to tell with girls.

Jane frowned. "You know, Father, Sarah really wants to come down and have dinner with us."

"How do you know this, Jane?"

"I know everything."

"The sad truth is that she does," agreed Tom.

"Does not," chorused Edward and Benjamin.

Mr. Mitchell did not like his dinner disturbed. "All right, all right. Cook made a wonderful meal, so let's do it justice."

Dinner was very pleasant, although why it was called dinner was a mystery to Will. "In the middle of the day we eat lunch, not dinner. But it's really good food whatever they want to call it," he thought as he ate happily.

"So, Will," asked Mr. Mitchell, "Where is your family?"

The question he was dreading. "My family?"

"Yes, where are they?"

"My mother is home and my father, uh, kind of left us." There, he said it. He never talked about it to anyone, but now in this strange situation, the truth seemed best.

"Oh . . . that's too bad." Mr. Mitchell coughed, looked uncomfortable and turned to his wife. "Elizabeth, dear, this is a very fine meal, and I am sure Nellie will serve an excellent dessert next. Will, just wait until you taste it."

"I wonder how Robs is today," asked Jane.

"We received a letter from him only a few days ago," answered Mrs. Mitchell, turning to Will. "As Edward mentioned, Robs is our second oldest son. He went to West Point until the North elected that Black Republican and decided to attack us."

Will was confused. "Black Republican?"

"Abraham Lincoln, of course. I'm sure you must have heard of him."

Will was quiet. He and Edward had just talked about Abraham Lincoln, but he never heard that he was African-American, and he certainly never heard that he attacked Virginia. He decided to risk speaking. "I didn't think he was black."

Everyone laughed. "That's just what we call him, silly," said Benjamin. "Don't your people say that?"

His people again. "They call him other things."

Again everyone laughed. Tom nodded and said, "Well, folks around here call him other things too."

Nellie came in with gingerbread that looked and smelled wonderful. Will ate heartily, and even accepted a second slice.

"Say, why don't you sleep here tonight?"

"Maybe Will has to go back home, Benjamin," Mrs. Mitchell said gently. "Will, would your mother worry if you stayed here?"

"She would worry more if I didn't," answered Will, thinking that his mother probably hadn't even noticed that he was gone yet. Since they moved to Connecticut she didn't notice much.

Everyone laughed again. "You sure have a way with words," said Edward. "I am only twelve, so I'm not enlisting now. I'm afraid that by the time I am old enough the war will be over. It's so unfair."

Will shook his head. "It may last longer than you think."

"I doubt it. Those Yankees can't fight."

"How do you know that? The Yankees were good fighters."

"Good fighters? Not true. They are shopkeepers, and what do shopkeepers know about shooting and hunting and living off the land?"

"Not all Yankees are shopkeepers. Besides, they had some really good generals at the end."

"The end of what? And how do you know so much about Yankees anyway," challenged Edward.

There it was. Another minefield. "You hear things," Will replied vaguely.

"Will is right," Tom said quietly. "We are hearing all sorts of things these days, few we should believe."

"Sometimes it's difficult to know what is truth and what is fiction," ventured Will.

Tom nodded. "You're right again. But it is true that we will go to war. We are just waiting for Virginia to secede."

"Maybe Virginia won't secede," Will answered, realizing how ridiculous he sounded as soon the words were out of his mouth. Virginia had been in the Civil War and he knew that.

"Yesterday, Lincoln called for 75,000 troops and there is no way that Virginia is going to fulfill her quota and contribute her men."

"Why not?"

"We will never fight against our sister Southern states."

Will looked at the faces around the dining room table, innocent faces completely unaware of the calamity that was about to overtake them. This war was going to bring death and devastation to the entire South and Will was suddenly desperate to stop it from happening. "Can't you just forget about all this?"

Tom shook his head. "We must fight, Will. We must defend our honor and our right to live as we choose. Remember Patrick Henry: 'Give me Liberty or give me Death.' He was a Virginian, too, you know."

"Why don't you stay a while," suggested Edward, "then you'll understand."

"What a good idea," agreed Jane. "We'll show you everything around here."

Will considered his choices. He could go back to the wheat field but the odds of figuring out how to get home from there were less than zero. He could wander around the countryside and get attacked for being a Yankee. Or else he could starve from lack of food. This Valley may be able to feed all of Virginia but without him having any idea how to turn crops into food he could eat, it sure couldn't feed him. On the other hand, he could stay with these nice people and eat good food and lots of it.

"Thank you. I would like to stay."

The day passed quickly and in the evening, after supper, which Will noticed, was more like lunch, Mrs. Mitchell said softly. "Will, do you want to write a letter to your mother?"

"I could text, I mean, I could write a letter with the text explaining where I am."

Mrs. Mitchell looked at him. "Will, is anything troubling you?"

"No, Mrs. Mitchell. Nothing at all." Will started to look through his pockets for his phone. "I must have lost it on the trip over here," he thought, "but there's no way it would work here anyway. I can't remember when cell phones were invented, but I sure know they didn't have them in 1861."

19

Will sat down and Mrs. Mitchell handed him a quill pen. He hoped he could figure out how to use it without getting ink all over himself. Of course, he wasn't used to writing by candlelight either. Somehow he managed to write a short letter to his mother:

Dear Mom,

I hope that you and Rebecca are well. I am staying with some very nice people in the Shenandoah Valley of Virginia. Please tell Mrs. Morris that I have chosen a topic and will present it as soon as I return.

Love,
Will

Jane looked over his shoulder. "Who is Mrs. Morris?"

His mother looked askance. "Jane, no lady ever reads another person's letters. It is rude and an invasion of their privacy. Please apologize to Will."

"I'm sorry, Will."

"That's okay. It's not much of a letter but, then, I'm not much of a writer. Mrs. Morris is my teacher."

"How come you're here if you're still supposed to be in school," asked Benjamin.

"I'll go back soon."

This seemed to satisfy Benjamin. Mary went over to the piano and sat down. As she played, the family gathered around and sang. "With no TV, I guess they have to sing. It's kind of cool in its way," thought Will.

"Come on, Will," said Edward when the singing ended and Mrs. Mitchell told everyone to go up to bed. "You'll stay with us in our room."

Chapter 2

As they got ready for bed, Will couldn't help but notice the way Benjamin was jumping around. "Hurry up, hurry up, you two. Mamma's coming and we've got to get to bed."

Will just stared at him. He never remembered being that eager to go to bed, not even when he was trying to play sick so he could get out of going to his miserable new school.

"Let's get into bed now before Mamma comes up to say good night," Benjamin repeated. "Remember, pretend to be asleep or almost asleep."

Before Will had a chance to ask why, Mrs. Mitchell came in and kissed her two sons goodnight.

"May I kiss you as well, Will? I know you must be missing your own mamma."

He nodded, thinking, "You don't know the half of it. If I can't find my way back, I hope I can stay here. On the other hand, there's going to be a fierce war here and I'm not even on your side. Or probably my ancestors would not have been, but for right now I guess I'm my own ancestor. That's weird."

When Mrs. Mitchell left, Benjamin quickly got out of bed. He opened the shutters and peeked outside. "Good, the moon and stars are bright. We'll be able to see."

"See what," Will asked.

"See the Yankees."

Yankees again. Against his better judgment, Will asked, "What Yankees?"

"The ones we're going to hunt."

"Shush," said Edward. "Get into bed and be quiet. Mamma could come back."

Benjamin climbed back into bed. "We're going to look for Yankees and kick them out of Virginia. Joseph thinks he's the only one who's going to fight Yankees but we're going to show him."

"Show him what?"

"Show him that he's not the only one who can fight Yankees. When Virginia secedes, he's going to enlist and he'll be off and fighting while we're stuck here," answered Edward. "So we're going to find us some Yankees and fight them before Joseph does."

Will couldn't think of anything to say.

"You're coming with us, right," Benjamin asked.

"Well . . ."

"Of course he's coming. Especially now that he knows our plan," Edward said in a slightly menacing voice. "Besides, why wouldn't Will want to come? We Southern men must stick together."

Before he was asked another question on where he came from, Will quickly said, "Of course I'm coming. Wouldn't miss it for the world. My shooting is a little rusty since I've not carried a gun in a while, but I'm coming."

That isn't exactly a lie, he thought. After all, I did shoot a rifle last summer in camp, didn't I? And what about all those video games I play?

"Father has muskets and we are going to sneak down and get them," said Benjamin, interrupting Will's thinking. "And he has enough powder so we can kill us a whole mess of Yankees."

Will sighed. Muskets and gunpowder. Of course, it's 1861. The only hope I have is that the Yankees will still be far away training in Washington, D.C., and none of them will be here.

Mrs. Mitchell did not come back, but the boys still waited. "You can't be too careful, when you're going to hunt for Yankees," Benjamin said seriously.

"Shush," his brother responded.

Finally, after what seemed to be hours, Edward decided it was time to go. Benjamin had fallen asleep, apparently worn out by all the excitement. "Too bad it didn't wear Edward out as well," Will thought.

Edward shook his brother. "Wake up; you can't fall asleep now."

"I'm not asleep. I'm just resting, so I'll be ready to fight."

"You were sleeping and we can't have that."

"Who made you the General?" Benjamin jumped out of bed, fists raised to fight his brother.

Will decided to intervene. "We can't fight among ourselves. We have to focus on the enemy."

"You're right." As both boys immediately responded, Will realized that he had lost the one advantage he might have had. If Edward and Benjamin fought each other, they might have forgotten about Yankees. Too late.

The boys dressed. "No shoes," said Edward. "They're too noisy."

"What do you think, we're Native Americans in the Old West?"

"What are you talking about," asked Benjamin. "Native who?"

"Forget it." Will looked down at his feet. Bare feet. Things keep getting worse and worse.

"All right, men, let's go." Edward led the way.

As they crept to the cabinet where the muskets were, Edward quietly opened the door.

"What are you doing?"

As the boys turned, Will's heart began beating very quickly.

It was Jane. "I caught you, all of you. I knew you were up to something, but I didn't know what it was."

Rallying, Edward said, "Get out of here. This is men's work. No girls."

"Oh, really? Well, then, where are the men? All I see are silly boys. I'm going to tell Mamma what you're doing. She'll tell Father and he'll be hopping mad. That'll end whatever you're doing with guns for good. Probably end you, too."

Edward thought about it. "Well, what do you want?"

"That's easy. I want to come too. Where are you going anyway?"

"We're going to shoot Yankees," piped up Benjamin, "and there's no room for girls."

"There is for this one unless, of course . . . ."

"All right, all right," Edward gave in. "You can come."

"But . . . ," Benjamin began.

"But nothing. If we want to succeed, we have to go now. If Mamma wakes up, it's all over. And she wakes up at the slightest noise. Father sleeps through anything, but we better get out of here and get out of here now."

Will saw the wisdom in this. He also remembered that at dinner Jane said she knew everything that goes on. Apparently, she did. Of course, he might not mind if Mrs. Mitchell stopped them. Maybe a little noise wouldn't hurt. "Hey!" he exclaimed.

"Quiet," everyone else said. "Do you want us to get caught?"

Duh.

Benjamin looked down at Jane's feet. "Take off your shoes."

"No."

"You have to." Edward scowled. "Let's just get out of here. The more time we lose, the more Yankees we lose."

They slipped out of the house quietly. "Should we take the horses," asked Benjamin.

"Of course not," his brother answered scornfully. "We need to go on foot because horses can be heard in the night."

They walked silently. "How are we going to find them if we don't know where they are," asked Benjamin.

Nobody answered.

Unaccustomed as he was to walking barefoot, Will's feet hurt. He looked over at the rest of his companions and saw that Jane, too, seemed uncomfortable. The boys seemed more accustomed to going barefoot.

"Ow," cried Jane. "I stepped on something."

"Probably a snake," answered Edward. "Maybe you should go back home."

"Good try, but I am prepared." She whipped out her shoes which she had been carrying, confident that Edward would never notice. Then Jane pulled out a pair of stockings and sat down on a stump to put her stockings and shoes on. "I can walk better and faster in shoes."

"No wonder there are no girls in the Army," grumbled Edward.

As Will followed, he wished again that he had been a better student in history class so that he might understand all of this. He looked around at his Southern friends and decided being with them was the best way to learn history. Although, it was a bit confusing.

"What's confusing," Jane asked.

Oh, no. He must have spoken aloud.

"Quiet," both boys commanded. "You'll wake the Yankee up if he's sleeping."

"You gonna shoot a sleeping man," challenged Will.

"No, of course not," Edward answered. "I'll just take him prisoner."

"And do what with him?"

"Take him home."

"That's a great plan," Will answered sarcastically. "I'm sure your father will welcome him."

"Look, are you in this or not? I'm tired of your complaints."

"I'm just trying to make you think about what you're doing here."

A noise startled them and Benjamin loaded his musket, fired and hit a squirrel.

"Great shooting," Will said, "If you're aiming for squirrels."

"Leave him alone," Edward said angrily, then turned to Benjamin and said, "What'd you do that for? Now you've warned any Yankees who might be around here."

Jane made a show of looking up, down, and left and right. "No Yankees. They're probably going to Harpers Ferry where Robs is. Or maybe they're heading over to Richmond."

"Why Richmond," Will asked.

"Because it is Virginia's capital, silly. A capital would be good to capture."

"I guess so. Say . . . I was wondering about something."

Edward stopped walking and looked upset in the moonlight. "Would the two of

29

you stop talking? We are not just playing around. This is serious. Yankees soldiers are coming to Virginia to attack us."

"But not today and not here," ventured Will.

"Go back home. You and Jane go. I don't need either of you."

Will thought about this. He was afraid Edward did need them, especially since Benjamin didn't have the best judgment in the world. Come to think of it, neither did Edward. And if they did get into any trouble, four people would be better than two.

"I want to stay. I'll be quiet."

Jane agreed. "I will be quiet, too."

They prowled around and passed by the creek.

"We can't go swimming now, right," asked Benjamin. "But it would be fun."

"We're not here for fun," Edward growled.

They heard the rustling of animals and they must have awakened some kind of bird, which angrily squawked at them. An owl hooted; a gray fox scurried by; and a raccoon family stared unblinkingly at them.

"I could shoot one of them," Benjamin offered.

Edward sighed heavily. "We don't want to make more noise than we already have. Remember? Even if there are no Yankees, we don't want to wake anyone up. All we need is . . ."

"Me?"

The four young people suddenly turned and saw Tom standing a few feet behind them, shouldering his musket. He didn't look very happy.

"What are you doing? I was fast asleep and I suddenly heard a shot coming from somewhere so I got out of bed — my warm bed, I may add — and I went searching. And what did I find? Idiots, and I'm related to three of them. What are you children doing?"

"I'm not a child," Edward said angrily.

"No? You could have fooled me!"

"We were hunting Yankees," Benjamin tried to explain. "And Edward said we had to be quiet so we can find them. And I thought I found them, but I shot a squirrel by mistake instead."

"Are you aware what would have happened if Mamma or Father woke up and found you missing? And what if you did find a Yankee? What were you going to do? Shoot him? Are you insane? Now, get back to the house, all of you. I would have thought that you, Jane, might have had a little bit more sense than your brothers. Will, I don't know you well enough, but what would your family think if they saw you now?"

Will frowned. "My family? They would probably think I had lost my mind if I told them this story."

"As would any sensible person."

"Are you going to tell Father," asked Benjamin plaintively.

"I don't know. What should I do with all of you? Take you as my prisoners, maybe."

Benjamin began to cry. "I don't want to be a prisoner."

"He's only saying that, Ben," Jane said soothingly. "Tom, we're sorry. It was a stupid idea."

"It was not," muttered Edward.

Tom spoke sternly to his younger brother. "Edward, you have no training as a soldier."

"Neither do you. You're a farmer. And neither does Joseph and he's enlisting and going in the Army."

Tom stopped walking and said, "You're right. I am a farmer and, until now, Joseph has been a student at the University of Virginia. So what is he doing? Not running in all directions with his musket. No, he is going to learn how to be a soldier. Robs wrote us from the Ferry and told us how hard he was working to help organize and drill the new recruits. He said they had to learn military discipline so they could fight well. War is not a game, Edward. It's deadly serious. People are injured and die in wartime."

"What about you, then? Why aren't you going," Edward challenged.

"I have a two-month-old baby and Father needs me on the farm. Don't you think I want to go? This war may be a very short one, although Robs seems to think it will last much longer. But if it's short, do you think I want to miss it? What will I tell my son when he is grown up? That his father stayed home to farm? He'll think he had a coward for a father. No, Edward, I will go. But my first obligation is to stay here right now through the summer harvest."

Edward looked sheepish. "I'm sorry, Tom. I am just so jealous of Joseph. I'm afraid that by the time I'm fourteen, the war will be over."

"You should only be that lucky," Will interjected.

Edward looked annoyed. "Why do you always say these ridiculous things? Don't you realize that our soldiers are tougher than any Union soldier that exists? And we have terrific officers, men who trained at Virginia Military Institute or West Point just like Robs did. Why are you always pessimistic when you really know nothing about us, not being from here? Say, where are you from anyway?"

That again. "What does it matter?"

"Maybe . . ."

"All right, enough," Tom said wearily. "Let's just go home."

"Are we prisoners," Benjamin asked.

"Only of your own conscience."

"What's that?"

"The voice inside you that tells you what's right and what's wrong."

"My voice is a little scared right now."

"It should have been scared a few hours ago. Come on, now. Move!"

* * *

"Why are you all so quiet? You all must be very sleepy this morning. Did something keep you up last night," Mrs. Mitchell asked, her face full of concern.

Edward looked down at his plate, Jane looked out the window, and Benjamin's lip trembled. Will thought that Benjamin was about to confess everything.

"Mamma," Tom spoke up suddenly, "don't you remember how I used to love to sleep when I was a boy? Surely you haven't forgotten the day I came home from the University and almost slept past dinner?"

"I remember that well," growled Mr. Mitchell. "Never have I seen anything like it."

"Boys just seem to get tired," Tom said vaguely.

Jane began to say something about girls getting tired as well, then thought better of it and said nothing.

Mrs. Mitchell nodded her head and then changed the subject. "I hope we get another letter from Robs today. One of us should go fetch the mail from town." Tom scowled and Will thought it must be hard for Tom to be the stay-at-home son.

"We'll get the mail when we go into town," answered her husband.

Will gulped as he suddenly thought of the letter he wrote to his mother. He hoped no one would remember that it had never been addressed or mailed. After all, what could he write for his address? Litchfield, Connecticut in the 21st century?

Fortunately, the mail was quickly forgotten and Tom looked over at his siblings. "When the three of you are finished with your lessons for today, I think that you will all be eager to help me as much as you can. I'm right, aren't I?"

"What about Will," asked Benjamin.

"I'll help all day, since I have no lessons," Will immediately volunteered.

"Isn't this nice?" Mrs. Mitchell beamed. "I know I can always count on you wonderful children."

There was some grumbling, particularly from Edward, but it was quiet grumbling and if Tom heard it, he was easily able to ignore the sound.

The day went by quickly, and Will was even more exhausted by the time supper came around. Even when he had played sports in school, he had not gotten this much exercise! A glance in a mirror had shown Will that his face was getting more freckled from all his time in the sun. He didn't have any suntan lotion to stop his pale skin from turning red, either.

Mrs. Mitchell looked at him with concern. "You look tired, Will."

"No, I'm not," he answered, then yawned. "Well, I guess I am a little bit. I'm not used to so much fresh air."

"Where do you live then? In a cave," called out Benjamin.

Everyone laughed, although Mrs. Mitchell said, "That's not nice, Benjamin."

After supper, the family filed into the parlor. It was growing dark, and Will automatically put his hand on the wall and groped for a light switch.

"What are you doing, Will," asked Jane. "Why are you touching the wall?"

"Just like to do that," Will answered, his mind racing furiously. "In my home we always touch the wall when we enter a room. It's for good luck."

"Oh. We don't do that here. I don't think they do that in Winchester either."

"It's an old family custom. Probably began with my great, great-grandfather who, ah, was a traveler and whenever he went to a new place, he needed luck so he could earn a living." Will was making up the story as fast as he could.

"What did he do?"

Will thought. "Everything imaginable. Yes, good old Gramps was quite a man. I remember him well."

"Wait a minute. You couldn't possibly have known your great, great-grandfather," Jane said reasonably.

"I knew stories about him. A lot of stories. My mother used to spend hours talking about him. And we have paintings of him. A lot of paintings. I see you have paintings of your relatives also. I'd be interested in hearing about some of them."

Jane looked up at the paintings of her ancestors and began to tell Will all about her family, just as he had hoped she would. Another minefield avoided. Good old Gramps could have been a bandit for all Will knew, since no one ever mentioned him, at

37

least not in his presence. He'd have to ask Rebecca if she knew anything about him. Just thinking about Rebecca suddenly made him a little sad. Not that he really missed her; he never even liked being with her, but he was used to her. It's kind of hard to suddenly have a new life, especially when that life is so old. He sighed.

"All right, Jane, enough," Edward said firmly. "Poor Will is probably bored to death listening to you."

"No, I'm not bored. Not too much anyway."

Once again, there was singing in the evening and before long, Mrs. Mitchell said, "It's time to get ready to go to bed. We rise early here and we all need our sleep, especially Will."

"Why Will," asked Benjamin.

"Because he is not yet used to our ways."

Benjamin turned to Will. "What time did you get up in the morning when you lived home?"

"About 7:00. School starts at 8:00 and I usually miss the bus so I have to walk."

"The bus?"

To his surprise, Jane answered. "His people speak a little differently. For example, I think bus must mean wagon and . . ."

Mrs. Mitchell intervened. "That's enough, Jane. Will is our guest and we do not criticize or even talk about the way he speaks. That's not polite."

"But . . . "

"No buts. I know how you like to begin long discussions to avoid going to bed. Not tonight, children. I am tired myself."

Mr. Mitchell looked concerned. "You are never tired, dear."

"Well, maybe I'm getting old."

"Never. You are as beautiful as the day when we married."

"But more tired. And more than a little worried. It is all this talk of war."

"Let's go to bed," Benjamin announced, "before they start getting lovey-dovey."

"They started already," said Jane as she began to walk up the stairs.

The next morning began as usual but, as the family was finishing breakfast, suddenly there were church bells ringing.

"It isn't Sunday; it's Thursday," called out Jane over the bedlam. "Why are the bells ringing?"

"Maybe Virginia seceded! I have to go to town to find out exactly what's going on," Mr. Mitchell said as he gulped his coffee down.

"I'm going with you," announced Tom amid a chorus of "Me, too." Sarah and Henry came down from the nursery with Betsy and baby Tommy, to see what was causing the excitement.

"All right, all of you settle down," said Mrs. Mitchell. "This is for grown-ups so let your father and I and Tom go together."

"We want to go, too," the older children shouted.

"It isn't only for grown-ups," Jane said gravely. "Joseph will enlist now and, if the war lasts long, so will Edward."

Benjamin jumped up and down. "I want to enlist too."

There were so many voices pleading that, finally, Mr. and Mrs. Mitchell decided that Edward, Jane, Benjamin and Will would go to town along with them and Tom, while Sarah and Henry would stay home.

"That's not fair," cried Sarah. "Jane gets everything and I get nothing."

Hearing his sister cry, Henry cried also and woke baby Tommy, who began to wail. Mary took him from Betsy and turned to Tom. "Be careful."

"I'm always careful and nothing is happening yet. Let's get going," he said, turning to the children, "There is still work to do on the farm, you know. Secession or no secession, the crops need tending."

Mr. Mitchell nodded. "That's my boy."

"What's going o[n]
Jane as they rode i[n]
already decided that
sympathetic. Edward
Tom was too smal
understand much of
refused on principle t(
adults, even if he liked
Mrs. Mitchell very much.

"Virginia has probably seceded but we'll know for sure soon. Everyone's been talking about secession for a long time, almost all of my childhood it seems, but now it's really going to happen."

"Why?"

"Because Mr. Lincoln calls the Confederate States of America a rebellion and we call it an independent country."

This was news to Will. He had never even heard of the Confederate States of America. Not that he paid that much attention in school, but he didn't think he could miss something as big as a new country.

"So the reason for forming this new country is to keep your slaves, right?"

"I think that must be part of it. But most people here in the Valley don't even have slaves. Tom says it is also about states having the right to govern themselves the way they want. He says that's in the Constitution."

41

ndered about all of this. Surely,
as more to the story. Then he
ght about the slaves. Of course, they
ould want to be free; no one wants to be a
slave.

"What are you two whispering about,"
asked Benjamin.

"Nothing," said Jane.

"That's what everyone always says when
they don't want me to know anything."

Edward glanced over at Benjamin.
"Ignore them. There are more important
things happening."

"Are we going to war," asked Benjamin,
yelling the words as loud as he could.

"Quiet," Tom answered. "Let's just get
the facts."

"I already know the facts," muttered
Edward morosely. "There will be a war and I
won't be fighting."

Will turned to him. "Why not?"

"Because I am not seventeen yet and my
parents would kill me if I lie about my age to
enlist. A lot of my friends say they're going
to do that, but my mamma said it would
break her heart."

"So you'll enlist next year," offered Will
unsympathetically.

"I won't be old enough."

"So, in a few years."

"What are you talking about? The war will be over in a few months."

"Not likely."

"You said that before and I don't want to hear it. You . . . "

Edward's words were suddenly drowned out as bells began to ring loudly again. Throngs of people lined the streets of the town. A friend of the Mitchells stopped beside the wagon and told them that a telegram from Richmond had been received. Will never saw such excitement.

"Virginia passed the Ordinance of Secession. We will be free at last!" shouted one man.

"No more Unionists," shouted another man. "No more talk of moderation. Hurrah for Virginia!"

Several men were busy hoisting a huge flag over a bank right in front of Will. They called the flag the Stars and Bars. Smaller flags were being hung from local homes. "This must be the Confederate flag that is replacing the Stars and Stripes," thought Will. "Man, they really are making their own country."

The next few hours were a blur. There was so much emotion that Will couldn't share or even understand. Suddenly, he was overcome. "I want to go home, but I don't know how to get back to Connecticut." Then he realized that just going back to Connecticut wasn't enough, because he didn't want to be in Connecticut in 1861. "All I want is to go back or, I guess go forward, to Connecticut and to the 21st century where I belong."

Will was exhausted as they piled back into the wagon to return to Willows.

"You're very quiet, Will," said Jane. "Is anything wrong?"

Edward glanced over at Will. "After seeing how excited we are, he knows that he's wrong and the war will end almost before it begins. Those Yankees won't want to fight us."

Will said nothing.

That night when he was almost asleep, Edward came over quietly and shook him. "Shush. Don't say anything that could wake Benjamin."

"What? Who?"

"Quiet. Just come with me."

Will shook the sleep out of his eyes and followed Edward, knowing he would undoubtedly regret it. He had a sinking feeling that Edward was up to something no good, and Will grabbed his shoes. He didn't want to be barefoot if they were going into the woods again.

"What is it," Will asked when they stepped into the upstairs hall.

"I'm going out again tonight, and I want you to come with me."

"Are you crazy? After Tom caught us the other night, you're going again?"

"Will, Joseph will enlist soon and I have to find a Yankee before he does."

The logic of this escaped Will. "What about Benjamin?"

"He won't wake up."

"What did you do, put Valium in his milk?"

"Valium? What's that? I thought about laudanum, but I can't do that to my own brother. No, Benjamin is a heavy sleeper once he's asleep, so we'll have nothing to worry about."

"Nothing to worry about? Just Tom and Jane and your parents, to say nothing about any of your roaming Yankees. Besides, why do you want me with you anyway?"

"You might hear me when I leave and then I'm not sure what you'll do. There's something a little strange about you."

Will tried to look menacing. "Maybe I'm a Yankee come to attack you and your family. You never know, do you?"

Edward looked sheepish. "Well, I didn't think that. Anyway, now that you know, I would really appreciate it if you came with me. If we do see someone, two people would be better than just me alone."

Will knew this was a bad idea, but what could he do? If he refused to go, Edward would think he was a coward and, anyway, Edward really did need him. Of course, if he said yes, he might get shot at by a Yankee, eaten by a wild animal or thrown out of the house by the Mitchells if they were caught. Some choice. "All right. But this time I'm wearing my shoes."

Chapter 3

They took a lantern and crept quietly out of the house. Will sighed loudly. "Here we are going into the woods again! You must have a death wish."

"Only death wish I have is for Yankees," growled Edward.

"What got us into trouble last time was Benjamin shooting off the musket and . . . "

"And you shooting off your mouth."

Will considered that. As rude as Edward was being, he made sense, so Will closed his mouth, determined to be quiet.

They walked for a long time before Will noticed that Edward was wearing shoes.

"So, you're wearing shoes this time," he said with just a hint of malice in his voice. "Guess Jane was right after all."

"And I thought you were going to be quiet this time."

Their voices must have scared a nocturnal skunk. She immediately reacted to their presence by facing them with an arched tail. Will let out a gasp and the skunk quickly turned around, took aim, and gave them a thorough spraying.

"Oh no," cried Will. "We'll stink."

Edward gritted his teeth. "No Yankee within a hundred miles will let us come near. We'll scare them all away."

"Good, then they'll go back North where they belong and we won't have any problems," Will said, then caught himself. "What am I saying," he thought. "Now Edward has me talking like a Southerner rather than the Northerner I am. Or was. Those Yankees, some of whom were my ancestors, came down here to save the Union, not conquer Virginia."

"You don't understand," Edward complained.

"I know; I know. You need to capture a Yankee before Joseph enlists. I get it, stupid as it is."

"Who you calling stupid?" Edward raised his fists just as they heard a noise behind them. "Don't move. Just turn around slowly."

There was a musket pointing straight at them, held by one soldier. A second soldier asked, "What did you fools do? Go hunting for a skunk?"

"We were sprayed," began Will.

"We could smell you a mile away! Now, who are you and what are you doing here?"

Both boys were quiet, trying to think of what to say when the larger man said, "Maybe they're spies. We better take them to camp. Hand over that gun now."

Edward did as he was ordered.

Will did not recognize their clothing. They were not wearing the Confederate gray or the Union blue he had seen on television so he wasn't exactly sure which side they were on.

"Move!"

The boys marched in front of them. "Let them get ahead," said one of the men, "far ahead."

"We can always shoot them if we have to. Probably a lot better than bringing this stench to camp."

"You can't shoot us," Edward wailed. "We're here to shoot Yankees."

"Yankees! Boy, where are they?"

Edward said nothing and felt the tip of a bayonet against his back.

"Leave him alone," Will yelled. "He's looking for a Yankee but he has no idea where they are. He wants to shoot one before his brother does."

The men looked at Edward with disbelief. "You boys are out here in the middle of the woods looking for Yankees? Why don't you go on to Washington if you want to find Yankees?"

The men thought this was very funny and both guffawed.

Edward frowned. "How do you know where they are? They could be anywhere. After all, if they plan to attack Virginia they could be right here in the middle of the Shenandoah Valley."

The men stopped laughing. "Maybe you know something you're not telling us."

Will sighed. Was his life going to end right here in the middle of the woods just because Edward's sense of pride was attacked? He tried again to explain, "You don't understand. He wants to find a Yankee before his brother does."

"I don't . . . " Edward began.

"Look, I know he's a little foolish, but he's a loyal Virginian," Will heard himself say, wondering where on earth he got those words.

"We'll see. Just keep walking."

They walked and walked until they reached an area where fires were burning low while some men were sleeping and others were standing guard. "Stay here," growled one of the men. "No one is going to appreciate this smell."

"What'd you bring them back for," called out a third man. "Think we'd like skunk for breakfast?"

"No, I thought you'd like these two kids nosing around looking for Yankees."

"Yankees? Ain't no Yankees here. We'd of seen 'em or heard of 'em. Boys, where'd you hear about Yankees around here?"

Edward began, "Well, we didn't exactly. We just thought maybe and we wanted to find them if they were somewhere here."

"What you gonna do with 'em if you find 'em?"

"Shoot them."

"Well, that's okay then. Zeb, whadda you have to go and bring 'em here with that skunk smell and all? If they're out hunting Yankees, then they're on our side. Ain't you, boys?"

"Of course," Edward immediately answered.

This was worse than the "where are you from" question.

"You, boy, why aren't you answering me?"

"Sorry," Will said. "I'm just wondering why you and these men are here in the woods and not in Harpers Ferry."

"Well, we're on our way there right now. We're heading for Winchester and we're gonna enlist, all of us. We're part of a company from home and we want to enlist together so we can all go to the Ferry to give our men a hand."

"Hey, get rid of those boys," shouted a very angry voice. "You woke me up with your shouting and their smelling. Boys, you want to find Yankees? All right then, we'll send you to Washington! Your smell will be a stronger weapon than anything else we have."

The men all laughed.

"May I have my gun back now," Edward asked.

"Sure. Go use it on a Yankee and get far away from here."

"How about next time taking the skunk to a Union camp?"

"How can they do that, Zeb? They can't find the Union camp!"

As the men hooted, the boys left the camp and headed through the woods back toward home. "They tried to humiliate us," Will said as they walked through the woods back toward home.

"Well, they sure succeeded."

"No they didn't. We won't let them. I'm used to guys like that because my school is filled with loads of them."

"Mine wasn't." Edward looked curiously at Will, then said, "I kind of feel like a jackass."

"You're not a jackass, and neither am I. Imagine a group of grown men dragging two kids in to stink up their camp. Now, I ask you, who are the jackasses?"

Edward laughed. "We'll have to clean up before we go inside, but I don't think this smell is going to come out. We're going to have to bury our clothes."

"These are the only clothes I have."

"I'll give you some of mine. Come on, we better get on home before it gets light."

The walk home was eerie and more than once, the boys were startled. Will thought he saw a lion once, but it disappeared before he could be sure. "Are there any lions here, Edward?"

"I've heard there are some bobcats in these woods, but I've never seen any."

"I think I just did."

"We probably scared him."

"And if we didn't?"

"Well, then we'll have to shoot him," Edward answered.

"Just like we shot the Yankees?"

Edward looked a little sheepish. "All right, I deserved that. Come on, we better get home before it gets light."

They walked as quickly as they could, trying to outrun the light that was slowly beginning to shine through the trees. Noises changed as some animals began to find places to hide for their long sleep and others slowly came out of their places of rest to find food for their morning meal.

"Come on," urged Edward.

Will hurried as he imagined Mrs. Mitchell's disappointment in them if she would discover them out at night rather than asleep in their beds. "What will your mother say if she sees us coming in like this?"

"I'd rather not think about it," Edward answered. "My father will be even worse. He hates it when his day is interrupted because he likes order."

"Then he must be increasingly annoyed these days."

"He is. Sometimes I think secession is more of a nuisance to him than a principle."

"And to you?"

"Do you have to ask? It's a just response to a North who refuses to respect us."

"And war?"

"That, too, is a just response."

"You have no idea what you are saying. You don't understand how many deaths will come from this war. There will be deaths on the battlefields and deaths from diseases. Men will die and women and children will starve and horses will die and land will be taken away. You have no clue about the carnage this war will cause."

"And you do?"

"I do."

"How do you know so much?"

Will was quiet as he struggled to find an answer that Edward could understand. "War is terrible."

"Which is just another way for saying that you are a coward."

"No, I'm not."

"Yes, you are. You even complained about the boys in your school. I think you are afraid of them but you don't have the guts to defend yourself and that makes you a coward. I don't want a coward talking about my war."

"It's not your war."

"It sure will be soon."

They walked on quickly, anger fueling their steps. Will thought hard about what Edward said and wondered if he really was a coward. Maybe Edward was right. Maybe that's why stupid Jack and his friends always picked on him. Suddenly, Will pushed Edward hard and he fell to the ground. Edward staggered up and punched Will. They rolled around, smelling of skunk and dirt and anger, pummeling one another until they both lay panting.

"Well, maybe you're not such a coward after all," Edward gasped. "Now let's get out of here before daylight comes and we get into more trouble."

They staggered on, finally coming to the creek just as the sun was beginning to rise over the mountains. Edward carefully lay down his gun and, without saying a word, both boys took off their outer clothes and ran into the water.

After they washed themselves as best as they could, Will shook his head. "We still stink. And what are we going to do with these smelly clothes?"

"We'll bury them," Edward said again.

"I just remembered something," Will said. "When our cat got skunked, my Mom bathed him in tomato juice. Got any tomatoes around here?"

"In the kitchen garden."

They raced to the kitchen garden and grabbed as many tomatoes as they could, smearing them all over their bodies.

"What's you boys doin?"

It was Nellie. Will froze and Edward pretended to laugh. "You caught us. It's a new game Will taught me. Seems as if they play with tomatoes where he's from."

Nellie was not amused. "That's wasteful. We use them tomatas to eat and cook with. Why do your people do that, Will? Don't they like tomatas?"

Will felt obliged to defend his people, absurd as it was. "My mother is allergic to tomatoes. Even the smell bothers her."

"Allergic?"

Oh, right, I'm in 1861 in the middle of the Shenandoah Valley. Who knows if they know about allergies here? "She gets sick from tomatoes so we . . . ah . . . got used to destroying them and it became a game we played."

"Why do you all plant them then," Nellie asked.

Man, I sure have to be careful when I speak. "My sister planted them. She, uh, loves tomatoes."

"G'wan back in the house. You boys are up to something and I smell skunk. Better wash good with them tomatas. Yo Mamma gonna kill you if you smell up her house."

Edward whispered, "Good try, but you can't get anything by Nellie."

"Will she tell?"

"I don't think so. She'll remember, though, and that may be worse."

Benjamin was still sleeping when they quickly climbed the stairs and into bed. Will was almost asleep when Benjamin shook him. "Get up, Will. You, too, Edward. You'll miss breakfast if you sleep."

"Rather have sleep than breakfast," Edward groaned.

"Me too," Will said.

Benjamin sniffed. "I smell something funny here. Almost like a skunk but not really."

"Get out of here," yelled Edward.

Before Benjamin could say anything, Will forced himself to smile. "Thank you, Benjamin, for waking us. We'll come down as soon as we can."

"Aren't you hungry?"

"We are," answered Will, thinking he really was hungry. Hungry and tired. It had been a long night and he envied the nocturnal animals settling into sleep just about now. "Meet you downstairs."

"I'm not going down," Edward said grumpily.

"Want your Mamma to come up? Or Tom? Who knows what they'll find if they come up here."

"We'd better make sure there's nothing for Mamma to notice," Edward warned as they went over to the basin and pitcher to wash their faces and arms with water and soap. Will asked to borrow a comb and tried to make his sandy hair look a bit neater.

Edward found some old clothes that fit Will fairly well once he rolled up the sleeves and legs. They hurried downstairs.

The boys took their seats at the table and Nellie gave each of them a withering look, which, fortunately, no one else noticed.

"Have you boys been fighting," Mrs. Mitchell immediately asked. "You both have bruises all over your faces."

Edward sat still as stone while Will wiggled in his chair. "This isn't my family," he reminded himself, "and if they ask me to leave, I'll just go. Where, though? Just a few days ago, at least I think it was a few days ago, I had a home and a family and now I have nothing but these people. I hope they don't throw me out."

"Well?"

Mr. Mitchell looked up. "Edward, your mother is speaking to you. Answer her."

"Yes, sir. Mamma, we were fighting."

"I am shocked. Fighting a guest in our home is unbelievably rude. I am very disappointed in you, Edward."

Will couldn't be quiet, not with the stricken look on Edward's face. He knew that Edward would never say it, so he did. "I started it, Mrs. Mitchell. I'm sorry, but I threw the first punch."

"Is this true, Edward?"

"Yes, Mamma."

"Well, then, perhaps, you can learn to turn the other cheek. I think I will have to punish both you boys because I cannot tolerate fighting in our home."

"You should have waited till the Yankees came and fighted them," piped up Benjamin.

"That is not the point," Jane said firmly.

"It's none of your business," Edward answered.

"Yes, it is. This is my home too, you know."

Mr. Mitchell had enough. "Tom and I have work to do. Listen to your Mamma, all of you."

With that pronouncement, he hurriedly left. Tom kissed Mary on top of her head and followed his father out of the room. Benjamin continued eating avidly while Mrs. Mitchell slowly finished her last cup of coffee. "Well, boys," she said. "What am I going to do with you?"

"I think," began Jane when her mother sternly interrupted. "This does not concern you, Jane. I am talking to Edward and Will."

"We are sorry, Mamma," began Edward. "We were stupid and it won't happen again."

"What was the fight about," asked Benjamin excitedly.

"Benjamin and Jane, please leave the room."

"I'm not finished yet," Benjamin said.

"You are now," said Mary. "Come with me, both of you."

Jane sighed loudly as she left the room.

"So, boys," Mrs. Mitchell continued, "what should your punishment be?"

"Do you want me to leave," Will asked tremulously.

"Leave? Of course not. I just want both of you to understand that fighting is wrong and that there must be consequences to bad behavior."

"I don't have to leave," repeated Will with relief.

"No, child. We want you to stay with us as long as you want. And, of course, as long as your mother agrees."

Will felt tears rising up in his eyes and he quickly averted his face. "Thank you," he mumbled.

"All right. It's clear to me that I have to give this some thought. Why don't we talk later? In the meantime, please spend some time cleaning yourselves. There is an unpleasant odor, almost reminding me of skunk. But how that can be?"

Later in the morning, Mrs. Mitchell called both boys into her front parlor. "We have an awful mess in the kitchen garden. Some animals must have gotten into the garden and eaten all the tomatoes! They made a terrible mess and I have decided that you boys should clean up the garden for your punishment. There is tomato pulp all over and whatever kind of animal it was, it tore into the other plants. I want you to replant what you can and clean up everything else."

Will thought this a more than fair punishment. "We will be happy to do that."

"Oh, and boys . . . "

"Yes, Mamma?"

"Next time you encounter a skunk, don't leave your clothes where anyone can find them."

Chapter 4

"I didn't realize we made such a mess," complained Edward as he shoveled and picked his way through squashed tomatoes.

Will just looked at him. "We weren't exactly thinking about messes. Actually, I'm not sure we were thinking at all."

"Boys, clean yourselves and get ready for dinner," Mary called out.

"To think I never washed at a pump before and now it's my regular hang-out."

"Hang-out, what's a hang-out?"

Will took a deep breath. "A hang-out is a place you spend time in, usually with your friends. Of course I don't have any friends so I don't hang out."

"Why don't you have any friends? You seem likable enough except when you're not, of course." Edward laughed to show he was only joking.

"Lots of mean boys in my town."

"Lots of mean boys everywhere. You have to show them you're tougher than they are, even if you're not."

"How do you know these things," Will asked curiously.

"I have three older brothers and Jane for a sister. If I don't act tough, they'll walk all over me."

"Hurry up boys. It's dinner time," Mary tried again.

"And now I have Mary, although she's pretty nice most of the time."

Will and Edward tried to rush through dinner so they could finish working in the garden and do other things. However, as Edward whispered from across the table to Will, "Rushing through dinner is like walking in molasses."

"I hear you whispering," exclaimed Benjamin. "When are we having molasses cookies?"

All eyes turned to Edward. Suddenly, before he could answer, there was the sound of horses and voices outside. Moments later, the dining room door opened and four tall young men walked in.

"Joseph," everyone exclaimed.

The tallest and the broadest of them came around to kiss his Mamma and smile a big warm smile at everyone. Joseph then shook hands with his father and Tom and said, "Hello. These are my friends from the University."

Introductions were made and places at the table were hurriedly set. "Is there enough food for all of them," Will asked Jane, who was sitting beside him.

"There's always enough food. We're on a farm in the Valley, remember, and the Valley feeds most of Virginia. Some farm we'd be if we couldn't feed our own family and their friends!"

"Do you get visitors often?"

"All the time," Jane answered. "They travel through here on their way to Winchester or Sharpsburg or even Baltimore. We like having people visit."

"There's no cooking like home cooking," Joseph said. "Why, at the University I sometimes just sit and think about all the good food we have here. Nellie, you've always made sure I eat well."

"G'wan with you," said a smiling Nellie as she brought in a tray to put on the table. "You sound just like yo' brother Tom when he come home from that same university. Always wantin' more gingerbread, wasn't you, Tom?"

"I remember wanting a lot more than just gingerbread," Tom laughed. "Brother, I know just how you feel. Do they still serve dessert only two times a week? I never understood that."

"Yes," answered one of the young men. "And it is just terrible because we are all used to dessert everyday."

"Well, I'm not going to the University of Virginia," announced Benjamin. "That'll show them. I would never go to a school that serves dessert only two times in a week."

The laughter around the table reminded Will how happy he was to be here. "So where are you from, Will," asked Joseph.

That question again. All right, here I go again. "I'm not from around here. I live outside of the Valley."

Joseph continued eating. "Slow down," his Mamma cautioned, "if you eat too fast you'll get a stomachache."

"Remember the time Joseph got sick at the table," Edward contributed.

"Well, now, Brother Edward, I really don't think anyone wants to hear about that." He turned to his friends and said, "Children say all sorts of things we don't want to hear, don't they?"

Tired as he was after last night, Edward reared up. "Who are you calling a child?"

Tom took control. "So why are you all here? In my day, we didn't get to go home except for Christmas."

"In your day there was no war." Joseph looked around the table. "Mamma, there is no easy way to tell you this so I'll just say it outright. The four of us are going to Winchester to enlist."

Mr. Mitchell stood up and shook hands again with his son, then shook the hand of each young man. "Good for you. This fight will be over soon if our men just go and do their duty. I'm proud of all of you."

"I am too," Tom said, "although I admit to being more than a little jealous."

"We need you here at the farm, son. Your Mamma and I depend on you."

"I know that, but part of me wants to get out there and finish what those abolitionists started."

Joseph turned to his brother. "Tom, you're the bravest man I ever met and the sacrifice you are making to help our family will never be forgotten. This war is all about family and country, and you have the family part while Robs and I have the country part. It's a hard question which is more difficult."

Overcome, Tom just nodded.

"So, Mamma," Joseph went on, "what do you think about me enlisting?"

"I am proud of you. Our cause is just and we mothers have no choice but to send our sons into battle for the honor of Virginia and the honor of the whole South. I know in my heart that God will keep all of His sons safe."

Will started to clap, then caught himself. As talk swirled around him, again he had a very strong desire to read a history book. "Maybe when I get back, I'll go and read that big Catton book. And if I don't make it back, well, then I guess I'll experience history firsthand here in the Valley."

"Will, are you daydreaming?" It was Jane. His sister always said that to him, but it didn't sound as annoying coming from Jane.

After dinner, Mr. Mitchell and his sons and Joseph's friends all went into the plantation office. Will assumed they would be talking about the war and Will knew he didn't belong in that conversation. This wasn't his family and these weren't his people. Besides, this wasn't his war.

Will walked outside to get some much-needed air. He was afraid things were going to get bad here and just thinking about it upset him. He wandered by the white fence and looked out at the cows roaming on the other side. It was a beautiful April day and a gentle breeze barely rippled through the trees. It was peaceful here and he suddenly wanted to freeze time forever.

Suddenly he thought he heard the sound of crying. He followed the sound and saw Mrs. Mitchell almost hidden by a large tree. This seemed so out of character for Mrs. Mitchell that he didn't know whether it would be kinder to go over to her or kinder to let her have her privacy. Will knew too much about being left alone and also knew that it was overrated most of the time. He went over and asked, "Are you all right, Mrs. Mitchell?"

As soon as he asked the question, he felt foolish. No one who crying is all right.

She wiped her eyes and looked up at him. "Ah, Will, I had hoped to cry in private."

"I'm sorry. I'll leave right away."

"No, it's all right. Please sit by me. If someone had to find me crying, I'm glad it was you because you don't need me to be strong."

Will was confused. "What do you mean?"

"Will, dear, my sons have to go off to war. Everyone says it will be a short war but I am not sure of that. The North has far greater resources than we have and once it gets mobilized, we may have serious trouble on our hands."

"Maybe they won't mobilize," offered Will, immediately wondering why he would lie to this woman he had begun to love as a mother.

"Because, dear, once fighting begins, it keeps going, almost as if it has a mind of its own. Like a hurricane, war doesn't stop until it finishes its course."

Will hung his head. She was right, of course, and it would change nothing if he told her all he knew. Besides, she wouldn't believe him anyway.

"My sons need to go off proudly. They need to know that I believe in them. They need to know that they are part of a family who will support them and care for them. And, most of all, they need to believe that God will keep them safe and that His love will carry them forward. If they see me cry, they will know that I am afraid."

Will thought quickly. He wanted so badly to find words to comfort this woman. As he sat quietly, much to his surprise, those words came. "I think it must take extraordinary courage to watch someone you love go off to war."

For a moment Mrs. Mitchell smiled. It was a brief smile, but nevertheless a smile. "Thank you, Will. Now, we must go back and face what we must. And speaking of things to face, anytime you want to talk with me, please do. I am always ready to listen to you and I have a feeling that you may have a few things you might want to talk about."

Looking at his shoes, he mumbled, "Thank you."

When they reached the house, singing greeted their ears. Joseph was playing a fiddle, his friend a banjo and everyone else was singing:

> *"Come all ye sons of freedom*
> *And join our Southern band,*
> *We're going to fight the enemy*
> *And drive them from our land;*

> *"Oh, wait for the wagon*
> *The dissolution wagon;*
> *The South is our wagon,*
> *And we'll all take a ride."*

There were many happy faces singing together. As Will met Mrs. Mitchell's eyes, they both nodded to each other and looked away. Jane was singing loudly as Benjamin was trying his hardest to sing over her. Sarah and Henry were beating on some kind of drum until Sarah lost interest and started to dance. Mrs. Mitchell joined in and Will began to back away when Tom beckoned to him. "Come on, we'll teach you the words. The chorus is easy."

It sure was. Will remembered his grandfather singing that song to him when he was a kid. Only it had different words . . . no enemy, no dissolution, and no South. Still it was interesting that the song was so old. Soon Will was singing along with the chorus and having a fine time.

"If I just forget where I am and where they're going, I'll be fine," he told himself. "Of course things would be better if I knew where I was going but, as Aunt Karen used to say, 'It is what it is.' " On that note, he sang louder.

The next day Will was up almost at dawn. "Probably because I went to bed so early. I was really tired after that ridiculous adventure with Edward," he grumbled and went downstairs.

He stepped outside on to the porch and a voice sitting in one of the rocking chairs said, "Much as I love them all, my family can tire a good man out."

Will saw Joseph smiling at him. "Well, they haven't tired me out yet so that may mean either I'm not a good man or else I really like them. I think if I were you I'd bet on the latter."

Joseph nodded appreciatively. "I'm enlisting today. I dreaded telling Mamma but she did fine. I guess with Robs at the Ferry, she's used to her sons in the army now."

Will said nothing.

"So, Will, have your family enlisted yet?"

"Not my mother."

Joseph laughed. "Tom told me you were good with words and, obviously, he was right."

"My family has had many soldiers," he answered. This was strictly true. Members of his family had served in World War I, World War II and Vietnam, and his cousin, Matt, was in Afghanistan right now. About the Civil War, Will didn't have a clue, but he thought that if anyone had fought, they would have fought on the side of the North. Unless there were some family stories he'd never heard.

"That's good," Joseph answered then added, "Will, I want to ask you to do me a favor."

"All right."

"You're an outsider here and may be able to see things that we can't see. I'm concerned about the Unionists that may live here."

Will gulped. Strictly speaking, he was a Unionist. "Why?"

"Before Virginia seceded just a little while ago, we had many men who still believed in the Union. They wanted us to remain loyal to the United States and it seemed then as if they might have been in the majority. However, when Lincoln called for us to contribute troops to destroy what he called the rebellion, most of those Unionists changed sides. They saw that we had to defend our rights."

"So?"

"So who knows who is giving information to the other side?"

"What do Tom and your father say about this?"

"They're both optimists and think things will go well. I'm not so sure."

They don't go well, but not for the reasons you fear. Aloud Will said, "I'd side with Tom and your father if I were you. Why borrow trouble?"

"Maybe you're right. Come on, let's go in to breakfast. Everyone should be up by now."

"What is your plan, Joseph," asked his father after they sat down and grace had been spoken.

"We," he pointed to his three schoolmates, "are meeting our other friends at the church and we're all going into Winchester together. We were part of a volunteer unit at school so we want to join the Confederate Army together."

"What about your parents," Mr. Mitchell asked one of the young men.

"We said our goodbyes a few days ago. Joseph lives closer to Winchester so we all came to Willows."

"You are very welcome here. We will go with you to the church and see you all off."

"Joseph," interrupted Mrs. Mitchell. "I would like a word with you."

"Of course, Mamma."

They went into the bedroom that Joseph had once shared with Tom and Robs.

"Now, I know you have to go today, but I think we first have to discuss what you plan to take with you. Nights get very cold when you're sleeping outside."

"We'll be in a tent."

"Still, it can be cold. I've prepared a list for you."

Joseph groaned. "Robs says the less you take the better."

"What does Robs know?"

"Well, he's a Captain and he was at West Point before the North went mad."

"He is not a mother. Now," she continued, pulling out a list, "you need an overcoat, a wool blanket, some extra shirts and extra socks. Then you'll need a needle and thread . . . "

"What for?"

"There are no servants in the Army. When something needs to be mended, you will need to sew for yourself."

"Some people have them. Mr. Pickens is bringing his."

"We are not the Pickens family and you will have no servant with you. I will continue . . . you will need bars of soap to keep clean and a hair comb. You'll need candles and," her lip trembled and she resolutely went on, "the Bible and . . . " here she faltered, and Joseph put his arms around her. "I'll be fine."

"I know you will. I just want you to be comfortable."

"No one is comfortable in war."

Ignoring him, she pulled out a game of checkers and a book of poetry. "You may get bored. Oh, I forgot, you need long winter underwear."

"It's April and the war will be over before winter."

"We hope."

"Mamma, we will beat those Yankees so fast they'll run back North before the summer's over. I promise you, all Virginia will be laughing and I'll be back at the University before you know it."

Mr. Mitchell walked in and took one look at his wife. "Come on, dear. The boys have to go and we want to see them off."

"But Joseph hasn't finished his packing."

"I will right now, Mamma. And Mamma . . . "

"Yes?"

"I love you."

Trying hard to hide her tears, she simply nodded and said, "I love you too."

The whole family went to the church and Will tagged along. Joseph's local friends were there and three of them were going to enlist as well. The young men greeted one another enthusiastically.

"I wish I were going with you," said an old man, his voice quavering with excitement. "I fought in my time but now I'm wanting to fight again."

"Now, Pa, you got to give the young men their turn. You already had yours."

Just then a very pretty young lady came over to Edward. "Do you know where Joseph is? I want to give him something to remember me by."

Edward threw up his arms in disgust. "Will, it's worse than I thought. Even if we had captured eight Yankees and shot a dozen more, this crowd would still be hurrahing the men who are enlisting instead of hurrahing us." His dark eyes flashed and his lips were pursed in anger.

As he stood scowling, an older lady came over to him and said, "Hello, young Edward. Who is your new friend?"

Edward pulled himself together and said, "This is Will Bradford, Mrs. Pritchard. Will, this is Mrs. Pritchard."

"Nice to meet you," Will said.

She nodded. "I do not believe that I know your family, Will. Where are you from?"

Will was uncomfortable. Mrs. Pritchard's eyes were looking straight at him. He began to shift his weight from one foot to the other.

"Well, let's not talk about that now. And, Edward, do not be jealous of your brother. Things are not always what they seem. Please remember me to your mother, Edward." With that, Mrs. Pritchard turned away, then came back and added in a low voice, "And, Will, you be careful, very careful."

After she had gone, Edward whispered, "Some people think she is a witch, but we all know there is no such thing as witches. Yet, there is something strange about her, don't you think?"

Will agreed and just then the Reverend stood up and the crowd fell silent. "Before we send these brave young men off to defend our people, our land, our way of life and our country, let us talk for a moment about courage. We must not take for granted the moral courage of these young men. We are grateful to them and we pray to God that He will guide them throughout their journey. Let us all pray."

There were several speeches and as Edward struggled with his envy, Joseph and his friends stood tall. Several ladies had worked together to make a flag for the men to carry with them. Lovely Miss Ann Bryant came forward to present their handiwork. "May you carry these colors bravely. We hope that this flag we have woven will inspire you to do great deeds for our country's honor and we also hope that while you are fighting for us on the battlefield, you will remember those who love and cherish you at home."

Edward nudged Will and rolled his eyes while Will did his best to ignore him.

"You are really a hero," Edward overheard Mary Sue Conway say to Joseph. "Please accept this floral arrangement I made in your honor."

Edward whispered, "If I don't get out of here, I promise to be sick. Come on, let's go for a walk."

Will had no choice but to follow. They skirted around the edge of the crowd.

There were a few more speeches and the band played. Will overheard a woman offer one young man fruit while someone else gave another young man three jars of jam.

"I wouldn't mind enlisting myself. I sure love jam," he said to Edward.

"Let's hope the war won't end soon so we will both have our chance!"

His words startled Will. "Our chance to die on the battlefield, to die from disease, to have our arms or legs amputated? I don't think so," Will thought. He knew that over seven hundred thousand men died in this war. As he watched the party atmosphere swell around him, he felt a choking pain in his heart. He had never, not even when his father left home, felt a pain like this before.

The men began to say their goodbyes. As they marched away, ladies waved their handkerchiefs in the air and everyone cheered.

"We'll knit socks and send them; we'll make them more uniforms and we'll write so many letters that none of them will feel lonely," Mary told Jane as they traveled home.

"How can they feel lonely when they are with their friends?"

"Friends are fine, but Joseph will miss his family," Mrs. Mitchell answered firmly. "I thank God he will see Robs up there at Harpers Ferry."

"I wish I were there too," mumbled Tom. "But I have to be with cows and wheat."

"Without food . . . " began Mr. Mitchell.

". . . there can be no life," everyone joined in.

"That's right. If I have said it once, I have said it one hundred times."

"That you have, dear," said Mrs. Mitchell, feeling suddenly better, "and with God's help, you will say it a hundred times more."

By the time they reached home, everyone was tired. It was a quiet supper and afterwards, Will began to think about war. This war was just beginning and people were still celebrating because they were sure that they were going to win. They had no idea what war was really like yet. Will never heard his mother's uncle say much about Vietnam, just that it was an awful war. He sighed.

"Is something wrong, Will," asked Mrs. Mitchell.

"I was just thinking about wars. There sure have been a lot of them."

"That's true," answered Mr. Mitchell, "but this war had to happen."

"Why?"

"The North refused to let us separate and form our own country. I suppose we were more important to their economy than they were to ours. After all, we have all the cotton."

Will thought about his last social studies class and remembered Mrs. Morris calling cotton, King Cotton. "I wish I had paid more attention in school," he said out loud.

"Why, Will, that's an admirable sentiment," Mrs. Mitchell said. "Now, when you return to school, you will pay more attention and that will make you a better student."

"I guess so," he mumbled, wondering if and when that would happen.

After supper, he decided to go for a walk. "Where are you going," asked Jane.

"I need a walk."

"I'll go with you."

"Not now, Jane," answered her mother. "Sarah has been asking for you and I would appreciate it if you would go to the nursery and help her get ready for bed."

"But Betsy can do that."

"Not tonight. Sarah really wants you."

"All right, Mamma," Jane said, then turned to Will and smiled. "I'll see you in the morning."

"Don't go too far," Mrs. Mitchell cautioned.

"I won't. I just need a little air."

Will heard her say to Mr. Mitchell that he was probably missing his home. Well, much to his surprise, he really was. He thought about all the mean kids in Litchfield and decided that he would like to go back home anyway. "After all," he thought, "I can't help anyone here. I know that there is going to be a terrible war but I also know that no one in the North or in the South was able to find a way to stop it from happening. Even President Lincoln couldn't stop this war, so how could I? I have no power here because no one would believe me. Maybe, just maybe, if I go home I can do something or change something. I used to believe that I was powerless at home, but, I didn't really understand what powerless meant. Here, I am really powerless."

Suddenly he felt himself being pulled up, shooting towards the sky where it was cold, very cold. He closed his eyes, waited for it to end, then banged hard against a floor. It was the floor of his hallway at home, and he lay surrounded by the books he had been carrying down from the attic.

He heard footsteps and his mother and Rebecca came in from the kitchen calling, "Will, Will, are you all right?"

He wasn't sure. He did feel a bit shaky and his body hurt all over. He struggled to sit up and look at himself. He looked the same as he did when he left, wearing old jeans and a t-shirt. He looked around. The house also looked the same. Behind the attic stairs was a hallway. His bedroom was the last room on the right. Rebecca's room was on the left, across from his room. His mother's bedroom was downstairs at the back of the house, near the bathroom and kitchen. Closer to the front of the house were the living room and the small dining room that they never used.

Will answered, "Yeah, I'm all right, but why am I here? How did I get here? Where are the Mitchells?"

"The Mitchells," asked his mother.

"Yes, the family who own Willows, the plantation in the Shenandoah Valley."

He saw his mother and Rebecca exchange glances. "Maybe we shouldn't move him," whispered his mother. "Go call 911."

"What are you whispering about?" said Will as he struggled to his feet. Rebecca reached out to steady him while his mother touched his forehead.

"What's the matter with the two of you? I just fell from the trip."

"Go call 911."

"No," Will shouted. "I don't need an ambulance. I'm fine, just a little shaky, that's all. Who wouldn't be after all that happened to me?"

"Will, what could have happened to you in our attic," asked Rebecca impatiently. "Stop faking."

"I'm not faking."

"Then we have to call an ambulance," his Mother said firmly

Will thought fast. They obviously wouldn't believe that he visited the Shenandoah Valley in 1861. He barely could believe it himself and it had happened to him! If they called an ambulance, chances are the EMTs wouldn't believe him and neither would the doctors and nurses at the hospital. They would think he had a concussion. Then they would lock him up for what hospitals call observation. Or, worse, they would give him pills so he would forget all about the Shenandoah Valley. He began to think more clearly and realized that he had only two choices. Choice one was to go to the hospital. Choice two was to pretend that the Shenandoah Valley never happened. Will decided on choice two.

"I feel better now. I don't know why I was talking about the Shenandoah Valley. Must have been this heavy book by Bruce Catton." He picked up the book and showed it to them. "I must have lost my balance and uh, it fell on me when I slipped."

"I don't know about school tomorrow," his mother said.

"I want to go to school. I'm fine."

"Now I'm really worried," she laughed. "You haven't wanted to go to school since we moved here."

"Well, I want to go now."

"He sounds fine," his mother said.

"Maybe too fine," wondered Rebecca. "He's eager to go to school. Will, what's up with you?"

"If I can't go to the Ferry and fight, I can go to school and fight."

"That's it. I'm calling 911."

"Mom, I'm just talking about Harpers Ferry where the young men of the Valley went after they enlisted. I'm comparing both as war of sorts. It's kind of a joke."

"A joke?"

"Yes, I've been reading this book of Catton's. Relax. Let's get out of the hallway now so I can get some sleep and be ready for school tomorrow."

"Well, I don't know," his mother hesitated.

"If you keep talking, tomorrow will be today and I will really feel bad from lack of sleep. Come on, ladies, let's go and forget all this."

"Ladies?" Rebecca looked at him. "You've never called me a lady."

"Probably because you've never been one before. But now you're being so kind and nice, I just thought of you as a lady."

"Why, Will, that's lovely," said his mother.

Close. Seems as if I have to be careful here, too. Well, if I can guard my words in 1861, I'm sure I can guard them even better here.

As they walked toward his room, Will's mother said, "Maybe a shower will make you feel better."

"Much better," he answered. "I've been looking forward to a hot shower since I first washed at the pump."

He noticed the look his mother and Rebecca exchanged. "Only kidding. I'm . . . uh . . . becoming immersed in the language of 1861. The pump was where they washed. Lunch was dinner and our dinner was their supper."

"Will, forget the shower and just go to bed. We'll see how you are in the morning."

Chapter 5

"Mom must really be worried about me," Will whispered to Rebecca at breakfast. "She never goes in late to work." He looked around the small kitchen. Everything was beige: beige cabinets, beige counters and a beige Formica table. Dull. They always ate in the kitchen, not like at Willows where they ate in the large dining room.

"Well, you gave us a real scare talking about some people called the Mitchells who lived in the Shenandoah Valley. What was that all about?"

Will thought about what to say. At Willows, no one ever pressured him for answers. Here, Rebecca and his mother just had to know everything all the time. They didn't respect his privacy; actually, here he had no privacy. Mrs. Mitchell, however, respected his privacy and, for that and much more, he missed her.

Rebecca tapped her foot. "Will, I'm waiting for an answer."

"I guess you'll just have to wait then. I'm carrying this big book on the Civil War because we have to bring in something we read and I don't want to miss the bus."

"Since when?"

"Since now. Bye Mom," he called out.

"Will, are you sure you're all right," his mother's voice rang out as he bounded down the steps outside. "I'm fine," he called out, "Bye."

"You made it for a change," the bus driver said to him.

"And good morning to you, too," Will answered, pleased to see the bus driver look surprised.

Good start. Edward would be proud of him. Well, let's see what's next.

He made his usual way through the groups of kids hanging around outside school. He got shoved as he went to his locker but since the bell rang and kids were scrambling all about, there was no one in particular to blame.

Will watched as Mrs. Morris talked to a group of students. "She always likes those kinds of kids, the smart ones," he thought.

"All right class, settle down," Mrs. Morris said as she called the class to order. "Today I want to briefly discuss my expectations for your research paper." There was the predictable groan from the class.

"They are so immature," Will said to himself.

"You were asked to pick a topic about the Civil War. You can use online encyclopedias, websites, books and journal articles. Just make sure that the online site you are using is a credible source. Stick with .org and .gov and stay away from student-created websites because you can't always trust their information.

"Thanks for the vote of confidence," Jack called out.

Mrs. Morris laughed.

Will frowned. Mrs. Morris always likes those kinds of kids, too, the troublemakers.

"All right, class," Mrs. Morris said, "when I call your name, please come to the front of the room, tell us your topic and name your sources. Michael, what is your topic?"

"Lincoln's assassination. I went to WhiteHouse.gov/about/presidents."

"Good. Jack?"

"The Battle of Bull Run and I used Civilwar.org."

"Next."

This went on until Will felt his eyes starting to close. He woke up immediately when he heard his name. He stood up, grabbed the Catton book, walked a little unsteadily to the front of the class, and said, "The Shenandoah Valley in 1861."

"That's a rather particular . . . "

"You mean peculiar," shouted out Jack.

Ignoring Jack, Mrs. Morris continued, " . . . particular topic. Are you sure you will be able to get the information you want on this topic?"

"Absolutely."

"Name one of your sources."

He held up the huge Catton book so the entire class could see it and everyone laughed.

"Hey, Willy-boy," called out Jack, "Is that the biggest book you could find? Ever hear of the internet?"

The class roared with laughter.

Will suddenly heard Edward's voice in his head telling him that he had to show the mean kids he was tougher than they were even if he wasn't. And he wasn't.

"This is a book," Will said calmly, then turned to Jack, "but you probably never read one."

A few students laughed half-heartedly, as if they didn't know whether or not they were supposed to laugh at Jack.

"Will, try it and see if you can find the information you need. All right, you can go and sit down now. Kayla, you're next."

As Will started to walk back to his seat, a foot stuck out and tripped him.

"Sorry," said Jack. "I don't know how that happened. Guess you just got under my foot."

Will made a big show of looking at Jack's foot. "Is that where you keep your brain? I figure you have one somewhere."

Again, there was some half-hearted laughter. This time Jack couldn't ignore it. "You better watch it or I'll kick your ass."

"Why? You tired of kicking your own?"

This time there was more laughter.

"I'll see you later, Willy-boy," threatened Jack.

"Looking forward to it," answered Will mildly.

He felt very good. He must remember to thank Edward when he saw him again. Will corrected himself: if he ever saw him again.

In the afternoon, he went to his usual classes.

I miss the Mitchells. I miss not knowing if Joseph got to the Ferry safely and what happened when he met up with Robs. I miss Mrs. Mitchell and Tom and Mary and Mr. Mitchell and Edward and even Benjamin and the children. And Jane, I miss her too. He sighed. I half-wish I were back there. I hope they aren't too worried about me. Probably not. After all, I came suddenly, so it's realistic to think I'd leave equally as suddenly. Realistic . . . maybe that's not the right word here.

Will got on the bus and headed home. The first thing he did, after eating his snack, of course, was to pick up the big Catton book and read. He wondered if something strange would happen again but all that happened was that he learned there were two very different societies in the United States. The North was more industrial and used free labor to work while the South was more agricultural and some people owned slaves who worked on the farms and did other jobs. Slavery seemed to have caused a whole lot of problems and he learned about all the ways the men in government tried to deal with it. "Man," he thought, "what a whole lot of compromises that didn't work."

"Will, it's time for dinner," his sister shouted.

"All right, all right, I'm coming. Stop bothering me."

"What are you so annoyed about," Rebecca asked him at the table. "Is it school?"

"What's wrong at school," his mother quickly asked, kind of like a dog suddenly picking up a scent.

"Nothing is wrong. I just miss . . . my friends."

"So, go on Facebook and friend them."

"I can't."

"Why not?"

"These friends aren't on Facebook."

"Well, I told you to sign up for after-school activities. You used to play soccer. They have a team here and you could play."

"I suck at soccer."

"So do three quarters of the other kids. It's not whether you win or lose . . . "

" . . . it's how you play the game . . . ," chimed in Will and Rebecca.

"You always say that," Rebecca pointed out, "but it's not really true."

Will was fed up with this conversation. "If you're in a war, winners live and losers die."

His mother looked at him carefully. "I wasn't talking about living or dying. We were talking about soccer, not war. Will, why are you thinking about war? Is something troubling you? I hear about bullies in school. Is someone bullying you?"

"I'm fine. And I'm not going to kill myself, if that's what you're thinking."

His mother inhaled sharply. "That wasn't what I was thinking at all. But if you're thinking . . . "

Oh, no, now my mother is going to go off on this. I was just thinking about the Mitchells and then I thought about war. And when I thought about war, I thought about people dying, but I can't tell her any of that.

"Will, do you want to talk to someone about your feelings?"

94

He almost laughed. What would I say? Doctor, I think I prefer 1861 so could you arrange a return visit? Now, I am going to have to calm my mother down. "Mom, I was just thinking about war because we're studying the Civil War in Social Studies. The Civil War was a war and in war, people get killed. You must have read about wars at some point in your life."

"Of course. All I have to do is pick up a newspaper and war is right there on the front page. But that's not the point."

"Yes, it is the point. My point. What's your point?"

Asking my mother that question might be a risky move. Most of the time, I never know what she is going to say even if I don't ask her opinion.

"I just want to know that you are all right."

"I am. Now if nobody minds, I am going to go play on the Xbox and do my homework."

"Perhaps you can reverse the order in which you do those two things," his mother suggested wryly. "And, first we're having dinner. I made the chicken you especially like."

"Sure, whatever."

Dinner was good; he really did like the special chicken dish she made every so often. After dinner, Will went to the TV in the living room and hooked up the Xbox. His mother walked in.

"Well," she said brightly, "Would you like me to join you in a game?"

Oh, no. She's trying to be my friend. What could be worse than this? "No, Mom. I like to play by myself."

"It might be more fun if we play together."

No, it wouldn't. "Mothers don't play these kinds of games. Why don't you do a wash or something?"

"Is that all you think mothers do?"

Now I've hurt her feelings.

"Mom, I'm fine. I don't have a concussion and I'm not suicidal. But I might become suicidal if you don't leave me alone. Actually, I might even become homicidal."

He looked at her face, "Mom, I'm joking. Just let me play. Please."

"All right, but remember to do your homework."

Nothing like a mother in General mode. I think I like it better when she works all the time and ignores me.

Will played Call of Battle and time melted away. He had to save his country from attack and he kept focus and took aim over and over again. He was relentless and working very hard when suddenly he felt someone shaking his shoulder. "What are you doing?" He jerked away. "Look what you made me do."

"You didn't do your homework and it's 10:00 now," his mother said angrily. "You will have to go back to playing on weekends only."

Will shoved the control toward her. "I want to play now."

"Well, you can't. Put it away or I'll take it away."

A standoff. Mothers always win and he grudgingly put the Xbox away. Will tried to argue, "If you gave it some thought, Mom, you would realize that this game is more important than math. Math problems are not important to anyone except to the teacher. This game I am playing is about war, which is real and important to everyone."

"Will," she cried, "What is happening to you?"

He had gone too far. "Nothing. I'm just talking. I'll do my math right now."

The week went by quickly; his mother calmed down and things returned to normal. He spent more time now online looking at Civil War websites and discovered many interesting things. For one, he learned that the Civil War was called the War Between the States in some places and the War of Northern Aggression in others. "Well, the

North did invade the South," he thought. "Of course their goal was to preserve the Union, but I can see how a Southerner could feel invaded. The Mitchells certainly did."

Thinking about the Mitchells led him to other websites and he spent his hours after school online.

"Are you getting into trouble on the computer," Rebecca asked him one day.

"No."

"I saw your light on last night."

"I'm doing research for my paper."

"At midnight?"

"It was a four-year war and I've only been at it a couple of days."

"You're weird."

"You're weirder."

"Just be careful," she said as she walked away.

"I'm always careful," he answered. That wasn't exactly true. He had stumbled into a few uncomfortable chats but quickly backed out when he heard more hate than he had ever heard in his life. The kind of talk that made even Jack seem sweet. Almost.

Since Joseph was heading off to Harpers Ferry when Will saw him last, Will decided to find out what happened there. He busied himself on the internet and, before long, found enough information to feel as if he was almost there himself.

Colonel Thomas J. Jackson came to Harpers Ferry to take charge and organize the volunteers since few of them had been in the army before. "Wonder what he did with Joseph?"

"Dinner, Will, come on."

"I'm too busy right now."

"Dinner, it'll get cold," shouted Rebecca.

"So, let it get cold. I have to find Joseph!"

"Joseph who?"

"Leave me alone. I am on the computer doing work that's important."

Suddenly the computer turned off. Outraged, he stood up, knocked over his chair, face red with fury, and faced his mother. "Oh, I thought you were Rebecca."

"I'm your mother and I want to know exactly who this Joseph is that you are looking for."

Will stood silent and picked up the chair.

"Will?"

Yankee ingenuity, that's what this calls for. "Well, Mom, Joseph is a friend I made who is also involved with the Civil War."

"Friend how? Where did you meet him? What do you know about him?"

Here we go. Might as well use what I learned in the Valley. "There was an after-school Civil War thing a couple of weeks ago and I met Joseph there."

"What kind of Civil War thing?"

"It was sort of a reenactment without costumes. We just . . . ah . . . chose sides and . . . uh . . . argued."

"Argued about what?"

"Stuff about the war."

"That sounds interesting, kind of like a debating club focused on the Civil War. I could see how you would like that. And how did you meet his family?"

"Mom, I need some privacy. A young man my age cannot tell his mother everything. But, if you must know, I went to his house after school one day. Joseph Mitchell is a fine, upstanding young man and I met his mother and father and sister and brothers. They are all what you would call respectable people."

His mother looked abashed and said, "You need to have friends that share your interests. I know how hard it has been for you to find any. If you ever want to have your new friend over, I'd love to meet him. And his family."

"Thank you."

"I'm sorry I shut off your computer. I won't do that again. Come downstairs and have dinner and you can Facebook or tweet or text or do whatever you do to contact your new friend and I won't bother you. Just make sure to do all your homework."

After dinner, Will raced to the computer and, after a few false tries, found out that Joseph was made a second lieutenant. "They made him an officer too! Robs is a Captain and Joseph is a Second Lieutenant. The Mitchells must be proud of both their sons."

He kept digging online, and found a picture of the Union Army burning the Arsenal at Harpers Ferry. "Wow, that's cool; the whole place is going up in flames. Hey, wait a minute. Robs must have been there and maybe Joseph too. This all is getting confusing. This is a tough war and it hasn't even started yet. For them, I mean. For me it started and ended over one hundred and fifty years ago. Talk about confusing . . . . "

"Sorry we are boring you, Will," said Mrs. Morris the next morning in response to a particularly vigorous yawn.

"I'm not bored, just tired."

"How nice that you had such an active weekend. Perhaps you would have preferred to sleep-in this morning," she said, her voice dripping with sarcasm. "However, since you are here, I hope you won't mind paying attention . . . "

Jack laughed, a mean kind of laugh. "Maybe Willy-boy pays attention to other things."

"Maybe I'll walk over and flatten you," Will answered, thinking Edward would be proud of him.

"Maybe you'll take a trip to Mr. Haber's office. In this class we do not threaten other students," Mrs. Morris righteously proclaimed.

"Yeah, yeah. All you do is watch as they try to bully me."

"Mr. Haber's office. Now."

Will stood up, collected his books slowly and left, head held high. In detention after school, he mentally composed a conversation with Edward.

"It didn't work. I got into trouble."

"It did work. Jack now knows you will stand up to him."

"Right. He attacks and I get punished."

"At least you have your honor."

Will stopped daydreaming and thought about honor. Honor was very important to Virginians, maybe to all Southerners. What if that was part of what this war was about? After all, the North had left behind its agricultural ways and was becoming more and more industrialized. The South wasn't, and the North really didn't respect that. It's kind of like when you decide to play a sport. Before I played soccer, I never thought about kids who didn't play. Once I started playing, I sort of looked down on those who didn't play even thought I didn't play well. Maybe the North felt something like that.

Except for slavery. I don't know where slavery fits in this war. When the war started, most Northerners didn't seem to care about slavery. They were fighting for the Union. Most Southerners didn't have slaves, but they were fighting to preserve a way of life that included slavery. That's kind of hard to understand.

"All right, Will. You can go home now."

Will looked at the time. He had been in detention for an hour. Good thing his mother wouldn't be home yet. Detention would be tough to explain.

He hurried through dinner and homework. "Yes, Mom, I did all my homework," he called out as he went upstairs.

"Good. Go to bed early for a change."

He nodded.

I am going to follow Joseph throughout the war. Joseph was part of Colonel Jackson's brigade at Harpers Ferry, which went from the Shenandoah Valley to the Battle of Manassas, which the North called the Battle of Bull Run. It seems as if the North named their battles after rivers or creeks and the South named them after towns or railroad junctions. Just another difference between them.

Will went straight to YouTube and typed in a search for the Battle of Manassas, since that's what Joseph must have called it.

He found thirteen videos to start with and then a whole lot more. He began to watch. Lots of smoke, noise, music and confusion. I'm not going to find Joseph here. These guys are only reenactors; they're not real soldiers. I don't want a pretend war; I want the real thing.

He scrolled down to look at some of the comments people posted.

"We whipped those Yankees at Manassas and still can take them on."
"The War was the North's fault. They should have just let us go . . . "
" . . . the South had nothing we Yankees want or need. Still doesn't."

Will stopped reading. Too much anger out there. Even now, over a century later.

He continued his internet searching. The first thing he read was that it was a warm Sunday in July of 1861 when hundreds of civilians came from Washington to watch the armies of the North and the South fight their first big battle. They came to picnic and see the show.

Will stopped reading and suddenly remembered tailgating with his father

104

outside the stadium at Yale University years ago. Even to his childish eyes, he knew that there was enough food and alcohol to make the game better, whichever side won. Of course, the picnickers in July of 1861 weren't at a game, but maybe they didn't know that yet.

Back in Washington, there seemed to be little doubt that it was going to be a Union victory. However, Will learned that the new recruits were poorly trained despite their firm belief that they would go "On to Richmond," the popular slogan of the time. Well, they didn't make it and thousands of men died. Boys really, some who forgot to fire and others who forgot that they were supposed to fight in a line. Some historians said this wasn't a real battle because the troops on both sides were so untrained. Maybe that's true, Will thought, but they sure died a real death. He decided then and there never to trust historians.

Joseph's Colonel, Thomas Jonathan Jackson, was now a Brigadier General with a new name: Stonewall Jackson. The fighting was fierce and ended in a Confederate victory. Will was happy for Joseph as he imagined Joseph chasing his enemies back toward Washington.

The Union retreat was completely disorganized. Thousands of soldiers dropped their weapons and bumped into one another as they ran back to Washington. Some even bumped into their own wounded! Union soldiers and supply wagons and ambulances collided with the picnicking civilians and their wagons and carriages as they all tried to get away.

Suddenly, a Confederate shell hit a wagon just as it was crossing over a small bridge. The bridge became blocked, and then nobody was able to move. It was chaos. As the Confederates cheered, the Federals (another name Will learned for the Union soldiers) tried to get away. Stonewall Jackson asked for more men to finish the Union off, but nobody listened to him. Confederate men were tired and happy. They had beaten the powerful Union Army.

Of course there was a cost, a huge cost, because many men on both sides died. Will read the number of casualties very carefully. The Union Army lost 2,896 men and the Confederate Army lost 1,982 men. Will was more determined than ever to look for Joseph but now that would have to wait. Out his window, he saw the sun beginning to rise so he shut down the computer, got into bed and quickly fell asleep.

Chapter 6

Will yawned three times at breakfast. "There is something a little stupid about having to go to school just so I can come home and do research on the computer all night," he thought to himself. "If I slept six hours now instead of spending six hours at school, I would feel wake up feeling good and, without having homework, I could do a lot more on the computer and even go to bed at a reasonable time tonight. Then I will do better at school tomorrow."

"I'm not feeling so good," he tried.

"Well, see how you feel after school," his mother said. "Maybe it's just a morning thing."

"Right, and maybe yellow fever is just an afternoon thing."

"Yellow fever? Who said anything about yellow fever?"

He sighed. "I'm just saying there's no such thing as a morning thing. You either feel sick or you don't and I feel sick now."

"How sick?"

"Well, I'm not dying if that's what you mean."

"It's not what I meant at all. Did you try your temperature?"

"I'm hot, very hot. And cold too."

"Maybe you should stay home from school and see the doctor."

Will knew this routine. If he said no, she'd send him off to school. If he said yes, he may have to go to the doctor. Yankee ingenuity was called for again. "Whatever you think is best," he said listlessly. "I just want to sleep."

"All right, get back to bed. Call me in the afternoon when you get up and if you don't feel any better, we'll go and see the doctor."

Yay! Will slowly walked up the stairs to his room as his mother watched him anxiously. He fell asleep as soon as his head hit the pillow and slept a solid eight hours. He woke refreshed, and made himself two big turkey sandwiches that he downed with two glasses of milk. He remembered to call his mother, assuring her that he was better and, finally, he went online.

Will told himself sternly, "I'm going to skip playing games today and I'm going to find Joseph."

He first went on a website about genealogy and ancestry but it cost too much money and he was afraid to use his real name. The National Archives looked interesting but not easily accessible. He then found a wonderful site with all sorts of military records called Fold 3. Here he was offered a free seven-day trial membership so he filed that idea for later. Finally, he worked his way to the University of Virginia Special Collections blog where he found daily letters from Union and Confederate soldiers. But still no Joseph.

After dinner, during which his mother scrutinized him to make sure that he was well, Will went upstairs again. Three hours later, he found it, the line that said Joseph had died. "No," he shouted, "It can't be, not Joseph."

Fortunately, Rebecca was downstairs in the living room with the TV blasting and his mother was in the shower, so no one heard his cries. "This has to be a mistake. Joseph cannot be dead."

He worked feverishly, hitting every site he could find looking for information about Joseph. Then he found archive.org, where he located letters from Confederate soldiers who served at the Battle of Manassas. Someone named Rawley Campbell was writing to Mr. and Mrs. Mitchell about Joseph's death:

"Yesterday I lost my best friend, your son, Joseph Mitchell. Joseph was killed bravely attacking the Federal artillery. It happened very quickly and he did not suffer. Joseph never turned away from a battle and was one of our best soldiers. He was also a good man and shared whatever he had with all of us. One time he gave me a pair of his socks because mine got wet and when I hesitated, he said, 'Go on, take it. It's my extra.'

"When times were hard, Joseph and I read his Bible together. We read 'Let Thy mercy, O Lord, be upon us . . . ' May God have mercy on this fine soldier and on me, his friend, who finds it very difficult to imagine going through another battle without him."

Tears fell from Will's eyes. "How could this happen? He just enlisted! I remember how excited he was with the parades and the bands and all the pretty girls. I can't believe something so terrible happened. I'm only five years younger than Joseph." Tears came faster now. "I remember when he told me I was good with words and he asked me to watch out for Unionists. I was the Unionist and now Joseph is dead!" Will put his head in his hands. "I just can't imagine how Edward feels now. I've got to get back to the

Valley now. Maybe if I keep repeating, 'Take me back,' I'll get there."

But Will stayed exactly where he was, in his house in Litchfield, Connecticut.

It was a long night for Will and he struggled to open his eyes when the alarm rang. He woke up and suddenly remembered. Joseph. He had a passing hope that it was all a dream, but looked over at his desk and saw the letter from Rawley that he had printed out. This was no dream. It was real and Joseph was dead.

Will felt heavy, like there was a weight tied to his body. He dressed and came downstairs where he was unable to eat breakfast.

"I'm not hungry."

"That's a first," Rebecca said.

His mother looked carefully at him. "Will, you don't look so good."

"I'm all right. Really."

It was something of an effort to move his body, but he left the house and went to school.

The day was something of a blur until he entered Social Studies. Will thought to himself, "I hope I won't have to give my report today. I don't know that I can."

Ella was the first one to give her report. She talk about Fort Sumter and explained that Fort Sumter was on an island in the middle of Charleston's harbor in South Carolina:

"You see, South Carolina had seceded from the United States of America. Other Southern states did as well. That meant they left America and created their own country called the Confederate States of America. Jefferson Davis was their President. The Confederate States of America really didn't like having a United States military fort in the middle of their harbor, especially since Fort Sumter flew the United States flag. Major Robert Anderson was the commanding officer at Fort Sumter. The Confederate states asked Major Anderson lots of times to leave, but he couldn't leave unless the President gave him orders to leave. And President Buchanan wouldn't.

"Then Abraham Lincoln was elected President. He also refused to allow Major Anderson to leave. Then the men at Fort Sumter began to run out of food. They didn't know what to do. They couldn't just go and leave the Fort to shop for food in Charleston. I guess Major Anderson must have complained to President Lincoln that he and his men were hungry. After all, if the President was keeping them there, the least thing he could do was feed them. So finally, President Lincoln said he would send food to them. Now, that made Jefferson Davis even angrier. He didn't want the soldiers to eat; he wanted them to leave.

"Jefferson Davis sent three men to ask Major Anderson to leave the Fort. Major Anderson refused. The men went back to Charleston. Then they rowed out again to warn Major Anderson that they were going to fire on the Fort. In the early morning, at 4:30 a.m. on April 12, 1861, the Confederates fired and the Civil War began."

"That was very good," said Mrs. Morris. "Class, let's have a discussion. I will begin by asking Ella why South Carolina seceded."

Ella looked uncomfortable. "Well, I only did research on Fort Sumter so I'm not sure of the answer."

"We've discussed this all before. Think."

Ella was quiet. "I guess maybe the Southerners didn't like the idea that they couldn't move their slaves into the territories."

"Very good, Ella. Class, remember that the United States at this time had states and territories, land which was not yet a state. Northerners didn't want these territories to have slaves in them. Southerners felt that the government had no right to tell them that they could not bring their property into the territories. You see, class, they considered slaves property."

No one said anything. Will looked over at Josh, the one African-American boy in their class. He didn't say anything either.

"Why do you think President Lincoln refused to allow Major Anderson to leave Fort Sumter?"

Will relaxed. Forts were easier to think about than slaves. He raised his hand. So did Michael.

"Michael."

"President Lincoln was just elected. If he allowed Major Anderson to evacuate it would mean that he was giving in to the Confederacy. He didn't want to do that."

"Why?"

"Because then he would look like a weak president."

"And why else?"

Michael was silent.

"What do you think President Lincoln thought about secession? Did he think South Carolina and the other Southern states had the legal right to secede?"

The class was quiet.

"All right. What do all of you think about secession? Is it right to just leave your country and declare yourselves independent? What if New Jersey decided to be its own country? How would we feel?"

"Lousy, if they wouldn't let us drive to the Shore," said Jack.

The class laughed.

"Well, that's true. If they were their own country, we would need a passport to drive through New Jersey. Any other reasons against New Jersey seceding besides the Jersey shore?"

"Yes, Maya?"

"Are you allowed to secede?"

"Excellent question. What do you think?"

"You joined the Union and said you'd always be together as one country. I don't think you should be able to leave because then you would break up the country."

"You are in good company. President Lincoln felt the same way. He wanted to preserve the Union. Anyone else?"

Aiden raised his hand. "Suppose you just want to leave. You joined because you wanted to, so shouldn't you be able to leave if you want to? We're supposed to be free, aren't we?"

"Another good answer. So, class, here you see two different interpretations of our Constitution. One says that states joined freely and should be allowed to leave freely and the other says that when states join, they make up a contract to stay together.

This was the basic disagreement about secession."

"Well, was the war about slavery or secession," Will called out.

"Good question, but next time raise your hand. What do you think?"

"I think they should have worked it out so they didn't have to fight."

"Why," called out Jack, "What's wrong with fighting? Of course, if you're a coward you don't want to fight, do you?"

"No one is talking about cowards, Jack-ass. I'm talking about dying. All those young men who were killed."

"Who are you calling a jackass?"

"Will and Jack, that's enough. Yes, Josh?"

"It's worth fighting over slavery. If there was no Civil War, my people would still be slaves and I wouldn't be here in this classroom today."

" 'My' people again," thought Will. "Is that what war is always about?"

"Class," said Mrs. Morris, "We have had a very good discussion but now we have to move along. Jack, why don't you give your report on the Battle of Bull Run."

Jack stood up and began. He gave a summary of the battle and then concluded with, "The Yankees almost won."

"You've made some very interesting points, Jack," said Mrs. Morris. "Who would like to start the questions?"

Will raised his hand. "Hey, Jack, you missed a few things. You missed the fact that the Yankee soldiers ran back to Washington, tripping over themselves and even over their wounded. That sure made them cowards to me."

"Cowards?" answered Jack angrily. "They fought hard."

"Running back home to Washington isn't fighting hard. Why didn't they stay and fight?"

"Because they were a little disorganized and maybe they needed more men. And, anyway, look at all the Confederate soldiers they killed. That was a good thing!"

Will thought about Joseph, strong and happy Joseph, killed by a Yankee soldier. He stood up. "You think so, do you?" Within seconds, he raced over to Jack and punched him hard, knocking him to the ground. Jack's nose started bleeding as he staggered upright. Meanwhile Mrs. Morris called for backup and as Jack began punching back, Will kept thinking, "This is for Joseph."

It was over quickly as two men separated the boys and held them firmly. "I'll take Jack to the nurse," one said as the other said, "and I'll take this one to Mr. Haber."

"If you broke my nose, I'll kill you," Jack threatened.

Will didn't care. He didn't care about anything except Joseph and he was vaguely proud that he avenged Joseph's death even though he knew he hadn't. Not really.

Mr. Haber did not say anything except that Will's mother was on the way. "Do you need to go to the nurse?"

"No, thank you," answered Will. "I'm just a little messy but I'm fine."

"I wish you boys could control yourselves better."

"What kind of example do you adults set? It's one war after another in this world."

Mr. Haber called for the school psychologist to join Will's mother and Mrs. Morris. "I hope Jack's family doesn't sue," worried Mr. Haber.

"Let them. I've been bullied by Jack for this whole year. Well, not anymore."

No one sued and Jack's nose wasn't broken. Will got suspended for a week. The meeting was, as Will complained, "a waste of time." Mr. Haber wanted it over with as little fuss as possible and, for once, he and Will were in complete agreement.

His mother asked Will only one question. "Why?" Will didn't answer. What could he say? I'm angry that Joseph was killed? His mother would ask when Joseph was killed and answering July of 1861 just wouldn't help things. In fact, it would probably make things worse. His mother took away his Xbox, his phone and the computer for a month. "But what if I have an assignment to do," he complained.

"You'll go to the library."

When Will came back to school no one said anything, not even Jack. School was almost over for the year anyway. He gave his report and no one asked any questions. Maybe there weren't any questions to ask. He saw the school psychologist, which was another waste of time. What could he say to a stranger? Why should he talk to a stranger? No stranger would care.

One day at dinner, his mother surprised him. "Will, how would you like to see your father?"

"My father? Why? He left us. He didn't want me so I don't want him."

"Look, Will, what your father did was wrong but it had nothing to do with you."

"Oh, yeah? I think it did. He didn't care about me. And why did he leave anyway? You've never talked about it to me and Rebecca."

"I know and that was wrong. At first I was very hurt so I couldn't talk about it to anyone. Then I was angry. Now, I think you may need him."

"Why?"

"A boy needs a father."

"Not this boy. If he doesn't need me, I don't need him."

Will left the room and went upstairs. He needed to be alone. His father? Why should he see him? He had walked out on them.

"Will." His mother came into his room without knocking. That was clearly an invasion of privacy.

"Will, I know this new school has been very difficult for you."

"Just because I hit Jack doesn't mean things are hard for me." Even as he heard himself say the words, he knew how ridiculous he sounded. "Please leave. I would rather be alone even if there's no computer and no Xbox here."

"What are you going to do?"

"Read about the Civil War."

"Did you know that your father had an ancestor in the Civil War? He was on the Confederate side."

"What! Why didn't you tell me that before?"

"You've only recently become interested in the Civil War. Besides, he was an embarrassment to your father and his family."

"Where was he from? I thought Dad was from Connecticut."

"Your Dad is from Connecticut, but way back his family was from Virginia."

"Where in Virginia? Did they live in the Valley?"

"I have no idea. That's one of the things you could ask your father if you agree to see him."

"He probably doesn't want to see us anyway."

"Oh, I think he does. Actually, he had suggested seeing you and Rebecca a few months ago but I said no."

"Why? You didn't ask us."

He mother looked very uncomfortable. "I was angry. He has another wife."

Will digested this. His mother was quiet while he thought about this news. Eventually, the Confederate soldier from Virginia trumped the new wife. "I'll see him, but I'll see him without the wife. He can take it or leave it."

His mother looked at him appraisingly. "Good for you. I'll contact him soon."

Will went to bed that night feeling somehow better than he had in a long time. He was not sure that he wanted to see his father, but he was sure that he want to learn everything he could about that Confederate soldier, his ancestor from Virginia. After all, he may have known Joseph.

Rebecca tried to be her usual know-it-all self, but couldn't hide her surprise at the news about the new wife. "What do you think she'll be like? Do you think she was the reason Dad left?"

"I don't care about her," Will answered. "I'll see Dad, once, but alone, without you."

Rebecca looked hurt. "Why?"

"I have to ask him a few things."

"What things?"

"I want to know about his Confederate ancestor who is also my ancestor."

"You really are crazy. Our father has just surfaced with a new wife and all you can think about is some soldier who died over 150 years ago. Why do you care?"

"Why do you care about a new wife?"

"Because she's our stepmother, dummy."

"Not mine. I'm only interested in my ancestor. Not Dad, definitely not the new wife and not any children if they have them."

"Children? You mean we could have a stepbrother or a stepsister? Maybe they even have a new baby! I didn't think of that. You're enough of a handful; I don't know if I can handle more children."

"You don't have to see him — or his new wife and kids, if they have any," Will said with as much dignity as he could muster.

The following week, Will's mother announced that his father would be picking him up and taking him to dinner on Wednesday.

"What if I'm busy on Wednesday," Will said truculently.

"Are you?"

"No, but that's not the point. If Dad really cared, he would call and ask me when I was available."

His mother looked uncomfortable again. "Well, actually, I told him not to contact you. I said I would ask you about Wednesday."

"And why did you do that?"

"I thought it might be easier for you."

"Stop making decisions for me," Will shouted.

His mother sighed. "All right, I was wrong. But do you want to go Wednesday or not?"

"I'll go, but only for the Mitchells."

"The Mitchells. What do they have to do with this?"

When Will didn't say anything, she went on, "Oh, right, they're those Civil War friends. That's why you want to see your Dad. So you can tell the Mitchells all about your ancestor. Will, I wish you'd invite them over one day; I'd like to meet them."

"Not now. Let me meet Dad first."

Jack and his friends must have declared a truce because no one bothered Will that week at school. As long as they left him alone, it was okay with him. Will wished he could tell Edward that his strategy for dealing with bullies worked.

It seemed to Will that Wednesday came very quickly.

"I hope you're planning to take a shower and change those jeans," his mother said.

"Why would I do that?"

"Well, you're meeting your father for the first time in over a year and . . . "

"His problem, not mine," interrupted Will. "He can take me as I am or not take me at all."

His mother frowned, but before she could say anything, the doorbell rang. She opened the door while Will busied himself reading.

"Hello. Good to see you," he said to Will's mother. "And look at that man over there. When I left he was a boy." He came over and stuck out his hand.

This is moving too fast. If I don't shake hands, I'll look stupid. A thousand thoughts rushed through his head. Will finally took his father's hand, careful to make his handshake as firm as his father's. "Your hair got a little white."

"That it did. For my sins."

Will didn't laugh.

They went outside and climbed into a Mercedes. "New car?"

"I had to drive something when I gave your mother the family car."

"Doesn't look as if you suffered with the trade."

His father didn't say anything for a while and they drove quietly. "So, Will, where do you want to go to eat?"

"I don't care."

"Do you like Italian?"

"Always did."

"All right, then. We'll go to Giovanni's, up in Bantam."

The ride was uncomfortable. "So, how have you been," his father finally asked.

"Okay."

"Well, it's been about a year."

"A year and five and a half months, but who is counting?"

"You always had a mathematical mind."

"Right. And I flew airplanes," Will took a deep breath to try to calm down, and thought, "Who's he kidding? My math was never that good."

They parked the car, went into the restaurant and were quickly ushered into a booth. A server took their drink order, a Coke for Will and a scotch for his father.

"So, how's soccer?"

"I don't play anymore."

"Why not? You were pretty good."

"I sucked."

"Dad . . ." "Will . . . " both he and his father spoke at the same time.

"Go ahead, Will."

"No, you go first."

"Look, I know you are angry and I don't blame you. I just want you to know that I'm sorry. I behaved badly toward you and your sister and your mom and . . . I just don't know what to say."

"That's it? That's your apology?" Will was tempted to run out of the restaurant and call his mother to pick him up.

"Will, if it makes you feel better or even if it doesn't, I did try to see you and your mother always said no."

"Oh, so now you deciding to go away was Mom's fault?"

"No," his father said steadily, "It was mine. After I left, I met someone else, Catherine, and we're now married."

"I suppose that you have a new family now too. How many children do you have?"

"Children? No, Catherine and I have no children together. She has a daughter who lives in Boston with her father. Will, lots of things were happening and work was going badly and your mother and I were having problems and I did the wrong thing. I just picked up and left. I did not act like a man should act . . . I ran away. There is nothing I can do about the past but I hope we can somehow have a future together and that one day you will be able to forgive me."

Will said nothing. The server came over to take their order. He hadn't even looked at the menu but ordered meatballs and spaghetti anyway.

"There is something I did want to talk with you about."

"Anything, Will."

"Mom said you had an ancestor in the Civil War, a Confederate soldier. I want to know everything about him."

His father looked surprised. "You want to know what . . . ?"

"Where he was from, what battles he fought, what he did in the War, everything you know."

His father looked at him and then started to laugh.

Will stood up. "I'm going home."

"No, please, Will, stop. I am not laughing at you. I am laughing at myself. I was nervous about seeing you and when you said you wanted to talk I imagined all sorts of serious things."

"This is serious."

"I know," his father said quickly. "It just wasn't what I was expecting. I'll tell you everything I know and I can even show you some of his letters. His mother kept them and they were passed down and eventually found their way to my mother."

"Where did he live?"

"Richmond, Virginia."

Will's face fell.

"Did I say the wrong thing? You look disappointed."

"I was hoping for the Shenandoah Valley."

"No, it was Richmond."

"What was his name?"

"His name was William Bradford."

"But that's my name!"

"I know." He smiled gently at Will, "I named you."

Chapter 7

"Well, how did it go," Rebecca asked as soon as he came back from the restaurant.

"I have a Confederate ancestor named William Bradford. He's your ancestor too."

"Great. Maybe we also have an ancestor who was in the Crusades! Who cares about our ancestors? I meant how did it go with Dad? What is Dad like now? Did he tell you why he left? Does he have any other children? I want to know what to expect when I go out to eat with him."

Will looked at Rebecca. She was eager but he could tell that she was a little scared. Funny, he never thought that Rebecca was scared of anything. He stood up a little straighter. Dad didn't scare him! "He has a stepdaughter, but she doesn't live with him. He has more white hair than I remember. He said he was sorry for leaving so suddenly, but I'm not sure he really means it. He lives in New Hampshire, about three hours away from us and he suddenly says he wants to see us once a month. I bet that won't last long. He's giving me some letters from our ancestor. I told him that I needed them right away, so he said he'll come back next week and give them to me. He says he'll have to find them, and I guess he's afraid to mail them in case they get lost. Probably he makes a lot of money in his new job, because he drives a Mercedes now."

Rebecca blinked. That was a lot of information from Will. "How does Mom feel about it?"

"About what," asked their mother as she came into the room.

"About Dad seeing us every month."

"If that's what you want, then that's fine with me. I've reconsidered and I think that children need a father. Will, was your father helpful to you?"

"Yeah. He's coming next week to bring me some letters from my Confederate ancestor, William Bradford."

She exchanged a look with Rebecca. "That's nice."

"Nice? It's awesome! I'm going to read now. It's fifteen and a half more days till I have my computer and Xbox back."

"Will," she called as he started going up the stairs. "Did you and your father talk about anything else?"

"Yeah, but nothing important."

* * *

School was almost over. It had been a whole year since he came to this awful town. And now he had finals. How stupid was that? You study to pass and then you forget what you studied just as soon as you can. No one talked to him at school anymore. That was okay; there was no one he wanted to talk to anyway.

"Are you studying," his mother asked worriedly.

"Always, Mom."

"Will, I'm serious. You have to do well."

"Why?"

"Will, stop it."

"I'm only kidding. Look, what else do I have to do? Of course, in eight more days I'll be able to live again."

"As long as there is no repeat of your fight with Jack. I wonder if that Call of Battle game contributed to your bad behavior."

"Undoubtedly. I watched and learned how to attack."

"Will!"

"Only kidding. There is absolutely nothing in Call of Battle that leads to fighting, nothing."

"Even though all you do in that game is fight?"

"You just don't understand."

131

The following week his father drove down to take Rebecca to dinner. He went straight over to Will and immediately said, "I couldn't find the letters, but I know I have them somewhere. I still haven't unpacked some of the boxes I brought with me when I moved to New Hampshire."

"You moved over a year ago. You probably threw the letters out, needing a new life and all," Will said bitterly.

"I know I wouldn't have done that. You'll have to be patient, Will. I promise I will find them and bring them to you."

There was a lot Will wanted to say, but he wanted the letters even more. He contented himself with, "I'm not holding my breath."

His father ignored him and said, "You know, I don't know much about William Bradford because he was kind of an embarrassment to my grandfather, being Confederate and all."

"Why? The war had been over a long time when your grandfather was alive."

"You know what William Faulkner said, don't you?"

"No, what?"

"He said, 'The past is not dead. In fact, it's not even past.' "

"What's that supposed to mean?"

"It means people have long memories."

"Isn't that a good thing?"

"Sometimes. Other times it isn't. There's a time to fight and a time to forgive and it's a tough call knowing when to do what."

Will thought about the implications of that in his own life and quickly changed the subject.

"Do we still have family in Richmond?"

"If we do, I never met them. Why all this interest in William Bradford, an ancestor you never even knew existed?"

"Maybe I need to find another relative since one of mine just up and disappeared one day."

"Ah, Will, you sure know how to throw a punch. I guess I deserved it. I am sorry about leaving so suddenly. I should never have left without saying goodbye. There is nothing else I can say. Maybe one day you'll forgive me."

"And maybe I won't," Will silently thought.

"Speaking of throwing punches, your mother told me about a fight you got into at school. Do you want to talk about it?"

To you? "No."

"That's all right. But if you ever do, I'm available. Here is my phone number, work, cell and home. Please call if you need me." He scribbled an unfamiliar telephone number on the back of his card.

"Fat chance of that," Will thought to himself. He grudgingly took the business card his father handed him. "I should throw that card back at him but I won't, because I need to find out more about this new ancestor of mine."

Will asked, "So, what else do you know about William?"

"That's about it. I never really thought about him."

"I'll find out more. I've gotten pretty good at looking up stuff about people online."

"Your mother said that you've become interested in the Civil War and that you have new friends who share your interest."

Right. And one of them died in the Civil War.

"All right, then. I'll see you soon and I hope you find what you're looking for."

* * *

School let out and Will had nothing to do. He refused to join the local summer soccer team and also refused to work as a counselor in the town day camp. Why would he? Many of the kids who made his life miserable this year would be there as well.

It was still six more days before he could go back online. What should he do? Will looked around his room and saw the Bruce

Catton book lying where he had left it. He turned to the chapter on Northern camp life. He learned about drills. Apparently they drilled all the time. When they weren't drilling, they were bored. He could relate to that. Close question as to which was worse, drilling or being bored. They also sang a lot and wrote letters home and played all sorts of games. Baseball began then. Of course, sometimes they fought in a battle and that sure wasn't boring. He wondered if he would have liked being a soldier.

"But how can I know if I would fight or run or even just hang back? I think I would fight but how could I know for sure?" Will mused.

Suddenly the answer to that question became very important. I hope I wouldn't be a coward. I fought for Joseph when it felt like Jack attacked him, so maybe I would fight for the men in my company. Why else would I fight? He thought about that question and decided he would fight for his home and his family.

At dinner that night he told his mother and Rebecca that if a war came, he realized that he would fight for them.

Rebecca sighed. "You don't know how to keep your mouth shut, Will," she whispered. "Now Mom is going to get all upset again."

"Why? I thought she'd be proud of me."

"Will," said his mother in her softest voice, the one that usually meant you were in trouble, "Will, why are you thinking about fighting? Is anyone bullying you still, even though school is out?"

"No. I am never again going to be bullied. I will stand up and fight!"

"That's my concern."

"It's probably only the books he's reading. You know, all that Civil War stuff," chimed in Rebecca.

"Maybe you should stop reading about the Civil War for a while," his mother suggested. "It may be upsetting you."

Why? Just because a young man died and I knew him and his family? "Mom, you're supposed to be upset by war. All that dying is upsetting."

"You know, I think it's time you talk to someone."

"Who?"

"A therapist. I have the names of some good ones and I think you might feel better if you talked about your feelings."

"I feel fine. Anyway, whenever I even mention my feelings, you just get upset."

"Well, that's why I want you to talk with a professional. Your father agrees with me."

"My father? The one who walked out without saying good-bye? He's the one who needs a therapist, not me."

Will finished his dinner without much appetite. Conversations with his mother did that sometimes. He went upstairs to his room and opened the Catton book. He read about slow-moving Major General George B. McClellan preparing to move up the Virginia Peninsula to Richmond in April of 1862. "I guess if the Union Army captured Richmond, the Confederate capital, they would win the war. Kind of like chess, only with real people."

The Peninsula was rainy and the ground was muddy. Apparently, McClellan had many more troops than his enemy, Joe Johnston, but McClellan refused to believe it. He always underestimated the strength of his army and overestimated the strength of his enemy's army. Wonder why? I read he used to drive President Lincoln crazy with his inability to get anything done. My mother would think that McClellan should have seen a therapist. Maybe she'd be right.

There was a knock on the door. "Come in."

It was his mother. "Will, I think you should stop reading that book."

"I think that's called censorship, only I can't imagine why you want to ban this book. Bruce Catton would be so upset to think that you consider his book dangerous. Good thing he's dead."

"I'm not worried about Bruce Catton; I'm worried about you. If you didn't read about this awful war, maybe you would think about other things."

"What things? My father? School? My exciting summer? Maybe I will expand that to my exciting life here in Litchfield?"

"That's just what I mean."

Realizing she was serious and knowing just how unreasonable his mother could be when she was serious, Will said, "How about I just finish this chapter? Then I'll read something else."

"All right. But I'm taking that book away from you after you finish the chapter."

He thought about discussing his rights, free speech and all that, but quickly realized it would be futile. His mother never cared about things like that. "O.K. Now leave so I can hurry up and finish this chapter."

"This is it," he thought when she closed the door. "I'm going to run away. I just have to figure out where to go. I might consider . . . " Suddenly he felt himself hurtling downward. He couldn't stop himself but he wasn't afraid. He just kept going until he landed rather harshly in the field near the Mitchell's home. He felt a little dizzy. He walked to the house with his eyes focusing straight ahead on the porch so the dizziness would go away.

"This is the same Willows, but it all looks different. The fence seems to have collapsed and there are tents over there where the garden used to be. Where is everyone? There's no one working in the fields."

Will climbed up the stairs and knocked on the front door. No answer. He tried again. Nothing. Tentatively, he turned the knob and the door opened. He peeked inside. It was dark, at least darker than he had remembered, so he stepped inside cautiously and called out, "Anyone home?"

"Yeah, someone's home. We are."

Will turned around and looked straight into the eyes of a Yankee soldier. "Oh. What's ah . . . going on?"

The soldier smiled a mean kind of smile. "Well . . . some might call it a war. Are you a friend of the folks who used to live here? Now, who are you?"

Will gulped. "I'm Will Bradford."

"Yeah, and what on earth are you doing here, Will Bradford?"

"I thought I was visiting, but I'll just leave and . . .

"Not so fast. Like I said, we're in a war so just maybe you're my prisoner."

"Leave the boy alone," called out another voice.

"I'm not a kid," Will yelled angrily.

"Suit yourself. Don't leave him alone."

"No, wait," Will said. "It sort of depends upon your definition of a kid."

Both soldiers stared at him.

"I mean, I'm fourteen but I don't feel like a kid. I was just coming here to see how everyone was doing because I was traveling through the Valley and . . . "

"Traveling now? Where are you from, boy?"

This question was definitely a challenge. If I admit to being from Connecticut, they might let me go. On the other hand, what fourteen-year-old is traveling to the Valley all the way from Connecticut in the middle of the Civil War?

"Well . . . ?"

Will decided to try what his Grandmother always called the lesser of two evils. "I'm actually from Connecticut."

The mean soldier nodded. "Actually, so am I. So, where in Connecticut are you from?"

"Litchfield."

"Isn't that nice for you? Something smells here, so I'm taking you in to my commanding officer."

The friendlier soldier frowned. "Wait a minute, Ben. Let's figure this out."

"You figure it out. Do with him what you want. I leave him in your hands."

Will watched him walk away. "Ben's always cranky before a meal," explained the soldier. "But he has a point and that's the fact that we have no idea why you're here. I think you need to do a little explaining."

Please, God, let me think of something. Then he got it! "I'm here looking for my ancestor."

"Your ancestor? Boy, my patience is running out."

"No, I don't really mean my ancestor. I mean my relative."

"What outfit is he with?"

"I don't know."

"Why did you come here then?"

"I think he's somewhere in the Valley. That's what we heard anyway. My family needs him."

The soldier sighed. "I don't need this now. We were on our way to Richmond to help General McClellan and then that Stonewall Jackson fellow started causing all sorts of problems here in the Valley so we can't leave. Jackson's a good officer, I'll give him that. We never knows where he's going to strike next! Now there's you, another problem. Tell me this minute why you're here."

Will didn't hesitate. "Jane and Edward Mitchell are my friends and I came to see how they were doing. Their brother, Joseph, was killed at Manassas."

"So were a lot of our men."

"I know, and that's terrible. It's all terrible. But I knew Joseph, sir, and I felt bad."

"You know that they're our enemy."

"They're my friends. The Confederacy may be our enemy, but Jane and Edward and Benjamin, too, are my friends. Can't you understand that?"

"Let me give you a bit of advice. Not too many men are going to understand that, not while these people you call your friends are shooting at us and killing our men. So, just keep your feelings to yourself. We'll say you came to visit and now you're leaving to go home. And for what it's worth, I'm sorry for the loss of your friend. That's the trouble with war; it's all about loss."

Will cried out, "Can't anyone stop it?"

"It is too late. Maybe they could have once, I don't know. Some men tried. South Carolina sure didn't when they fired on Fort Sumter and started the war, but that's all well and gone now. We just have to go on and win. The sooner we win, the sooner it will be over and people can go back to living their normal lives."

They were both quiet for a few seconds. Then the soldier spoke, "Come on with me.

I'll walk you past the pickets to the road. It's not safe around here. Go back wherever you came from and forget your friends. That's the best advice I can give you."

"Thank you."

They walked together silently. "I'm leaving you now, boy," said the soldier. "Take care of yourself."

"You too."

"I'll try my best. I hope you find your relative and stay safe."

Will watched the soldier walk away. He felt a little bit like the Scarecrow in *The Wizard of Oz* as he looked both ways and wondered which way to go. "This way, that way, which way should I go? No GPS, no computer, eeny, meeny, miney, mo," he rhymed to himself.

No one was around except groups of Yankee soldiers camped on fields, now filled with rows and rows of tents instead of crops. Men sat outside the tents and played cards, talked, read, and wrote letters home. Far away, Will heard the sound of a fiddle. He decided that he better get going before another nosy soldier came over to him, but where should he go? Then it came to him . . . the church. "I will walk to the church where the Mitchells used to go and I'll find someone who knows where they are."

Satisfied, Will set out at a brisk pace, wishing he had brought some food with him. Before too long, he came to the small town he remembered. Last time he was here, Joseph and his friends came to enlist and everyone treated them like heroes.

When he came to the church, he was surprised by all the activity. He wondered if it could be Sunday, then looked around more carefully. There seemed to be men and women going in and out and he watched a man, obviously wounded, being carried inside.

"Can I help you?"

He turned toward the voice and saw a young woman looking concerned. "Are you lost? The hospital is over there," she said pointing to the church.

"Isn't that the church?"

"Well, now it's a Yankee hospital, although some of our men are inside too."

"What happened here?"

She stared at him. "What do you mean what happened? We're in the middle of a war, of course, and troops keep passing through here to get to Winchester."

"What troops?"

"All troops, Federal and Confederate."

Will digested this information, and then asked, "So what date is this anyway? I forget."

The young lady looked at Will curiously. "It's May. Do you want the year as well," she asked sarcastically.

"Why turn down information," Will said gamely, hoping she would be able to tell him the year. After all, the Civil War lasted for four years.

"1862."

"And why are you out here all alone," he asked boldly, remembering that women (or ladies as they were then called), rarely went anywhere alone.

"I am a teacher and I used to teach at the Comstock Female Academy. It closed because of the War and since there are few schools left here anymore, I am now a private tutor in the home of a good family."

"What happened to your home?"

"It was burned. And what about you? You look too young to be a soldier. Where is your home?"

"Gone as well. By the way, do you know a family named Mitchell? I'm looking for them."

"I think so, but I wouldn't know where they are now. I am sorry, but I am going to help the wounded soldiers and I don't have much time to talk."

"But, wait, who can I ask about the Mitchells?"

"Ask any one of the older ladies. They know everyone," she called out as she walked away.

Will debated whether or not to follow when someone called his name. "Will Bradford. That's who you are, isn't it?"

"Yes, ma'am," he answered, looking straight at an older lady wearing a heavy bonnet with a long kind of curtain pinned up around it that could, he supposed, be let down to hide her face. It was not down now.

"Do you remember me?"

Before Will could think of an answer, she said, "I am Mrs. Pritchard and I never forget a face. I know you. We met at the church when Joseph left. You're the boy who disappeared just after he enlisted, aren't you? Poor Joseph. How sad that we are sacrificing all our brave young men. May God in His mercy save us."

Will nodded. "I am looking for the Mitchells. Do you know where they are?"

"Poor, poor Mrs. Mitchell. She was younger, but I remember her fondly from our school days. I have sad news to share. After Joseph was killed at Manassas, Sarah and Henry passed away. Henry went first, the scarlet fever. At first he looked like the sun burned him, then a redness with tiny bumps spread all over his body and, finally, the red streaks came. Just about then Sarah got the same sunburn and they both died within days of each other."

"But they were fine when I was here, and that was only one year ago!"

"It was the scarlet fever," Mrs. Pritchard repeated. "There was nothing anyone could do."

Will didn't know what to say. Antibiotics can cure scarlet fever. Will knew this because one of his classmates in his old school got that fever, took antibiotics and got better. Imagine, here in 1862 there were no antibiotics to help Sarah and Henry.

"You look so upset. Will, I am almost afraid to tell you the rest."

"There's more?"

"I'm afraid so. The Yankees came and camped at Willows. Wherever soldiers go, illness follows and the Yankees brought the very sick ones inside the house. Soon Mr. Mitchell took ill and passed away and then they ordered Mrs. Mitchell to leave. She went with Edward, Benjamin and Jane to live in her family's home in Winchester where she grew up."

Will was reeling with all this bad news. "I don't understand. I was here just a while ago. What happened to Tom and Mary and their baby?"

"Tom joined Robs and is now with Stonewall Jackson somewhere in the Valley.

He sent Mary and the baby to Richmond to Mary's Grandmother Patterson. We hear that they are fine."

"I still don't understand," he repeated. "I had such a good time when I was here. We had adventures and we ate good food and . . . . " He was suddenly unable to speak anymore.

"Will, come with me; you need to sit down." She put a surprisingly strong hand under his elbow and led him to a small house where Yankees were lounging on the front porch and stairs.

"Shoo," she said to them. "I'm bringing home a sick boy."

Only one soldier moved to make room for them to climb up the front steps into the house. "Some of them have manners," she said loudly, adding pointedly, "And some of them don't."

Mrs. Pritchard led him into the house and down the hallway. "Now, you sit down right here in what was my parlor, but is now some kind of office for one of the generals."

"I don't understand . . . . "

"Oh, they just up and took my house, said they needed it for some kind of headquarters so I told them the best I can do is share it with them but I won't move."

"And they let you stay?"

"Well, some of them learned manners from their mammas back home. Yes, I am staying. Now, let me fix you a cup of tea. With the blockade, we don't have much in the way of tea but I hid some as soon as the war began. Have no coffee though. Tried making it with wheat, then with corn and, finally, with rye. It's not too bad. Heavens, if I can say that I've probably forgotten what real coffee really tastes like."

She bustled out of the room. In a little while, she came back with a tray. The sight and smell of the food made Will's mouth water. He couldn't even remember when he ate last.

"Now, young Will, drink this tea. Nothing is as good for shock as tea and you have had a real shock. 'Course some say whiskey is just as good if not better, but I don't hold with drinking. Never did. I fixed you some cold chicken and these beans from my garden. The Yankees here raid my garden, try to steal my chickens and if they are not stealing, they are trampling the vegetables with their horses and boots. It's been a trial, I tell you."

The tea did make him feel better.

"Your color is back, Will. Now eat."

He did as she commanded and had to admit he felt better. When he had finished, she smiled. "Feeling better?"

"Yes, Ma'am, I am." As soon as he said the words, he remembered that Joseph, Sarah, Henry and Mr. Mitchell were all dead. "How could they all be gone?"

"It is not for us to know, Will. God does as he sees fit."

"This wasn't God. Joseph was killed by these Yankees here and . . . "

"And what? Who are you going to say killed good Mr. Mitchell and those babies?"

"I don't know: I just don't know."

"Will," she added more gently, "We don't none of us know. None of us. We just have to accept what is and do the best we can."

"But it didn't have to be. There are antibiotics, I mean medicines, for scarlet fever."

"Not here there aren't, and if they are somewhere else where we can't get them, then we have to leave it alone. Will, I don't go holding with some story you told the Mitchells about how you came to be here."

Will felt a tinge of fear. Was she a witch like Edward suspected? Were there such things? Could she possibly know the truth?

She went on more gently. "I don't know where you really came from and it isn't my business anyway. But I'm an old lady now and I've seen too many things to believe just whatever I'm told. Wherever you are from, Will Bradford, keep it to yourself. Never tell and never confuse your place back there with your place here."

"I don't even know why I'm here," Will cried out.

"Then you are in good company. Does anyone of us know for sure why we are here? I expect we are all here to do some good and maybe, just maybe, to bring a little love into this sorry world. Now, that's all I'm going to say on the matter."

"But what should I do now? I want to find Mrs. Mitchell and Edward, Jane and Benjamin."

"So, go and find them in Winchester."

"I guess I can walk to Winchester?"

"Yes. Just be careful on the road."

"What road?"

"The Valley Pike, of course. Just follow it and it will lead you to Winchester."

Will had seen a map of the Valley Turnpike in the big Catton book he had read at home. It was the only paved road in the Valley and it went all the way from Martinsburg in the north to Staunton in the south. The odd thing, Will remembered, was that the locals said they were going "up" the Valley when they were going south and "down" the Valley when they were going north.

The Valley Pike was the road everyone used. Farmers traveled to market, businessmen traveled to customers and merchants traveled to their buyers. Ordinary people took the stage up and down the Valley Pike while wealthy people took their carriages. Now Union and Confederate soldiers were traveling up and down the same Valley Pike and Will couldn't help but wonder what would happen when they met. He guessed they would fight each other. Who would he meet? Would he have to fight? If so, who would he be fighting?

"Stop worrying. You will be all right."

How did she know he was worried? He looked at her suspiciously.

Mrs. Pritchard laughed. "Now, you stop giving me that look. It wasn't magic. Anyone in your place would be worried. And, Will . . . ."

"Yes, Ma'am?"

"Remember that we cannot choose our troubles, but we can choose how we react to them. Be strong. Take strength from your people and your God. They will be with you."

Will felt ashamed of his previous thoughts. "Thank you for everything. I wonder if I will ever see you again."

The older lady shook her head and smiled. "That's just another one of those things we can't know, Will. But we can know we helped each other and we can remember that when we need a bit of kindness. Go now, and God be with you."

"Where do I go?"

"That way," she said pointing. "You can't miss the Valley Pike. It's the busiest road in these parts."

Chapter 8

Will started walking. By the time he came to the Valley Pike, his feet were hurting from blisters that felt as they were growing bigger with every step he took. Will looked around and wondered which way to go. He saw a group of Union soldiers hurrying by and joined them. "Is this the way to Winchester," he asked.

He received no answer. "Where are you going," he asked in a louder voice to the next soldier who passed him.

Again, there was no answer.

Will was desperate. Finally, he pushed the man next to him with a "Sorry. I didn't mean to do that." When the man scowled at him, Will quickly said. "Where are we going, anyway?"

"You been drinking too much applejack?"

"What do you mean? I'm not drinking anything and what's applejack anyway?"

"It'll make you drunk and mind you, keep away from it." Then the soldier grumbled, "Babies. They let babies in this war."

"I just want to know where we are going," Will asked plaintively.

"Winchester, where else?"

"And we are going because?"

"We are retreating. Them Secesh whipped us at Front Royal."

"Secesh?"

"Rebels, Confederates, traitors, whatever you want to call them. Anyway, we had to retreat and now we're heading to Winchester."

"How do we get there?"

"Follow the Valley Pike, the way we're all doing."

"Thank you."

The man shook his head. "Young'uns don't belong here."

Will thought the man was probably right, but he continued walking anyway. There were mountains to the east and mountains to the west but farms dominated the land around him. The land was green and lush and it would have been very pretty, he thought, except for all those Union soldiers running with their rifles.

Then there were the dead men and the dead horses. Will had never seen either a dead man or a dead horse before, and the sight was far from pretty. And there was the smell. Between the smell of the gunpowder and the smell of the bodies, living and dead, Will began to feel more than slightly ill.

Of course, the noise didn't help. There were the cries of men and the cries of horses. It seemed as if dying wasn't easy. He hurried along, careful to avert his eyes from all the horrible scenes surrounding him. Finally, he forced himself to look around. "Isn't anyone going to help these hurt men," he cried aloud. Then, suddenly, he realized that it was up to him. He, Will Bradford, was probably the only one with no reason to run, so it was up to him to stop and help at least one of the hurt soldiers.

At that thought, Will stopped walking and two men immediately bumped into him, knocking him over. "Watch where you're going," one of them called out. "You're out of uniform," growled the other.

Will got back up and looked for someone he could help, someone who was still alive. He heard a young man calling out, "Water, water" and he ran over to the soldier.

"Sorry, I don't have any water, but where are you hurt?"

"Everywhere."

Will knew he had to do something, but he had nothing . . . no water, no bandages, no skills. How could he help this young soldier who was sitting in the middle of the Valley Pike where he could easily be run over?

"Can you stand?"

"I don't know. Maybe."

Will helped him to his feet and half-pulled, half-dragged the man off the Pike, remembering to be gentle in case something was broken. "I'm coming back," he assured the young man after he had found a safe spot for him to rest, out of the way of the soldiers, the horses and the wagons. "I promise."

Will looked around and noticed that there were broken and upset wagons everywhere. All he needed to do was find a wagon that was not burning, occupied or already looted. After a few tries, Will found one. Two of the large wheels lay broken and useless. Pieces of the canvas top were half torn off so he took some, figuring they might be of use. He found some kind of bandages and took that as well. He continued rummaging around until he found some food and a bottle of whiskey. "I once saw a movie where whiskey was used to disinfect a wound," Will remembered, so he took the bottle as well.

After taking all he hoped he'd need to treat the wounded soldier, Will spied some peaches which had fallen out of a basket. He grabbed them and put them in his pockets. "Always did like peaches," he thought to himself, wondering how he could be thinking about eating any time soon.

Walking back, he saw a canteen on the ground, right next to a dead soldier. He didn't hesitate to pick it up and quickly ran back to the young man lying by the side of the Pike.

"Here, drink this." Will lifted the man's head and helped him drink water from the canteen.

"More," demanded the soldier. Will remembered reading somewhere that water should be given slowly. Was that only for dehydration? Was this soldier dehydrated? He didn't know but gave him more water anyway.

"Thank you."

"You're welcome. What hurts you?"

"It's my leg." Will looked down and noticed blood on the man's right leg. He ripped part of his own sleeve off and applied a tourniquet like he had learned to make last year in health class. "I think we need to get you to a hospital, but how and where?"

"A hospital? No, not a hospital. They might amputate my leg. No hospital!"

Will remembered reading about all the amputations they did during the Civil War. No wonder the man was afraid. He'd be afraid too. Most patients died either from surgery or from an infection that they got after surgery.

"I'll get you some kind of help, even if it's not in a hospital."

"I'm Charles Walker with the 5th Connecticut," he said, and promptly passed out.

Will looked around. "What am I going to do now? How can I get him where someone can treat him? What's the point of being from the 21st century if you can't figure things out in the 19th century? I can't use technology so I'll try to use what's left of my brain. Let's see, I know there are stretchers, but for that we need two men. Then there are wagons but the empty ones are useless. Of course, there are horses . . . horses, that's it! With all these dead men, surely there is a horse to spare."

He made sure Charles had not awakened and carefully hid the canteen. After all, a thirsty man might steal it. "Well, I can't save them all," he reasoned. Then he got back on to the Pike. Men were still running but there, across the Pike, was a horse calmly grazing on the side of the road. He hurried over, then stopped, not wanting to scare the animal. "Here, horse," he tried, but the horse didn't even look at him. He suddenly remembered the peaches. "I know horses like apples, but maybe this one might like a peach." Will reached into his pocket and pulled out one of the peaches. "Here, horsey.

Try a peach." He held out his hand and much to his amazement, the horse came over and began to eat. "Good girl." Will carefully took the reins and led the horse back to the soldier. After all, since he was already a food and whiskey thief, why not add horse stealing to his record?

Will tied the reins to a nearby tree the way he had seen it done in movies and bent down to have a closer look at the leg. He loosened the tourniquet and saw that the wound had stopped bleeding. He washed his hands with the whiskey and probed the cut to make sure there was no bullet stuck inside.

"What are you doing," cried out an agitated Charles.

"Relax, this isn't fun for me either. I'm trying to make sure you don't have a bullet or something stuck in there."

"Do I?"

"I don't think so. Look, my knowledge of medical stuff is from another time, but I really think we should somehow try to disinfect it and the only way I can imagine without antibiotics is alcohol."

"Anti . . . what?"

"Oh, that's a term for the medicines my family use."

"Herbs?"

"Kind of. Anyway all we have is alcohol and I know it will hurt but I don't know what else to do."

"Then what? Where is my Company?"

"I don't know."

"Say," Charles suddenly asked suspiciously, "You're not one of them Rebels, are you? You don't have a uniform and you look kind of young but these days you never know."

"I'm fourteen years old and I'm from Connecticut."

"Oh . . . well, I'm not fourteen years old but I'm from Connecticut as well. Danbury, Connecticut."

"I'm from Litchfield."

They both started to laugh.

Charles shook his head. "Guess we're neighbors of sorts."

"But you can never tell anyone," Will said anxiously. "Please promise. No one here can know where I'm from."

"Running away? I understand. Your secret is safe with me. This is sure one hell of a place to meet. Go ahead. Use the damn alcohol."

Will rolled up a piece of canvas and said, "Bite this hard. The alcohol will hurt."

Will poured half the bottle on the injured area, which seemed to be only a flesh wound. Afterwards, he made a bandage as best as he could and then took another piece of canvas to wipe the sweat from Charles' face. "Can you stand?"

"For a little while, if you help me."

"I have a horse but I'm not really a rider. I only did it a few times when I was in camp."

"Camp? What camp?" Again the soldier looked suspicious.

"Camp Mohegan in upstate New York."

"What camp is that? I thought you weren't in the army. Oh, forget it. Let's just get out of here. Who ever heard of riding only a few times? How do you get around? You can't only use wagons."

"I can."

Will resolutely ignored the look of disbelief on Charles' face. He helped Charles struggle to his feet, then they both got on the horse together, Charles in front and Will behind him to support him if he got weak and started to fall. "Your job is to guide the horse," Will told Charles, "Mine is to stay on. Now, we'll follow the Pike and head to Winchester."

The ride was a nightmare. Charles explained that Stonewall Jackson had made a surprise attack in Front Royal and overwhelmed the Union soldiers stationed there.

"I was with General Banks at his headquarters in Strasburg and no one there believed that Jackson had much of a force. We didn't know there was a Louisiana brigade fighting with him. After the attack, all the troops evacuated to Winchester. All of us, that is, who could."

"I see," answered Will as he looked around the Pike. "I guess Jackson is coming after you . . . I mean us."

"Those Rebels will stop at nothing to win a war they started for no reason other than to allow some rich planters to keep their slaves. I don't understand them. Over half of the men fighting don't even have slaves."

"They feel like you invaded their state and their homes."

" 'Course we did. They wanted to destroy the Union."

Will decided this was not the best time for a political discussion on who or what started the war. They just had to reach Winchester. He felt Charles' body go a little limp.

"Are you all right?"

"I just suddenly got very tired."

"Stay awake; we're almost there," he said, although he had no idea how far it really was to Winchester.

The long Union wagon train, the horses, and the foot soldiers all added to the din of

163

the crowded Pike. Will sensed the urgency; it was in the air. You could feel it as it spread from soldier to soldier. The Union Army had to reach and hold Winchester before the Confederate Army came to take it back.

Will hurried because he doubted that the Confederates would appreciate his rescuing a Union soldier even if he did have a Confederate relative. Then again, he was sure the Union Army wouldn't appreciate that relative.

"Hang on," Will called out as Charles began to slip further. He stopped the horse, rolled up some more canvas and tied Charles to his own body. He took hold of the reins and prayed that the horse would obey him. She did. Will just followed the crowd and cheered along with the rest when he saw Union General Banks and the defensive line he drew just south of Winchester in his attempt to stop Jackson.

"Now, what do I do," wondered Will. "I have a half-conscious Union soldier and I'm looking for the Mitchells. I could sure use my computer right now."

"What have you got there," screamed a soldier to him.

"A wounded man."

"Go on through to the Union Hotel Hospital over there."

Will rode through the line and suddenly his horse stopped. "Please, please don't stop," Will said and untying the canvas holding Charles to him, got down. Charles slumped, looking very pale. Will faced the horse. "Look, Peaches, that's your new name, please don't stop. Of course I'm not sure where you should go, but we have to go somewhere."

The horse looked at him. She made a noise. "Maybe she's thirsty," thought Will. "Great. I'm in the middle of a war without even knowing what side I'm on and I have a thirsty horse." He took off Charles' cap and poured a little water from the canteen into it. Peaches drank and seemed to want more. "I don't have much more but I'll give you what I have." Peaches drank all the water. When Will mounted the horse, Peaches was on her best behavior and they nobly entered Winchester and found their way to the hotel that was now serving as a hospital.

Will tethered the horse and helped Charles get down and sit on the ground. Suddenly, a voice called out, "Will? Is that you? Can it be?"

It was Mrs. Mitchell. As she came over to him, he wanted to collapse in her arms. "Mrs. Mitchell! What are you doing here?"

"What am I doing here? I think the question is what are you doing here? I'm taking care of wounded soldiers and it looks like you have one right there."

Charles half rose.

"Should I take him up the steps?"

"No, you come on to my family's home and we'll take care of him there. We all do our best in the hospital, but he will do better in our home, believe me."

"Of course I believe you. I always did."

"Is that your horse?"

"Well, I sort of took it. She was alone on the Valley Pike and we needed a horse. What do you think I should do with her now?"

"We have been under a Union occupation since March and if I have learned anything, Will, it is that the Union Army believes there is no such thing as private property anymore. They say all our property belongs to them, so I say keep their horse and even things up a bit." She let out a gasp. "Will, listen to what I am saying! It is hard enough to witness all the pain and suffering I see around me, but it is almost harder to see myself become filled with all this anger. One day I may be able to forgive the Yankees for fighting this war, but I don't know if I will ever be able to forgive them for turning me into someone I no longer recognize."

"Mrs. Mitchell," Will said quietly, "You are a good person who is doing all that you can do under extremely trying circumstances. Please, believe me."

"I hope you are right, Will. Now, let's get going and take that soldier to my home."

"That Yankee soldier," Will reminded her. "You are kinder than you realize."

She smiled. "Let's go."

"You really don't mind," Charles asked weakly.

"Why would I mind? I take care of dozens of soldiers, both Union and Confederate, every day. Anyway, Will brought you here and Will is my friend."

"Thank you, Ma'am. I am Charles Walker, 5th Connecticut."

They made their way through the town, Charles riding while Mrs. Mitchell and Will walked. Winchester in May was filled with leafy trees, green lawns, vivid flower gardens and apple blossoms blooming. Yet none of this beauty was able to hide the sense of occupation, the smells of the wounded and the lack of sanitation as more and more people crowded into the town.

Here and there Will saw a U.S. flag flying over a house. Mrs. Mitchell observed Will's puzzled look. "As I mentioned before, we have been taken over by the Union Army. They pick a house for one of their general's headquarters and they fly their flag over that house. Their horses trample our gardens;

their soldiers milk our cows,; and sometimes they steal our chickens, regardless of the fact that none of this is officially allowed. It is most trying."

Mrs. Mitchell never complained when he was visiting at Willows, so Will realized how stressed she must be now. He asked about the servants from Willows and learned that none of them came with the family to Winchester.

"Not even Nellie?"

"She wanted to, but she said that her family felt they would be better off if they followed the Union Army. I miss her."

They slowly made their way uphill to a two-story house that faced the road.

"So far our house has been spared, but the Union Army could decide to occupy it anytime they want. It is terribly upsetting. I grew up in this house. My ancestors lived on this small piece of land for well over one hundred years, ever since they first came here from Scotland. Now, I'll go inside and call Edward to help you bring Charles up the steps."

Will couldn't imagine what he was going to say to Edward. Whatever it was, it would certainly be awkward.

"Hello, Will." Edward faced him. "Who is your friend?"

"I am Charles Walker, and I am with the Union Army."

"I noticed. Sure you want to come in here?"

Charles hesitated, then said, "If you'll have me."

"Not willingly. You should thank my Mamma. She feels the need to help everyone."

Edward and Will managed to assist Charles up the steps. "I don't feel very steady."

"Maybe it's all the whiskey."

Edward frowned. "Whiskey?"

"That's a joke. I poured half a bottle on his cut."

"Come in," Mrs. Mitchell said from the doorway. "Edward, take Charles in to the front parlor and I will examine his leg. Will, you can wait here. The children will want to see you, I'm sure."

Will was not so sure. After all, he left very suddenly and without any explanation.

"Will, you're back!" It was Benjamin. "Why did you leave like that? Didn't you like us anymore?"

More awkward than he could have imagined. "Hi, Benjamin. I'm very happy to see you."

Not easily swayed, Benjamin went on. "You just disappeared. One day we were playing and the next day you were gone. That wasn't very nice."

"I'm sorry, Benjamin. It wasn't my fault."

"Hello, Will." It was a frowning Jane. Now he knew he was in trouble.

"To what do we owe the honor of your company?"

Big trouble.

"Jane, I'm very sorry that I left so suddenly."

"Around here we say goodbye before we leave. It is called manners. And we write letters to say thank you after we visit. And we . . . "

"I couldn't say goodbye. I was . . . sort of . . . kidnapped."

Looking at the doubt on her face and the excitement on Benjamin's, Will went on. "It's true. There were forces beyond my control that took me away from here."

"Yankees," asked Benjamin.

"Kind of. I really didn't want to go, please believe me."

"But you did," cried out Benjamin. "And we looked everywhere for you."

Edward came into the room and looked embarrassed when he heard his brother's words. "Not our business. You were free to come and go. Still are."

Will knew enough to know that he had hurt their feelings, but he didn't know how to explain. He tried his best. "I know, but I couldn't help it. Honestly."

"There always was something a little strange about you," Edward said. "I never knew exactly what. Now you turn up with a Yankee friend. Could you be a spy?"

"A spy! Absolutely not. I don't spy for anyone. And as far as Charles is concerned, he isn't my friend. He's just a person I saw on the Valley Pike. He was in pain and I went to help him. We're supposed to help our fellow men."

"Not if they're Yankees."

Mrs. Mitchell came into the room. "The leg will be all right; it was only grazed and because Will used the whiskey, I don't think Charles will have any other problems. I gave him some laudanum and he's sleeping now."

"Here?"

"Edward . . . "

"And what if he was the one who killed Joseph? What then?"

"Edward, I will mourn Joseph for the rest of my life, but because I am a mother, I know that Charles' mother would be happy to know that I am taking care of her son. If Tom or Robs were hurt, I would want a mother to care for them as kindly as I am caring for Charles. Don't you understand that we ladies are fighting this war in our homes and in our hospitals?"

171

No one said anything.

"Will," she went on, "Where are you staying?"

"I don't know," he mumbled. "I just came to Winchester to find all of you. I went to Willows first but it was filled with Federal soldiers so I went to the church and an old lady named Mrs. Pritchard told me you were in Winchester so I came here."

Mrs. Mitchell smiled. "Not so old, I hope. Lavinia Pritchard and I were girls together. I'm glad she sent you here to find us. You will stay with us, of course, and so will Charles while he is recuperating."

Edward glared. "Recuperating so he can join his Company, right?"

"Our very own Dr. McGuire and some of the Union surgeons are working together to treat the soldiers, all the soldiers. When this war is over, I expect people will long remember that Winchester was a medical haven for soldiers on both sides."

Again, no one could think of anything to say. Then Will took a deep breath. "I want you all to know that I just heard about the passing of Mr. Mitchell, Joseph, Sarah and Henry. I cannot really understand it all. I mean they were good and I . . . I . . . just don't know how something so awful could happen."

Jane thawed a little. "We don't know what to say either. It is terrible."

"There is much on this earth that we do not understand. Come on now, let's get to work. Jane, help me in the kitchen. Edward, go and put Will's horse," she paused and smiled at Will, "in our small stable, then go and milk the cow. Right now we are grateful to her for whatever milk she gives us." Will followed Edward outside.

"Of course, a lot has changed," Edward told Will as he milked the cow, "but you already know that if you saw Willows. I will go back someday and I will chase those Yankees off our land."

Remembering all the Federal soldiers he saw, Will had his doubts.

While they washed up together, Will couldn't help but remember Willows and better days. They went inside the house.

"Charles will join us as soon as he wakes up," Mrs. Mitchell told the children. "His color is back and he seems to be resting well."

Edward scowled but said nothing.

The hours went by quickly and Will was relieved to see that it was like old times again. Benjamin still was annoying; Jane still knew everybody's business and Edward was still angry with the Yankees.

"I am going to see how Charles is doing," Mrs. Mitchell said. "It's almost time for supper. Jane and I have been cooking with whatever we can find in our garden and can afford to buy. Everything is so expensive these days! And with the servants no longer with us, we have had to learn how to cook and do all sorts of things we never did before."

She went to the room where Charles was, then came back out and called to Will, "Charles needs some help."

Will went into the room,. He had never helped an injured man with dressing and so forth before, but Will smiled gamely and did what he could. When Charles was ready, they both joined the family at the table.

Will ate with great appetite, and Charles joined in with gusto. "Best food I've had in a long time," he said. "Our camp food can be dreadful."

"When Stonewall Jackson comes, we'll see Robs and Tom," cried out Benjamin excitedly.

Mrs. Mitchell looked at him and shook her head. "I don't know."

"Why not?"

"He'll be fighting," Jane told her little brother. "When you fight, you can't take the time to visit. Can you, Charles?"

Charles frowned. "I can only tell you about my experiences as a Union soldier." Edward made an angry sound but Charles resolutely went on. "Most of the townspeople are hiding anyway, so you usually don't even see them. Maybe your brothers will stop by after the battle, depending on what happens. I wasn't in any shape to visit anyone when your Will rescued me. Of course my home is far away, so I don't have anyone to visit here."

"Where do you live," asked Jane.

"I live in Connecticut."

Everyone looked up. "Connecticut!"

"There must be so many people up there."

"Is it crowded and dirty?"

"Do you have lots of factories?"

And then from Benjamin, "Why do you hate us?"

Charles said, "Wait a minute. I don't live in New York City. That's where it's crowded and dirty. I live in Danbury. It's farm country, kind of like here. And we don't hate you; we just love the Union. That's what this war is all about, the Union and keeping it together."

"You can't keep a body together when its spirit is far apart," said Mrs. Mitchell softly.

"What is it like there," asked Benjamin.

Charles thought a moment, "Not that different from here. My father is a farmer and I'm a farmer too."

"Do you like it here in Virginia?"

"Well, Benjamin, I don't really know Virginia as a place to live. I only know it as a place to fight. I just do my job, but I can't wait until this war is over and I can go back home again."

"Do you have brothers and sisters," Jane asked.

"I have two sisters and I had one brother. George was killed at Bull Run."

"Just like Joseph."

"Yes."

"So, why are you all fighting," asked Edward. "Why didn't you just let us go?"

"I told you already. We're fighting to preserve the Union."

"But we want out of the Union."

"I know. I guess that's why we're at war with each other."

There didn't seem to be much else to say.

"I suggest we all go to bed and see what the morning brings," Mrs. Mitchell said. "I am going to put you, Will, in the front parlor with Charles. There's room there."

As Will tried to settle into sleep, he kept hearing the sounds of wagons and troops and cavalry moving outside. Just as his eyes finally began to close, Charles moaned and sat up. "Where am I?"

"Shush. We're in a safe place and your leg will be fine. Go back to sleep."

At breakfast the next morning, everyone was very excited. It was now May 24th, the day after Stonewall Jackson's victory at Front Royal.

"We heard that our troops captured over $200,000 worth of supplies," said Jane happily. "We're not allowed to show our excitement, though, or the Union Army here in Winchester will shoot us."

"I doubt it," said Charles. "We don't go around shooting women and children."

"Maybe not you, but that's what we hear. I also heard that the Yankees told the Negroes that Jackson is going to kill them all. And someone told me that you all will burn Winchester down to the ground."

Charles only stared at her. "That sure is a lot of information before 9 o'clock in the morning."

"I've been awake since 7 and I went outside to hear what the neighbors have heard."

"Don't listen to Jane. She eavesdrops on everyone and what she doesn't hear, she makes up," Edward said, then realized with horror that he was taking the side of a

Yankee over his sister. "Of course she's probably right in this case," he amended.

Mrs. Mitchell smiled. "If we believe all the rumors we hear, we will be in a constant state of panic. I prefer to believe what I see and what I see is a very warm day, filled with sunshine. Benjamin, you need to pick some of the vegetables in the garden."

"If the Yankees haven't stolen them yet," Edward said.

"And," Mrs. Mitchell went on as if she had not heard him, "Charles has to walk more to make sure his leg is better and Will can help Edward do his chores. Oh, and, Edward, please clean our shotgun and bring it here as part of your chores. I also suggest we all stop and pray for God to protect us."

"But who is God going to protect," asked Benjamin, "Charles or us?"

"The wonder of God is that He can protect us all."

After their morning prayers, Mrs. Mitchell turned to Jane. "Jane, today I would like you to come with me to the Union Hotel to help take care of the wounded soldiers."

"Good. You never took me before. Maybe we'll learn more about what happened yesterday at Front Royal. It would be interesting to hear the details."

"Not from the Federals," cautioned Edward.

"We will bring lemonade to the soldiers," she went on, ignoring her brother. "They must be thirsty."

As Jane prepared the lemonade, Will said, "Let me taste your lemonade and I'll tell you if it's good enough."

"I know you, Will Bradford. You just want a glass of lemonade. Of course it's good enough," she answered with a toss of her hair, "but I'll give you a glass anyway. Isn't it amazing? Ladies always get the best jobs."

"What do you mean?"

"I get to go to the Union Hotel Hospital and see all the soldiers."

Will had seen more than enough wounded and dead soldiers as he traveled on the Valley Turnpike to Winchester. "A hospital can be pretty grim," he told Jane.

"Grim? I think it will be fun, all those handsome young men wanting to talk with me."

Will didn't answer. Nothing was fun about this war.

A few hours later Jane and her mother returned. Jane ran upstairs before Will could even say hello.

"What's wrong with her," he asked.

"The first thing that she saw was a porch filled with dead bodies, some with their names written on pieces of paper pinned on

179

to their jackets," Mrs. Mitchell answered. "Then she asked me if Joseph had a paper with his name pinned on to his jacket. When I told her that Joseph didn't need paper to identify him because he had his brother to bring him home to be buried in our family's cemetery, she burst into tears."

"I'm sorry," said Will.

"We all are," agreed Charles.

"Are we," yelled Jane as she came halfway back down the stairs. "If we all were so sorry, there would be no dead men. You, Edward, all you want to do is kill Yankees. And you, Charles, all you want to do is kill Confederates. Why can't you all just stop killing?"

No one answered.

"And," Jane went on as tears ran down her face, "All Mrs. Winston could talk about was that before the War, I wouldn't have been allowed to be with strange men and here I was pouring lemonade and talking with them. One soldier even had a fiancée somewhere in Pennsylvania. He told me that I reminded him of her. Her name is Emily and she has brown eyes like mine. Do you think he will ever see her again?"

"I hope so, Jane," her mother answered.

"What can we do? All this is terrible."

"We can take care of the wounded and pray that it all ends soon."

"Is there nothing else?"

Mrs. Mitchell didn't answer. Jane went on angrily, "There has to be something else we can do; there has to be."

Jane turned to Charles. "I saw your wounded men. It was awful."

"I know. I saw them too."

When Jane looked confused, he said gently, " . . . on the battlefield."

There was tension at dinner and Charles told them all it was time for him to leave.

"Where are you going," Jane asked.

"I must join my Company, or what's left of it. I'll go over to the Taylor Hotel and find out where I am supposed to go."

"This is so strange. Here you are having dinner with us and soon you will be fighting against us. I don't understand anything," she cried out and suddenly burst into tears again.

Will was uncomfortable. After all, he had brought Charles into this house. Before he could say anything, Mrs. Mitchell went over to Jane. "Come on, dear. We will step out on the porch and get some fresh air. It was a very hard morning for you."

"It's not just the morning; it's everything. Nothing is the same anymore and Father is no longer here and Sarah and Henry and Joseph and . . . "

"I know, dear. We all know."

"What's going to happen to us?"

"That I don't know, but I do know that we have one another and we have to put our trust in God."

"It's not enough."

"It has to be. It's all we have."

"Well, I am going now," said Charles, standing up. "I want to thank you for your kindness to me."

"Will we see you again," asked Benjamin.

"I don't know. Probably better if you don't."

"That's kind of sad."

"Yeah, it is."

When he left, Mrs. Mitchell said to her children, "Come on, now. There is work to be done. If they are fighting right here in Winchester, we better get the chickens and our one remaining cow some place safe. And our horses."

"I want to ask you about something." Will felt very uncomfortable, but pushed himself to speak. "It's about Peaches. She is . . ."

"She is a he," laughed Edward. "I'm not sure how you missed that."

Will looked embarrassed, but rallied. "When it comes to horses, I try not to look at them too closely. Anyway, you all know that my riding skills are . . . um . . . not very good. I wonder if anyone here might be willing to teach me how to ride?"

"I will," volunteered Jane immediately. "I'm a good teacher. I used to teach the slave children to read, back when we had slaves and lived at Willows."

"I didn't know you could do that in Virginia."

"Well, a lot of people did it, even though I suppose it was against the law. Mamma says that some laws are supposed to be broken and, anyway, all my students learned how to read."

"How did you know what books to use?"

"I used my own books and the Bible, of course. Anyway, I am sure I could teach you to ride. Riding is much easier than reading."

"Not for me," Will said darkly.

"Just tell me when you want to start. You already have a horse who knows you, so that's good."

"Why?"

"You want the horse to be comfortable with you."

"I'm more interested in me being comfortable with the horse."

The next morning, Jane took Will and Peaches to a nearby field. "I'm going to teach you the right way to get on and off Peaches." She showed Will what to do and had Will practice. "That's very good. After all, if you can't get up on a horse, how can you ride? Let's take a break for dinner and come on out here afterwards."

"To ride? I kind of liked just getting on and off."

Jane giggled. "Can't get very far if you're standing still."

"So how are the lessons going," asked Mrs. Mitchell as they sat around the table and ate.

"Fine. I learned how to get on and off Peaches."

"How did you get around without a horse," Edward asked, and then laughed, "What did you used to do . . . fly?"

Everyone joined in laughing and Will answered, "Someone always took me wherever I needed to go."

"Oh, then you must have had a driver with your wagon or carriage."

"Something like that. Where I come from, boys my age are considered too young to travel by themselves."

"Strange," muttered Edward.

"No, it's not strange," interrupted Mrs. Mitchell, "It's just different."

Jane ate quickly and was very impatient to get back to the lessons. She wasted no time when they got back to the field. "Now, I will show you how to brush Peaches and saddle him and put on a bridle."

Unlike Jane, Will was not enthusiastic. "What if she, I mean he, doesn't like it?"

"He already does, I think. Remember, he is a well-behaved horse so he must be used to all this. It's you I have to train."

The next day Jane brought her own horse to the field. "I'll ride our horse, while you ride Peaches." She showed Will how to stop and turn and how to make Peaches go faster and go slower. It was very hard work for Will, and he was uncomfortable most of the time.

Benjamin thought it was all very funny. "I can ride better than you, Will, and you're so much older than me."

Will gritted his teeth.

He practiced more every day and got very sore.

"Maybe he should give up," Mrs. Mitchell said to Jane.

"Do you want to quit," Benjamin asked Will.

"No."

Since Yankee soldiers were all around, it was only a matter of time before one of them noticed the lessons. Before long, a group of them came to watch and soon they were taking bets on Will.

"Hey, kid, I've got money riding on six days until you can ride so you better hurry."

185

"Naw, do just like you're doing. I bet me a fiver that it'll take you to the end of August."

"How about to the end of the war," called out another one.

Will refused to give up. Under his breath he repeated, "If all those jerks can learn to ride, so can I."

"Well, Jane, teaching Will is not as easy as you thought," challenged Edward. "Maybe you should quit teaching."

"I'm going to be a teacher when I grow up and right now I'm going to teach Will how to ride if it's the last thing I ever do."

"I don't know about you," Will grumbled, "but it just may be the last thing I ever do."

Jane rode her horse while Will rode Peaches and they went around and around together until Jane began to feel sorry for Peaches. Finally, she had an idea. "Will, let's try this. Close your eyes and I'll lead Peaches."

"Close my eyes! Are you crazy? Why would I want to do that?"

"Just do it. I promise I will lead Peaches and nothing will happen to you. You need to feel Peaches and move with him, not against him. Let's try it."

Will balked so Jane took off a large handkerchief and put it around his eyes.

"He looks like an Indian," laughed Benjamin.

"They wear bandanas around their heads, not their eyes," Will growled. "They need to see what they are doing and so do I."

"Please try it. I know it will work," pleaded Jane.

"All right, but if I fall and die, it's on your head."

Jane giggled. "It won't be on your head where you'll be landing."

They practiced for what seemed to Will an eternity, but after a while he began to understand what Jane was trying to do. He suddenly forgot his fear, forgot Jane, forgot the Yankees and the rest of his audience and felt almost a part of Peaches. They started to ride together not as boy and horse, but as one entity and, before he knew it, everyone was cheering. He took off the blindfold and said, "Come on, Jane. Let's ride."

Chapter 9

Before six o'clock the next morning, Will awoke to the sound of loud firing. He rushed out of bed, looked out the window and saw fires burning and fighting in the street. There was a battle going on!

Suddenly he heard someone pounding on the door. "Wake up, wake up."

"I'm up, Benjamin. Why are you screaming?"

"I'm screaming because Stonewall Jackson is here and he's going to free us from those mean Yankees! Maybe he'll even send them away from Willows and we'll be able to go back home."

"Maybe."

"Benjamin, don't go waking Will," said Jane as she peeked into the room, then hastily withdrew. "Sorry."

"I'll be out in a minute."

Will dressed hurriedly and thought that this was a very strange way to start the day. Of course, he admitted to himself that all mornings have been strange since he came back. And afternoons, and evenings, too. But this one . . .

"Close the front door," he heard Mrs. Mitchell call out.

"I want to see what's going on," Benjamin said.

"Let's look out the window instead," Mrs. Mitchell answered.

"I want to join the soldiers," Edward announced. "I am too old to be cowering in a house with women and children."

"Who are you calling a child?" challenged Benjamin.

"You."

"Stop it, both of you. Edward, we will discuss this later. Right now, we had better have breakfast."

"Mamma, how can you talk about breakfast?"

"Jane, we need to eat. I do not know what is going to happen. We may win or we may lose and have to watch the Federals take over this house just the way they took over Willows. We do not know anything, but we have to do two things. First, we have to pray to the Lord. This is Sunday, His day of rest, and if we cannot go to church, at least we can pray in our home. Second, we have to feed ourselves so we are prepared for whatever may happen."

Will agreed. "You are right."

"Who are you to say that? We still don't know who you are or where you come from. For all we know, you could be one of them." Edward pointed toward a mass of Federal troops that lined the nearby hill.

"Are you crazy? I am not one of them. I am fourteen years old and I have an ancestor who shares my name who is fighting somewhere here in Virginia."

"An ancestor?"

"I mean a relative, a . . . cousin I guess."

The noise of the cannon and muskets cut off further conversation. The fighting raged and the Mitchells watched as men fell wherever they stood. Suddenly there was a rush of men running down the hill. They kept running and running as Confederate riflemen used them as targets. Finally, Mrs. Mitchell could take no more and insisted that the children sit down to eat.

Only Benjamin was hungry. "Mamma, you're right. We need food. Maybe I'll be on the Pike fighting with Stonewall today. He may need me."

"If he needs you," Edward said darkly, "we're in big trouble."

"Mamma, my mouth is very dry," said Jane.

"Drink some water."

"It's not that kind of dry. It's a different dry."

"When we are scared, sometimes our mouths feel dry. Still, drink some water."

"My mouth isn't dry," offered Benjamin. "And I'm not scared."

Edward glared at his family. "The biggest battle Winchester ever saw, and we are eating breakfast and discussing dry mouths.!"

After they finished eating, everyone ran back to the windows and immediately saw that a nearby building was on fire.

"What if it spreads," Jane cried out. "What if they burn our house down, too? Maybe we should evacuate."

"It would be more dangerous to go outside," Will pointed out. "Everyone's shooting."

"Will's right," Edward admitted grudgingly. "We can get ready to leave if we have to, but right now we should stay here."

"I think we should retreat to the cellar. It is much safer down there," Mrs. Mitchell shouted over all the noise. "A bullet could come through one of the windows at any time."

"The cellar," cried out Benjamin, "and miss seeing everything?"

"It's bad enough that I am not out there," complained Edward angrily. "I am not taking cover in our cellar."

All the children nodded their heads as Jane said, "I agree."

"Me too," Will chimed in.

"No one asked you," Edward retorted.

Mrs. Mitchell turned toward her son. "Edward, that was very rude. All right, I give up. We will stay right here. It might be worse to hear the fighting, but not be able to see what is going on. Besides, if the fire spreads, we will need to be prepared to leave quickly."

Guns and shells were firing in all directions. Cannons boomed and it was hard to see what was happening with all the smoke that seemed to be everywhere.

"Look, look over there," cried Edward.

Suddenly there was General Jackson himself, riding down Loudoun Street, right out in front, ahead of all his men.

Into the streets came the soldiers. As Union men ran, Confederate men ran after them. Arms and knapsacks, clothes and blankets, boots and food all went flying as the Federals lightened their load so they could run even faster.

"Come on," shouted Jane, opening the front door. They ran into the street cheering loudly. The Stars and Stripes was taken down from the occupied houses and the Stars and Bars was hoisted up. It was chaos as hundreds of Yankees ran north toward the Potomac while hundreds of Confederates chased after them. They chased them on horseback, they chased them on foot and those in the artillery even unhitched their horses to ride after them.

"Go get 'em," shouted Benjamin. "Hurrah, hurrah!"

"Go back where you came from," cheered Jane.

Many of the Union soldiers were taken prisoner. Everyone watched as they were marched past the Mitchell's house to the Court House, now being used as a prison.

"This is the best Sunday ever," Edward cried out.

"I hope the Lord agrees," said Mrs. Mitchell softly.

Jane nodded confidently. "He will."

Columns of men marched by and the people of Winchester lined the streets cheering. Women ran back into their houses to get food to offer to the hungry soldiers.

"Mamma," called out Robs as he suddenly walked up and grabbed his Mother in a big hug.

Mrs. Mitchell looked up. "Robs, Robs . . . you are all right. Thank God." They all headed back toward the house.

"Tom will be coming soon. We can't stay long, though."

"You did it, you did it," shouted Edward. "We're free!"

Jane, overcome, ran over and hugged Robs as Benjamin grabbed his legs. "Stay, don't go. We miss you."

Robs gently freed himself and saw Will. "I heard that you're helping my family. Thank you."

Will smiled and shook Robs' hand.

"This is what I've dreamed about since I left home," Tom called out as he came running. The Mitchells gathered around him and Mrs. Mitchell wept. "Mamma, why are you crying? Robs and I are here safe and sound and we had the pleasure of driving those Federals north across the Potomac where they belong."

"I'm so happy that you both are here."

Benjamin folded his arms. "I don't cry when I'm happy. You're silly."

"Don't call Mamma silly," Jane told him.

"That's all right. I am silly," answered Mrs. Mitchell. "I am just so happy that my boys are here."

"Not for long, Mamma," Robs reminded her. "We are just stopping for a short time. And, by the way, do you think you can spare two hungry men a bite to eat?"

"A bite? We can prepare a feast!"

Tom laughed. "No time for a feast, but a quick meal would do quite well."

"What about a slow meal," asked Benjamin.

"A quick, wonderful meal is better than a slow, terrible meal any day of the week."

"These days I'll take food any way I can get it," added Robs.

"Don't you get enough food, Robs?"

"Sometimes. In the Valley we do. You know, food is one reason we need to save the Valley. We grow so much food here that the whole army depends on us."

"What's the other reason?"

"The Valley is my home."

The Mitchells went into the house and Will stayed on the porch, figuring they should have their reunion in private. Jane came and pulled him inside while the family crowded in the kitchen.

"I'll make you griddle cakes, your favorite."

"No time."

Mrs. Mitchell and Jane almost emptied the larder and Robs and Tom fell upon the food with great enthusiasm.

"Benjamin, don't eat so fast," Mrs. Mitchell admonished her youngest son.

"A quick meal is better than a slow one. Tom said so."

"Not exactly, Benjamin," laughed Tom.

Before they left, Edward asked Robs if he could talk with him in private.

"Yes, we can talk on the porch. But make it quick." The two brothers stepped outside.

"I want to join the army. Is that quick enough?"

"I think it's too quick."

"Robs, I'm serious. I'm almost fourteen and I am very tall. I'm even taller than Tom and almost as tall as you. I can shoot very well; you know how good a shooter I am. I can ride and I'm smart so I would like to join."

"We told you to wait until you were seventeen. That still stands. You can join in three years. Meanwhile, take care of Mamma and the young ones."

"They don't need me. The Confederacy does. They need all the good men they can get."

"I think we can do without you," laughed Robs.

"Why? I'm a good fighter. Ask anyone at school."

"Edward, fighting classmates is a very different than fighting Union soldiers. This is a war and you are too young to be in it. Wait until you grow up!"

"Well, I'll just see about that!"

Will was standing by the front parlor windows and overheard the beginning of the conversation. He quietly backed away, and hoped Edward and Robs hadn't seem him. He headed into the hall.

Edward came into the house looking like thunder.

"What's the matter, Edward," asked Benjamin. "We won!"

"I didn't."

Robs and Tom kissed their mother, hugged everyone else and walked toward the front door.

"So soon?"

"We are at war, Mamma," answered Tom.

"I pray to God that there will be peace in the Valley soon."

Tom nodded his head. "And I pray to God that we drive every last one of those Federals not only out of our Valley, but out of all Virginia and out of the rest of our Southern states."

"And I pray we hurry up and move," Robs added, "because it won't look good if we are among the stragglers. The General will be most unhappy and no one wants to make Stonewall Jackson unhappy."

They walked out into the jubilant crowd.

After they left, Mrs. Mitchell said, "Come on. We'll put all this food into baskets and give it to every soldier we see."

Again, they hurried outside and gave food to passing soldiers who grabbed what they could and marched on with a "thank you" and a smile.

Jane noticed their neighbor, Mrs. Winston, weeping silently on the other side of the street. "Mamma, why is Mrs. Winston crying? It's a great day."

Mrs. Mitchell walked over to her neighbor and learned that Mrs. Winston lost her son on this morning, this great morning in Winchester. She came back and told the children.

"Is it still a great day?"

"Yes, Jane, it is. But it is a sad one, too, because so many of our men have fallen. We have to cheer our victory and mourn our loss," Mrs. Mitchell said, as the family headed back to the house.

"How can Mrs. Winston do that? Does her heart have room to cheer?" Jane asked as they went inside.

"Why do you ask all these strange questions?" Edward scowled.

"Don't you have any questions?"

"Only one, and it's already been answered."

* * *

The next day, there was a knock on the door and Will opened it to find a young boy on the front steps.

198

"I have come to see Benjamin," announced the boy. "We are friends. My name is Joseph just like Benjamin's brother, only his brother was killed at Manassas. But I am called Joey and Joseph was always just Joseph."

"Well then, Joey, please come in. He is somewhere around here . . . ."

"I will find him. We have had a great victory, and Benjamin and I must celebrate."

"What are you going to do," Will asked, genuinely curious.

"We will play war, and we will be the soldiers who freed Winchester."

"Who will be the Union soldiers?"

"They will have to be pretend. No one ever wants to play them so we make them up. Did you ever play war?"

"All the time."

"Who did you play with? What side were you on?"

He couldn't explain games like Call of Battle, or laser tag either, for that matter. He'd better stick to good guys and bad guys. "I was always on the good side. Look, here comes Benjamin."

Everyone was in such a good mood, despite all the wounded who, once again, flooded Winchester. Everyone, that is, except Edward.

"What's the matter with Edward," Jane asked Will. "He should be happy but he seems angry."

Will shrugged his shoulders. "Hard to tell."

"I asked him, but he wouldn't answer except to say that he'll show Robs and the rest of them. That's strange because we were all so happy to see Robs. Maybe he is jealous that he didn't get to kill any Yankees. Remember when you were here last time?"

Will remembered and didn't like it. Edward was a little too impulsive for his own good and Will also remembered how he talked the rest of them into following him. He hoped Edward would forget all about his talk with Robs. But, then, he had also hoped that his father wouldn't leave and that the Civil War wouldn't happen. So much for his hopes.

The next morning, the Mitchells learned that their army had almost reached Harper's Ferry and was pushing toward the Potomac.

"Are they heading for Washington," asked Jane in awe.

"What do we want with Washington," Edward asked. "We just want to get rid of those Federals so they'll leave us alone."

"But if we attacked Washington, they might get scared and then they'd leave us alone for good."

Will knew the answer. "Jackson doesn't have enough men to attack Washington. It'll never happen."

Edward turned toward him. "How do you know so much?"

Good question, one I will not answer. Aloud, he said, "The Union Army has more men. Why would you attack their capital? You have a great fighting army, but they have more men and more resources so you have to be careful where you use that army."

Edward didn't answer.

The next day brought disappointing news. President Lincoln was sending many more troops to fight Jackson.

"Well," reasoned Jane, "He must know how great a general Jackson is and that's good."

Will shook his head. "No, it isn't."

"Why not?"

"More troops mean more fighting. The Union has more men. You want less fighting because you cannot afford to lose so many men. You can't replace them."

"And the Union can?"

"Yeah, it can. Between the immigrants that keep coming and the North's greater population, they can keep this war going longer than you can."

Edward glowered. "So speaks the wise know-it-all. Why don't you just go on to Richmond and advise President Davis?"

"I should," Will answered.

"Or maybe you would like to confer with General Robert E. Lee?" Edward said sarcastically. Will just shrugged.

On Wednesday they heard that Lincoln had sent even more men to the Valley to catch Jackson.

"We'll show them," shouted Benjamin. "We'll get them all. Me and Joey will fight them all, every single one of them. Let them bring all the men in the North, every last one of them, and we'll show them how tough we are."

Everyone was now tense, Will noticed. The news was not good. Each day brought another rumor and each rumor had Jackson retreating.

"Mamma, is Stonewall Jackson going to leave us to the Federals again," Benjamin asked. "We didn't like that and I thought we were going to be able to go back to Willows." He started to cry.

"Come here, Benjamin, come and sit on my lap and we will weep together," said Mrs. Mitchell.

At breakfast on Saturday morning, the Mitchells heard the army, Jackson's army, was coming through town again only this time they were retreating.

"Why does everything happen at breakfast," wondered Jane.

"I don't know, dear," her mother answered. "Maybe it is because soldiers wake up early."

There was a banging at the door and all the children rushed to answer. "Tom, it's Tom! He's here again," they all shouted.

"Where is Robs?" Mrs. Mitchell looked anxiously at her son. "What happened to Robs?"

"Robs is fine. He's an important officer, remember, not like me. He had to go ahead to Strasburg last night and get ready for what we're doing next. But I'm here. Have you any breakfast for this tired and hungry soldier?"

"Do I have breakfast for my oldest son? Sit down, sit down."

"What was it like, chasing the Federals? Were they scared," asked Benjamin.

"Were they scared? You bet they were. They ran like the devil, sorry Mamma, and we chased them all the way to Harpers Ferry. They kept going and we kept going until we reached the Potomac River and learned that thousands more were coming our way. I'm not sure exactly where we are going now, but we will follow old Stonewall until the death."

His mother gasped. "I hope not."

"Me too, Mamma. I meant that he is a great leader and we will follow him anywhere."

After Tom finished eating, he said, "I have to say goodbye again. I finally got a letter from Mary. She and baby Tommy are well in Richmond and she sends her best and hopes you come to Richmond to stay with her if things get too difficult in the Valley."

"Do you think they will," asked Edward.

"No, I think we will continue to drive out the Federals. This is just a temporary setback."

All too soon, Tom left and once again the Mitchells were outside handing out food to passing soldiers.

It rained the next day. "Are those more cannons I hear," asked Benjamin. "They are so loud."

"That's thunder," Edward told him. "And now it's hailing."

"I wonder if the rivers will flood," Mrs. Mitchell said, more to herself than to anyone else. "Things were going so well just a few days ago. Now . . . . "

The Union Army came back to Winchester in full force and it rained even more.

"How will our army find their way with all this rain," wailed Benjamin.

"Don't worry. They know the Valley a lot better than our enemy does."

No one in Winchester quite knew where Jackson was, but it was said that he was somewhere in the Valley planning another surprise attack.

There was a knock on the door. It was a Union officer asking to search the house.

"Why?"

"Just to make sure."

"Sure of what," demanded Edward.

"Enough of that insolence, boy. Step aside."

It was a quick but thorough search.

"If you tell us what or who you are looking for, we can make your job easier," Mrs. Mitchell said.

"We are looking for Confederate flags. We saw them hanging when we left Winchester and we want to make sure that they won't be hanging ever again."

"You mean," asked Jane innocently, "even when Stonewall Jackson returns?"

The officer just looked at her and then left.

"Where is our flag," asked Jane.

"We left it at Willows. It is hidden where the Yankees won't find it."

"But if it's at Willows, we can't have it either."

"We will one day, don't worry."

Out in the street, the Stars and Bars once more was taken down and the Stars and Stripes was hoisted up. The family went about their chores, but nothing seemed normal to Will. "I'd almost say we were waiting for something," he thought.

After the noon dinner, Edward announced that he was planning to visit his friend George and spend the night at his house.

"How come," asked Benjamin.

"To get away from my nosy brother."

"Edward," admonished Mrs. Mitchell. "That was uncalled for. Please apologize to Benjamin."

"I'm sorry. I was only teasing anyway. George and I have things that we want to do."

Jane looked interested. "What?"

Edward gave her a look. "Things."

"It is a great pity the Academy closed, or you would be busy at school," Mrs. Mitchell said. "But, then, it is a pity about a lot of things these days. Yes, all right, you can go off and spend the night with George."

"Can I sleep in your bed," asked Benjamin, all excited.

"I don't care."

"Well, I care," his mother interrupted. "The answer is no."

"But, Mamma, Edward said I can."

"That's enough, Benjamin."

Will was no longer sleeping in the parlor. The room he had been sharing with the Mitchell boys seemed strangely empty without Edward. He felt a little uneasy without knowing why and that made him even more on edge.

Will went to bed earlier than usual and fell fast asleep. But his dreams were all of battlefields and shooting and he woke up feeling tired and uncomfortable.

It was an ordinary day until close to suppertime when Mrs. Mitchell asked Will if Edward was back.

"No, I haven't seen him."

"He should be home by now. Would you do me a favor and run over to George's house and tell Edward to come home."

"All right. You will have to tell me where George lives."

"I'll go with you," piped up Jane.

"Me too," said Benjamin.

Mrs. Mitchell sighed and said half under her breath, "I hope this war is over by Fall so Edward's school can reopen and Miss Agnes will return to teach Jane and Benjamin. These children need school and so do I."

"Mamma? Can we go?"

"Go ahead. But before you go, why don't you first pick some raspberries and take them to George's family since we have so many. And while you are in the garden, dig up some of the baby potatoes for supper."

While Will worked, he had a bad feeling that wouldn't go away.

As they were leaving, Mrs. Mitchell called out, "Be careful of all the Union soldiers. They're everywhere."

"That's true, Ma'am," called out a soldier who was sitting under a tree nearby. "We are back in Winchester and we plan to stay here. Nice raspberries. Think I'll pick me a few."

No one answered him, and Will and the children hurried away.

They walked by Union soldiers encamped on lawns all over the neighborhood.

"Look at that," Jane pointed.

There in the middle of Mrs. Winston's flower garden were horses tied up and grazing. "They shouldn't be allowed to do that. Poor Mrs. Winston. It isn't enough that they killed her son, now they are destroying her flowers," raged Jane.

Will privately agreed, although he realized that flowers were the least of the damage that the army could do and, so far, this army had seemed fairly tame. For an occupying army, that was.

When they arrived at George's house, all seemed quiet. They knocked on the door and a young boy opened the door.

"Hello, Harry," smiled Jane. "Is Edward around?

"No, we haven't seen Edward today."

"But he came here yesterday."

Harry and George's mother came to the door. "Come on in, children. And you must be Will. Or do you prefer William? I have heard a lot about you."

Will couldn't think of anything to say, but Jane, never at a loss for words, chimed in. "We are so pleased that Will is here with us. Mamma sent you these raspberries from our garden."

"Thank your Mamma for me. Now, what's this about Edward?"

Will spoke up. "He told us he would be visiting George."

"George? Let me call him and see. Harry, go and get George, please. I believe he is upstairs."

George came hurrying down with a clatter. "What's this about Edward? I haven't seen him for a few days."

Will's heart sank. He had been afraid of something like this ever since he overheard

Edward's conversation with Robs. That fool boy must have gone off and done something stupid. He shook his head. Who knows what trouble Edward would get into?

"Where could he be," asked Jane worriedly.

Will and Benjamin said nothing.

"Well, you children better go home and talk to your mother. I always thought she was too lenient with her boys and now with your father gone, well . . . . "

"Let's get out of here," Will whispered to Jane and shepherded them all outside, leaving George's mother still talking.

"Where is Edward," Jane asked.

Benjamin began to cry. "The Yankees got him."

"Hush, I'm sure there is a reasonable explanation. Right, Will?"

"I don't know, Jane."

They made their way home slowly, afraid of what might have happened to Edward and afraid of telling Mrs. Mitchell.

"Where is Edward," she asked as soon as they entered the house.

"He wasn't there, Mamma, and they don't know where he is." Benjamin started to cry again.

"What? What are you talking about? Of course, Edward is with George. Where else would he be?"

No one said anything.

"Oh, no, something has happened to Edward."

Looking at her anguished face, Will felt he had no choice but to speak. "Mrs. Mitchell, may I talk with you privately?"

"Will, what on earth do you know that you have not told me," asked Jane, giving Will a nasty look. "I am staying right here and not moving because you are talking about my brother."

"I'm staying too," announced Benjamin.

"What is it, Will? What do you know about Edward," urged Mrs. Mitchell.

"I don't know anything, but I'm guessing."

"Guessing what? Will, this is serious; stop playing games."

"By accident I overheard Edward ask Robs if he could join the army. When Robs said no, Edward was very upset and maybe even felt humiliated the way boys do when someone tells them that they're only a boy and they sort of think they're a man."

"What are you saying? Will, where is Edward?"

"I don't know. I am just guessing," he repeated miserably.

"Guessing what? Tell me."

"I know," Jane suddenly shouted. "Edward ran off to join the Confederate Army!"

"What," cried Mrs. Mitchell. "That's impossible. Will, what do you think?"

Wishing he could be anywhere else but here, Will took a deep breath and said, "I think Jane may be right. It's either that or . . ."

"Or what?"

"Or he's at Willows."

"Willows? What on earth would he be doing there?"

"I don't know exactly."

"I know," Jane announced. "Edward is always saying that he wants to go back home and chase the Yankees away. What if that's what he's doing?"

"But that's ridiculous. How could he do that?"

"He did it last time, remember," piped up Benjamin. "He went after the Yankees and we all helped him."

"What last time," asked Mrs. Mitchell. "What are you talking about?"

No one answered at first, but she insisted. "This is not a game. A vicious war is going on and I lost one of my sons already. If I can help it, I am not going to lose another son! So, you all better tell me what Benjamin is talking about right now."

The story came out haltingly at first, but then everyone began to speak quickly. When they had finished, a dazed Mrs. Mitchell said, "I am very disappointed in all of you, but we won't speak of that now. At this time, we have to figure out how to find Edward."

Looking around at what was left of the family, Will knew what he had to do. "I'll go," he said quietly. "I will find Edward."

"How?"

"I will take Peaches and go to Willows."

"But how do you know he is there?"

"I don't. It's my best guess."

"I want to go too," Jane said as Benjamin chimed in, "Me too."

"I am going alone."

"But, Will, what would your parents say? You are under my roof, and I don't want to put you in harm's way."

"I am already in harm's way and my parents . . . I think they would be proud of me. Even my father."

Chapter 10

"Big words," thought Will as he saddled Peaches the way Jane had taught him. "I wonder how my father would really feel about what I am going to do. Actually, I wonder how he would feel about anything I do. I don't know him anymore. Makes me wonder if I ever did."

"I'm not sure you should start out so late," Mrs. Mitchell said as she watched him prepare to go. "Why don't you wait and go in the morning?"

"I don't want to run into too many people. I think it may be safer to go now."

"Well, take the lantern and, please be careful. Luckily, the moon is full tonight and it's not raining. I can draw you a map from here to Willows. I rather pride myself on my drawing."

"Thank you, but I already know the way to go. Remember, I first went to Willows when I was looking for you."

A strangely silent Jane came to watch him leave.

"Go and get those Yankees," said Benjamin. "If me and Joey were going with you, we would kill them all and capture Willows and bring Edward back home!"

Mrs. Mitchell hugged Will, then he walked over to Jane. "Wish me luck."

"I do; you know that. I only wish I could help."

"Jane," Will said softly so the others wouldn't hear, "You have to help your mother. She puts on a brave face but I know her and I know she is terribly worried. You have to stay strong for her."

"You're right. I can do that. I only hope that Edward is at Willows."

"So do I. If he just went off with whatever part of the Confederate Army he saw marching by, we may never find him."

"Do you think that they would have let him join?"

"I don't know. He's pretty big for his age, so maybe they would. Look, let's not get ahead of ourselves. I'll text you as soon as I find him."

"You'll what?"

"Oh, I mean . . . I'll . . . come home as soon as I find him."

Jane looked at Will oddly. "Sometimes you say the strangest things. Anyway, may God go with you, as my Mother says."

"My grandmother used to say that too." Thinking about his Grandmother was somehow comforting. "Goodbye, everyone."

At first it was very peaceful, with nothing but animal sounds. Then there was an occasional sound of a rifle in the far-off distance. Actually, he wasn't even sure it was a rifle. Will thought, "If I allow myself to think about Willows and what is ahead of me, I might get scared. Instead, I will think about my life here in Winchester. I like it. I could do without the war, of course, but no one bothers me to do my homework and no one tells me I should join a team and, most of all, no one makes fun of me. Here, I get respect. Maybe I can figure out a way to stay."

"What do you think, Peaches, should we stay?"

Peaches didn't answer, so Will took that as a yes.

Mrs. Mitchell had given him plenty of food and water to carry in a knapsack. Will thought it must have belonged to a soldier who died in her care. The thought was sobering. She had offered him a shotgun as well, but he did not want to leave the Mitchells without a weapon if they needed one. Besides, he figured he would seem more innocent without one and he wasn't sure how to accurately shoot the thing.

"Maybe that should be my next lesson. I wonder if those Yankees would bet on me like they did when I was learning to ride or if they would just take it away." He guessed they would just take it away. Mrs. Mitchell had also given him a blanket, which he rolled up and put behind him.

When he had been riding long enough to feel hungry, he and Peaches pulled off the Pike to eat. He ate some of what Mrs. Mitchell had given him, gave water to Peaches, and lay down to rest. He fell asleep thinking, "This is the life. Outside, under the open sky . . . eating when I want . . . no one around telling me what to do . . . . "

"Hey, boy, that your horse?"

Will woke up to the sight of a disheveled-looking man carrying a large musket with a bayonet on the end of it. It was not comforting to realize that the bayonet was pointing straight at him. "Which side are you on?"

Tempted to answer, "Which side do you want me to be on," Will said nothing.

The man poked him with the point of the bayonet and said, "Answer."

"I am on no side."

"Everyone's on some side. Now, which side are you on, boy?"

"I'm not from around here. I'm from far away and we aren't in this war."

"Everybody's in this war. The whole country, the whole world."

Was this the time to argue history? Will didn't think so. "My family and I are not in the war."

"You one of them Dunkars?"

"Dunkars . . . are they like the Quakers?"

"They don't believe in fighting, just let everyone else do their fighting for them."

"No, I'm not, but don't some of them take care of the wounded and things like that?"

"Some do, some don't."

Will decided to make an attempt at friendly conversation. "So, what are you doing here? Are you in one of the armies, Confederate or Union?"

"No," the man shouted. Will instantly regretted his choice of subject. "Why should I be in anyone's army? I come from the mountains of the West," he pointed toward a mountain range in the distance. "We were forced to fight for them Confederates. I ran away and got taken by the Union Army. They tried to force me to fight too. I weren't having none of them either so I ran away. Guess they're all after me now. I don't care. I got to hide and I'm trying to get back home. If I still have a home."

"Would you care to share my food," Will asked.

"Yeah. Good thing you wanted to share or else I'd have just taken it all."

Will could think of nothing to say to that.

After the man ate and Will silently blessed Mrs. Mitchell for the large amount of food she provided, the man cleaned his teeth with the point of his knife. Then he said, "Good food, better than I got in either army. So, what's a boy like you doing out here on the Pike?"

"Traveling."

The man smiled, kind of a mean smile. "Well, I've heard tall tales in my time, and I know when I am being fed one. You gonna tell me, or am I gonna make you tell me?"

That wasn't as difficult a choice as Will might have thought. "I'll tell you. I am looking for my friend, Edward, who really needs my help. The Yankees took over his home and he had to move away. But now I think he decided to go back to his old house and try to get his home back. And I think he will probably get himself into real trouble."

"Are you jesting?"

"No, I'm not making a joke. It's the truth. I'm going to either try to stop Edward or, if I am too late, rescue him."

The man thought for a while. "Well, then, where's your gun?"

"I don't have one."

"How you going to rescue him without a gun?"

"I haven't figured that out yet. I kind of thought I'd find out where he is and then figure what to do."

The man laughed. "Now, that's funny. Here I am running away from two armies and you are going to attack a bunch of Yankees with nothing and no one to help you. And I think I've got problems!"

He stood up, stuck out his hand and said, "Best of luck to you, boy. If you succeed, then I guess anything can happen. Got to admire your pluck. Yes, sir, I gotta admire you."

He stood up and started to walk away, then he turned and came back. "I'm gonna warn you about something. There's them guerrillas somewhere around here. Both armies hate 'em 'cause they steal from 'em both. They care about no one but themselves and they're mean as sin. If they see you with this nice horse here, they'll likely steal him and kill you. Be careful."

"What should I do to avoid them?"

"Just be careful."

"But how . . . " Will called out after the retreating man who called back, "If you can rescue your friend without a gun, you can do anything."

"That wasn't the most relaxing meal we ever had, was it, Peaches? It's time to go."

As he rode, he thought about how comforting it was to talk with an animal, particularly one as intelligent as Peaches. Animals never talk back, never disagree with you, and are always very much in support of whatever it is you say.

They continued on for miles and miles, until Will was sore and tired. Eventually he found a spring and let Peaches have a long drink. He drank from the spring as well, hoping to save water from the canteen for later in his travels. The sun began to set and the sky became a mass of orange with reds and pinks streaking through. Soon the last of the colors faded and the darkness came. As night came on, he was grateful to the moon for its light.

Will decided to pull Peaches off the Pike and get his bearings. He took down the lantern that was hanging on Peaches and lit it. He had been quick to tell Mrs. Mitchell how well he knew the way, but it was dark now and the Valley Turnpike looked bigger and somehow less friendly than it had during the day. He tied Peaches up and gave them both some more water.

"I beg you, sir. May I share some of that water?"

Will was startled and looked up to find who was speaking to him. He saw a man who was as dark as coal. Was he a slave? Had he run away? Was he what they called a freedman?

"Yes, please take some."

The man drank sparingly and said, "They need water too."

Will peered around and saw partly concealed in the bushes a woman and three little children — all looking very scared.

"This is all I have, but you are welcome to drink. Just leave a little for my horse."

When they finished, the man said, "I thank you, kind sir. Now we will be on our way."

"Where are you going?"

"To freedom."

"Are you following the Union Army?"

"The Union Army?" He gave a strangled kind of laugh. "We are no longer slaves. We have set ourselves free and free men do not want to be in any of those contraband camps. We hear how our people are treated. Might as well stay back home for that."

"What do you mean? Doesn't the Union Army feed and house you and treat you better than you've ever been treated?"

The man smiled bitterly, "What sounds good to the ear, can feel bad to the body."

"What do you mean?"

"Enough. We'll be on our way."

"Wait a moment. I have some extra food. Would you or your family care for some?"

The man hesitated.

"Please. I want to share."

"We will take a little for the children. Thank you."

Will handed some of his food over to the man. "May I ask you a question?"

"You may ask. I will see if I answer."

"Why is freedom so important? If your owners treated you well, why wasn't that enough?"

"Ah . . . a philosopher."

"You don't sound like a slave."

"And you don't sound like a school boy from around here. My master was a good man and I served him well. He allowed me to learn to read and shared his books with me, so I am educated. It is what he would have called a mixed blessing, since the other Negroes would have little to do with me. Too much power can corrupt even the most 'well-meaning' people and not all slave owners are well-meaning people. Some of them are just plain mean.

"As to why I am leaving, it is simple. No one likes to be a slave. Freedom is a natural human impulse; just read your Bible. From babyhood to old age, people want to be free to make their own decisions. Sometimes they make poor decisions, but if I am going to make a mistake, let it be my mistake, not my owner's."

"You put it well. It also explains why teenagers fight with their parents."

"Teenagers? Who are they?"

Will thought there was no harm in explaining. "Young people. Like 13 to 17-year-olds."

"If I may be so bold, where are you from?"

"Far, far away."

"I thought so. You should be careful."

"Why do you say that?"

"You are different, and it is dangerous to be different. Especially in these times."

"You be careful, too. I was told that there is a group of men who see themselves as guerrillas but are really thieves who steal from everybody."

"Thank you."

Will frowned. "If I may ask, where are you going?"

"To Washington."

"Why Washington?"

"I want to see this President Lincoln who is at war for my people."

"I met a Yankee soldier who said the United States is at war to keep the Union together. I met him right here on the Pike."

"That is only half the truth."

"Why do you say that?"

"Tell me, young man, what if there had been no slavery here in this country? I want you to imagine that my people stayed in Africa and your people hired white men to work. No slavery ever. Can you imagine that?"

Will nodded.

"Now," continued the man, "Would there have been a war? Of course not. You know that without slavery the North and the South would never have fought. So, I will go and see President Lincoln and thank him because he is leading a war to help me and my people be free."

"I'm sure he will be surprised to see you but, from what I've read about him, I am sure he will be gracious. You are an unusual man."

"And you are an unusual boy."

"Good luck to you," said Will.

"And to you, too."

It was still dark as Will mounted Peaches. And lonely — it would still be a few hours until dawn. The moon was full and the road seemed to go on and on. He kept being startled by weird noises; at least, weird to Will, and he was a little on edge. He decided to go to the church where the Mitchells used to worship, even though it was now a hospital. Somewhere around there, he might be able to figure out what he was going to do next. "I've got to get on to a different road. People keep popping up near the Pike and I want to make sure I don't meet those guerrillas."

Looking for the way to the church was a challenge as trees created oddly-shaped shadows that looked real and alive. And scary. Will kept Peaches to a slow walk and tried to remember which way to go.

A tree on his right leaned toward the west and he decided that was the way. It was. Soon he entered the village and found his way to the little white church. He went behind the church, tied up Peaches, sat down on the ground and, to his surprise, wept. When he finished, he wiped his eyes with the leaves of a nearby tree and took a deep breath.

"Come with me," said a voice. "You must not stay here. It is not safe."

He turned around and saw Mrs. Pritchard. He remembered that she was Mrs. Mitchell's older friend and that she had fed him when he was here last. It seemed years ago, but really couldn't have been more than a few weeks ago.

"Hush now. Follow me. I will ride Peaches and you must walk by me."

"How did you know his name?"

"What? You must have told me last time."

"But I didn't have a horse then."

"The Valley is small, Will. What we say here travels up and down the Pike almost before we have even finished talking. When we get home, I am going to have to pretend that you are my cousin so as not to make the Union soldiers suspicious. Now shush. This is not the time for conversation."

They came into her house and she exclaimed loudly, "My cousin has come back to visit. Where can he put his horse?"

A large unkempt soldier was lounging in the parlor. "A horse? Our army can always use an extra one."

"Don't get up. I wouldn't want to trouble you with manners," she said sarcastically. "Now, go and get your commanding officer."

The soldier stood up slowly and mumbled, "Why on earth the General puts up with you I'll never understand. If I was in command, I'd have you shot."

"That's why you're not in command," she answered tartly.

"Should you talk to him like that?" whispered Will.

"No, but his narrow-minded stupidity bothers me. It actually bothers the General as well. We have become friends of a sort, General Pellam and me. We understand each other. Maybe it is because we are two old people who are bound to do our duty in a situation neither of us would have chosen. I hate to lie to him, but I will have to tell him that you are my cousin. These days it's too dangerous to be a random boy."

"So, Mrs. Pritchard. Who have we here?" A tall man with the appropriate bearing of a general walked into the room. His eyes twinkled, but his manner was grave as befitting a general.

"This is my cousin's son, William Bradford, but we all call him Will."

"How do you do, sir," Will said politely.

"And where are you from, William?"

"He is from Connecticut," answered Mrs. Pritchard.

"Connecticut? Then he is a Yankee, aren't you, boy?"

"Yes, I am," he said defiantly, looking straight at Mrs. Pritchard.

"Always glad to have another young man on our side, especially in these rebellious parts." He, too, looked at Mrs. Pritchard. "You never told me about your Connecticut relatives."

"I don't think of him as my Connecticut kin. I just think of Will as part of my family. Since we were all one country before this war began, half of us have kin where the other half lives."

The general smiled. "Common kin we may share, but not, I fear, common sense.

That attribute is sorely lacking in these times and I am afraid few besides you and me, Mrs. Pritchard, know that. However, it is what it is. Now, what shall we do with your cousin? How old are you, boy?"

"I'm fourteen, sir."

"Too young to fight and too old to play. So what do you do with yourself?"

Was that a trick question? I certainly can't say I've hunted Yankees and now I am rescuing a Confederate friend. "Well, sir, frankly I am a bit bored."

"I appreciate your honesty. My men get bored at camp sometimes. I sincerely hope you do not indulge in the kind of pursuits that they indulge in to alleviate their boredom. So, what are you doing here?"

Before Will could answer, Mrs. Pritchard spoke. "He is visiting me and will stay here tonight and tomorrow night, then go on back home to his family. I am very grateful for his visit."

The General wrote something and signed his name. "Here is a pass if anyone troubles you. I hope you reach your home safely."

"Thank you, sir."

After the General left the room, Mrs. Pritchard said, "I see you are carrying a knapsack. I will fill it up with food before you leave in the morning. Now, would you care for supper? I know it is late, but growing boys usually have large appetites."

"Wouldn't mind some food myself," called out the unpleasant soldier.

"You help yourself to my food all the time. I call it stealing, of course, when you grab my chickens or take vegetables from my garden. Then there were the times your men tried to milk my cow, something expressly forbidden by the General. So, soldier, I will not willingly prepare food for you or your men."

"One day, lady, we will order you out of this house and I will be pleased to know that you have become one of those wandering refugees, those people who lost their homes and go from place to place seeking food and shelter."

"Better an honest refugee than a common thief. Come, Will. Let us leave this young man whose mamma would be ashamed of his rudeness."

The soldier started to rise but the Adjutant immediately came over to intervene.

"We are sorry for the trouble we have caused you. Please accept my apology on behalf of those men who do not have the manners we in our army try to instill."

Mrs. Pritchard simply said, "Thank you," and Will followed her out of the room.

As she put out milk and bread, she said, "I cannot always silence my tongue. It is a weakness. The General and the Adjutant are good men, but they cannot control everything that goes on around them. I am particularly upset today because they tied up their horses in my garden and trampled all my flowers. But damage to gardens is not the worst of this war, is it, when bodies are being broken and families torn apart?"

Mrs. Pritchard watched while Will ate and drank. "All right, Will, now that you have eaten, we will retire upstairs and you will sleep in the nursery which is, thankfully, not occupied by Union soldiers."

They went up the stairs together and as soon as they were in the nursery, Mrs. Pritchard said, "So, why are you here, Will? What has happened?"

"Edward ran away and I'm going to try to find him and bring him back home."

"Where do you think he is?"

"Back at Willows."

"You may be right. I have heard rumors of an indiscreet attack."

"You know something about Edward?"

"I believe so. I was not sure who they were talking about, but now I realize it must have been Edward. It seems as if he went and found a hornet's nest on a tree near Willows. He put some kind of a bag around it, cut it down and threw it into the parlor which is now the Colonel's headquarters. The bag opened up and hornets swarmed all over, stinging the Colonel, his Adjutant and many soldiers. They caught Edward almost immediately and he is going to be sent to prison."

"For throwing a hornet's nest?"

"For attacking the Colonel, for attacking his headquarters, and for causing tremendous inconvenience, as soldiers had to deal with hornets swarming all over the house."

"But prison?"

"They are very angry. He is being held until they can send him over to Fort McHenry in Baltimore."

"Can your General help him?"

"I don't think so. The Colonel thinks they have to make an example of Edward so other young men will not follow in his footsteps."

"Does Robs know about this? Or Tom?"

"I doubt it. Edward's name was never mentioned so even if they heard about the incident, they would have no reason to connect it with their brother that they just saw in Winchester."

"This is worse than I imagined. How am I going to get him out?"

"We will think of a way."

Will was very relieved to hear her say "We."

"In the morning I will try to find out whatever I can about Edward. I have to be careful, though, because I do not want to get you into any trouble. Or myself. Let us go to sleep now. Morning will come soon enough."

Despite his troubles, Will slept well and woke up to the smell of frying bacon.

"I figured this would rouse you," Mrs. Pritchard said.

"Smells good," said one of the soldiers, as he helped himself to a piece of bacon.

"You get your rations from the Army."

"But they sure don't taste as good as your meals."

Will sat down and ate quickly. "What are we . . ."

"Well, dear cousin," Mrs. Pritchard interrupted loudly. "Come outside and we will go to the fields and pick what these marauding soldiers left us."

Will followed her outside.

"We can talk if we do it quietly and quickly. I don't want anyone to hear what I am about to say. Early this morning I found out that Edward is being held in the smokehouse over at Willows."

"I know exactly where it is," Will replied.

"Good. I have an idea but it is risky."

"What is it?"

"There is a band of guerrillas around here. They may respond to this situation if we give them an incentive and present it as a challenge. I will give you some of the silver I have hidden in these fields. It should be enough to interest them, but it will be up to you to convince them to go to Willows and rescue Edward."

"But where can I find those guerrillas?"

"That part is easy. I know where they are camped. The hard part will be convincing them to help. You will have to be the one to do that convincing, even though I happen to know one of them quite well. You may use my name, but I cannot come with you."

Will didn't hesitate. "It's a good idea. I will go and see them."

"All right. But first we have to dig up the vegetables and somehow dig up the silver without anyone seeing us."

Will thought about this. "Why don't we take those baskets over there and put the silver on the bottom and then cover the silver up with lots and lots of vegetables that we pick. That way none of the soldiers will be able to see what we have underneath the vegetables."

"Good idea."

The two of them worked together to harvest the food that was ready to be picked. "Are you sharing today," asked a soldier as he came over. "I'm sure our cook could use some of those greens."

"Your cook could use a little more than my greens in the kitchen from what I hear from your men," she answered tartly. "Go on with you. I have the General's permission to work in my own fields."

"It is galling that I actually need permission to pick my own vegetables," muttered Mrs. Pritchard to Will when the soldier left.

Will was distracted in the afternoon, so much so that one of the soldiers asked him if he had a lady friend he was missing. That gave the other soldiers a good laugh and gave Will increased motivation for the task that lay ahead.

At supper, they made table talk under the bored eyes of the soldiers. "Don't you have anything else to talk about except Brother So-and-So and Sister So-and-So and their doings?"

"If we do," Mrs. Pritchard answered, "We have forgotten it since you men came to live with us."

"Ah, needling my men again," said the General as he walked into the room.

"I know I shouldn't, but it is very tempting since they annoy me so much. You know the saying, 'needs must when the Devil drives.' "

"Nice to know that it is the Devil's words, not your own. Look, I know they can be annoying, but since they have occupied your home, why don't you just ignore them? After all, if I can, so can you."

Mrs. Pritchard laughed. "It is good that you have a sense of humor. I imagine a General needs to laugh sometimes."

"If I cannot laugh, I will have to cry and, honestly, I much prefer to laugh."

This night, Will had trouble sleeping when he went to bed. Mrs. Pritchard had given him detailed directions to the guerrilla camp and he went over and over them in his head until he could almost recite them backwards. "I am not scared. Not really. I just hope that I am up to this. It is more challenging than anything I have ever done, and it makes standing up to Jack and his friends back at school look so easy. No guns there."

Sleep finally came but, all too quickly, the smell of bacon once again wafted up to his room.

"If I have to wake up, this is a fine way to do it," he told Mrs. Pritchard.

"Why don't you join us and fight like a big boy," the now-familiar soldier said. "Heard you were from Connecticut, so maybe we can use you. That is, if you shoot and ride like a man, not a boy. Looking at you, though, I doubt it."

Will decided not to respond. He had more important things to do than argue with a jerk.

Mrs. Pritchard handed him his knapsack. "Here, Will. I have given you a few things to eat when you get hungry."

"How about me," called out the soldier.

This time both of them ignored him.

She gave him a hug and said, "God bless you, child."

Will returned the hug and went on his way. Peaches seemed in good spirits, well-fed and watered which must, Will reasoned, make him happy. After all, food and drink make people happy. He passed wheat straw that stood tall and knew it was only a matter of time before one or both of the armies would be around to cut them down and carry them off. That was the problem here. The Confederate and Union armies had little respect for farmers and just helped themselves to whatever they wanted.

He then left the farms and headed into the forest. The landmarks Mrs. Pritchard told him about were there, and Will had no trouble following them.

When he had gone far enough, he got off Peaches and took out the white flag of truce that Mrs. Pritchard had made for him. Even though he saw no one around, he held it up with one hand and led Peaches with the other. His heart was beating furiously, but he held his head high.

"Halt!"

Will stopped.

"Who are you and what do you want?"

"I am Will Bradford. Mrs. Pritchard sent me to speak with the leader of the guerrilla camp."

"We use the word partisans, not guerrillas."

"Sorry. I want to speak with the head of the partisans, then."

"Oh, you do, do you? Why should we let you?"

"Because I come bearing gifts and requesting aid."

"Let him through," said a man with a full head of red hair and a bushy red beard. "I am the man you seek. I am Big Red. Put away your flag and ride your horse and follow us."

Will did as he was told and was led through the forest through twisted paths and around freshly-cut trees. He doubted that he would be able to find his way back but he took note of a few markings that he hoped he would be able to remember.

"Get off your horse now and tie him up. We will walk."

They walked through the woods and Will knew he could never retrace these steps. When they came to a clearing, Will was surprised to find a small village. It was rough and crude, but there were places to cook and places to eat and sleep and it had all the things one might need for an extended stay.

"Sit," said Big Red, "and state your business. If it wasn't for Mrs. Pritchard, we would not be talking now."

Will didn't want to contemplate what they would have been doing. "I need your help."

"Why?

"My friend did a stupid thing and attacked a Union camp with a hornet's nest."

Big Red stared at him. "A hornet's nest? Men, you have got to listen to this . . . "

Several men gathered around.

"I know it was stupid but you have to understand that the Union army was camped right in his house and he wanted them out."

"That I sure can understand," laughed one of the men. "We all want them out . . . out of the Valley, out of Virginia and out of the South."

"But this was his home," Will said a little defensively.

"And the South is our home," added another man.

"Anyway," Will went on, "My friend was caught and they are going to send him to prison and I want to rescue him."

Big Red looked at him carefully. "Well, what do you want with us?"

This was it. Will knew he had to speak the truth. "I can't do it alone. I need help."

Big Red nodded. "It takes a strong man to admit to needing others. Look at us. Alone, we cannot fight the Union army. Together we can attack them the way we attacked the British Army during our American Revolution. We are following in their footsteps. We attack their railroads, we disrupt their supplies, we stay hidden so they never know when we will appear. We partisans are bad for their morale and what's bad for the Union army is good for the Confederacy!"

The men cheered.

"Now, why should we help you?"

Will hesitated. He didn't want to insult these men by offering them the silver. On the other hand, they probably needed the money it would bring. Causes, noble or not, still need money to finance their operations. Feeding all these men, for one thing, could not be easy although they probably mostly lived off the land. Will spoke. "I think you should help me for two reasons. One, there is a boy in trouble and only you can rescue him. Two, Mrs. Pritchard gave me some silver to give to you as a thank you for your help."

"Keep your silver. We will help you just because you need us. Now, what is the name of the boy and the name and the location of his plantation? I need all the information you have."

"He is Edward Mitchell and his mother and Mrs. Pritchard are old friends." Big Red looked a little more interested now, so Will continued, "He is being held at the smokehouse at Willows. I know where Willows is because I stayed with the Mitchells last year."

"I know Edward," said one of the partisans. "I was friends with his brother, Joseph, who was killed at Manassas. The Mitchells are good people."

"All right, now," Big Red said. "We need to make a plan."

"How about using hornets," laughed one of the men.

Big Red smiled. "Well, we know that doesn't work so let's try something else."

"Bees?"

They all laughed again.

Big Red turned to Will. "Are you willing to take an oath of loyalty to us, the Partisans?"

"Yes."

"All right then, let's plan our next raid! Willows it is!"

Chapter 11

"What do you think, Little Man? What ideas do you have?"

Although he didn't like being called little, Will did appreciate being called a man. He thought for a moment. "I think we have to use distraction. If we can pull the soldiers away from the smokehouse, then one of us can go and rescue Edward."

Big Red nodded. "Distraction usually works. What kind of distraction do you have in mind?"

The question surprised Will. Somehow, he didn't expect Big Red to ask for his advice.

"Well, Little Man? We are waiting."

"We could set off some explosives, whatever kind you have in this time."

"What do you mean by in this time? What other time do we have?"

Not much gets by Big Red. "I mean here, where we are now."

"As it happens, we don't want to waste what we have. Not that your friend is not important, don't get me wrong, but we may need explosives for bigger things. The same with powder."

By now Will knew that powder meant gunpowder. He looked around and thought. "I know. Why don't we burn a wagon? Fire always brings people running."

Big Red nodded again. "Men, tell Will why I am asking for his suggestions. Rats, you start."

"Rats? The man sure has a way with nicknames," thought Will.

Rats began to speak. "One reason is to make sure that he is really with us, not just letting us do all the work."

"Well put. Owl, what do you say?"

"I say a man has the right to help plan a rescue if it's his friend we are rescuing. And he better be there too," Owl growled menacingly. "None of this we work and you thinks. No, we all work and we all think."

"Excellent. Owl is expressing the philosophy of our small partisan band. We all contribute. We all take risks and we all fight. I am the leader, the elected leader, but this is an egalitarian operation."

At Will's shocked look, Owl smiled, "He went to the University of Virginia. That must be where he learned them big words."

The men laughed and Will joined in uncertainly.

"A wagon," Big Red repeated. "If we found a wagon in good condition, we might appropriate it, but we have no need for a broken wagon. Until now that is. All right, so who has a plan?"

Big Red reminded Will of a teacher he had in his old school. The man always asked questions and expected his students to somehow figure it out. He seemed to tell them nothing, but Will thought he learned more in that class than in any other class. Strange how that worked . . . .

"Let's begin this way. Who has either an idea or else something to contribute to this venture?"

The men threw out different ideas. "We can just take a broken wagon. They are all over the Pike."

"And if we're stopped," asked Big Red. "What then?"

Will suddenly looked up. "I know. I have a pass signed by the General who is staying with Mrs. Pritchard. I can show that."

A shout went up.

"That, Little Man, is a valuable item, even more valuable than that silver you are carrying."

"Why aren't we taking that silver," a man asked.

"Fingers, we do not take anything that belongs to our friends. We only take things from our enemies."

"We have plenty of those," Fingers said. "Both Yankee and Rebel."

"Correct. And we take not take only from the rich. We take from everyone who does not willingly share what they have with us."

"And do you give to the poor," asked Will, thinking of Robin Hood.

"That we do. Ourselves. We are the poor, the new poor."

As the men laughed, Will said nothing.

"Ah," Big Red mused, "I see I have offended you. Perhaps if you understood that we never steal from women who are alone on their farms, you would feel better. Of course if their men are there, then we have no problem."

As the men laughed again, Big Red broke off a twig and drew a map on the ground. "Once I wrote with pen and ink on fine paper and now I write with twigs on the ground. But, men, remember, it is not how you write but what you write. I am as good a mapmaker as Jed Hotchkiss! He drew a map of the Valley for Stonewall Jackson."

"Do you know Stonewall Jackson or any of the other Generals," asked Will, momentarily diverted.

"No, I don't. Right now most of the Generals do not appreciate our band. They think we are undisciplined and have no honor. What they do not understand is that they were trained at West Point where ideas of battles come from Napoleon . . . big and grand with lots of killings."

"Like Gettysburg."

"Like what? What is Gettysburg?"

Will began to panic. He forgot that Gettysburg hadn't happened yet. Will looked around for a diversion and took out his pass. "Do you want this?"

"I do, but you hang on to it for now. Little Man, you bother me. There is something about you that is unusual. Where are you from? Tell the truth now, Little Man, because I can smell a lie fifteen feet away and running."

"Litchfield, Connecticut."

"A Yankee," cried out Owl. "Let's kill him."

A shout went up and Big Red put out his hand. "No one gets killed in this band without due process. The floor is yours, Will."

"I am here because I came to see my relative, William Bradford, who is fighting for the Confederates. I left Connecticut to look for him."

"Why?"

Good question. "I have had some trouble at home. My father left us and we had to move. I am not happy where I am in Litchfield, so I thought I would go to another place."

"You ran away," Big Red said flatly.

"I guess I did."

"Have you found what you are looking for?" Big Red asked.

"I don't know. I'm not sure what I am looking for except maybe William Bradford, who I really don't know."

"Where is your father? Is he in the Union Army?"

"No. He doesn't care much for any army."

"Like us."

"No," Will answered passionately, "Not like you. You care about your men. My father doesn't care about me, or my sister, or my mother."

"Will, you do not know that."

"I do. If he cared, he wouldn't have left us."

No one spoke for a moment until Big Red began. "You are an idealist. Once I was one, too. An idealist sees the world in black and white. He knows what is good and what is evil and there is not very much in between the two. But, in the real world, there is gray that lies between black and white. You want certainty, Will, but you might as well learn right now that there is no such thing. A man like myself can defend a poor widow on Monday and steal from her son on Tuesday. Am I good or am I bad? Truth is, I am both. To the widow I am a hero, and to her son I am a villain."

"I don't understand," began Will.

"I know, son, I know. Now we have to get back to work. Let us forget philosophy, forget Litchfield and Gettysburg, forget Rebels and Yankees, forget everything but figuring out how to free your friend. Look," he pointed at his map drawn in the dirt, "this is my plan. The men will attack Willows from here while you and I break into the smokehouse." He went over the plan again and again, until Will felt his head reel with exhaustion.

"We must rest now and at first light, Little Man, you and Rats go and take our wagon and load up whatever you find on the Pike that would be good for burning."

"I'm not going with a boy," complained Rats.

"A boy with a pass to move about freely. That's not just any boy." He pointed, "Little Man, you sleep over there. You have to learn to get your sleep when you can if you work with our band."

Will was sure that he would never be able to sleep with all that was going on in his mind, but before he knew it Rats was shaking him awake. "Get up. The sun is just rising and we've got to get going."

He stood up shakily. Big Red walked over. "Today we have much to do so get some food and eat quickly. And Rats?"

"Yeah?"

"Little Man is leaving the silver in my care. See that he returns safely."

Rats glowered until Big Red said, "Rats, I am counting on you. This is his first military operation so it is your responsibility to see that it goes well. And, Little Man, follow Rats. He knows what he is doing."

After a hasty meal of corn cakes and ham, Will and Rats walked quietly through the forest until they came to the clearing where the horses stood in a makeshift corral.

"Peaches," called out Will as the horse came over and nuzzled him. "You're a good boy." He turned to Rats and asked, "Did someone feed him?"

"Course. Whaddaya think? We need our horses and we treat 'em good. Your horse ever pull a wagon?"

At Will's shrug, Rats said, "Didn't think so. We gotta get these other two ready 'cause they know what to do."

Feeling somewhat insulted on behalf of Peaches, Will just followed Rats.

"You got that pass," Rats asked when the wagon was ready.

"I do."

"Give it to me."

Will thought about that. "No." Rats' face turned a mottled purple, so Will quickly added, "If we are stopped, the soldiers will believe me better than they will believe you."

"And why is that?"

"I am a boy and I can explain how I got it. What can you say?"

Rats didn't answer and they set off.

They reached the Valley Pike and saw half-broken wagons lying on their side along with the usual remnants of battle. Will observed one boot, one shoe, a dented spoon, a cup, half a barrel, and a lone cap with a hole through the middle. He thought he saw blood on the ground but he hoped that was only his imagination. They quickly piled up the wood from the broken wagons and put them inside their wagon. Just when their wagon was filled and they were ready to leave, they heard a voice.

"Halt."

Will stopped and turned around. Two Union soldiers stood facing him, one waving a gun almost in his face. "Yes?"

"What are you doing?"

"We are dismantling these wagons as General Pellam ordered."

"I know nothing about this."

"I am William Bradford," announced Will, "and this is my assistant. We do odd jobs for the Army down the Valley in Winchester and this is what we were ordered to do today."

"Why should we believe you? Got anything in writing?"

"I have a pass from the General if you want to see it." Will started to take the pass out when one of the soldiers waved his hand. "Forget it. Just hurry up and get out of here."

Will was eager to oblige and he and Rats headed off quickly.

"Whew! That was close," said Will.

"I've been in closer fixes than that."

Will refused to be drawn into a conversation about Rats' jams. "The turn-off is around here. We have to get to the church first and somewhere behind there is where Big Red and the rest of your band is meeting us."

"I know the way. It's over there," Rats pointed. "We gotta go way past the church."

Will gritted his teeth. "That's what I just said."

As they rode, Will clutched his pass, ready to show it to anyone who might ask. Finally, they reached a small clearing in the woods and Rats stopped the wagon.

Big Red walked over. "I see you got here without any problems."

"Two soldiers asked us what we were doing here and I told them I had a pass from General Pellam and . . . ," babbled Will.

Ignoring him, Big Red went on, "We have everything we need now. One of our men scouted Willows and it should be even easier than I anticipated. We will plan it for suppertime when everyone is eating. Now, have you considered what Edward is going to do when we release him?"

Will looked surprised. "Go to his Mother's house in Winchester, where else?"

"Little Man, you haven't thought this through. There are Yankees all over Winchester and he surely will not be safe there. They will send him back to Willows or else they'll send him to prison in Baltimore."

"But won't they realize that Edward is not even fourteen years old yet?"

"We are in a war, Little Man. It does not matter if your attacker is fourteen or thirty-four. He is still your attacker. Yankees do not take well to invasions and your friend invaded their territory."

"But it was his home," protested Will.

"Not any longer. Now it belongs to the Yankees."

Will was quiet. How strange war is. It kind of changes everything. Sometimes it's even hard to figure out who is good and who is bad. He said passionately, "Those Yankees who took Edward's home were terrible."

"Not much worse than the Confederates who are going around taking farmers' crops to feed the Confederate army. A plague on both their houses, as Shakespeare so aptly said. Food and water and rest now. No alcohol. We want no muddled thinking. Owl brought Peaches here for you and you will ride him and come with me to release your friend. We all will meet up back at camp after we free Edward and then we can celebrate."

The atmosphere was genial as the men ate, talked and joked.

"So, Will, are you ready," asked Owl.

"I don't know. I feel a little funny. Not exactly scared, but not relaxed either."

"First-time nerves. Everyone gets them, but gets them only once."

Big Red came over to Will. "We all separate now. Get your horse and follow me. Do you know how to use a gun or a bow and arrow?"

Will shook his head. He didn't think his experience shooting in his computer games counted in the real world.

"Don't they do that in Litchfield, Connecticut?" Big Red asked.

"Not really."

"So, I won't have anyone to help if things go bad. Well, just listen to me. Your job is to get Edward out and on your horse and ride like the wind back to our camp."

"What about you?"

"I have some things to take care of. All right, men, it's time to show those Yankees what we are made of and who we are! Let's ride."

Will felt his heart pounding in his chest.

The men scattered and Will found himself riding with Big Red through the back roads to Willows. As they approached the plantation, Big Red gestured for Will to follow. They tied up their horses and proceeded on foot. Soon they were close and suddenly Big Red pulled out a bow and arrow. "For the pickets guarding the encampment," he whispered. "Quieter than powder." They waited.

Suddenly a huge commotion began as flames leaped up into the air in the distance. Men began shouting and running. Big Red nodded to Will and quickly sent a arrow right through the heart of one of the men on picket duty. Before the other man could see what was happening, he shot his arrow and killed that man as well. "Good job, if I do say so myself." He then took his ax and gave Will a sturdy piece of wood. "Let's hurry now to the smokehouse."

Together he and Will broke down the door while the flames grew nearer. "Stand back, Prince Albert," he called out. "We are here to rescue you."

Within seconds, they flung the door open and Edward stood blinking at them in disbelief. "Will," he said in amazement. "Will, is that you?"

"Time for your reunion later. Here comes Owl. Go with him and meet us at camp. Little Man, ride like the wind."

"Who, what . . . ," Edward began.

"No time to talk. Move quickly."

Edward mounted Peaches and Will climbed on behind him. They followed Owl and rode faster than Will had ever ridden. When they past the church, they heard the sound of cannonading down the Valley and rode even harder. It was a ride that Will would never forget. The trees seemed to spur them on and the wind carried Peaches along. Finally Owl gave a signal and slowed down. Will followed and soon they dismounted and tied up their horses.

"Water 'em down," commanded Owl. "They're gonna be mighty thirsty after this ride."

He pointed to the river. Will found a bucket and filled it while Edward followed him shakily. "How did you know where to find me?"

"Just did. Where else would you go if not to your home? Can you give me a hand with Owl's horse?"

"Who or what is Owl and where are we and . . . "

"I'll explain after we water these horses. Peaches never had a ride like that."

"How do you know that?"

"I just do."

Owl sat down to rest. "Will, you and your friend water and feed the other horses here. The food is over there."

"Why is he giving us orders," Edward asked. "Who is he anyway?"

"Just one of the men who rescued you. If he hadn't, you would be off to Fort McHenry in Baltimore."

"I'm sorry; you are right. I guess I'm a little bit dazed. After we finish, please tell me what is happening and how Mamma is."

"Worried. That's how your Mamma is."

"I'm sorry. I just had to fight and . . . "

The sound of hoof beats and men laughing and talking loudly interrupted them.

"Got some more horses for you to water, Little Man," said a smiling Big Red. "You can head to camp after the horses are comfortable."

Tired as he and Edward were, they worked hard, even rubbing down the horses.

Finally they were done and walked the convoluted route that led them in circles to the camp in the woods.

"Where are we going," Edward asked Will, forgetting that Big Red had told them shortly before.

"To the camp," Will repeated patiently.

"I hope they feed us. I am hungry."

Before they reached camp, the smell of barbecuing meats wafted through the trees. They arrived to see a hog on one spit and a side of beef on another.

"So, boys, how did we do?"

"I am impressed," said Will. "Where did you get all this meat?"

"From Prince Albert here," answered Big Red. "Thank you for contributing to our supply of food."

"But what did I do?"

"Well, we figured you would much rather that we have your family's stock than the Yankees, so we took whatever we could and brought it here."

"You are right. I hate those miserable men who stole my house, my farm and then locked me up in my own smokehouse."

"Little Man, introduce us properly," commanded Big Red.

"Big Red is the leader of this band of partisans. Big Red, this is my friend, Edward Mitchell. Edward, this is Big Red."

Big Red stuck out his hand. "Always pleased to meet a fellow rebel. Now tell me exactly what you hoped to accomplish. I understand that you used a hornet's nest. Is that true?"

"Sadly, it is," answered Edward. "I did not think things through carefully. I knew I could cause a huge commotion with the nest, but I didn't stop to think what would happen next."

"What did happen?"

"They got stung and came running. Then they captured me right away. I tried to run, but there were too many of them. They were very angry."

"I don't doubt it," laughed Big Red. "Well, you tried your best and that is to be commended. Of course, your lack of experience showed. I always plan ahead. That is the key, Prince Albert."

"Sir," Edward asked timidly, "Why do you call me Prince Albert?"

"After Queen Victoria's husband, of course. I have names for everyone, because we do not want anyone knowing who we really are. It just seems safer to give names that no one at home would recognize. My Mamma, naturally, does not know me as Big Red. And Will is not known as Little Man anywhere else, are you, Will?"

"No, sir."

"So, boys, let us eat and enjoy ourselves and tomorrow morning we will plan what to do next. Always remember, Prince Albert, planning is the key to success."

"I am still confused," Edward confessed to Will as they lay down to sleep later. "Who are these people?"

"They call themselves Partisans, but I think that people who don't like them call them Guerrillas, because they fight in guerrilla style, sort of hit and run."

"I don't know what you are talking about. Whoever they are, why are they helping me?"

"I'm not sure. Maybe because I told them Mrs. Pritchard asked them to or maybe because they just wanted to stick it to the Union Army again."

"Or maybe," said the deep voice of Big Red, "just maybe I can remember being young myself and doing foolish things like Prince Albert here. Now, go to sleep. Mornings come early around here. Oh, and if you don't sleep, try lowering your voices so other can."

Edward and Will just looked at each other and burst out laughing when Big Red walked away. "Remember how Mamma always used to tell us to lower our voices at night? Big Red and Mamma using the same words! Imagine!" They laughed and laughed until they finally fell asleep under the spell of a hot June night in a clearing in the woods.

"Git up. No loafers here," shouted a voice as the sun rose. "Git on down to the river and bathe yourselves. No stinking up our camp. And wash your clothes, both of you."

"You didn't tell me about this," grumbled Edward. "At least in prison I didn't have to wash and no one cared how long I slept."

"Want to go back?"

"Not on your life."

"How about on yours," suggested Will with a smile.

"Git out of here. Go on and jump in the river."

They splashed about and swam until they exhausted themselves and were hungry.

"That food smells almost as good as Mamma's cooking," said Edward.

"Know what you mean. My Mother is a good cook, too. Or, at least, she used to be when she had more time."

"Where is your Mamma," Edward asked curiously. "You never talk much about her.

"Back home in Litchfield."

"Litchfield?"

Will shook his head at his stupidity, until he realized that the Partisans all knew he was from Connecticut.

"It's in Connecticut."

"Connecticut! You're a Yankee?"

"No, I'm not. I'm just a person caught in the War without a place, without a home and without a time."

"What . . . "

"Git on over here, boys," shouted Owl. "Food's on and we have work to do."

"But Will," continued Edward. "I don't understand."

"Well, neither do I. Just know that I care a lot about all of you and I want the killing to end. Now, let's go and eat."

The makeshift tables were laden with huge amounts of food. Will and Edward began to grab some, but Big Red shook his head. "Grace first, boys. We have to thank the Lord for this repast."

"Repast," whispered Will. "What's a repast?"

"It's a meal," Edward whispered back. "Big Red sure does like fancy words. For some reason, he reminds me of someone I once met, but I can't remember who it is."

After grace, the boys ate heartily. "I sure missed good meals in the smokehouse," Edward said as Big Red came over to them.

"I see you boys are enjoying the food. That's good. We should enjoy the good things that we are given. Now, Prince Albert, what do you think you will do next?"

"Next? I'll go home to Winchester."

"Will you try to fight the Yankees again?"

"I want to, but not this way. I need men to help me, but the Confederate Army says I'm too young to join. Even my brothers agree with that."

"And you? Do you agree?"

"No," Edward answered passionately. "I am young, this is true. But I am tall and strong and a fighter and I am not afraid. Well, I am sometimes, but that never stopped me from fighting."

"I have a proposition for you. Why don't you join our band of partisans? Youth has energy and excitement. You are too impetuous, but we can help direct your enthusiasm to success rather than failure. And, you must realize that it is not safe for you to go home. Your home is the first place the Union Army will go to look for you."

"But why will they look for me," Edward asked.

"You are an escaped prisoner. They cannot just let you go. Prince Albert, I want you to consider my proposal."

"I don't have to consider it. I accept."

"Ah, impetuous youth. Before you accept, I want you to spend a week with us, working alongside my men and seeing if you will fit in here. Remember, we have no servants here. We do all our own work, something you probably never did."

"I can work as hard as anyone else."

"But have you ever? And will you now? You will find out during this week."

"And me," asked Will. "What should I do?"

"Much as I enjoy your company, you have to go home. I don't mean to Litchfield, at least right now. No, now you have to go back to Mrs. Mitchell in Winchester. You have a pass so you should not have any trouble. Spend the day here and go tomorrow morning."

"But what will I tell Mrs. Mitchell? I told her I was going to bring Edward home."

"I would like to see Mamma," Edward admitted.

"Little Man, explain to Edward's mother that he is with friends and cannot come home because he broke out of a Yankee prison. Make sure you tell her that you saw him and he rode off to . . . let's say Lynchburg, with these new friends. I promise that I will arrange for you, Prince Albert, to see your mother again when it is safe for you to do so. I will do this whether or not you stay with us. If you decide to leave, I will try to arrange a hiding place for you. And I also promise you, Little Man, that I will not try to delve into the mystery of Litchfield."

Big Red looked at Will's stricken face and laughed. "Little Man, my advice to you is to develop a poker face. It will stand you in good stead as you go through life."

"And what is your advice to me, sir," asked Edward.

"Think. Think before you act. All right, boys, off with you. Prince Edward, there is a mess to clean up. Go and make yourself useful. Little Man, I want to talk with you alone."

"Take care of yourself, Edward," said Will. "It's a brave thing you are doing."

"Brave? I think it's called survival. It's you who were brave, Will. You came out here, found these men and somehow got them to rescue me. Thank you."

Will was embarrassed. No one ever called him brave before. He didn't feel brave. He was just doing what he had to do. He waved as Edward walked off.

"Will," Big Red came over and stuck out his hand. "Good job."

As he shook hands, Will felt suddenly shy. "Thank you for everything."

"You know, Will, there is another piece of advice I want to give you. I want to ask you to think about forgiveness. This is a hard world but if we ever hope for redemption, we have to learn to forgive."

"Redemption?"

"Redemption. If we cannot forgive others, Will, how can we expect God to forgive us?"

Will looked confused and Big Red just shrugged his shoulders. "Never mind. Just remember my words, because one day they will mean something to you."

Chapter 12

After supper, when darkness fell, one man picked up his banjo and another his fiddle and they began to play. They sang many songs but, for some unknown reason, it was the spirited sound of "Dixie" that made Will suddenly think of Litchfield and his mother. He felt uncomfortable and pretended to yawn.

"I'm going to bed," he said quietly to Edward, only to find that Edward was already asleep right there by the fire.

In the morning, Will said his goodbyes.

"Anytime you need us, just come and get us. You know the way," Big Red told him. "Now, here is Mrs. Pritchard's silver. Thank her for the offer and tell her I will come by one day and expect a meal instead."

"Why did you take the silver if you weren't going to keep it?"

"I took it for safekeeping. Conceal it well as you go, and help Mrs. Pritchard hide it when you get there. You never know who might try to steal it. Godspeed, Will, and be gentle with your people in Litchfield."

"How do you . . . "

Big Red smiled. "And, Will . . . "

"Yes?"

"Remember what I told you about forgiveness."

Will nodded. "Goodbye and thank you, sir. See you later, Edward."

He now knew the way and easily walked the circular route to find Peaches. The ride was uneventful and he reached Mrs. Pritchard in the late morning. He saw that her house was still full of Union soldiers.

"Why, Will, you must have left at the crack of dawn to get here so early."

"I did."

"So, the boy is back," grumbled one of the soldiers. "Don't like all this coming and going. Shouldn't allow it in a war."

Ignoring him, Mrs. Pritchard drew Will inside and said loud enough for anyone to hear, "Come upstairs with me. I want to show you what I made."

She led him to her bedroom and handed him a beautiful flowered quilt. "This is one of the quilts that I made to raffle off and raise money to buy our boys ironclad gunboats to fight for our seaports. Now that our seaports have been taken by the Yankees, I will send it to Mrs. Mitchell who can send it on to Tom or Robs. It will keep them warm when we get to those cold winter nights."

"War isn't gonna last till winter," said a soldier as he stepped into the room. "Them Rebs don't have it in them."

"Shoo. This is my home and my room and I am allowed to give away a quilt. Shoo, or I will tell General Pellam about your rude behavior."

"I'm going. Whoever heard of giving a quilt in June, especially here where it is hotter than . . . "

"We don't want to hear such talk," Mrs. Pritchard shouted after him. She turned to Will and pointed to five yellow flowers sitting in a carefully stitched bouquet and lowered her voice. "Tell Mrs. Mitchell that I have sewn something under these flowers for her. It is a present to make up for the one she lost at Willows."

"Yes, ma'am. And speaking of Willows, it all went well."

"I heard." Mrs. Pritchard laughed. "The soldiers here are very angry. Feel like they were made fools twice over, first by Edward and his hornets and then by the Partisans and their rescue."

"Their leader gave me back the silver to return to you."

"He would."

"You don't sound surprised."

269

"I know him. All right, I will hide it again after dinner. I have noticed the soldiers get tired after eating their big meal and have no desire to go out into the hot sun. Must be their cold Northern blood. They often close their eyes, even on guard duty. When they do, I will go outside and, if they say anything, I will tell them I am picking vegetables since we have little else to eat these days. But right now, I want to give you something to eat. You must be hungry after all your adventures."

Rather than tell her how well he ate, Will just said, "Yes, ma'am, thank you."

General Pellam walked in as they were eating.

Mrs. Pritchard smiled. "Want to join us? I have enough."

"Only if I can contribute. I brought you coffee."

"Coffee? That I have been missing. Your blockade of our seaports has denied us the two things we ladies need. One is good fabric, which we used to import from the North and Europe, and the other is coffee. I admit I miss the coffee more than I do the fashionable fabrics. So, thank you very much for your contribution. Now, please sit down."

As the General ate, he said, "Nobody makes corn bread the way you do."

"Thank you. So, how are you today?"

"Could be better. That escape from Willows hurt our Yankee pride."

Will almost choked on his eggs. "What escape," he managed.

"Some boy threw a hornet's nest into the parlor of a plantation we are using as our headquarters. Of course, our soldiers caught him immediately, but yesterday the guerrilla band that operates around here went and freed him. The whole thing is bad for morale."

"Well, General, people aren't happy when their homes are occupied by foreign troops. You can't really blame them, can you," said Mrs. Pritchard as she poured him coffee.

"If they hadn't started this war, we would be out of their homes and back in our own homes and everybody would be happy."

"So do you think you will catch this boy?"

"No. Too many people around to hide him. Of course, we'll check with his mother, but that will be a waste of time. If we ever find him, we'll send him off to Fort McKinley immediately."

"But he's only a kid," ventured Will.

"If he fights us, then he has to be treated as an enemy, and we put our enemies in prison. Or we kill them."

With this sobering information, Will quickly finished his meal, thinking how

271

different the food was from what he was used to at home in Connecticut.

He helped clear away the dishes they had used. He hoped the General would forget about Edward, the rescue and, most of all, the pass he had given to him. If word about his part in the rescue ever got out . . . Will didn't want to consider the consequences.

Soon it was time for him to leave.

"Send my love to Mrs. Mitchell and the children," said Mrs. Pritchard. Will was aghast at her slip and hoped that the General wasn't paying any attention.

Of course, the General did notice the name. "Is that the same Mrs. Mitchell who is the mother of Edward?"

There was no point in lying. "Yes."

"And you are going there to visit them? Do you know anything about Edward's disappearance?"

This time there was a point in lying. "No, I don't."

"Well, if you see him or learn about his whereabouts, I expect you to tell one of our men. As a Yankee, Connecticut born and bred, you know where your loyalties lie, don't you?"

"Yes, sir."

He climbed back on to Peaches for his trip down the Valley to Winchester. As he rode, he was scarcely aware of the wagons and horses that passed him. All Will was aware of was the feeling in the pit of his stomach. There were so many loyalties these days. There was the Union Army, loyal to the United States of America. There was the Confederate Army, loyal to the Confederate States of America. There were the Partisans, loyal, it seemed, to themselves. Then there were the mountain men loyal to their place in the mountains. And, finally, there were the slaves, some of whom were loyal to Abraham Lincoln and were hoping that he would grant them freedom.

And here he was, a Northern boy from the 21st century traveling in 1862 to be with a Southern family. It was all very confusing.

The sound of Union soldiers marching and singing the "Battle Cry of Freedom" took him out of his musings.

"The Union forever, hurrah, boys, hurrah!
Down with the traitor and up with the stars!
While we rally round the flag, boys,
Rally once again,
Shouting the Battle Cry of Freedom."

By this point, Will knew the words to both Union and Confederate songs. It was a singing war, and the men seemed to sing all the time. Will wondered if they sang while they fought but figured they would probably be too busy for that.

He reached Winchester undisturbed and wished the trip had taken longer. "How am I going to tell Mrs. Mitchell that I didn't bring Edward home," he wondered. "If I didn't like her so much, I would just keep riding." Again, he thought of Litchfield and, from where he stood right now, Litchfield was looking better and better.

He rode up to the house, gave Peaches some water, and knocked on the door.

"You back," called out a soldier from the porch. "We didn't miss you."

Will ignored him as Jane answered the door. "Will, you're back! Everyone, Will is home!"

Mrs. Mitchell and Benjamin came running. "Will, how are you? Did you find . . ."

Will quickly interrupted her, "Mrs. Mitchell, please." He pointed to the soldier on the porch and put his finger to his lips, shook his head, and whispered, "Let's go where we can talk privately."

Mrs. Mitchell led Will and the children upstairs to her bedroom. "I think they won't hear us here, if we talk quietly. Now, did you find Edward? Where is he? I thought you would be bringing him home. What . . . "

Will interrupted the flow. "Edward is fine, but he cannot come home."

"Cannot come home? Why? What has happened?"

"Edward threw a hornet's nest into the parlor of Willows."

"Good . . . " Benjamin started shouting, and Jane grabbed him and put her hand over his mouth. From behind Jane's hand, Benjamin tried to get out, " . . . for Edward!"

Jane whispered, "Didn't Will just say to talk quietly!"

Will continued talking, "Not so good, actually. The hornets stung everybody, and they caught Edward and locked him up in the smokehouse while they were waiting to take him to Fort McKinley. He was rescued and . . . " here Will was on delicate ground, "he escaped."

"Where is he," asked Mrs. Mitchell immediately.

"From what I heard, he was heading for Lynchburg." Will hated using Big Red's made-up story, but he didn't know what else to do. "Edward is well, I promise you. You see, if he comes home, the Union Army will arrest him again and, this time, they may punish him harder because he escaped once already."

"But he's my son. I must see him. We will all go to Lynchburg. I have a cousin there."

"You can't," Will said, starting to worry that Mrs. Mitchell might do something rash.

"Why not?"

"Because I don't exactly know where he is."

"What do you mean?"

He tried again. "This had to be done in secret because the Union Army sees Edward as an enemy. Many people were involved in his rescue. I trust them because Mrs. Pritchard trusts them, but even she doesn't know where Edward is."

"Lavinia Pritchard? What does she have to do with this?"

"She helped me find the man who helped Edward. I don't know his real name but he told me that once the Army forgets about the hornet's nest, he will see that you and Edward meet."

"I am so confused. When can I see Edward?"

Jane interrupted. "Mamma, if Edward is considered an enemy of the United States, we don't want the Union Army to find him. If you go and visit him, they may follow you. After all," she continued reasonably, "where else would a mother go but to find her son. So, if you really love him, you will leave him alone."

Mrs. Mitchell burst into tears.

"I will find him," said Benjamin, remembering to speak softly now.

"Then the Union Army will find you and put both of you in prison," said Will. "Right now the best thing we can do is nothing. Later, when the war is over, you can see Edward."

Mrs. Mitchell stood and walked over to the window. Her eyes seemed to see beyond the soldiers who were camped on the lawn. "This is such a shock. But after Joseph's death, all I can say is thank God that Edward is alive. I will pray for him and for all the other sons who are in this awful war."

The rest of the evening passed quietly. No one talked about Edward because the children were afraid of upsetting their mother again. Just as Will climbed into bed, he heard the sounds of soldiers singing from somewhere close by. He smiled and turned over and went to sleep.

The next day began just like any other day. Will missed the excitement of the being with Big Red and his men, but admitted to himself that he was more relaxed here. After breakfast, he suddenly remembered that he had never given Mrs. Pritchard's quilt to Mrs. Mitchell. He had rolled it up with the blanket that Mrs. Mitchell gave him when he left to find Edward. Now he retrieved it and took it to Mrs. Mitchell as she sat sewing.

"Mrs. Mitchell."

"Yes, Will?"

"I forgot to give you this quilt that Mrs. Pritchard made. She said to give it to Robs or Tom to keep them warm."

"Why, thank you, Will. It is beautiful. I made a gunboat quilt too, but I sold it to help raise money to buy an ironclad for our Navy."

Will remembered learning about the Merrimac and the Monitor at school.

Mrs. Mitchell sighed. "That did not work out well, and our seaports were captured." She sighed again. "I will write Mrs. Pritchard a letter and thank her. I know that Robs or Tom will appreciate her quilt, especially when the winter comes."

"Maybe the war will be over by then," said Jane as she came into the room.

Mrs. Mitchell just shook her head despondently. "We can only pray."

"She also said that she hid something under those yellow flowers over there," Will pointed to the bouquet sewn on the front.

"This is a beautiful quilt. I hate to rip her stitches, but how else can I see what she hid for me?"

Mrs. Mitchell worked quickly and pulled out something that was tucked in between two layers of fabric. She opened it up and saw a small Confederate flag. Mrs. Mitchell gasped. "Our flag was confiscated by the Yankees when they took over Willows." She examined it carefully and found two tiny letters stitched in the bottom left hand corner. "LP for Lavinia Pritchard. How kind of her to make me a new flag. Will, you must take it."

"Me? No, I can't."

"You must. If they find it here among our possessions, they will be very angry and I fear the consequences. You can hide it in your things and take it with you when it is time for you to go."

He looked at her. "How do you know I will have to go?"

"I never believed that you went away because you wanted to leave us. I know you have a family somewhere but, for some reason, it is difficult for you to stay with them. I do not want to intrude but, as a mother, I must urge you to go back home when you can. I know your mamma is missing you. Only this time, Will, please say goodbye before you go."

Will felt tears in his eyes and furtively brushed them away. "I don't know if I can do that because I'm not sure when I will go."

"So, say goodbye now."

Jane stood up. "I was angry with you when you left, Will. Now I see that you couldn't help yourself. Your family needed you. Your other family."

"You will always be my family, too, my Valley family," Will answered.

Benjamin jumped up and down eagerly. "Can I come with you?"

"They need you here. And I'm not going right now."

"When, then?"

"I don't know, Benjamin. So I will say goodbye to you, too."

Mrs. Mitchell looked at Will very carefully. She rose, kissed him and said, "May God be with you."

That night a new group of Union soldiers camped out in the yard.

"Years ago, my family had a flower garden that was the envy of all our neighbors. Now, we have soldiers camped on our lawn. The flowers are gone and so is everything else."

"Not everything, Mamma. You have Jane and me and Edward, even though he is somewhere miles away. And you have Robs and Tom somewhere else and even Will. You have him too."

"You are right, Benjamin, dear. Thank you for reminding me of all that I have."

"Mamma, the Federals do make good music," Jane said. "I like to hear their songs."

"I'd rather hear 'Dixie,' but I know what you mean," answered her mother.

Just before he fell asleep, Will heard soft singing from somewhere outside.

"There's no place like Home, boys
There's no place like Home.
Be it ever so humble there's no place like
Home!"

Will sat up and thought about home, his real home in the 21st century. "I wonder how Mom and Rebecca are doing? I wonder if they are worried about me. I wonder . . . "

"Home! Home! Sweet, sweet Home
There's no place like . . ."

And Will came home to Connecticut. Just like that. As the notes of the song floated through the window, they took him far away back to his home. With a gentle landing, Will suddenly found himself near a pile of hay that was close to a stable. It was night, but the moon shone light upon the ground.

"Where am I? Wait a minute." He looked around. "This is the stable we pass whenever Mom drives out of town to the farm where we get fresh milk and eggs."

A voice called out to him. "Who is there?"

"I'm Will Bradford. I live on Sedgwick Lane in Litchfield."

A tall woman with long, straight, silver hair came over. "What are you doing here at this hour of the night?"

Will improvised. "I was hiking and I guess I got lost."

"Hiking at night?"

"It was foolish, I know. I just wanted an adventure."

"Well, I guess with school out, you must be a little bored. How old are you anyway?"

"I'm fourteen, ma'am, almost fifteen."

"That's a hard age. Too old to play and too young to find work. Know anything about horses?"

"I ride."

"Ever take care of one?"

"Yes. They're a lot of work, but I like them."

"Well, one of the boys who works for me just quit and I've had a hard time finding someone to replace him. Want a job?"

"Yes. Thank you."

"Of course, we will have to check with your parents. Why don't I give you a ride home and we can talk tomorrow. I'm Mrs. Johnson, by the way."

"Like I said, I'm Will Bradford. Pleased to meet you."

Will got into her station wagon. As they rode through the dark country roads that led to town, Will wondered what his mother would say this time.

"Would you like to meet my mom," he asked Mrs. Johnson, hoping desperately that she would say yes. She might create a good diversion and he learned from the partisans that diversions work. Maybe not with mothers, though.

"It's too late. I will come by in the morning." She drove off.

Will walked across the front lawn and reluctantly climbed the steps to the front door. "Mom, I'm home."

"Will, is that you? Where have you been?"

"I was out walking."

"Walking? All this time? Are you crazy?"

Lighthearted, lighthearted. "Actually, I got a job for the summer."

"A job? What kind of job?"

"Working at the stable we pass when we buy milk and eggs."

"The Johnson stable? Why would they hire you?"

"Thanks, Mom."

"No, I mean you don't ride horses so what would you be doing?"

"Well, I do ride horses, but I think I would be mostly feeding and watering the horses and cleaning up."

Momentarily diverted, his mother thought about the long summer that stretched out ahead of them. "A job would be a good thing."

"Mrs. Johnson will come by tomorrow to talk with you. Where is Rebecca?"

"I was trying to sleep," Rebecca said crankily as she came downstairs. "I heard you talking all the way from my bedroom." She yawned. "Where have you been? Mom's been worried sick. She was afraid it was like the other time when you were hallucinating."

"I wasn't hallucinating. I had been reading and I get very involved when I read."

"Since when?"

"Since . . ."

"Oh, stop it, you two. I am so tired of your squabbling. Will, you have to understand that Rebecca and I were worried about you."

"Sorry," he mumbled.

Rebecca smiled. "How about I make some hot chocolate for all of us?"

"That's an offer I can't turn down," Will answered.

Sitting around the kitchen table, Will felt good. This was his family, not the Mitchells. This was where he really lived, not in the Shenandoah Valley. And definitely not in

1862. "Hey, Rebecca, I got a job for the summer."

"Really? What are you going to do?"

"Work in a stable."

"A stable? You don't ride horses."

"Actually, I do. And I'll be doing more than riding. I'll be grooming them and feeding them and exercising them."

"When did you learn to ride?"

"A while ago."

His mother and Rebecca both stared at him. Rebecca was the first to recover. "When?"

"What I do I like to keep private," he improvised. "Mom was teaching and you were busy cheering or whatever it is you do when you jump around. So I just decided to learn to ride." Then before they could ask any questions, he said, "I'm very tired. Mom, when Mrs. Johnson comes by in the morning to talk with you, I'll try to be up and finished with breakfast. I'm going to bed right now."

His mother looked anxious, and he had the strange impulse to hug her. He couldn't bring himself to actually do that, though, and left the impulse behind him as he went to his room.

Despite his good intentions, Will slept late and came to the kitchen to find Mrs. Johnson having coffee with his mother. "There you are. Good morning," Mom said.

"Good morning. I would like to try coffee this morning since it was so hard to get coffee when there was an embargo."

"An embargo," asked Mrs. Johnson.

"You know, when the Union troops guarded the Southern seaports and didn't let fabric or coffee through."

"They didn't let a lot of other things through as well," Mrs. Johnson said. "Are you interested in the Civil War?"

"Yes, I am."

"I would imagine that living on Sedgwick Lane is very satisfying to you then."

Will was confused. "I don't understand. What does Sedgwick Lane have to do with the Civil War?"

"You don't know? General John Sedgwick was a Union general. Sedgwick Lane was probably named after him."

"Did he actually live here?" Will's voice croaked with excitement.

"That I don't know. You could find out at the Historical Society."

"What Historical Society?"

"You don't know a lot about Litchfield, do you? We have a wonderful Historical Society where you can learn a great deal about Litchfield history. It's right on the Green which, even you must know, is only a short walk from here. And the adjacent museum has a Civil War exhibit going on right now."

His mother gave him coffee and said, "Will is very interested in the Civil War. Here is your coffee, dear. Do you take milk and sugar?" She turned to Mrs. Johnson and said, "Will always surprises me. I never knew that he rode horses or drank coffee."

There was an uncomfortable silence. Will again tried for lighthearted and said, "Actually, I have never had coffee before, but I want to get used to drinking it because so many people seem to like it. I will try it with both milk and sugar."

"That's a lot of sugar," commented his mother as she watched him pour three heaping spoonfuls into his cup.

He began to drink and kind of agreed with her. It wouldn't do to say so, though. "Good coffee."

"How will you get to the stable," Mrs. Johnson asked.

"I can ride my bike."

"Do you want to start tomorrow?"

"Yes, I would. Thank you."

When Mrs. Johnson left, his mother said, "You keep me on my toes, that's for sure."

"Well, since you like to dance, I guess it's all right," Will answered and went back to his room to play a few games. It seemed as if only a few minutes passed when his mother shouted, "Will, come on down for lunch."

"I'm busy."

"You have to be hungry by now! You only had that sugary coffee for breakfast, and it's noon. I'll make you a cheese sandwich."

Will looked at his watch. It was noon all right. Will thought about all the noon dinners he had in the Shenandoah Valley in 1861. There midday meals meant meat and potatoes and cornbread and pie. Of course, a lot of that changed when he went back in '62, but thinking about a cheese sandwich depressed him. Maybe he could go out and buy something to eat. That kind of depressed him, too, since he had no money.

The thought of spending a whole summer with his mother home, not teaching her little first graders, depressed Will even more than no money and a tasteless cheese sandwich. The stable and his new job suddenly looked even more promising.

Rebecca sat down. "Tomorrow I start my job as a counselor at the Rec camp."

"Big whoop."

"Will, that is rude."

"That's who I am, a rude dude." Will thought that was very clever and laughed until he noticed that no one else was laughing. "I start my job tomorrow also."

"I've been thinking more about that job," Rebecca said." Just exactly when did you learn to ride? And where did you get the money for lessons?"

"A nice girl taught me for free."

"Right. And I'm Taylor Swift."

Why is it that when you speak the truth no one believes you? "You win. I didn't have any lessons. I was born with the talent."

"No one is born to ride."

"I was."

Although she tried, that was all the information Rebecca could get out of Will on the subject of his riding. Finally, she gave up.

"So, what time are you leaving in the morning," his mother asked. "I can take you since I'm not teaching this summer."

"No, I'll use my bike. I have to be there at 7 so I thought I'd leave around 6:30. Well, of course if you really want to take me I won't turn down a ride."

"We'll have to put your bike in the van so you can bike home. I'll be busy later because I have to go into Waterbury to see . . . ," she droned on. "and if you need to get back before I do . . . . "

Will thought it was all too complicated and remembered Will's Rule #1: never get adults involved with anything important. Maybe not even anything unimportant. "It's all right. I'd rather bike."

That settled, Will went upstairs again. Before he went to sleep, he set his alarm.

He awoke at 6:15, grabbed three Entenmann's doughnuts and hurried out the door. There was no one around as he rode his bike over the quiet open roads. The air smelled fresher and the land looked cleaner at this hour.

He came to a gate and got off his bike. Before he could figure out what to do, it suddenly opened on its own. "Cool." He biked right over to the barn.

"Hi, Will. Glad you came on time. Put your bike over there," Mrs. Johnson pointed to a bike rack, "and I'll give you the run down." She was leaning on a car, smoking a cigarette. He watched as she finished her cigarette and carefully put it out and into some kind of container. He followed her into the barn.

"Let me first tell you about this place. I'm the owner. We are a 15-horse barn; 12 horses board here and 2 are lesson horses. If you can add, you know that's 14, so if you're wondering about the other horse, I'll tell you. Habit is my own horse and he makes number 15. We have another trainer besides me, a couple of part-time guys, two working students and you're one of them. Cal is the other one. Now, let's get to the money. I don't pay much. Never have; never will. You'll get enough to get by, but that's all. What I do is, instead of a high salary, I offer you lessons and rides in exchange for work. So what do you say?"

Will silently considered, "On the one hand, I would like more money. On the other hand, no one is exactly beating down my door and offering it to me. My choice is being home with Mom all day or being out here with horses."

Will made up his mind, and told Mrs. Johnson, "I'll take it."

"Good. Cal will show you the feed room and explain the routine to you. After they eat, you turn the horses out into the field where they stay for about an hour and a half. While they are in the field, you do all sorts of things, mucking the stalls, replenishing hay, sweeping the aisles of the barn, doing the laundry. There's a lot of laundry."

"What do you wash here?"

Mrs. Johnson chuckled, a hoarse, throaty laugh. "Not ourselves." She laughed again and Will smiled uncertainly. "We wash saddle pads and towels, lots of towels. Believe me; you'll be doing loads and loads of laundry. I run a clean barn."

Will looked around. It was clean, very clean. Actually, it was much cleaner than his room, maybe cleaner than his entire house.

"And the horses . . . when do I ride them?"

"I'm getting to that. You ride them for exercise — theirs, not yours." Again Mrs. Johnson laughed her deep laugh. "You take them out to the trails and ride. You brush them, clean their feet, you know . . . keep them looking and feeling good. Be sure to ask about each horse before you do anything because, like people, they're not all the same. Any more questions?"

Will could think of so many that he said nothing.

"All right, then. Let me show you how we do things we do around here."

Will learned that there was a right way and a wrong way to do almost everything. He let Mrs. Johnson drone on while he thought about the camp and Big Red and the men and their horses. Those horses couldn't care less about right and wrong ways of doing things. They ate and were happy. Suddenly he thought about Peaches and felt sad.

"I assume you know how to do a wash," Mrs. Johnson asked, interrupting his reverie.

Startled, Will immediately answered, "Yeah, I know how to do laundry."

He washed and folded towels until Cal came into the barn. "Great to see someone else doing the wash, for a change. Hi, I'm Cal."

"I'm Will."

"Most of us who work here are horse people. Do you have a horse?"

"I used to, but not any more."

Cal looked uncomfortable. "Sorry."

"It's okay. Peaches was a good horse."

"Peaches?"

Will shrugged. "Hey, what's in a name?"

Cal laughed. "Too much Shakespeare, I think. What do you say we have lunch at one?"

"Sure, except I forgot to bring my lunch."

"We can go to the deli; it's not too far. Joe let me open an account and then, well, he sends my bill to my mother and she pays."

"Good plan, but I don't know that my mother will go for it. Whenever you want to go, it's fine with me."

They worked until Cal said, "Let's go now. I'm hungry." They got on their bikes and rode off. "Are you sure we don't have to tell Mrs. Johnson that we're going?"

"I do this everyday. She's fine with it."

They came to a deli that stood alone on a road with nothing but trees around. Will wondered how anyone could find it but, apparently people did, since there were many cars in the unpaved, dirt parking lot. He followed Cal inside. "Joe, this is my new friend, Will. He's working with me at the barn."

Joe waved and said, "What'll it be, boys? Cal is a turkey, ham or roast beef man. What's your pleasure?"

Will looked at the wall above the counter displaying the sandwich choices. "I'll go for turkey and cheese."

"What kind of cheese?"

First-class deli. Will was pleased. "Munster, thank you, and a coke."

"Polite too, like Cal. Want to open an account?"

"Sure." Without it, I'd starve since I never thought to bring either money or food this morning.

The boys went outside. They sat on a rickety table that looked as if it must have been around since Litchfield men first went south to fight in 1861. "So what do you like to do, besides ride," Cal asked.

"Civil War things."

"Really? Like reenactments?"

"Kind of."

"That's interesting."

The boys went on to talk about other things and when they headed back to the barn, Will realized he was having a good time, maybe the first good time since he moved to Litchfield.

He finished out his shift, said goodbye to Cal and got on his bike to ride home. The ride home was exhausting. Will didn't realize just how tired he was until his feet could barely pedal. It had been a long day. Besides being tired, he was hot, sweaty, and thirsty.

He reached home, put his bike away and looked forward to a shower and collapsing. "Maybe I'll forget the shower and just collapse."

Somehow he had enough energy to get through dinner, but when he got upstairs to his room afterwards, he fell fast asleep. He was so tired when the alarm went off in the morning that he slept right through it until a very angry Rebecca came in the room and screamed, "Shut that loud thing off."

On his second day at work, Cal began to instruct Will on what to do and what not to do. Will yawned. "A horse is a horse."

"Not on this farm. Here we have a responsibility to each horse. Mrs. Johnson is very particular about that because she says that people trust us to take good care of their horses."

Will yawned again. Cal was getting bossy.

"Every horse has his own bucket," Cal went on.

"Why? Afraid they won't share?"

Cal just shook his head. "Some of them get different food."

"How come? Picky eaters?"

"I don't know. I'll take you to the feed room and show you what they eat."

Will was surprised how much could be crammed into a small room. Red and green buckets filled with food were stacked on the floor along with huge bags of Purina feed and containers of all different sizes.

"What happened to good old-fashioned hay?"

"We use hay but we feed them other things as well. You must know we can't only feed them hay. If we did, they'd get 'hay bellies' and become fat."

Will didn't know. At Big Red's the horses were fed whatever was around: hay, wheat, grass or whatever feed they had managed to forage or "appropriate."

"If a horse needs medicine, we crush it up and put it in his feed," continued Cal.

"Why would they need medicine," Will asked.

"Some have stomach problems; some need them for their muscles or joints or stuff like that."

"They sound spoiled."

"They're not. The people around here may be, but not the horses."

"Take them over the people, huh?"

"Any day."

"Know what you mean."

Cal looked serious. "The best advice I can give you is to ask questions when you don't know something. Don't take short-cuts. Not that you would, but don't ever pull a horse out of a stall if you don't know him. Horses can get spooked by all sorts of things. And never lead a horse without a lead rope. That drives Mrs. Johnson crazy."

"Why?"

"We've had horses break away just because some kid was too lazy to put the lead rope on the halter."

"Thanks for the tip."

"So, will you get another horse," Cal asked.

Will could just imagine asking his mother to buy him a horse, then to pay to board and feed it. That sure wasn't going to happen. "I don't know."

"Let's ride together one day."

"Sure."

"When do you do those reenactments? I might go with you one time."

Will just smiled and replied, "They don't do them too often around here. It's not like we live in Virginia."

"Why Virginia?"

"Virginia had a lot of the action. You could almost call Virginia one big battlefield."

"Is that really true?"

"Sort of. Tons of battles were fought there."

"How come you know so much about Virginia?"

"I used to go there. For visits."

Chapter 13

To his amazement, Will was beginning to feel comfortable in Litchfield.

"So, how is your job," asked Rebecca a couple of evenings later when they were having dinner.

"Good. Yours?"

"Well, I like it but I wish there were more cute male counselors. Any cute girls where you work?"

"Several, but they all have four legs, a tail and are way taller than I am."

The early morning bike ride to the barn was getting easier and, as Will became more familiar with the horses, he began to relax.

"Never get too relaxed," cautioned Cal. "Horses can surprise you."

"Not Jim-Jim."

"Well, no, probably not him. He's what we call a 'broke animal,' a lesson horse that is so tame you can ride him blindfolded."

"Been there, done that."

"What?"

"Nothing. I don't think the boarded horses are so hard to handle either."

"Well, listen to you. Four days on the job and you already know all the horses."

"What's to know?"

"I'm telling you, don't get too sure of yourself."

It was a cool morning and Will was restless as he prowled around the barn. He walked over to Habit and began talking to him.

"He likes you," said Mrs. Johnson as she hurried by. "Bring him out and over to the field. He's got a lot of energy this morning and can use an extra run."

"You do like me, don't you," Will murmured to Habit. "Come on, let's go outside. I'm going to take you out just with your halter 'cause I don't think you want to bother with a lead rope. What does Cal know anyway?"

As Will led Habit out of his stall holding on to the side of his halter, Habit suddenly reared up and bolted. With a single fluid motion, Habit pulled himself free and ran right out into the field. Will ran after him but Habit was too fast for him.

"What happened? What did you do," called out Cal as he came running.

"I didn't do anything, Cal. I just took him out the way Mrs. Johnson told me to."

"Not the way I told you to," yelled a very angry Mrs. Johnson. "When I told you to take him out, I naturally assumed you had the sense God gave you and would use the lead rope for more control. I even told you that Habit had a lot of energy this morning. How could you take him just with his halter?"

"I used to do it all the time with my horse."

"Well, you can't do it with mine. You are careless but, right now, all I can think about is Habit. Let's go get him and bring him back to his stall."

They tried to cajole him, to trick him and to outsmart him, but Habit enjoyed his freedom too much to pay any attention. Finally, Mrs. Johnson went to the stable and came back with a red feed bucket filled with pellets of grain. She shook it hard and Habit, always alert to the sound of food rattling in his bucket, came running.

Slipping the lead rope on to his halter, Mrs. Johnson murmured soothing sounds to her horse as she led him back into his stall. Habit paid little attention. It had been a good morning for him with extra food and an extra run.

It was not such a good morning for Will, though. He was sure that he would lose his job.

"Not only were you careless, but you were careless with the boss's horse," Cal said as he threw up his hands. "I warned you but you refused to listen to me. How come?"

"I don't know. I was stupid. Now Mrs. Johnson will probably fire me."

Cal shrugged his shoulders. "You better go and apologize fast."

Will nodded and walked back to the barn. Habit was in his stall munching with enthusiasm and Mrs. Johnson was in her office. He knocked on the door.

"Yes?"

"I uh, I um, I came to apologize."

"Why?"

"What do you mean?"

"What are you sorry about?"

Will thought for a moment. He knew he had to be truthful. He had been used to a more casual way with horses but, if he really remembered, Big Red had his rules too. "I thought I knew more than I did and I figured I handle horses pretty well. I did the wrong thing and Habit could have gotten lost. I'm very sorry. Do you want me to leave now or stay till the end of the day?"

Mrs. Johnson looked carefully at Will. "I am going to give you a second chance."

Looking at Will's surprised face, she went on, "But if you take any shortcuts again, that will be it and you will be fired. Go on now and make yourself useful."

"I don't know what to say. I am so grateful for another chance, I . . . " Will felt like crying.

"Go, I don't have time for this. And, Will, you do handle horses well, so don't ever disappoint me again."

"I'll do my best not to, ma'am."

"Scoot."

"Are you fired," asked Cal, when Will headed over to where Cal was working.

"No, she gave me a second chance. Cal, you were right and I was wrong. I guess I don't know everything about horses."

"Hey, let's get to work. We have to go to the deli for lunch and we're already behind schedule."

* * *

Before long, it was Monday, Will's day off, and he had nothing to do. The prospect of staying home was not appealing, so he decided to check out the small museum on the Green.

"Good morning," said a friendly voice. "Are you here to see the Civil War exhibit?"

"No. Well, maybe. I'll see it for what its worth."

"Some of us think it's worth quite a bit. You're Will Bradford, aren't you?"

Will looked closer. He thought the girl might have been in his Social Studies class.

"I'm Maya Donner. We were in Mrs. Morris' Social Studies class together, the one where you punched Jack."

"Yeah, well, that may not have been my finest moment."

"On the other hand, it may have been. Jack is pretty mean and not just to you."

Will was surprised. He took another look at Maya. "What are you doing here?"

"This is my summer job. I sit at this desk and tell people where to go." She giggled. "I don't mean it like that."

"What do you think of the exhibit?"

"I think it's pretty good. You have to pay to see it, though."

"How much?"

"If you're a student, it's $3.00."

He opened his almost-empty wallet and took out the money. Most of his meager salary was going to Joe's Deli, but he had to admit that the sandwiches there were awfully good.

"That's good for admission to the Historical Society also."

The Historical Society! He forgot about General Sedgwick. "I'm going to go to the Historical Society first."

"Really? What are you researching?"

"My street."

"Remember to turn off your phone while you're here," she said with authority.

Will turned his phone off and hurried away before Maya could ask him any more questions or give him any more instructions.

"May I help you," asked the librarian as he entered the domed building.

"Yes, thank you. I am interested in learning about the street I live on, Sedgwick Lane. I heard it might have been named for the Union general, General John Sedgwick. Do you know anything about that?"

"No, but I can help you find out."

She gestured for him to sit and disappeared behind a door. While Will waited, he looked around. There were several people working at long tables.

Before very long, the librarian came out holding several books, one of them almost larger than she was. "I have deeds and documents and books all pertaining to your street. Let's look together."

There was no mention of General Sedgwick.

"Well, I think we can safely say that Sedgwick Lane was not named for the General. A merchant named Theodore S. Sedgwick seemed to have owned that land in 1874 and his son built a house on it twenty years later. There is no mention of General Sedgwick."

"That's too bad."

The librarian looked at Will's disappointed face. "The Sedgwicks settled this part of Connecticut so even if Sedgwick Lane was not named directly for him, he probably was a distant relative of whomever it was named for." She continued, "Do you think you are a descendant of the Sedgwick family?"

"No. I'm just interested in my street, that's all."

The librarian gave Will an odd look. Will knew that look well. It was time to say something stupid — for some reason, stupidity always seems to reassure adults. "I just thought I might find something that belonged to the General on Sedgwick Lane."

The librarian smiled that smile adults give you when they think you are too young to know anything. "Young man, anything of value would be long gone by now."

"Why am I wasting my time in an historical society anyway," thought Will as he walked out. He turned his phone back on and did a search. Within seconds, he discovered that General Sedgwick led an historic 34-mile march to Gettysburg. "I can find out almost anything I want online, anyway. Except about my street."

* * *

"Find what you wanted," asked Maya when he came back to the museum.

"Not really. I'll just look around here for a while."

He learned that the town of Litchfield gave extra money, called a bounty, to men who volunteered for the Union Army, but gave no money to men who were drafted. He also learned that volunteers could choose their own officers but men who were drafted could not. Since they all would probably end up in the Union Army anyway, volunteering seemed like the way to go.

"What was life like for these Union soldiers who were so far away from home," wondered Will. He walked into the next room and found some answers right in front of him. Huge posters of letters from Union soldiers to their wives, mothers, sisters, brothers and children covered a large wall.

Fort Henry, Tn.
February 6/62

My Darling wife,

I have not heard from you for two weeks and I am concerned. I hope you are well and your silence is only because of our irregular mail. How I long for the day when this War will be over but I take comfort in knowing that I am doing my part to save our country.

I miss you and little Tommy and Lizzie. Today is Lizzie's birthday and she is with me in my heart. Tell her I did not forget and ask her to save a kiss for me.

Thank you for sending the dried apples. George and I paid someone to make them into pies and we ate and enjoyed them.

We hear that there will be a big battle here in Tennessee. I trust that God will answer our prayers and grant us victory and end this cruel war.

Your loving husband,
Caleb

Port Republic, Virginia
June 7/62

My dear mother,

I am not well and wish I were at home where you would take good care of me. Since that cannot be, perhaps you can send me some butter in a tin with preserves and, also, a little sugar. I would also like another towel as well.

Virginia is not like Connecticut. It is terribly hot and steamy and Virginia ladies treat us as if we were criminals. They turn their faces away from us and will not answer if we speak to them. I hear in New Orleans some ladies spat at our soldiers and others threw the contents of their chamber pots out their windows and aimed for our men.

I guess I should be grateful that I am in Virginia and not in New Orleans, but I would rather be home.

May God grant us the victory we deserve.

Your affectionate son,
Robert

Fredericksburg, Va
December/1862

My Darling Wife,

How can I describe the events of last evening? It was as if God Himself sent an angel down to us suffering soldiers just to give us all one moment of peace.

It was after the Battle of Fredericksburg. We lost many good men in that Battle and our hearts were weary and hurting. We were camped on our side of the Rappahannock River and it was twilight, that time when day ends and night begins. It is a hard time for us men because it is quiet and in the quiet we are missing home. Maybe that's the reason the regimental bands try to play at this hour, to ease our lonely hearts.

Anyway, the Confederates were on the opposite side of the Rappahannock. Their bands were also playing and soon a contest developed between their bands and our bands. We played our songs and cheered and they played their songs and cheered.

As it got dark, suddenly, very suddenly, both bands began to play "Home, Sweet Home."

My dearest, it was as if the world stood still. We were all quiet until the tune ended. Then everyone cheered, but cheered as they had never cheered before. We Federals and those Rebels, all together we cheered and yelled and cried as one man, not as enemies separated by a river.

Maybe we could have shaken hands then and ended this war forever, but we didn't, and today we went back to killing each other.

Your loving husband,
Tom

310

Will left the museum and walked home slowly. Just as he came to his house, he saw an unfamiliar car in the driveway. He opened the front door and there was his father with a woman. "Hi, Will. I've brought you the letters."

Shoot, he had forgotten all about those letters. Why today? He wasn't in the mood for his father and that person with him.

"This is my wife, Catherine. Catherine, this is my son Will."

"Hello."

Catherine smiled a phony smile. "Aren't you the handsome one? You take after your father, don't you? I heard you have a new job in a stable. Do you ride horses?"

He thought, "No, I ice skate with them." Since he couldn't say that, he settled for, "Yes."

"Isn't that wonderful?"

His father beamed while Will wondered how long that woman's phony smile would stay in place. He guessed until she left.

"We are going to spend a weekend in the City and your father wanted to drop these letters off," she said as his father handed Will the letters.

That's another thing I hate besides a phony smile, people who call New York City, THE CITY, like it's all in caps.

"Oh, which city is that," Will asked.

Now that smile looked a bit strained.

"New York City, of course," answered his father testily. "Where else?"

"Milwaukee?"

She positively tinkled, "Oh, dear, your son is so cute. Milwaukee!"

Cute, my ass. Will smiled back, showing his teeth. "Well, thank you. I better go and shower."

"Will," his father called him back, "When does Rebecca get home? I want Catherine to meet both my children."

Isn't that nice? "I don't know. She works at the Rec camp. In this family everyone works," he added, pointedly looking at Catherine.

"Well, I work," she said, that smile definitely fading.

"Good for you." Will started for his room and heard the key in the door. Rebecca was home. Great. Now she'll gush or something. He left them alone and went to take a shower. But first he took the carefully-folded letters and put them on his desk for later. He might have wanted to talk with his father about them, but with that Catherine around, there wasn't going to be much to say anyway.

He decided to play computer games until his father left.

"Will, dinner," shouted Rebecca after their father and Catherine had left and his mother had come home.

"How was your day off," his mother asked energetically.

"What did you think of Catherine," asked his sister immediately.

Both of them waited for his answer. "Okay, I guess," he said.

They continued to badger him, but he had nothing else to say. All he wanted to do was finish dinner. Then perhaps there would be peace and quiet and he could read the letters.

He escaped just as soon as he could, and took the letters, unfolded them, and held them to the light. Reading them was not going to be easy. First of all, the words that had been written on the folded part of the letter were faded. Also, William Bradford must have been short of paper because after he wrote on the front and back of his letter, he then wrote on the top, the bottom and the sides of the paper. And then to make things even worse, his handwriting was poor. "Kind of reminds me of my own writing," Will thought. "Maybe I better work on my penmanship just in case we have a war. On the other hand, I can always text from the front. I guess that would depend on what front. If I'm sent back to Virginia . . . ," his thoughts trailed off and he began to read.

Kernstown, Virginia
March 22/1862

My Dear Laura,

I got my ambrotype taken a few weeks ago and I will send it to you as soon as I can. It is a good likeness. Please show it to Mamma and tell her that I am thinking of her but I cannot afford another three dollars for a second ambrotype so she will have to share yours.

It is cold here. It snowed a few days ago but now there is sunshine. They say tomorrow will be another great Battle. May God grant me life so that I can fight even harder for our just Cause. Our dear friend, George, was killed and it grieves me deeply. He fought bravely until a ball hit him. I am grateful that our son, Will, is a cadet at the Virginia Military Institute. We need well-trained officers and as much as I hope this War ends soon, if it doesn't, the Confederacy will need him.

Don't count on my returning home anytime soon.

Please send my love to Mamma and Sister Sallie.

Your husband,
William

"He called his son Will, just like me." Will was so excited he could hardly breathe. Will looked up the word ambrotype and discovered it was some kind of photograph. Maybe someone in his family still had it and he could actually see what this William Bradford looked like. He rushed to call his father but then remembered that he was in THE CITY with that Catherine person. It would have to wait.

Meanwhile he opened the next letter.

Frayser's Farm
June/1862

My Dear Wife,

I barely hear the cannonading anymore since there is so much of it. We marched eighteen miles yesterday and most of it was through mud and water.

Thinking of you and Will sustained me through that long march.

There is a lot of camp talk about the Yankees giving up and going home. Personally, I doubt it. From what I see, I think this will be a very long war.

Your loving husband,
William

"William Bradford was smart," Will mused. "Look how he predicted how long the war would last. I think I am like him."

Will opened the last letter slowly.

Fredericksburg, Virginia
December, 1862

My Dearest Wife,

We have been engaged in a battle in Fredericksburg.

Our brigade fought much of the night and into the following day when we were able to drive Hooker back across the Rappahannock River. Our losses were heavy but their losses were much heavier. It was a great victory.

I shall share a true story. The Yankees camped on their side of the

River and we camped on ours. No one was fighting anymore. As the day began to sink into night, the Yankee band came down to the River to play. Our band did the same.

There we were, on opposite sides of the River, both bands playing their hearts out with their men cheering them on. And then the Yankees played "Yankee Doodle." After they finished, we played "Dixie" and then, suddenly, together, both bands began to play "Home, Sweet Home." Men from both sides of the River grew silent, stood erect and smiled, laughed or cried. Then, when the song ended, everyone cheered.

Dear Laura, after that song, if the Rappahannock River had not separated us, we men could have ended the war right then and there. But it was not to be.

Your loving husband,
William

Will held the letter and stared at it. "It's the same letter." He repeated this to himself as if in a daze. "This letter is the same as the letter written by that Union soldier. It must have really happened. When both bands played 'Home, Sweet Home,' the soldiers, Union and Confederate, all wanted to shake hands across the Rappahannock River and just go home. But they didn't, and the War kept on going. And all the other letters were kind of the same as well. They all wrote about missing their home and families and how right their cause was. Why am I so surprised? Once, all these men were part of the same country. They couldn't find a way to work things out so they split up. I wonder if they can ever get back together again?"

He shook his head the way a wet dog does. "What am I talking about? Of course they got back together. The North won the war and the South became part of the United States again." He shook his head again, marveling at his own stupidity. "How could I have forgotten that, even for a second?" Then he thought, "But how were all of them able to forgive each other? And what about the slaves? Could they ever forgive?"

As he tried to remember the little he knew about what happened after the war, he fell asleep and dreamed about men swimming across the Rappahannock River to shake hands.

When the alarm clock rang, he was groggy and took four Entenmann's donuts instead of his usual three. "I need something strong to wake me up this morning and there's no time to make coffee. Besides, I don't know how."

*　*　*

Will got used to the routine of his job and the days went by quickly. He loved exercising the horses. That and lunch were the best part of his day, although nothing really annoyed him now the way so many things did at school.

"I think I would have joined the cavalry," Will announced Sunday night at dinner.

His mother looked at him. "What cavalry?"

"The cavalry in the Civil War. The Confederacy had the better cavalry at first but the Union Army caught up with them later in the war."

Rebecca hooted. "So, which one are you going to join?"

"Rebecca, don't encourage him," said her mother firmly, remembering what she called Will's flights of fancy regarding the Civil War. Those moments were never very far from her mind whenever Will brought up the Civil War.

Rebecca nodded her head. "Will, you're not in the Civil War and you never were. Besides, you would never have been accepted in the cavalry."

"Why not?"

"You're too young. You're only a kid."

By the time the next Monday morning came, Will was ready for his day off. He was walking toward the War Monuments that stood on the Green when he heard someone calling his name. He stopped and turned around.

"I thought I'd never catch up with you," panted Maya. "Where are you going?"

"I'm going to look at the Monuments."

"Didn't you ever see them before? I thought you were so interested in war."

Will found her very irritating. "I am not interested in all war, just the Civil War."

"So? There's a monument to that War here, too. How come you never saw it before?"

She was even more irritating today than she had been last week. With as much dignity as he could muster, Will said, "If you must know, I don't like Litchfield so I didn't pay attention to things here."

"Well, it may be where I live, but I'm not in love with it either."

Unwilling to share anything else, Will just said, "I am going over there now."

"Good. I'll go too."

"Don't you have to be at work?"

"Not yet. I have time to go with you to the Monuments."

"All right," Will answered grudgingly.

"Well, don't act so excited."

"I . . . uh . . ."

Maya just laughed.

Will walked to the Green and went straight over to the big cannon. He touched it, then looked around and saw the monuments.

"See this big one?" Maya pointed. "It says, 'In honor of the men of Litchfield who rendered service in the World War, 1917-19.' Notice it said 'The World War.' They didn't know there was going to be another one."

"Maybe there's always another one. Here's the World War II monument," answered Will, interested in spite of himself. "And Korea and Vietnam."

And suddenly there it was, right in front of them, a tall Civil War monument. The words "PRO PATRIA" were carved into the stone and four American flags stood around the bottom of the monument. "At the very least, they could have put one Confederate flag there also. I mean there were a lot of men who died for that flag as well."

"This monument is for Litchfield men only. Besides, those men who fought against the Union are considered traitors here," Maya said somberly.

"Traitors? Why?"

"They rebelled against the government."

"Yeah, like George Washington."

"No, not like George Washington," Maya said angrily. "Look, I know you have some sort of loyalty to the South, but you live here now."

"Maybe that's my problem."

"Maybe it is."

They glared at each other.

"What does 'Pro Patria' mean anyway," asked Will. "I never took Latin."

"Can't say my Latin's very good, but I think that means 'For the Fatherland.' "

"Question is which Fatherland," mused Will. "The South felt the United States had changed so much it was now a different country."

"That's ridiculous."

"Well, that's how they felt in Virginia in 1861."

"Just how do you know that?"

"I met . . . I mean I read things they wrote."

"Come on," Maya said, "Let's look at the rest of the monument."

On each of the four sides of the monument, the words "Roll of Honor" were carved above a list of the Litchfield residents who were killed in action during the Civil War.

"See that church over there," Maya said, pointing to a large, majestic white church across the Green. "The Litchfield families who were lucky enough to get the bodies of their sons returned had their funerals there."

"Doesn't seem so lucky to me."

"Luckier than not knowing."

Will thought about Mrs. Mitchell. She took comfort in knowing that Robs brought Joseph's body home. How awful to die on a strange field and lay there all alone, left to rot. No one should die like that. "I guess you're right. So why do you think these men fought anyway? Not the ones who were drafted later in the war, but the ones who volunteered in the beginning."

"Their friends volunteered."

"That's true. Joseph and his friends all volunteered together."

"Joseph. Who's Joseph?"

"Just someone I once knew."

"And the North wanted to keep the Union together," Maya added. "The soldiers fought for the Union."

"True." He began singing, "The Union forever, hurrah, boys hurrah. Down with the traitor and up with the stars. While we rally round the flag, boys, rally once again, shouting the battle cry of freedom."

"What song is that?"

"That's 'The Battle Cry of Freedom.' Obviously a Union song. I know most of the Civil War songs. They're kind of catchy."

Maya looked curiously at Will. "You know, some of the soldiers fought against slavery, especially after Lincoln signed the Emancipation Proclamation."

"That was in January of 1863; I'm not there yet."

"What do you mean?"

"I mean I'm studying and not yet reading about 1863," Will improvised.

"You're a little strange, but I kind of like you."

Will was mortified. He didn't know which was worse, to be called strange or to be liked by Maya. "Well, I'll see you."

"Where are you going?"

"Home."

"Sedgwick Lane?"

"Probably, but you never know. Maybe Virginia."

Chapter 14

Will wondered why he told Maya that he might be going back to Virginia. "Must have been seeing that Monument," he thought. "Kind of made me think about the Mitchells."

He was quiet at dinner, so quiet that even Rebecca noticed. "What's wrong with you? Daydreaming about the cavalry?"

Will didn't bother to answer.

"I'm going out to dinner with Dad tomorrow," she continued. "Are you coming with us?"

He had forgotten about the dinner. "Maybe. Is that Catherine woman coming too?"

"I don't know. She's not so bad," Rebecca said, then remembered her mother. "Well, Mom, I'm not saying that I like her. I just . . ."

"Rebecca, and you, too, Will, please don't feel that you have to dislike Catherine because of me. She didn't do anything to me. Dad didn't even know her when we separated."

"So, why did you and Dad split up? You never told us," Will asked suddenly as the words just kind of spilled out of his mouth. He stared at his plate while he waited to see if she would reply.

His mother was silent, then she spoke very quickly. "I guess I should have discussed it with both of you, but it was too hard to talk about. When you were little, things were fine, But as the years went on your father and I started arguing. It seemed as if all the good things we had, except for you two, were disappearing and all we had left were our disagreements that just kept on growing. Finally, it split us apart."

Will looked up. His mother had never talked about the divorce before at all, at least not when he was around. "So what happened? I mean why did you have to split up? Whose fault was it?"

"Oh, Will, not everything can be explained as one person's fault. It took me a while to realize that."

"I don't understand."

"Sometimes there isn't a clear right and a clear wrong. Sometimes you can't blame one person and make him the bad guy. Sometimes, things just happen."

"I don't understand," Will repeated.

"Look, when we got married, your father and I were very much in love. That's usually why people marry. But we had our differences even then. I liked to go to bed early and your father liked to stay out late."

"You got divorced because you couldn't agree on a bedtime?"

"Will, dear, it isn't that simple. I'm just trying to explain that there were disagreements. I liked to go to church; your father always said that his church was the land and the sky and that he felt God's presence stronger in the outdoors than he did in a closed building. These are just a couple of examples. Basically, we never settled our differences and they finally got so big, we had nowhere to go but to separate and create our own lives apart from each other."

Will got excited. "Like the Civil War," he exclaimed. "The North got industrialized and the South wanted to stay as they were. They grew further and further apart until they finally split!"

"Well, I don't know if it's the same. Your father and I never went to war."

Rebecca and Will looked at each other. "Yes, you did," Rebecca said quietly. "You used to fight all the time. I remember."

"You're right; we did fight a lot. Things just kept getting bigger and bigger and we couldn't compromise anymore. But at that point, we were barely talking to each other, so how could we compromise?"

"But there are some things that you can't compromise, right," asked Rebecca. "You always tell us to stand up for our ideals."

"I know. But everything we care about is not an ideal. Some things are simply habits and we have to figure out what we can compromise and what we can't. Your father and I never did that, and every single thing we argued about became more important than learning how to live together."

"Like the North and the South."

"I don't know, Will. Not everything relates to the Civil War."

"But this does."

"Whatever. Now, let's talk about pleasant things. Rebecca, tell me something good that happened today."

As Rebecca complied and talked about her day, Will began to think furiously.

"Will, Will, earth to Will," called out Rebecca.

"What?" Will snapped back to reality.

"Mom wants to know about your day."

"I went to see the Monuments, and saw one of the girls from my school. She volunteers at the historical society." Will explained.

Rebecca and his mother looked surprised. Rebecca asked, "What is her name? Are you going to see each other again?"

Will clammed up, "I have other things to do now."

His mother replied, "Please help with the dinner clean-up first."

"Stay away from the Civil War," cautioned Rebecca as Will started to help her clear the table.

"Why?"

"It means trouble."

"You're right about that. The War means trouble for a whole lot of people. You know, I think I'm going to take a walk right now."

"A walk," his mother exclaimed. "At this hour? Why?"

"Because it's the middle of the summer and I have nothing to do and I want to go out and get some fresh air. Sometimes there is no pleasing you, Mom. You tell me to go outside when I'm on the computer and now when I want to go outside, you don't want me to go. I'm old enough to know what I want to do. You have to learn to accept that."

"I have too much to do to bother with this nonsense. Go on and take a walk but remember you have to get up early so don't stay out late."

"Yeah, yeah."

Will put his dishes in the sink and immediately headed out the door. He walked down the driveway and turned to look back at the house, the new house as he usually called it. It was a simple two-story brick house with a breezeway between the house and the garage. He could see his mother loading the dishwasher under the window as Rebecca washed the table behind her. It was a peaceful scene, one that Will needed to escape from right away before he got too comfortable. He never wanted to forget all that he had seen in Virginia.

Walking down Sedgwick Lane toward the Green, Will looked at the carefully-tended gardens. Summer vegetables were growing and flowers were in full bloom. "These people are so lucky and they don't even know it. They don't know anything about watching soldiers battle it out on their own lawns and gardens. Bet those vegetables wouldn't have lasted long in Winchester. The Confederate soldiers would have eaten them or the Union soldiers would have destroyed them."

He headed straight for the Monuments. There was no one around as Will stepped in front of the Civil War Monument. He read the names of the battles: Fisher's Hill, Cold Harbor .... Will suddenly thought about General Sedgwick and his epic 34-mile march to Gettysburg. He wondered what it would have been like to be on that march. Suddenly he began to feel dizzy, the ground started to shake and Will felt himself move faster and faster.

When his mind was functioning once again, he had no idea where he was and his tongue hurt. He touched it and his finger came away with blood on it. "I must have bitten my tongue on the ride to wherever I am." He looked around. He was on the ground, off to the side of some road where men were camped. Actually a lot of men. There were men crowding the camp as far as the eye could see. He stood up and began to walk around.

"No mail. No newspapers," complained a young soldier. "Well, at least we're in Maryland now where the ladies are a whole lot better to us than the ladies were in Virginia. Hey . . . what are you doing here?"

Will thought quickly. "I'm relaxing."

The soldier lost interest and moved away.

"After our long march from Virginia, I can't think of a nicer place than 'Maryland, Our Maryland,' " another soldier said with a laugh.

"Isn't that a song," asked Will.

"I am making a joke. The song is 'Maryland, My Maryland' and I said 'Our' because we left Virginia and we are finally on Union soil. Oh, forget it. No good if you have to explain a joke."

He, too, wandered off.

"What are you doing here, boy," called out a soldier as he lifted Will by the scruff of his neck, the way a mother cat grabs her kitten.

"Just chilling."

"If you are chilly here, you are very, very sick. It's got to be one of the hottest days of the year."

"And what year is that?"

"1863. It's July 1ˢᵗ if you must know."

"And," Will asked hesitantly, "exactly where am I?"

The soldier looked at Will with a mixture of fear and concern. "What do you mean where are you? You're near Manchester, Maryland, camped out with the Sixth Corp."

"Why am I here?"

"How should I know why you are here? I barely know why I am here. I think you better come with me. Are you ill? Do you have a fever?"

"I don't think so. Why?"

"Because there is something very strange about you."

"So, tell me," Will asked brightly, "Why are all these soldiers here in Maryland?"

"Just why are you asking all these questions?" The soldier cocked his head and suddenly said, "You could be a spy."

"Not again!" Will laughed. "Been there, done that."

"What do you mean by that? There is nothing funny about spies. You sound mighty suspicious to me."

"I am not a spy. I'm from Connecticut."

"I don't care if you're from the moon; I'm taking you to see Uncle John."

The sun was setting and here and there Will saw the glow of light from whatever it was the men were smoking. "In these times they didn't know how unhealthy smoking was," he thought, and then remembered that war wasn't any healthier. He stumbled.

"Move."

"I didn't do anything," he whined, then remembered that soldiers don't whine. Will held his head up high.

"You," the soldier said to someone else in blue, "Watch him."

Being in front of a man holding a rifle pointed toward him is not particularly conducive to conversation, but Will tried anyway. "So, where are you from?"

There was no answer.

"I'm from Connecticut," Will continued. "I used to live in New York but now . . . ."

"No one cares where you live, so be quiet."

"You are rude."

"And you are nothing but a child. At least our drummer boys know how to keep quiet."

That hurt. But before he could think of a witty reply, the first soldier returned and unceremoniously ushered Will into a tent where a muscular man was playing solitaire.

"This is the boy."

"Hmmm. Just sit him over there." Uncle John pointed to a stool. "You can leave," he told the soldier and then he went on with his game. "I don't like to lose my concentration."

Will was quiet. He didn't want to be responsible for breaking the man's train of thought. Uncle John looked pretty old to Will since there was some gray in his beard. He also looked pretty strong and tough. His eyes were focused on his cards. Finally he called out, "That's it. I win."

He turned and looked closely at Will. Those dark eyes of his seemed to penetrate right into Will's head. "So, son, what is your name?"

"William Bradford, sir, but everyone calls me Will."

"Well, Will, what can I do for you?"

"I don't know, sir. I'm not even sure why I'm here. That soldier called me a spy but

I'm not. Really and truly. I'm from Connecticut."

"Connecticut! That's my home state. I'm from Cornwall-Hollow and there's no where else I've seen that can match its beauty. When I think about Cornwall, I am proud to be serving her people. Where are you from?"

"I live in Litchfield."

"Litchfield! Why, we are practically neighbors."

"I didn't always live in Litchfield, sir. I used to live in New York."

"Well, New York is a fine place, I'm sure. It is not Connecticut but it must have its merits."

"I didn't want to leave New York. My father left us and my mother got a job as a teacher in Litchfield, so my sister and I had to move to Litchfield with her."

"Hmm. That is difficult. You know, son, you are a long way from Litchfield. What are you doing here?"

"That's just it, sir. I don't know."

Will found himself looking into Uncle John's kind eyes and suddenly he began to talk. "I was restless and needed to get away, even though my mother tried to keep me home."

"Mothers, even my own mother, have been known to do that."

Will looked up in surprise. He couldn't imagine this old man with a mother. "Do you have children too?"

"These men you see are my children. They are all the sons I ever wanted."

Will nodded and went on with his story. "I walked over to the Litchfield Green. I don't know what happened, but the next thing I knew I was here." That is really the truth, except for the time travel, but he doubted anyone, even this nice Uncle John, would ever believe what really happened.

Uncle John sighed. "That is a rather strange story. My best guess is you hitched a ride in someone's wagon, got hurt somehow and fainted. Men can lose their memory when they hit their head. Usually the memory returns."

"It doesn't seem dark yet," said Will, trying to change the subject. "Why are the men sleeping?"

"They are sleeping because they are tired. And you are right; it isn't night yet. July days take their time going into night. It's almost like the Bible says, the sun stands still."

He was quiet for a moment and Will decided to wait patiently.

Uncle John continued, "General Hooker sent us to Maryland in case the Rebels were planning to attack Washington. Our Sixth Corps is the biggest Corps in the Union and we were ready for battle. Then, suddenly, General Hooker was replaced by General Meade. General Meade is now the Commander of our Army of the Potomac."

"Why was General Hooker replaced? Did he make too many mistakes?"

"You'll have to ask President Lincoln that. His decision, not mine."

There was a commotion outside and two men entered the tent. One of them looked pointedly at Will. Uncle John nodded. "I have to meet with some of my men. There seems to have been a new communication from General Meade. Please excuse me. Just make yourself comfortable."

Will said, "Thank you," as Uncle John left the tent. He felt very tired himself and lay down on the floor and fell fast asleep. He woke up when Uncle John and another man came rushing in, but he didn't think that he had been asleep very long.

"Wake up, Will," Uncle John called out. "We just got word that Lee is not going to attack Washington. We are going to head to Pennsylvania, where reports say Lee is now."

"How do you know that's where he is?"

"We have fine intelligence. Although we are too far away to hear the sounds, apparently a battle has already begun in a small town called Gettysburg."

337

"Gettysburg. Oh, no, that's awful," said Will.

"Awful? Why? Have you heard of Gettysburg?"

Will didn't know what to say. Everyone all over the world had heard of Gettysburg where so many men died. Will once read that over 51,000 men were killed, wounded or missing. He mumbled, "I just heard the name."

"Don't look so downcast, son. We will get there as soon as we can to help the Union win. Lord knows, we could use a victory right about now."

"You aren't leaving tonight, are you, sir?"

"We certainly are. It is our duty to go wherever we are needed."

"But, sir, it's almost dusk! I thought no one marched at night during wartime."

"Not usually, that's true. But this is an emergency. We will move out right away."

"How far is it to Gettysburg?"

"About 34 miles, so we better get started."

"Are you afraid," Will asked.

Uncle John smiled. "No, son, are you?"

"Me," asked Will. "Why should I be afraid?"

"Some boys would be afraid if they found themselves all alone in the middle of a war. But you are not afraid. Now, why is that?"

"I don't know. I am afraid some of the time, but I am not afraid now."

"If a man had no fear, he would have no courage. Courage is not the absence of fear but the strength to carry on in spite of fear. And do you know why we carry on?"

"No. Why?"

"Because it is our duty. A man must do his duty to his God, to his country, to his family and to himself."

"But what is my duty? You are a soldier and you must lead your men to war. What am I supposed to do?"

"Well, son, you are asking a good question, one that only you can answer. I suspect when you think about it, you might see that it is your duty to go home."

"I don't know how to go home."

"You will find a way. Now, we must go. I suggest you come with us to Gettysburg and once there, take shelter in a church or school . . . . "

"Or wherever the children are," Will said bitterly, remembering the guard's comment.

"As you like. Remember, son, you must do what causes the least trouble for our army. You wouldn't want us to have to feel responsible for you on the battlefield, would you? That might distract us from the Rebels. No, son, you can go with us if you promise to stay off the battlefield."

Will didn't think that was much of a choice, but he liked the old man so he answered honestly, "I'll try my best."

"I can't ask for anything more," Uncle John answered with a smile.

As he stood up, a soldier entered and saluted. "General Sedgwick, sir, I fed Cornwall and he is ready."

"Probably readier than I am. This is Will. He is coming with us to Gettysburg and then you will find shelter for him."

"Sir?"

"Yes, Will?"

"Are you a General?"

"I am indeed. I am General John Sedgwick, Commander of the Sixth Corp."

Will's mouth almost fell open. "General John Sedgwick! Why you are famous."

"I wouldn't say that."

"Yes, you are. I am so happy to meet you, sir."

"Pleased to meet you too, Will."

"The other soldier called you Uncle John so I assumed you were his uncle," Will went on, gushing like he had just met a celebrity.

"The men all call General Sedgwick, Uncle John," answered the Adjutant. "That's because he cares for all of us the way a good uncle cares for his nephews."

"Thank you," the General said with a smile. "Now in case your next question is

340

about Cornwall, I will tell you he is my horse and a better one cannot be found anywhere. All right, men, enough. Let's move out. Find Will a wagon and put him in it."

"A wagon? I can walk."

"No, you cannot," said the General. "You haven't drilled like a real soldier and Gettysburg is much too far. But you can do something a lot more important than walk. Can you write?"

"Yes, of course."

"I thought so. You can be our witness. Write it all down, everything you see and everything you hear. One day people will see this march as part of our heroic struggle to save the Union and I want it all written down."

"It was; it was," Will wanted to cry out. "There is even a monument to you and the men of the Sixth Corps who marched to Gettysburg." But, of course, Will knew he could say none of this. So he said, instead, "Yes, sir."

And the march began.

Chapter 15

Will was furnished with paper and a pencil. "Both are getting mighty scarce these days so mind that you are careful not to waste or lose 'em," warned the soldier. He still seemed to believe that Will might be a spy.

Will wasn't alone in the supply wagon; two men were with him. They were too ill to march and too well to go in the ambulance wagon, so they were taking a breather, as one of them said. Will would have called it a break.

"What are you, some sort of writer," asked the older man, who said he was from Massachusetts.

"You can say that," acknowledged Will.

"So, what are you gonna write?"

"I don't know," Will answered. "I'm going see what there is to see."

"Won't be much," said the second man. "It's going to be dark soon. How are you going to write in the dark?"

"If the Sixth Corps can march in the dark, I can write in the dark."

"Heard there was fighting at Gettysburg today and General Reynolds was killed. Guess those Rebels are winning again," the older man complained.

"It's only the first day. Don't count the Union out just yet," cautioned Will. It sure was strange. Here he was heading to the most famous battle of the War, and he already knew the outcome.

General Sedgwick had been ordered to reach Gettysburg by four o'clock on July 2nd, so he had no choice but to keep the men moving on the Baltimore Pike. There was no moon that night, Will observed, only a few barely visible stars in the sky. Between the joggling of the wagon and the lack of light, he wondered if he would be able to write legibly.

"They can't stop, can they," asked Will.

"What do you mean?"

"If they stop to rest, the men will fall asleep. If they keep going, they will move as if they are in a trance. One foot goes in front of the other, but the body is half asleep."

"Why don't you go into a trance and fall asleep yourself," growled the older man. "I'm resting now before they make me walk again."

"How can I sleep? I am a witness. If they can march half asleep, I can at least write half asleep."

"I don't care what you do, as long as you do it quietly."

Quiet was something Will couldn't imagine in an army. What with artillery rumbling along and wagons rolling and men marching, how could this man complain that Will was noisy?

The night was warm. The men were tired and complained their bones ached. The more they traveled the less they talked, so Will assumed they were too exhausted to speak. He heard singing, though, and sang along with them. It was eerie to hear the words of "John Brown's Body" juxtaposed against the harsh sound of feet hitting the road.

Will jumped out of the wagon to march with the men for a little while. He felt their urgency and heard their whispers: "We cannot let the Union down."

Finally, in the early morning, they took a break. It was a short break. There was barely time to boil coffee before the bugler called for the men to continue their march. Will resumed marching with them.

"Had to drink my coffee too fast, but I ain't marchin' without coffee."

"Whoever heard of marching at night?"

"We have no choice. Those Rebels are on our land now. If we don't whip them here, they'll be in New York City soon."

"So what? Who cares about New York City?"

"Your town and my town could be next."

The day grew even hotter. Suddenly he heard the sounds of cannonading in the distance. That must be from Gettysburg, he thought.

The men of the Sixth Corps pushed on. Will could see their faces tired and sweaty, their eyes half closed, their bodies dripping with sweat and their feet limping, painfully crippled with blisters. The day grew even hotter. The thick dust from the turnpike, combined with the fierce heat, made Will choke. He climbed back into the wagon, but it wasn't any better there. Could be it was even worse.

When they reached the border between Maryland and Pennsylvania, the men from Pennsylvania cheered and sang loudly along with the bands. They were here to defend their state, their homes and their families.

The Sixth Corps approached the town of Littlestown and saw flags waving in the distance. They were given a hero's welcome with women running out of their homes, bringing food and buckets of water to the exhausted men. Will declined to eat, but drank thirstily.

How could they fight, after a march like this? Will thought about this for a while until he realized that he didn't have to worry. Uncle John would take care of his men.

"We're resting; we're resting," cried the exhausted men when the General gave them another break. "That's Uncle John. He never lets his men down." But, again, it was only a brief rest.

As they approached Gettysburg, Will looked around from his perch in the wagon and saw a fearsome sight. Bodies were strewn all over fields everywhere. Dead and dying men lay together with dead and dying horses. Their combined groans reminded Will of his 4th grade Sunday School teacher's pictures of hell. Will had nightmares about that for years and here was the picture, real and right in front of him. And the smells . . . they were so awful that Will tried to breathe only through his mouth. It was even worse than when he was on the Valley Pike and found Charles, the wounded soldier. Will started to write down descriptions of all he was seeing and smelling.

"And how are you faring, Will?"

Will looked up from his scribbling and saw General Sedgwick riding his horse alongside the wagon.

"I am fine, sir. How are you?"

"Fine. Been cleaner and better rested, but never more ready for battle."

"Are the men ready," Will ventured.

"They will be after they rest a bit. They know that we are saving the Union here at Gettysburg. I will see you later, Will. Right now I am going to be with my men."

Will watched as the General, wearing a funny round hat, rode up and down the lines. On anyone else, that hat would look silly, Will thought. On Uncle John it just looks like . . . Uncle John.

Uncle John met the deadline and arrived at General Meade's headquarters by four o'clock as he had been commanded. Before he left to set up his headquarters on the northern slope of Little Round Top, Uncle John went over to Will. "Will, get off the battlefield now and take yourself to a safe place."

"But where," Will stammered.

"Somewhere in town - although I'm told shells are flying everywhere and there isn't a place that's really safe. Try a home. Usually, they become hospitals."

"I know."

"Oh, do you? Someday when this is all over, you and I are going to have a talk, young man. I know you're not a spy, but there's more to you than meets the eye."

Will swallowed hard.

"Right now, I want to go over a few things with you. Somehow talking with you clears my mind."

Will stood a little taller as Uncle John continued, "You know, our Army didn't do all that well yesterday. The Rebels had more manpower than we did but, of course, that's going to change now that my men are here. You see, Will, the fact is the Union will never run out of men. Over time, the South will. They have no reserve manpower. When they win a battle, they don't even have enough men in reserve to follow it up. Eventually, we will have to win this war and I hope it is here at Gettysburg today. Apparently, Gettysburg was not supposed to be the scene of the battle, but when armies collide, they have no choice but to fight."

Will nodded. "I hope you stay safe today, sir."

"That is not in my hands; I simply must do my duty," said General Sedgwick. "All right now, I'm off to direct my men to give support to a place called Culp's Hill and something called Cemetery Ridge and wherever else General Meade needs them."

"Why do your men go all over instead of fighting in one place," asked Will.

"We are the reserve corps for the Army of the Potomac. Our job is to go where the Army needs us. Give me what you wrote, Will, and write about whatever you find in the town. We'll meet again after this battle ends. May God go with you, son."

"And you too, General Sedgwick." Will handed him the pages he had finished writing. He hoped he had not made many spelling mistakes and that the pages were readable. It had been hard to write neatly in the wagon.

"I prefer Uncle John."

Will thought for a moment. "Not when you are going into battle. Your men need a General more than they need an Uncle."

"How wise you are. We will have that talk soon," he answered and went off to lead his men.

* * *

It was a long afternoon. Will walked to Baltimore Street and ran into hordes of people trying to leave. It was confusing because some roads were clogged with people leaving town and other roads were clogged with soldiers coming into town. Wounded men lay everywhere. Suddenly, from across the road, a boy beckoned to Will to come over to him. Rifle bullets called Minie balls were raining down, and between the roar of the cannon and the whizzing of the balls, Will thought it safer to follow the boy.

It turned out it wasn't a boy at all, but a girl dressed in boy's clothing.

349

"Why are you dressed like a boy?"

"There is no time to talk. Come with me to my house. You will be safer there than wandering in the street."

"How did you know that I was wandering?"

"I saw you from the window, even though we are not supposed to be close to the windows."

"How come?"

"In case you have not noticed, there is fighting going on here and no one wants to be standing at a window when a shell or bullet comes through the glass. Even if it was shot at a house by mistake, people can be killed or injured."

"That's right," thought Will. "I remember now. No one was supposed to hurt civilians during the Civil War. That, at least, was a good thing." Will asked the girl, "Is it all right with your family if I come with you?"

"Yes! Just come on before we get hurt," urged the girl.

He followed her into a small house.

"Did you bring the boy, Joanna?"

"Yes. Here he is, Ma."

"I am Will Bradford from Litchfield, Connecticut, ma'am," Will said politely.

"I am Mrs. Greene and this is my daughter, Joanna Greene. She is dressed as a boy because I was concerned about her going outside if they knew that she was a girl."

Will didn't think much of her logic. No one would bother a girl, but you never know with a boy. He decided not to answer.

"Are you lost," she asked.

"Kind of. I lost my Uncle."

"How sad. Everything is sad these days," said Mrs. Greene. "There is so much loss, I'm afraid. And now this. If Mr. Greene ever does return, what will he say about Gettysburg? It will never look the same again and no one will ever remember why."

Tell that to the hordes of children who still have to memorize the Gettysburg Address, thought Will. But he said nothing.

"If you have no one, I guess you might as well stay here. You will have to sleep on the floor because the beds are given to the wounded." She sighed. "There are so many wounded."

"Are you using your house as a hospital? Mrs. Mitchell did that in Winchester."

Oblivious to Will's comment about Winchester, Mrs. Greene just continued talking, "I put six boys upstairs and one died so I can take in another wounded one. The worst was when the doctor came and took off an arm and a leg from two of them. He wanted to leave them on the porch. Can you imagine? An arm and a leg on my porch?

Sometimes I think that this is all a bad dream and I will awaken soon."

Joanna looked anxiously at her mother. She put her arm around her and said, "I will go and tend to the wounded, Ma. You stay here with Will."

"No, take Will with you. Maybe he can help."

"Come on, Will," Joanna said, as she led him upstairs. "Why are you just with your Uncle, anyway? Where is the rest of your family?"

"Back in Connecticut."

"Then what . . . "

Much to Will's relief, the cries of one of the soldiers interrupted her.

"There, there," Joanna said, as she knelt down to put a compress on the soldier's forehead. "You'll be all right soon."

She moved toward Will who asked, "Will he?"

"Will he what?"

"Will he be all right?"

"I don't think so. He is burning up with fever. Who knows, though? Only God knows and He doesn't seem to be here in Gettysburg today."

"Yes, He is," said a voice that was vaguely familiar to Will. "Just because bad things are happening does not mean God is no longer with us."

"Another one down with fever," whispered Joanna to Will, adding, "I am going to try to engage him in talk to see if he is hallucinating."

Joanna went to stand by the wounded soldier, "So, sir, how do you know where God is?"

"I know because I have seen goodness under the worst of situations. I saw a Confederate general stop to help a wounded Union general. God was there. I saw a boy take me to safety when we were retreating down the Valley Turnpike. God was there. And, dear child, God is here with you and your mother as you tend to all of us wounded soldiers."

"Charles," called out Will excitedly.

The man looked toward the doorway where Will was standing. Will came close to the bed and said, "It is you. I'm Will Bradford, don't you remember me?"

"Of course. I was just talking about you and how you gave me water on the Valley Pike and listened to me when I said I didn't want to go to a hospital. I was afraid that a surgeon in a hospital would remove my leg. So now a surgeon in a house removed my arm! An arm for a leg." Charles shook his head and laughed wildly. "Yea, though I walk through the valley of the shadow of death, I will fear no evil, For Thou art with me . . . " Then he nodded off.

Will walked over to him and touched his head. "He doesn't feel hot."

Charles suddenly tried to get up. "I feel my arm, Will. That must mean they didn't cut if off, after all. I feel it; I do." He fell back again and went silent.

Will was confused. He looked at Joanna, who said, "That's called phantom pain. They all seem to feel it when a limb is amputated. Somehow they still feel the limb."

"Will he be all right? I know a lot times the area gets infected."

"I don't know. I just know that since his arm was removed within a day of his injury, it is much less likely to make him sick. See all I have learned in just two days? If the battle lasts much longer, I may qualify to be a surgeon!"

Joanna went to see to her other patients. Will asked if he could sit by Charles' bedside. "Go ahead, it will do him good to see you when he awakens."

Will lost track of time as he sat quietly, barely hearing the sound of the cannonading anymore. There was so much firing that Will feared the firepower would engulf the small house. He reached out and touched Charles. "You are not alone," he said. "I am with you."

Charles roused and said, "I know. Thank you. Remember how we were roommates in Mrs. Mitchell's house? Well, we are roommates again! Imagine, in July of 1861, I enlisted for ninety days. And here I am, still with the 5th Connecticut two years later. How many days is that, Will," Charles asked, but fell asleep again before Will could answer.

The fighting seemed to go on forever. In these days, Will knew, men had to see their target in order to hit it, so there wasn't much fighting during the darkness of night. Will thought he heard the sounds of battle somewhere to the east but, if he did, the battle was short and didn't last very long.

"Courage is doing whatever it is you have to do. My father always told me that," whispered Joanna.

Will turned around and saw that her blue eyes were full of tears. "We lost another soldier. His name and address was pinned to his uniform and I need to write to his family. They will want to know. I would if it was my brother or father."

Will went to her and, without thinking, just put his arms around her. They stood together for a moment, the girl from 1863 and the boy from another time, lost on the second day of the Battle of Gettysburg.

"Joanna, Joanna," called one of the wounded soldiers.

Joanna pulled away and shook herself. "I am coming," she answered and hurried away.

Will felt this powerful urge to shout at the top of his lungs, "Go home, all you soldiers. The worst is going to come tomorrow." Then he would take Joanna and her mother and go home to Litchfield. But, instead, he walked back over to Charles' bedside and sat down.

Charles slept fitfully and Will stayed by his bedside for a while, and then began to help with the other patients. He emptied basins and learned not to look, he changed bandages and learned not to breathe through his nose, and he learned not to think of each patient as a person with a home and family far away. Instead, he saw them as his job and, that way, was able to do what he had to do.

Around 3 a.m., Will heard rain. "That suits this day," he thought and went to sleep. He slept fitfully and when he awoke, the rain had stopped and the long night finally ended. It was now Day 3 of the battle of Gettysburg.

Will went down to the kitchen, where Mrs. Greene was baking for the soldiers. At first he declined to eat any of their meager food, but she said kindly, "You've been a soldier this night. I don't know what we would have done without you. You need to keep your strength up for whatever we may face next."

Will looked down and took the bread with a quiet, "Thank you."

"Maybe today will be better," offered Joanna. She had changed into a dress and could no longer be mistaken for a boy.

"No, it won't," Will wanted to shout. "It will be worse, much worse." But he said nothing and headed to the door.

"Where are you going," asked Joanna.

"Out to the field."

"To the battlefield? How old are you anyway?"

"I'm almost sixteen. Why?"

"Aren't you a little young to be all alone in the middle of a battlefield? At least soldiers have other soldiers and officers to take care of them."

Will looked straight at Joanna. "There's not much taking care at Gettysburg, is there?"

"Maybe not, but don't go. We need you here."

"They need me out there," he cried and pointed toward the door. "I have to save any soldier I can save."

"What about Charles, you saved him, didn't you? Don't you want to see him again?"

"Please tell him goodbye. I have to go."

"But they are fighting out there," she screamed at him.

"I know."

"Why are you going?"

"I need to help. Please give me some bandages and anything else you can spare for the soldiers on the field."

Mrs. Greene took a linen tablecloth from the cupboard and said, "I've been saving this for something special. I guess there's nothing more special than saving our soldiers, is there?"

Joanna pulled off her petticoat with a flourish. "Here, take this too."

Will was embarrassed and immediately turned away.

"Don't worry, Will. If we rid our land of these Rebels, I'll make another petticoat and that one will be even finer because perhaps it will be for my trousseau. Come on and help me tear these up so you can use them as bandages."

They worked quickly and when they were finished, Joanna said, "I know you need to go but I will miss you."

He touched her gently and said, "Joanna, be safe. Listen to your mother and stay away from windows."

"Ah, but if I had listened to her, I would never have met you."

"Joanna, I'll always remember you."

"Well, I kind of hope we will see each other again, don't you?"

Will smiled. "Hope is a good thing." He waved to Mrs. Greene, and went out into the morning.

It was getting very hot as he began to walk out of town. If that early morning rain had cooled anything down, you sure couldn't tell it now. Whether it was the heat or his fear of what was coming, Will began to sweat profusely. He suddenly saw two Confederate soldiers sitting by the road. One held his head in his hands and the other was vainly trying to stop a wound from bleeding. Will walked over to them.

"I have some bandages and I know how to make a tourniquet. Can I help you," he asked.

"Why would you help us," drawled the man with the wound.

Will knew the answer to that question. "In honor of my relative, William Bradford. He's from Virginia and he's fighting near here. Also in honor of my friend's brother,

Joseph, who died at Manassas. And also . . . "

"That's enough. Just help me. I got hurt sometime yesterday I think. These days just sort of roll one into the other around here."

Will worked deftly as the man talked. He recognized that this kind of talking was a combination of shock and pain.

"Where is your Company?"

"What Company? We're all scattered. Some of us are dead or wounded and lying on a field."

"What are you going to do now?"

"We're going to find my cousin. He's with the 8th Virginia."

"No, don't do that," screamed Will. "Don't go and find him."

"Why not?"

"The 8th Virginia fought with General Pickett."

"What are you talking about?"

"Just listen to me. You have already been in a bad battle on Day 2 of Gettysburg. You don't want to be in the worst one yet, do you? So, stay away from the 8th Virginia."

The other soldier stood up and grabbed Will. "What do you know, boy, that you aren't telling us? Why shouldn't we find Cousin Robert? What are the Federals planning that we don't know about and how do you know whatever it is you think you know?"

"I don't know anything. I just know that this will be a bad battle and they have more men than you do and . . . "

"Is that all? We're still better fighters than them any day of the week. Don't you know we just beat 'em at Chancellorsville? Before that it was Fredericksburg and we beat 'em there too. Yesterday was just a loss like you get in any battle. A lot of killing, but today we will beat them again."

"How do you know?"

"We are planning a cannonade like no other cannonade, one that will completely destroy their artillery and drive their men crazy. Then when they're at their weakest, we will charge them and destroy them!"

Will could think of nothing to say. He wanted to tell them the truth, that the Confederates will be destroyed, not the Federals, but, again, he said nothing and just walked on.

In the early afternoon, it began, a fierce cannonade with maybe 150 Confederate guns all firing together from Seminary Ridge. It was as if fire consumed the land in front of him.

As he watched smoke turn the field dark and fire light up the sky, he thought of the words of the prophet Jeremiah, his favorite prophet in Sunday school when he was a kid.

"Behold, a storm of the Lord is gone forth in
     fury,
Yea, a whirling storm;
It shall whirl upon the head of the wicked."

Will saw more pain than wickedness here in Gettysburg. He walked on and went behind the Confederate artillery line where the men were waiting for the order to charge. He sat down near an officer and said, "What if your cannonade doesn't make the Federals quit? Maybe you shouldn't make the charge."

"Hey, kid, I do not give the orders around here."

"But maybe you could . . . "

"I cannot do anything except watch my men die. If I'm lucky, I might die too."

"So you know . . . "

"I don't know anything except that we are about to advance over a mile of open field against the Federal army who holds the high ground. We were supposed to start early in the morning but something must have gone wrong and now it's late. None of this is my decision."

"Is your artillery so good? What if it overshoots? That happens a lot." Will knew it happened here on Day 3 of Gettysburg.

"Go away, kid. We have enough problems without you making up new ones."

Will left and decided to do one final thing to stop the charge . . . find Major General George Pickett himself.

But he was too late.

It was the middle of the afternoon and the sky was clear and the day was hot, close to 87 degrees, when the charge began. Confederate men fixed their bayonets and moved forward to charge the little clump of trees over on Cemetery Ridge. They crossed a mile of open field and just kept walking. When they came close enough, Union troops began to fire and they kept on firing as Confederate men kept on coming up to that ridge. They kept on marching and the Federals kept on shooting.

"No matter how many men the Confederates kill, the Union Army will bring in other men in to replace them," General Sedgwick had told Will. "We have reserves and they don't."

Will watched the General's words unfold in front of him.

The battlefield was indescribable even though Will had read enough accounts of this battle to know that many people tried to describe it. But no one got it right. No one really captured the smell of the dying, the cries of the wounded, the blaze of heavy fire, the whistling of bullets, the flying shells, the screams of men and horses sounding like the groans and wails of souls in torment.

Will looked around. There were supposed to be all the Confederate divisions on that field, but some of them just didn't come. Confederate artillery was supposed to cover the men and support their charge but it didn't. There were supposed to be fresh horses and more equipment but there weren't. How can everything go so wrong?

Everyone fought, even the cooks. Will watched the color bearers, those young men, boys really, carrying their flags proudly, all falling down under a rush of fire. When weapons failed, fighting became hand-to-hand, but the fighting didn't stop. Blood soaked into the ground so deep that Will knew the stain would never completely disappear, no matter how many years would pass.

Then it was over. It had lasted about an hour or so and it was Pickett himself who called retreat. There was great confusion as men scattered around with very few officers alive to give them orders.

The field was a mass of dead and wounded men and horses so Will walked over to help. He passed those who were beyond his skill and applied tourniquets randomly.

"You, over there." Will turned and saw a man come toward him. "Help me save who I can."

"Are you a doctor?"

"I am."

"They need you here," Will said quietly.

"They need a lot more than me but God seems unavailable today, so I will have to do."

Will worked tirelessly until his legs were ready to buckle under the weight of so many hours. He learned to administer chloroform over a soldier's nose and mouth so that the surgeon could operate. He watched in horror as one surgeon licked a piece of silk to get it firm enough to thread through a needle.

"Stop," he called out. "You need to clean that thread before you put it in a soldier."

"I just did. I used my spittle."

Will knew he was from another century and no one would listen to him and that trying to explain the need for sterilization was a waste of time, but he tried anyway.

"Sir, that soldier will heal a lot better if you clean his wounds and clean your instruments with soap and water or even with whiskey. You just wiped your knife on your apron which is filled with the blood of other soldiers. You can't do that."

"And you can't tell me what to do. Go away. I don't need you here."

"You do. I can help if you will just listen."

"Get out, or I will have you thrown out."

Will left, taking care to step over bodies, not on them. In the distance, he saw General Sedgwick sitting on a log and he hurried over to him.

"General Sedgwick, it's me, Will. You're all right!"

"Well, why wouldn't I be? I might as well have been home for all the good I did here at Gettysburg. I had no men under my command and I felt useless."

"But your men did good and that's thanks to you. You trained them. They fought everywhere at Gettysburg and they won. The Union couldn't have won without your men, sir, and because of that, you should be proud of yourself."

"Hard to swallow for a man like me, Will."

"But, sir, you once told me these men were your sons. That's what a father does. He lets his sons go and he is proud of their successes. My father let me go, but he never was proud of me."

General Sedgwick looked Will straight in the eyes. "I am proud of you, Will."

"Are you proud of your men?"

"I am. Thank you, Will. Now, if I may, I'd like to ask you a question."

"Of course," Will replied nervously. "Anything."

"Where are you really from? I accept that you live in Litchfield now, but you sound different from the boys I know from that part of the woods."

"I . . . "

"Will, if your original home was in the South, as I believe it was, then I understand your reticence. We are in a war and past loyalties to our enemies will not be well received. Keep your own counsel, Will, as you are doing and, God willing, after the war when the Union is back together, you can speak about your birthplace without fear or shame."

"Thank you, sir."

"We'll speak of it no more. Good luck to you, Will."

Dismissed, Will walked away, thinking that the older man got it right in one sense. "He knew that I didn't belong here. Of course, how could he know that my real home is 150 years away in the future? Somehow, after Gettysburg, that home is looking better and better."

Will sat down for a moment and the next thing he knew he was gone and Gettysburg

was a place of the past. He woke up
expecting to be home but he was definitely
not in Litchfield.

Chapter 16

"When is our time going to come? Tell me that, Will. When?"

Will looked at the angry boy in front of him and then turned his head away in confusion. This wasn't Gettysburg or Litchfield or any other place he had ever been.

"Again I ask when is it going to be our turn?"

What am I supposed to say? Here I am looking at a boy about my age in some kind of fancy uniform with brass buttons and stripes and I don't have a clue what he is talking about. He looked down at his own clothes and saw he was wearing the same uniform.

"Well?"

"I don't know," answered Will truthfully. "I'm afraid I haven't a clue."

The boy pushed a lock of his dark hair away impatiently. "I cannot wait anymore, I tell you."

"So what are you going to do, James? Run away to fight," asked a second boy as he entered the room, nodding to Will. Will nodded back. "Can't you calm your roommate down, Will? We can hear him throughout the barracks."

I have a roommate! Is this high school? College? But what about the uniform we're all wearing. Maybe it's a military school of some sort.

Will's musings were loudly interrupted.

"Oh, you can hear me, can you," asked James angrily. "Well, good. If my voice is loud, it's loud because I have something to say. You, John, talk with nothing to say."

Will decided to intervene. "Look, we are in the middle of a war and we are all edgy."

"Edgy . . . never heard that word. What does it mean," John asked.

Before Will could answer, James interrupted again, "You just said it very well, Will, when you said we were in the middle of a war. That's exactly the problem; our country is in the middle of a war — but we are not! We want to be right there fighting in the middle of a battle, but they won't let us. They say cadets are too young, but all of us are at least sixteen years old now."

Cadets? "But there are color bearers and drummer boys who are younger," protested Will, remembering Gettysburg.

"Precisely my point."

The three boys were quiet.

"So, where are we," asked Will, without thinking.

James shook his head. "Well put. Where exactly are we? Nowhere, that's where we are."

"You are wrong," John answered. "We are at The Institute, the Virginia Military Institute and we are proud to be here."

Will searched his memory. "Isn't that in Lexington?"

"What's wrong with you today, Will? You're acting a little strange," answered an exasperated James.

"He is acting strange?" John laughed. "I would say all your yelling is stranger. Actually, though, if I think about it, Will, you do seem a little preoccupied. What is wrong?"

Nothing, except I don't know how I got here and I don't know what I am doing here and I can't imagine why I am wearing this uniform. Actually, I can imagine. I seem to be a cadet! "I'm just tired, that's all."

"Tired of waiting, I bet," said James. "Yesterday when that soldier handed us the flag he had captured, I felt ashamed."

"Why," John asked. "That was a nice thing he did."

"It was, but we should have captured that flag ourselves!"

"Here we go again," John answered.

Before things could escalate further, Will picked up a book and said, "I guess we have to study, don't we?"

"Study, study, study," mimicked James. "Sometimes I think that's all you do. What is it today, Will, Chemistry or Natural Philosophy?"

"I can't imagine," answered Will, more honestly than James knew.

John laughed. "Don't pay any attention to James. Anyone who gets as many demerits as he gets is hardly a reliable authority on studies. Look," he added in a more serious voice, "We are training to be officers. The Confederate Army needs us because they are losing so many men on the battlefield. We can't lead until we are fully trained. People's lives will depend upon our leadership and we had better be good."

There was a sudden quiet in the room. "My brother was killed at Gettysburg and I am going to avenge his death," James said passionately.

"I lost two uncles at Sharpsburg and a cousin at Malvern Hill and my brother is in prison in Baltimore. You don't have to lecture me about loss," answered John. "And, Will, of course we all know your story."

Will took a deep breath. What was his story?

372

"You lost your father and that's a terrible loss. My uncle said that William Bradford was the best officer they had. He was killed trying to save his men."

William Bradford was his father! Wait a minute; that can't be. I already have a father. William Bradford must be my great, great, great-grandfather!

"This is getting confusing," Will said aloud.

"What is," asked John.

"Everything," Will answered, then thought to himself, "If William Bradford wrote about his son the cadet, I must be that cadet! This is the strangest thing that's happened to me yet!"

"Will, you look like you tripped a landmine. What's wrong?"

"Nothing. I, uh, am happy to know that William Bradford died a hero!"

John nodded and said gently, "Yes, of course. William Bradford was a real hero. You must be very proud of him."

"So many heroes on both sides lost and gone," Will murmured.

John looked at Will curiously. "What do you mean? Ours is the only side with heroes."

Right. Say that at Gettysburg. "Heroes come in all shapes and sizes and even in all locations."

The cadets were uncomfortable with the conversation. "You're not thinking straight, but who would be thinking straight after losing a father," John said quietly. "Let's not talk of these things anymore. Why don't you come with us tonight to visit the Misses Davis."

"Why?"

"You'll meet some very nice ladies," drawled James with a smile.

"I'm not interested in ladies."

"Never found one you liked, not even a little bit?"

"Well, there was someone named Joanna once, but I don't want to talk about her now."

"I'm going sketching with Miss Mary on Saturday," James announced.

"You," scoffed John. "You cannot even draw your name legibly. Now if Ezekiel was going that would be another thing."

"Moses Ezekiel may be a better artist, but I have special gifts when it comes to the ladies."

"Maybe you'll find your gift for engineering if you look hard enough."

"An artist of my caliber cannot think about lowly things like class."

"Well, since I am not of your caliber, I think I will go and study now."

When John left the room, Will felt a tremendous need for air. "I'm going for a walk."

"A walk," said James in disbelief. "Don't you get enough exercise here? After that two-hour drill and those two charges across the parade ground, I think you would have had enough exercise! Why we practice pretend charges when we could really charge Union soldiers, I can't imagine."

"I just need to clear my head."

"My head never needs clearing."

Too many possible replies popped up in Will's mind, none of them flattering and none of them kind. He left without saying anything.

As Will walked around, he looked up at the mountains. Same mountains he saw when he last visited the Valley. Somehow that was reassuring. His mind was reeling. Now that he knew who he was supposed to be and where he was, he needed to find out when it was. It wasn't cold and it wasn't hot. The grass was green and trees were in bloom. Maybe it was Spring. He looked around at the buildings. They were a kind of tan stone with narrow windows and almost looked like a fortress or even a castle. Will walked over to a large field. He guessed this is what James had called the parade ground. He tried to imagine what it must look like when it was filled with cadets. James said they drilled and practiced here. Will nodded approvingly. It was a big space.

He walked back to the barracks deep in thought. "Say, James, what date is today?"

"Don't you know? Why it's May 9th."

"1864, right?"

"No. Actually, I heard it was 1764."

"Very funny."

"Well, tomorrow is the big day. The first anniversary of Stonewall Jackson's death and there will be no academics for us."

"I'm glad you put his death before your vacation from class."

James gave Will a look of reproach. "Don't joke about Stonewall Jackson. Had he lived, things would have been better for all of us. Remember, he was a professor here, a great soldier and General Lee's right hand man."

"I know," Will answered somberly. "He was killed accidentally by a Confederate soldier. Kind of like friendly fire."

"What are you talking about?" James thought for a moment. "I get it. You fire on your own side by accident. That's a good term; I never heard it before."

That's because it originated during the first World War. "I hear a lot of things," Will said lamely, hoping James wasn't interested enough to continue the conversation.

He wasn't.

"Sure you don't want to come tonight?"

"I'm sure."

"Your loss. Bradford, you are missing out on your best years."

* * *

Will awoke on May 10th every bit as excited as the rest of the cadets. This was an important event and he was part of it. There was a huge crowd at the cemetery where Stonewall Jackson was buried and Will listened to the speeches and helped raise the flag over his grave.

Since the cadets had the rest of the day off, Will mingled with them and began to feel very comfortable. This was nothing like being with Big Red in the Valley or with General Sedgwick at Gettysburg. Or even with Joanna or the Mitchells. "This is like school only you do more physical things. I think I can get used to being here if I don't get to go back home."

He spent time with John and Ezekiel and his roommate Jefferson and a few of the other cadets. They seemed to be a nice group of guys, better than the guys in his school in Connecticut. "Maybe I'll stay here," Will began to be excited at the prospect. "The War is going to end in another year and I'll wait it out at the Institute with all the other cadets. Nothing much is going to happen here."

"We better turn in," someone said when night finally came and ended this very exciting day. But before most of them were asleep, drums began to beat. It was the long roll, the call that cried "Emergency!"

"What the . . . ?"

"What's going on?"

"Another drill? Why? This was our day off."

The cadets dressed in a hurry and tumbled out of the barracks. It was dark but they were able to see a few officers reading a piece of paper by the light of a lantern. They stood at attention when the adjutant turned to them and began to read the dispatch aloud. It was from General Breckinridge, giving an order for the cadets to move toward Staunton and join him and his troops to stop a Union invasion of the Shenandoah Valley. The cadets were ordered to be in Staunton by May 12th and were given two days to get there. From Staunton, they would march another three days before they would reach the invading Union soldiers.

The cadets broke into a spontaneous cheer. Finally, they were going to be in a battle, a real battle!

378

"What happens now," Will whispered to John.

"We go and march to Staunton. After all, we're supposed to be ready to fight at a moment's notice, aren't we?"

"I have a feeling that this is going to be a long moment," commented Will.

"Well then, I guess we'll just do what we're assigned to do. Like always."

Will listened carefully when he was told his assignment. It was going to be a challenge to keep up with the other boys, because he'd actually had so little training.

"What's your job, Bradford," James asked as he hurried on by.

"Rations. I'm getting the bacon and the beef together to take with us."

"Get us a lot. We're sure going to be hungry after all that marching. Staunton's more than 35 miles away."

"What are you going to be doing?"

"Me? I'm off to the artillery. You know, I'm an old farm boy so I'm used to horses. I don't reckon you want to trade jobs, since you aren't so handy with horses."

Will let that pass. He knew he probably had as much experience as James did with horses, but evidently his ancestor, Will, didn't. Besides, he didn't want to go into any explanations of where and how he rode. "Some things are better left unsaid," he thought, "especially when you travel the way I do." Will hurried to fill the wagons with food.

Some cadets stayed up late writing letters home.

"What about your Mamma, Will," asked John. "Aren't you going to write to her?"

"I thought about it, but I decided to write her after the battle."

"But what if . . ."

"Yeah, I know. But I don't want to worry her before it's necessary. She's," he hesitated as he wondered how to describe his real mother and the mother he was supposed to have here in 1864. "She's a little emotional," he finally said.

John nodded and sighed. "Most mothers are."

Between packing their haversacks, writing letters home and whispering with excitement, few of the cadets slept much that night. They got up in the early hours of the morning and ate breakfast by candlelight because it was still dark outside. Actually, Will wasn't sure that they were candles; he'd never seen anything like them and he guessed that they were some sort of replacement candles that the Confederates had concocted. At least they gave off some light.

Suddenly, there was another announcement.

"We need cadets to guard the Institute so twenty-seven of you are not going to Staunton."

No one wanted to stay back.

"I better be going," said James as he gritted his teeth.

"Me too," shouted other cadets.

A cry of disappointment went up as each of the twenty-seven names were called. Will didn't know whether to be relieved or disappointed when his name wasn't called. "I guess I'm going to be in a battle. I hope I don't have to fight anyone I know well. Or even anyone I've ever met before . . . ."

"Bradford! Quit daydreaming."

"Even here I get accused of daydreaming!" Will thought soberly, "I better not daydream during the battle or I'll be dead."

"Bradford!"

"Yes, sir!"

By 7:00 a.m., the cadets were ready. 264 of them began to march down the Pike toward Staunton. They were going to march 18 miles on the first day, then they would camp. The next day they would march another 18 miles and finally reach Staunton.

"I remember this dust," Will said to John. "Last time I was on the Valley Pike, I coughed and got blisters. It's not my best memory."

"When were you on the Valley Pike?"

"Quiet," called out a voice and Will mentally kicked himself for mentioning the Pike. John couldn't know about Charles. He would never understand why Will rescued a Union soldier.

The cadets were in high spirits as they crossed a creek.

"Look at me," yelled James. "I can make this old wooden bridge really move!"

"Stop it," said John. "You'll get us all in trouble."

By the time they camped, many of the cadets, including Will, had blisters on their feet. Sometime during the night, it began to rain. It was a hard rain and it kept on throughout the next day.

"This isn't marching," complained one of the cadets. "It's wading through mud."

"Just keep moving," called out a voice.

They reached Staunton the next day and joined the Confederate soldiers that were waiting there.

"I'll bet you're glad to see us," said James to the first soldier he saw.

"Why is that?"

"We're here to help."

"Well lookie here, men," he said gesturing to a group of men sitting around.

"We got here a bunch of polished jackasses coming to help us."

"Guess they aim to teach us a thing or two. Boys, how many battles you been in?"

"This is our first," a cadet said proudly.

"Your first," the soldier repeated as the rest of the men laughed. "You sure are looking pretty for your first battle, now aren't you? Did you dress up special?"

The men laughed again. "Maybe you're gonna play 'Pat a Cake' and do some bakin' while you're here."

"Naw, they're going sing 'Rock-A-Bye Baby' and put themselves to sleep."

"What about 'Baa, Baa Black Sheep'? They ain't nothing more than a herd of dressed-up sheep!"

"What about just shutting your mouth," called out one of the cadets.

Just as one of the soldiers stood up to answer, an officer came over and ordered the cadets to continue marching. They marched until they camped again for the night and the next morning they were up early and marching again.

The rains continued. Will was wet, tired, and uncomfortable, but very happy to be marching with the cadets. "I don't know why I am fighting; I don't know exactly who I'm fighting and I don't know where I'll be fighting. But what I do know is that I'll be fighting alongside these cadets and I don't ever want to disappoint any of them. I guess that's what I'm really fighting for. I'm fighting for them!"

The next day, they marched again.

On Saturday, they finished their march and made camp. It was still pouring, but they could see in the distance the fires from the Union camps. Will knew it wouldn't be long before he would "see the elephant," a term that meant a soldier's first battle.

Will mused, "It's a good thing I read so much online, or else I would never know these things. But . . . what if I run? I don't think I will, but I don't know for sure. Up to now, I've been an observer, not a fighter. Uncle John made me a reporter, not a soldier. Now, I am going to be a soldier, a real soldier."

"I'm going to be in a battle," he cried aloud out to John.

"Hard to avoid," John answered with a smile. "But who would want to avoid it?"

"No one," cheered the cadets.

Will was too excited to sleep and was still up at midnight when the long roll of drums sounded. The cadets were ordered to rise and take their places. Captain Preston said a prayer and soon the cadets began to march again.

Hours later, they met groups of soldiers eating breakfast and waited for the teasing to begin. It began, "Do you miss your mama yet?" and someone else piped up, "Here come the 'Rock-A-Bye' babies."

This time the cadets ignored them. They had bigger things in mind as General Breckinridge himself came by. The cadets cheered him and then fell quiet as he motioned for silence. The enemy was close, very close, and the less noise everybody made, the better.

General Breckinridge made it clear that he would rather not use the cadets, but would if he had no other choice.

"I hope we get in," whispered James.

Will said nothing. Out here on this Sunday morning, he heard the sounds of fire in the distance and suddenly remembered Gettysburg. Will felt afraid. "I don't want to be scared. I have to see the elephant; I have to see the elephant; I have to see the elephant," he kept repeating over and over to himself.

The order finally came for the cadets to move. Will looked around. They were now with the second line of fighting men and were no longer the reserve line. They would fight.

Will forgot that he was scared. Here he was at New Market, Virginia, alongside cadets from the Virginia Military Institute and they were all depending on him to do his job. He would not fail them.

They started to move and the Union guns started to fire. All thoughts disappeared from Will as he faced the enemy. As the shells came, the cadets pushed forward. At one point Will was conscious of crossing a ravine that was almost four feet deep, but for the most part, he was only conscious of the sounds of the artillery in front of him. And the smoke, the black smoke that seemed to be everywhere. A cadet next to him dropped and Will kept moving forward. Another one dropped, struck by a ball, but the line closed and they kept moving forward. Whenever there was a gap in their line, there was a cadet right there to fill it, closing the line in to the center.

But they were only the second line. It was the first line that faced the worst.

There was more rain. Mud was up to their ankles in some places, slowing them down, but never stopping their advance. Will was very aware of General Breckinridge riding up and down to cheer them on and Will stood as tall as he could whenever the General rode by.

Then things started to go bad. There was a big gap in the center of the first line where the 62nd Virginia suffered terrible losses.

Even with such a huge hole in the middle of their line, General Breckinridge still did not want to put the cadets in to fill the gap. Yet there was no one else available.

"Put the boys in . . . ," the General finally said, "and may God forgive me for the order."

The cadets went in. As they approached a house, they felt the fury of fire. Balls and shells crashed all around as bullets whizzed by. Will saw James down on the ground, stopped, bent down, but saw he was too late. Almost in a trance, Will passed the house and marched along with the other cadets through the orchard and across the wheat field that was soaked from heavy rains. There was mud everywhere. Will's left shoe got stuck in the mud and as he pulled it out, he and another cadet saw three other shoes buried down deep in the thick and oozing mud.

John was hit and yelled out to Will, "Don't stop for me. Go for me. Get them for all of us."

Will felt the sweat run down his face but didn't waver as he kept on moving forward.

Smoke filled the field and it was hard to see the enemy clearly as the cadets tried to fire. Their ramrods, made of wood, were soaked and some of them couldn't be pulled out to reload. But the cadets persevered.

And then, suddenly, the Union soldiers began to retreat.

"Look," shouted Will, "They're leaving their artillery!"

"Let's grab what we can," shouted someone else.

There was no way the artillerists could protect all their guns when the infantry had retreated, and the cadets triumphantly walked away with a twelve pounder.

The Battle of New Market was a victory for the Confederate soldiers and all the cadets, who suddenly became soldiers on the fields of New Market that day.

After the battle was over, Will searched everywhere for John. He stumbled upon a classmate who had a gaping hole in his head with one eye torn out of its socket. Will stared. "He was so alive just this morning. We worked together to pull our shoes out from the mud."

Will found two more of his classmates and his heart was filled with so much pain, he feared it would break. "I know you cannot die from a broken heart, but how do you live with it? And where is John?"

Will finally found John in a field hospital at the other end of the Pike.

"John," Will began.

"Don't looked so upset, Will," John answered. "I will have a story to tell for the rest of my life."

"You will have a life then? Oh, I'm sorry. I shouldn't have said that."

John laughed. "I will have a life. The good Lord saw fit to spare me and all I have is a grazed shoulder. It's a bit painful, but nothing I cannot handle. Not like poor James." John shook his head. "I still can't believe that James is gone."

"He wanted to fight so badly."

"And that is the good thing . . . he got to fulfill his dream even if it cost him his life."

Both boys were quiet.

John spoke first. "I'm not going back to the Institute. I'm going to Richmond to fight."

"I am going back to the Institute," Will answered immediately. "I owe our fallen classmates that much."

"And I owe them a fight for the Confederacy. Come on, let's go into town now."

"Are you up to that?"

"I sure am. It will make me feel better than being here."

Will had to agree. There were a lot of seriously-wounded soldiers here and his job was now over. He had fought like a man and like a soldier.

"I guess I finally saw that elephant," he thought.

Will helped support John, and they began to walk together.

"Look around. Every building and home seems to have been turned into a hospital," John said somberly.

"That's what happens after a battle," Will answered. "There are never enough doctors and hospitals, so ordinary people have to become extraordinary and open their homes and hearts."

John looked at Will curiously. "You know, you suddenly know much more than you used to know. Must be all that studying you do."

"Must be," Will agreed. "Say, look over there at those horses. They've been abandoned by some Union soldiers. Let's take them."

As they rode grandly into town, the ladies of New Market cheered them.

"What's the matter, Will? You're scowling. Smile pretty for the ladies."

"I was just remembering Joseph, someone I used to know. He went off to Manassas and was killed. That was in 1861 and it seems so long ago."

"It was. We were children then; now we are men."

The veteran soldiers seemed to agree and treated the cadets as old friends when they came by. They hung out with them for a while, and then Will decided to leave.

"I guess those soldiers know we're not 'Rock-A-Bye' babies anymore," Will said proudly.

"We never were," John answered. "Good luck to you, Will."

Will nodded, shook John's hand, and began walking away.

Chapter 17

It seemed as if Will hadn't been walking very long when he became tired and stopped under a tree for a short rest. Suddenly he woke up and there he was back in Litchfield, in the middle of the Monuments.

"Still here," a voice asked. "It's 5:00 p.m. and I'm going home and you are still here." It was Maya. "Were you here all day?"

"Of course not," Will answered.

"What did you do then? I thought this was your day off. Surely even you could think of something better to do than stare at war monuments."

"Hey, I've done a lot since I last saw you. I fought in the Battle of New Market. Is that enough for you?"

"I think you're really nuts. I don't know why I waste my time."

Will just shrugged his shoulders. Being around Maya was very tiring. Maybe if he ignored her, she would go away. Besides, his head hurt and he thought he was missing some memories . . . like about a year's worth.

"What are you going to do now?"

"Go home and sleep."

"Sitting around must exhaust you. I guess you're glad school is over and you're going back to the stable."

"What do you mean going back to the stable?"

Slowly and patiently as if talking to a child, Maya said, "Well, since you were working at Mrs. Johnson's stable last summer and she had the bad judgment to hire you back this summer, you must like the job or else you would have done something else. You know, I switched from the museum to the historical society, and I like the historical society much better. It's interesting looking things up and . . . "

He thought furiously. Last summer was Gettysburg, so this must be the summer after New Market. And the memories of the last few months were coming back . . . school . . . exams . . . his mother saying that he could work at the stables this summer if he passed . . . Rebecca's graduation . . . "What else would I do?"

"I don't know. Do some Civil War thing. Maybe you could work at the historical society with me."

Will shuddered at the thought. Imagine seeing Maya everyday. "I prefer horses."

"To me?"

"I didn't say that. I meant to indoor work. I am indoors enough during the school year. And now, I must return home."

"Return? You sound as if you went far away."

"I told you I was in . . ."

"I remember . . . the Battle of New Market. All right, Will, I've had enough. You don't have to make up stories to get rid of me."

"What do I have to do then?" Will remembered that she had tried to be friends with him all through the last school year, although Will hadn't encouraged her.

"Just be yourself."

When he opened the door to his home, he found a package on the hall table that was addressed to him.

"Did you see the package," Rebecca called out.

Will picked it up and saw the return address. It was from his father.

"It's from Dad," Rebecca said as she came into the room. "What did he send you?"

"I'll open it later."

"Open what later," asked his mother as she came into the house. "I'll never understand how I have more work to do when it's summer and I am not teaching than when it's the school year and I am teaching. I just spent hours shopping for a refrigerator."

"What's wrong with our refrigerator?"

"Will, haven't you heard the noises it's making? I called the repair man and he said we need a new one. It's upsetting because they cost so much."

Will looked at his mother with affection. "At least we have a refrigerator even if it is noisy. Imagine having to go out to an ice house."

"Why would we do that," chimed in Rebecca.

"How else could you keep things really cold? Life here is much easier than in the days of the Civil War."

Seeing his mother's anxious look, he quickly added, "I'm only kidding."

"Don't joke around like that, Will. The Civil War isn't good for you."

He resisted the temptation to ask who exactly it was good for, and, instead, took his package to his room. It was a book about horses in the Civil War with a note from his father.

Hi Will,

Thought you might enjoy this book since you enjoy both horses and the Civil

War. Hope to see you on the 23rd when I'm coming down to visit.

Love,
Dad

"Well, I sure hope he knows that he can't me buy me with a book, even a good book," Will said aloud. He put the book aside, then changed his mind and picked it up and started reading. Before he could get very far, his mother called him to supper.

As he looked around the table, he marveled that nothing had changed.

"Did you ever think about time," he asked conversationally.

"What kind of time, a good time or a bad time," Rebecca asked.

"Just time. Doesn't it ever seem to you that a day can be a lot longer than 24 hours?"

"Sure." Rebecca answered, "When I was studying for my SATs, the days seemed endless. I'm glad I went away to college, though; it's a whole lot better than high school."

"That's right, you graduated last year. How was college," asked Will.

Rebecca looked at him curiously. "We've discussed this before. I already told you that I love college."

"Speaking of college," his mother quickly chimed in, "this summer would be a good time for you to begin studying for the SAT, Will. You have no school so you have more time."

"See, there it is again. How can you really have more time? Is a day twenty-four hours or can it be more elastic?"

His mother frowned. "Elastic? What are you talking about?"

"Mom, don't pay attention to him. Will says weird things to get attention."

"No, I don't, Rebecca," Will answered. "Anyway, I don't know if I want to go to college."

"What do you mean? You have to go to college."

"Why?"

"Will, dear," his mother began in that tone he hated. "Of course you'll go to college. You can study history and learn all about the Civil War."

"I know enough about the Civil War to know I don't want to study it. Besides, you always say bad things about my interest in the War."

Rebecca clapped her hands. "Hallelujah! Will has given up on the Civil War."

"The real question," Will answered, "is not if I have given up on the War; the real question is has the Civil War given up on me?"

"What do you mean?"

"Just pass the potatoes, Rebecca. That's all I am going to say on the subject."

In the morning, Will rose early, got on his bike and rode to the stable. Everything was the same as it was last summer, almost everything anyway.

"Say, Cal, where is Jim-Jim?"

"That's right, you don't know. I forgot that you don't work here during the school year. Jim-Jim died. He was twenty-five and Mrs. Johnson said it was his time."

"That's too bad; he was a good horse."

"Tuxedo is our new horse. He's a little temperamental, but Mrs. Johnson says he'll be fine."

Will liked being at the Johnson stable and he was sure the horses liked being here too. "Ever think about battle horses," he asked Cal as they sat at the same rickety table behind the deli eating their sandwiches.

"Not really, but now that you mention it, they must have had a tough time."

"They sure did. In Gettysburg alone thousands of horses died. And they didn't all die quickly. Some of them died slowly and the sound of their screams still comes to me sometimes in my dreams."

"But you never heard them," Cal said.

"Yeah, I did," began Will until he caught himself and continued, "well, not literally, of course, but those reenactments I went to were pretty realistic."

"How realistic can they be? No one is really fighting."

"You'd be surprised. Anyway, back to horses," he said, quickly changing the subject. "People don't realize how important horses were in the Civil War. Everyone used horses. The cavalry, of course, but also the artillery. Horses pulled just about everything from ambulances to supply wagons. They even hauled stuff the engineers needed to built bridges across rivers. Without horses, oxen, and mules, no one could move anything."

"I never thought about it before, but you must be right. After all, there were no trucks and no aircraft, so all they had were animals." Cal asked, "I suppose you heard men dying as well?"

"Yeah, I did. Right now, I'm going back in to buy another drink. Want something?"

As Will paid for his coke, he thought that if he could only learn to keep his mouth shut about the Civil War, life here in Litchfield would be fine!

The days went by with a monotonous regularity that Will appreciated.

"How's life at the stables," Rebecca asked one day.

"What could be bad? I like horses and I like Cal."

"In that order," she teased.

"I don't know." Will thought for a moment. "Cal's a good guy, but with a horse it's like you're with the friend you always wanted, always knew was out there, but never met. And you don't have to think or do anything; you're just yourself."

Rebecca didn't laugh. "Maybe you found something good for yourself. You might become a veterinarian someday."

"See, that's what I mean. Why do people always think of something else you could do instead of just being happy with what you are doing? Horses would never do that."

"Stick with them, then. I was just trying to be helpful."

Will sighed.

The next day was cloudy. As he biked over to the stable, it began to drizzle. The drizzle turned into rain, but it was a soft, summer rain and Will liked the feel of water on his face and arms. By the time he reached the stable, the rain had let up even though Will knew it would begin again. There were puddles of water and mud all around. He stowed his bike and walked into the barn.

He looked at all the horses, murmured hello to a few of them, and went to find Mrs. Johnson.

"Good morning, Will. Don't stand around, busy day, so get going."

"To her it's always a busy day," Cal whispered.

"I see Tuxedo is in the paddock."

"Yeah. Mrs. Johnson said he needs a little more training so someone is going to work with him."

"I'd like to try."

"Go ahead. I'm sure she'll let you."

After getting permission, Will approached Tuxedo very slowly. Tuxedo had a straight black tail that nearly touched the ground and a shiny brown coat. He looked at Will with sweet eyes and ears that faced forward as if to better hear whatever Will was saying. Will talked in a low voice and held out a carrot. At first Tuxedo shook his head, then he cautiously approached.

Will marveled at the sight of such a large animal, seemingly timid and shy.

"Hey, I get it. I'm shy too. But, then, I'm sure as not as beautiful as you."

He watched the lean and sleek body with long, skinny legs come toward him. He waited. Tuxedo took the carrot and munched.

"Good carrot? A good carrot for a good boy. I'll save the second one for another time."

Tuxedo finished his treat and pushed his large head toward Will's body. Slowly, very slowly, Will patted his neck. "I had a horse once. His name was Peaches, and he also liked being patted. He would have liked carrots, too, but we didn't have any to spare."

When Will opened the gate and stepped out, Mrs. Johnson was standing in front of him.

"Nice work, Will. You're good with horses, all right. I think you should spend more time with Tuxedo. He just needs the human touch and he'll be fine. Go back this afternoon after laundry."

"No problem."

After that day, Will began riding Tuxedo. Each day he would take two carrots and put them in his pocket. Sometimes he gave them both to Tuxedo and other times he ate one himself.

The rains continued on and off for the next week, but other than eating their lunch inside on a Formica table rather than outside on a rickety wooden table, there was no change in Will's routine.

It was after lunch when Will noticed a car pull in near the barn. A blond woman with a young child got out and walked toward the barn.

"Where is Mrs. Johnson," she asked Will.

"In her office, I think."

"Well?"

"Well what?"

"Well, aren't you going to get her for me?"

Will just looked at the woman. He turned away and took his time walking to the office to see if Mrs. Johnson was there.

Suddenly he heard Mrs. Johnson walking from the other direction, shouting. "What is going on and who the hell let this child loose?" She came toward the woman while she dragged a child by the hand.

"Let go of my child," the woman yelled.

"Gladly. How dare you let a child wander around here? What is she — two years old?"

"Emma is three."

"Great, so she's three. Do you have any idea how she could hurt herself in a barn, to say nothing of spooking the horses?"

As soon as Mrs. Johnson said that, the child started to scream, making the horses so uncomfortable that they pinned their ears back and their large eyes looked even larger. Will noticed that some of them were retreating to the very back of their stalls. He wished he could retreat with them.

"Get that child out of my barn!"

"Your barn," said the woman as she picked up the screaming child and yelled, "You must be Mrs. Johnson. I came to talk with you."

"Will, back at your chores. I'll handle this," Mrs. Johnson ordered.

Will went to the laundry area, and he and Cal watched from the door.

"I will be happy to talk with you, but, first, calm your child down. Her screaming is not good for the horses."

"Or for me," muttered the woman. She reached into her purse and hurriedly pulled out a big cookie. Emma grabbed it and greedily began eating.

"I want you to give riding lessons to my other daughter. I think she will have real talent with horses."

"Why do you think that?"

"Well, she likes horses."

"Riding is discipline and hard work, not just liking horses. If your daughter is up to it, bring her here and we'll see."

"May I walk around a bit to see where she will be riding?"

"Yes. I will have Will or Cal show you around."

"Will," whispered Cal, "you go. I don't want to."

"You'd rather fold laundry than be outside?"

"I'd rather do anything than be with them. Besides, you're better with people."

"Me?"

"Yeah. Even after you messed up with Habit, you were able to apologize and get Mrs. Johnson to give you another chance. Last guy we had was fired before he could say he was sorry."

"Maybe he wasn't. I was."

"Still, it's not easy to say you're sorry."

Before Will could even think about that, he heard Mrs. Johnson calling. "Will, come and show Mrs. Andrews around." Moving closer to him, she said quietly, "Try to move it along so we can get rid of her and get you back to your chores."

Cal gave Will a knowing look and went back to what he was doing. Will nodded and walked outside.

"I'm told your name is Will. I am Mrs. Andrews. I want to see where my older daughter will be riding."

"First, I'll take you to the ring where we give lessons," Will said.

"And after that? I want to see everything!"

"Where do we go now," asked Mrs. Andrews after she saw the ring. "What's over there where that beautiful horse is?"

Will didn't answer. Out of the corner of his eye, he saw another car pull up to the barn, and he paused to see who it was. Then he heard Mrs. Andrews call as she hurried on, "Emma, slow down. Here, have another cookie." He raced after her.

"That's the paddock," Will answered as he followed Mrs. Andrews. "It's where the horses go to graze and run around and play."

"That one is a beautiful horse," she repeated. "Will my daughter be riding him?"

"Tuxedo is not a beginner's horse."

"I doubt she'll be a beginner long. Let's go inside."

"Inside?"

"Yes, inside the paddock," she answered impatiently, "I want Emma to pat the horse."

"Not this horse. Tuxedo is not ready to be around young children. At this point, we can't let anyone but trained people approach him."

Will was vaguely aware of hearing voices behind him, but before he could turn around to see who was there, Mrs. Andrews angrily said, "I don't understand. I am the customer and I want my daughter to pat that horse."

"I'm sorry. He is a little temperamental, and I cannot allow you inside."

Mrs. Andrews crossed her arms and said unpleasantly, "You are rude. I will report you to your . . ."

Will heard an unfamiliar noise and turned around to see Tuxedo pawing at the ground. Will looked across to the other side of the paddock and there was little Emma climbing through the slats in the wooden fence. She began advancing toward Tuxedo. Tuxedo reared up on his hind legs as the child began to scream in fear.

Will and Mrs. Andrews started to run toward them. Will was vaguely aware of footsteps behind them. He climbed into the paddock and immediately got between Emma and Tuxedo so Mrs. Andrews could grab her child, who was now crying hysterically.

"Get her out of here," Will ordered Mrs. Andrews. Will stood very still and began to talk to Tuxedo in a soft voice. The horse stopped rearing and started to run. Will walked into the middle of the paddock and rummaged in his pockets. He found a carrot and took it out. He held it toward Tuxedo and continued to talk quietly. Tuxedo stopped and watched Will from a distance. Will didn't move. Slowly, very slowly, Tuxedo came toward him. Tuxedo took the carrot and then gave Will his neck to pat, as if to let Will know that he didn't blame him for what had happened.

"What a good horse you are," Will crooned. "I think we should put that kid in a stall instead of you."

"Good work, Will," Mrs. Johnson said very seriously as she came over. "I knew you had it in you. I'm going back to the barn to make sure Mrs. Andrews leaves, but, first, I want you to say hello to someone."

Will turned around.

"Hi, Will."

His father stood outside the paddock.

"You must be very proud of your son, Mr. Bradford. I certainly am. I will leave you both now. Nice to meet you, especially on this day when you were able to see what your son is capable of doing."

As she walked away, Will said, "Dad, what are you doing here?"

"I can't make it on the 23rd, so I decided to stop by and see you at work, your work. Will, you were incredible. Weren't you afraid? That big horse and that little girl . . ."

"It all happened so fast, I didn't have time to be afraid. All I knew was I had to calm Tuxedo down and get Emma out. Dad, look at your shoes."

They both looked down. Mr. Bradford's shoes were oozing mud.

"I guess I shouldn't have worn loafers to a stable. I wasn't thinking; I just wanted to see you."

"Why?"

"Believe it or not, Will, I love you. I know I haven't been a good father, but I want to try to make it up to you. Please help me learn how."

Looking at his father's face, Will suddenly felt as if he was the father and his father, tears in his eyes, was the child. Will looked away. He had never seen his father cry.

"I'm sorry, Will. I'm not asking you to forgive me, but I am asking you to give me a second chance. I made a lot of mistakes."

Will didn't answer. He thought about mistakes. Did he make a mistake when he started the fight with Jack? He didn't think so. Did he make a mistake when he followed Edward to hunt for Union soldiers? Probably. Did the Union Army make a mistake at Manassas when it sent untrained soldiers out to fight? Yeah. And what about all those spectators who came out to watch? That sure was a mistake. Then there was Pickett's Charge at Gettysburg. Maybe that was another mistake. And the soldier who accidentally shot and killed Stonewall Jackson . . . a giant mistake.

Will looked up at his father. "Hey, Dad," Will answered. "We all make mistakes."

His father grabbed him in a big bear hug, whispered, "Thank you." He slapped him on the back and said, "How about going out to lunch?"

"Well," Will answered doubtfully, "I usually go with Cal."

"Bring him along. I'd like to meet your friends, all your friends. How about the Mitchells next time?"

Will smiled. "Let's start with Cal. The Mitchells are away, far away."

Chapter 18

The summer days just seemed to fly by and Will was happy at the stable. He formed a bond with Tuxedo that almost made him forget Peaches. Well, not quite, but almost. "That was another lifetime ago," he thought one evening, "And now I live here. Still, I can't help wondering how things are going in Winchester."

Will shook his head and laughed at himself. "What am I saying? I know how things went. Badly."

He decided to make an early night of it, and climbed into bed. Within minutes, or so it seemed, he was back in Winchester again.

Will made his way through the streets to the familiar house on Loudoun Street and stared. There were bullet holes in the walls and the porch was sagging. The steps needed repair and the windows were all shuttered. It wasn't the house he knew; it was what his grandmother would have called a poor relation.

"Will. Is that you?"

He turned and saw Jane standing in front of him. She looked older, but probably so did he. She opened the door and entered the house, motioning for him to follow.

"Why are you wearing that uniform? Is it one of ours? I cannot imagine that we have any shiny buttons left anymore."

Will looked down at the brass buttons on his cadet uniform. One was missing and one was literally hanging from a thread. The uniform itself was torn and looked as if it had seen better days. "I am or, rather, I was a cadet."

"A cadet?"

"At The Institute, the Virginia Military Institute over in Lexington. We fought a battle in New Market. It was my first battle and some of my friends died. But we won."

"We heard about that battle. You must be proud of yourself. But we also heard that the cadets were furloughed back in June after that awful Union General David Hunter attacked The Institute and burned many of the buildings."

"I didn't know about that."

"Yes. The barracks were heavily damaged and the library was looted."

"But I thought I'd be going back there."

"There is little left to go back to right now; the Federals made sure of that."

Will tried to digest this. "I see so many wounded men. What's going on here now?"

"Grant made a new army and called it the Army of the Shenandoah. He put Phil Sheridan in charge and he told him to follow our Jubal Early to the death. So that's what we're all seeing: lots of death."

Will digested this, and then said, "How is Edward? Do you ever hear from him?"

"Don't you know anything," Benjamin called out as he came into the room. He was taller than Will remembered, almost as tall as Will himself. "Edward came one night when it was dark and we visited. He has a beard now. It's a small beard, but he likes it. Then he had to go back. He said he is giving hell to the Union. That's what he said, I didn't say it."

"You may not have said it, but you sure like repeating it," Jane said in exasperation.

"No, I don't. I'm just telling Will. And Edward and the rest of the band he's with gave you know what to the Federals. They took lots of supplies from their wagons and they really made them angry and gave them . . . ."

"Benjamin, stop it. Will doesn't need to hear that again."

"Yes, he does! Edward is now going to give hell to Sheridan."

413

"Benjamin, I am going to . . . " began Jane when Will interrupted quickly, "Where's your mother?"

"At the hospital, either the Taylor Hotel or the Union Hotel. She's always taking care of one soldier or another."

"And who is taking care of her?"

Just then, the door opened and Mrs. Mitchell came inside. She looked tired, but her eyes lit up when she saw Will. "Will, dear, you have come home."

Will's heart melted. "You're right. I came back to my Winchester home. I have missed you all."

Immediately he was engulfed in Mrs. Mitchell's arms. "Thank God you are safe. Now, we have to get you out of that tattered, dirty uniform and into clean clothes. We still have some of Edward's clothes. Go upstairs and change."

Will changed into Edward's clothes, rolling up the sleeves and pant legs as he did years ago when they had washed themselves with tomatoes after being skunked. "Edward and I were kids then," he thought. "Hard to believe it was only three years ago."

"What are you doing up there, you slowpoke," called out Benjamin.

"Benjamin!"

Will came downstairs laughing. "At least some things stay the same. Tell me, what do you hear from Tom and Robs," Will asked, almost afraid to hear the answer.

"As far as we know, they are fine. They are with General Lee somewhere near Petersburg. Mail, if we get it at all, is very slow and there are so many rumors that it's hard to know what to believe. But Edward came home to visit a few weeks ago and he looked wonderful."

"I told Will that already," called out Benjamin, "and I told him that Edward told us that he is giving hell to the Union."

"That's enough, Benjamin. Apparently, those words were the highlight of Edward's visit for Benjamin." Suddenly, she added self-consciously, "It is hard to keep tidy doing the work that I do." She removed her bonnet and smoothed down her hair. "I never would have imagined that I could get used to the suffering I see."

"It's not the suffering we get used to, Mamma; it's the healing. And some of them do heal," Jane said.

"Many of them, dear, and we must remember that. Jane has become a very good nurse, Will. She really has a gift."

"I'm not sure it's a gift; sometimes I think it's a curse. But seeing the faces of the soldiers, helping them feel cared for and safe makes it worthwhile. They want to live and I want to help them."

Her mother just nodded, then turned to Will. "Of course you will stay with us, Will."

Will smiled with relief and said, "Thank you," then added, "I've been worried about all of you here. How is everyone?"

"I don't know. Gettysburg was very hard. We lost too much of our family there."

"I didn't know. I am sorry."

Will couldn't think of anything else to say. He thought about Joanna and her family and Charles and Uncle John. "It's a terrible war."

Jane shook her head. "I know. Some people say that the war started because of slavery; others blame secession. Then still others blame Lincoln. Then there's state's rights and the sanctity of the Union and who knows what else and what does it matter anyway? We're in the middle of a cruel war which just won't end."

"I'm hungry," said Benjamin. "When is dinner?"

"Soon," answered Mrs. Mitchell. "Go and pick what you can from our meager garden and there are a few potatoes down in the cellar that the soldiers missed. Bring them upstairs as well."

"I'm not hungry," began Will, reluctant to take their food since they had so little.

"Yes, you are. Everyone is hungry, but we do the best we can. Do you know I heard that coffee is now $16 a pound and flour is $150 a barrel in Richmond? When this war is finally over and we somehow have money again, I am going to have pancakes and coffee all day long."

"Me too," said Benjamin. "I am going to have 14 pancakes, maybe 20 pancakes, maybe even 100 pancakes!"

"You do that, Son. But right now go and see what you can find in the garden."

It was a quiet day. Will was grateful to be with the Mitchells and wanted to help them in any way possible.

"Let me repair the steps," he suggested. "While you and Jane are out nursing, Benjamin and I will work on these rotting steps."

"I'd rather be fighting," grumbled Benjamin.

"Easy to say if you haven't been in a battle."

"But I want to be in one. I'm almost ten already."

Will decided not to respond to that. "Come on, Benjamin, someone's going to get hurt on these steps."

"They'll get more hurt from a Minie ball."

"Yeah, well, I can't do anything about that. At least this I can fix. Maybe."

"Listen to Will," Mrs. Mitchell said. "Jane and I are going off to the hospital now."

"Let's find some lumber, Benjamin."

Just then, neighbor Joey appeared.

"Whatcha doing?"

"Hey, Joey, come and help us."

It took them most of the afternoon, but they did the job. When they finished, Benjamin and Joey started to jump up and down on the steps. "See, they're strong now!"

"Well, this is my first time doing carpentry, so let's not test it too vigorously."

The boys paid no attention and went on jumping. "I'm jumping on a Yankee," called out Benjamin. "He killed Joseph."

"I'm jumping on one too," Joey sang out. "This one killed Uncle Tommy."

Will walked away.

Everyone was tired at suppertime and ate without enthusiasm.

"I remember all the food we had at Willows," Benjamin said. "One day I'm going back to kick all those Yankees out of my home. Just like Edward tried to do, except I'll do it right."

"Well," interrupted his mother, "Right now we're here and thankful for what we have received."

Very early in the morning, Will awakened to the sound of cannonading. He stumbled out of bed and gingerly pried the shutter open. Artillery wagons and supply wagons and soldiers rumbled by. "Wait a minute," he thought. "Didn't I see all this before?"

"Wake up, Will, wake up."

I remember this for sure. "I'm coming, Benjamin."

The cannonading continued and the sounds of musketry seemed to get louder.

"From the sound," Will said, "I think they're very close by, maybe not even a mile away."

"This is the third battle in Winchester," Jane shouted over the noise. "Why can't they just leave us alone?"

She put on her bonnet and cape. "Where are you going," Will asked.

"I am going out to help."

"I will come with you."

"What can you do?"

"Anything that you tell me to do."

Running through bursting shells, they looked for soldiers to treat. Jane led the way to the hospital, stopping to make sure that those lying about were dead and not in need of care. Will followed her lead. They worked tirelessly in the hospital.

"Take a rest," one of the surgeons said.

"Can't. There's no rest for the wounded."

Fighting raged until nightfall when General Early's defeated army came marching through Winchester. Now there were even more wounded and they littered the streets, as Winchester itself once again became one giant hospital, with hotels, churches and homes opening their doors to the wounded.

* * *

"I am so tired," Will said as he sat with Jane and Benjamin in the parlor. "It's been three days of non-stop nursing. Then we come home and take care of the wounded we have staying here. I need a long, hot shower."

"What? Rain showers aren't hot," asked Benjamin.

"I was talking about a different kind of shower . . . it makes you clean. And makes your muscles feel better."

Jane gave a wan smile. "Like hot springs, only you climb down into springs. Our Grandmother went to one for her health years ago, before the War."

Jane continued, "Sometimes I don't know that we'll ever get clean again. Not that Benjamin would mind skipping baths . . . ."

Benjamin was bored with talking about cleanliness. "We didn't give them hell," Benjamin said sadly. "They gave us hell."

No one had the energy to criticize him. Three days later there was another battle at Fishers Hill, and Early once again retreated.

"What happened," Benjamin asked. "Why did we lose?"

"Because we have fewer cannons, fewer artillerymen and hardly any horses with life in them anymore," answered Jane.

"Why?"

"Because the North has more of everything. Will warned us about that once, remember?"

"Will, how did you know that," Benjamin asked.

My history books? Can't say that. "I've spent time in the North and I learned about their economy. They had, I mean they have, many immigrants coming in from foreign countries, which gives them many more men. Then they have more industry and loads more money than the South has."

"You were in the North? When," asked Benjamin, momentarily diverted.

"A long time ago, a very long time ago when I was young."

"You're young now."

"No," Jane answered, "he's not. After all this, none of us are young."

"I am."

"Well, Benjamin, I guess you still are. Come on, let's fix supper before Mamma comes home. She stays at the hospital later than anyone else I know. I am going to roast some of those apples she thought she was hiding. If we can find some vegetables to go with it, we will have a fine supper."

Benjamin frowned. "I want chicken or meat."

"We're saving the chickens for their eggs and there is no meat anywhere. Come on now, you like roasted apples. I know you do."

Will wished he could bring them some of the food they had in his pantry at home.

He walked outside and picked a few vegetables that had somehow managed to survive. There was a chill in the air and Will hurried. It was September 27th and the nights were getting colder now.

Mrs. Mitchell stopped by the garden on her way into the house. "Will, please come in as soon as you pick the vegetables."

He looked up. Mrs. Mitchell was very pale and her hands were trembling. He gathered the remaining vegetables and followed her inside. "Have you fed our patients, Jane?"

"I have, Mamma. We are lucky that Merry still gives some milk and that the Yankees have not stolen her. I heated the milk up by the fire and I mixed in cooked potatoes for them. Depending upon what vegetables Will gathers, I will make a soup for tomorrow."

"You have done well."

Jane scrutinized her mother and did not like what she saw. "Is anything wrong, Mamma? You don't look well."

"I have heard something that is so terrible, it must be unbelievable, yet I very much fear that it is true."

Amid shouts of "What, what's happened," Mrs. Mitchell simply said, "They are burning the Valley."

"What do you mean? Who is burning what in the Valley?"

"Barns and haystacks and cattle and sheep and fowl all are systematically being destroyed. A plague of locusts have descended upon us; only, this time, it was a plague sent not from God, but from General Sheridan and his men."

Mrs. Mitchell picked up the family Bible and read, " . . . the land was darkened . . . and there remained not any green thing, either tree or herb of the field . . . "

She closed the Bible and cradled it against her body. "This is what is happening now. The whole Valley is being ravaged by fire and soon there will be nothing left that grows."

"How do you know this?"

"I heard it from our soldiers and from their soldiers. You know how quickly news flies around the Valley. I also heard it from Mr. Easton who heard it from his son. His son lost both his legs in the War and had to lie helpless in his home as his farm was burned to the ground around him."

"Mamma, please sit down," Jane said, ushering her mother to a chair. "Will, do you know anything about this?"

Will did. He had read all about the fires in the Valley. Forever after it was called The Burning. Grant wanted the Valley destroyed, " . . . so that crows flying over it . . . will have to carry their provender with them."

"But, what exactly is burning," cried out Jane as she repeated her earlier question.

"The Valley," answered Will.

"What? The whole Valley?"

"No. Just everything that allows the people to survive. All the grain, all the barns, all the livestock, all the mills are being burned. Grant wants to destroy everything in the Shenandoah Valley because he believes that the Valley is the heartland of the Confederacy. Later historians will debate this, but most Valley people will remember the thirteen days when their livelihood was slaughtered and destroyed right in front of them."

"Thirteen days?"

"Yes, it went on for thirteen days."

"Will, you are scaring me," cried out Jane. "What are you talking about? Who are these historians and how could you possibly know them?"

"Ignore me, Jane. I am upset and babbling nonsense."

There was a knock on the door. Mrs. Mitchell opened it and saw a wide-eyed Joey standing with his mother who was frantically waving her hands.

"What's wrong?"

"They're burning our fields. Robert came from our farm outside Winchester to tell us that the Yankees set fire to the barn. And they're killing the sheep, all of them."

"Oh, no. All your hard work for nothing," groaned Mrs. Mitchell.

"What can we do? I complained to an officer here and he laughed. He said we started this war so we deserved anything we got."

"Can we see anything if we go outside," Benjamin asked.

"The fires are too far away," Will answered, but he thought he could smell the smoke. No one else said anything, so perhaps it was all in his imagination.

"Mamma, you don't look like yourself. Why don't we sit down and have supper."

"Supper? Dear Jane, I feel no hunger; I feel numb. It is all too much to bear."

"Will they burn Willows," Benjamin asked.

Will shook his head. "I doubt it. If Willows is still occupied by Yankees, they probably want to preserve it for themselves."

The days that followed were very hard. Will and the family worked tirelessly at the hospitals, and were given food for themselves and their patients by a kind Union officer.

"Why does he give us food," whispered Benjamin.

"Why do we take care of his soldiers? It's because we are human beings despite this dreadful War," Mrs. Mitchell told her son. "Even in the midst of destruction, there can be some kindness. There has to be."

As the days went by, the wounded soldiers began to leave. Some were moved to hospitals when they had space, or, if the men were furloughed due to their injuries, they tried to make their way home.

September moved into October and on the 13th day the burning finally ended. That night after supper, there was a knock on the door. It was a man Will did not recognize.

"Mr. Moore," Mrs. Mitchell said. "How nice to see you. Please come inside."

"Mrs. Mitchell, I came to bring you news before it leaks out all over Winchester. I thought you would like to know."

"Is Robs or Tom . . . "

"No, my dear Mrs. Mitchell, it does not concern them. In fact, it might not be anyone you even know."

"I don't understand."

"It's about Big Red's band of men. It appears that they captured a wagon train and made off with a great deal of supplies. Some of the men were taken by Union soldiers but Big Red got away."

Mrs. Mitchell moaned. "And where is Edward?"

"I have no idea if Edward was among those who were captured or not."

"How many were captured?"

"Six or eight, but that's not the worst part."

Mrs. Mitchell took a deep breath and said, "Get on with it, Mr. Moore. Tell me what is happening."

"The Union wants to hang these men in order to show what they will do to partisans who raid Union wagons and make off with their supplies."

Jane put her arm around her mother. "What can we do?"

"I don't think there is much anyone can do, but I did want to make sure you heard it from me rather than from the people who make up rumors."

"Thank you for coming to tell me, Mr. Moore," said Mrs. Mitchell as she rose. "Please give my regards to Mrs. Moore."

"I will. And, let us hope for the best. I will pray for you."

When he left, Mrs. Mitchell excused herself. She came back with a traveling bag and a look of determination that the children knew very well. "I am going to find Big Red's camp and make sure that Edward is safe."

"What if he's not safe," Benjamin asked.

"Well, then, I need to know that too."

Will frowned, and then came to a decision. "I will take you and the children. I am sixteen years old now and I have fought in a battle."

"I am not a child," Jane said mechanically.

Will ignored her. "Mrs. Mitchell, I doubt that Big Red's camp still exists, but I do know where it is and I can take you there. It's probably time for all of us to leave the Valley anyway."

"Why?"

"Things are going to get worse."

"How much worse can they get," Jane asked bitterly.

"When will we go," asked Benjamin, a note of excitement creeping into his voice. "Can we take Joey with us?"

"No, we can't take Joey. Joey needs to stay with his family."

"If we can't stay at Big Red's Camp, where would we go after we left there," Benjamin asked again.

Everyone was quiet, trying tried to figure out the best place to go.

"Appomattox," Mrs. Mitchell cried out suddenly. "I have cousins there. I have cousins in Richmond as well, but I cannot imagine that Richmond is any safer than the Valley."

Will thought quickly. Richmond was the Confederate capital and way back in 1861 when the war began, Union soldiers wanted nothing more than to capture Richmond. 'On To Richmond' was the popular slogan. That never changed and they still wanted Richmond. "No, Richmond is not safe. But Appomattox . . . I don't know."

"Why not? I know they supplied a lot of men for the Confederate Army, but Cousin Louise writes that it is peaceful there. Nothing much happens in Appomattox."

Nothing but the Surrender in 1865. "I don't know. I think Appomattox is too far away and the trip will be too long. Where else can we go?"

"How about Staunton," Jane suggested. "We can stay with Aunt Mary and Cousin Sue."

"You just want to see Cousin Sue," Benjamin said, making a face.

"Well, I do want to see her, but Staunton is closer than Appomattox. We can go up the Valley on the Pike."

Mrs. Mitchell looked thoughtful. "Maybe Jane is right. I know my husband's family will welcome us."

"By the way, I have been meaning to ask this question ever since I first came here."

"Yes, Will, what is it?"

"Why do you say 'up the Valley' when you go south and 'down the Valley' when you go north? It is usually the other way around."

"I have no idea. That's just how it is," answered Mrs. Mitchell, momentarily distracted.

"All right then, let's get ready for our trip. Forward, march," Will said as Benjamin began marching around the room.

Mrs. Mitchell stood up. "I don't want to put the children in danger."

"We are in danger already, Mamma, and if what Will says is true — and what he says is usually true although I don't fully understand why — then we really should go."

"When?"

430

Will thought for a moment. "As soon as possible. We have to take some provisions with us."

Jane shook her head. "What provisions? We have nothing."

"That's not entirely true," answered Mrs. Mitchell. "I hid some apples in the attic and . . ."

"We ate the apples," Benjamin wailed.

"I saw what you took and you did not take all of them. I hide things very well. To continue, we still have more potatoes buried downstairs and we can gather whatever we have in the garden and pantry. We have to remember to bring along some warm clothes because late September nights can get cold. And we must take some medical supplies. Jane, you'll put the quinine somewhere inside your skirt."

"Why?"

"So no one will steal it from us. I'll take my kettle and . . ."

"The idea, Mrs. Mitchell," Will said gently, "is to take as little as possible."

"Well, I'm not taking the silver. It's still here in the yard where I buried it back in 1861."

"I'm taking my scrapbooks," Jane said.

"And I'll take Betty."

"We are not taking a cat on a wagon."

"What will happen to her," Benjamin cried out. "The Yankees will kill her."

"No, they won't," Will answered. "They didn't kill animals."

"They killed Joey's sheep."

"They killed livestock; that's different."

"How do you know they won't kill Betty?"

"I just know." Will began thinking about what they were about to do. When they left Winchester, the Mitchells would have no home anymore and they were going to be traveling from place to place. Since he was casting his lot in with them, that would make them all refugees. He began to think about being a refugee.

"How do you know, Will," Benjamin repeated.

"Will is daydreaming," said Jane with a roll of her eyes. "Will, pay attention!"

Will laughed and then laughed harder. Even here in the Shenandoah Valley in 1864, he was accused of daydreaming.

"Why are you laughing, Will," asked Benjamin.

"Sometimes you just have to laugh," Will answered.

Mrs. Mitchell looked thoughtful. "Maybe we should spend the first night with Aunt Cornelia, the second night with Mrs. Pritchard, the third night with Mrs.

Tompkins, then the next day we will be ready to travel on to Staunton."

"That's right," thought Will. "This will be a long trip, and it will take a lot longer than it would on horseback. I once read that 10 miles was a day's travel in a wagon."

"To continue," Mrs. Mitchell went on, "I hope Mrs. Pritchard's house is not completely taken over by Yankee soldiers. The last letter I received from her took over six weeks to get here and Mrs. Pritchard said she feared she would no longer be allowed to remain in her own home. She said there was a nice Union general, but he was leaving for somewhere else, and those who remained were barbaric."

Will silently agreed, and suddenly remembered that he must still have the pass that nice general gave him. When he was asked to show it, the soldier did not take it away from him. Now, where did he put it? It had to be somewhere in the house.

"I have something that is as valuable as food, well, almost anyway," said Will. "I have a pass."

"What's that," asked Benjamin.

"It's a piece of paper that will allow us to travel without Union soldiers causing trouble for us."

"Where is it?"

"That's the problem. I can't remember where I put it, but I'm going to look right now."

He rummaged frantically through the dresser in his room, then remembered that when he was here with Charles in 1862, he had first slept in the front parlor. He searched that room but couldn't find the pass anywhere. Desperate, he called to Benjamin. "I need help. Crawl around on your hands and knees everywhere you can think of and find any papers you see and bring them to me."

Benjamin smiled. "I can do that. I'll crawl all over the house and find the pass."

"Go."

"Yes, sir, Captain Will."

True to his word, Benjamin crawled in and out of corners diligently. He had dust on his hands and a cobweb in his hair. "I am so embarrassed," Mrs. Mitchell moaned. "Who knew there was so much dirt in my home? Honestly, I do clean and dust."

After almost an hour, Benjamin called out, "Look at this. Is it the pass? Did I find it?"

Everyone rushed over. "Yes, Benjamin, it is," exulted Will. "You are a hero. Without this pass, our journey would be much more dangerous. Thank you."

Benjamin stood tall as he handed the precious pass over to Will. "Is this all it is? I've seen this in the corner before. I just didn't know that it was anything important."

Mrs. Mitchell shook her head. "So much for my cleaning. Benjamin, what else is stuck in our corners?"

"Dust."

Will joined in the laughter. "All right, tomorrow we'll start our trip and go up the Valley."

"Yay," called out Benjamin.

"Should be down the Valley," Will muttered to himself, "not up."

Chapter 19

They were finally on the road. It was not easy for Will to persuade Mrs. Mitchell to leave behind many of her beloved items, but when the wagon overflowed, even she recognized that there was no choice. Jane was upset about leaving the piano because she loved to play. It was not an issue, however, since it was very clear that there simply was no room for a piano in a wagon, especially this wagon.

Joey's family, of course, saw them packing up the wagon and came over to see them off. They volunteered to look after Betty and milk the cow while the Mitchells were gone.

Benjamin finally said goodbye to his cat, "Catch all the mice you can, Betty, and stay away from Yankees."

"If any Yankee tries to get Betty," Joey said firmly, "I'll protect her!"

No one was happy to leave Winchester, and no one was in a good mood as the wagon started.

Jane looked appraisingly at Will. "I guess you're our escort now. You seem to be the best we can do."

"What do you mean, escort?"

"Surely you remember that ladies were not permitted to travel without a male escort before the war. Now that there are no men left, we may have to travel alone. Someone might say that we're lucky to have you."

"You have me too," Benjamin cried out.

"Again, how lucky we are."

Will just looked at her. "I am confident that I can do whatever it is the men in your family did to protect you."

"They did nothing, and I am equally confident you can do the same."

"Well, someone is very cranky today."

"Why shouldn't I be cranky? Here I am in a wagon leaving behind everything I ever knew to see family I don't want to see and . . ."

"I thought you liked your Cousin Sue."

"She's better than my Aunties."

"I would guess that so am I?"

Jane began to laugh. "All right, Will, I'll give you that."

Will joined in laughing. "Why are you and Will laughing," asked Benjamin. "What's so funny?"

"You."

"No, I'm not."

"Yes, you are."

They traveled hard. The once-luscious Valley was ravaged. Buildings lay in ruins. Will looked up at the Blue Ridge Mountains still standing tall and unaffected by the brutality in the valley below and felt a strong urge to turn the wagon toward them and disappear in their comforting shadows.

"Look at that gristmill all torn up."

"How about those corncribs over there?"

"It's all terrible," cried Jane. "And it's too much."

Mrs. Mitchell brought out the family Bible. "Let me read from Jeremiah. It is very appropriate for today, wouldn't you say?"

> *"For I will bring evil from the north,*
> *And a great destruction.*
> *A lion is gone up from his thicket,*
> *And a destroyer of nations*
> *Is set out, gone forth from his place;*
> *To make thy land desolate . . . "*

Will looked around. It certainly was desolate. He remembered reading that Sheridan had boasted about destroying 2,000 barns, 70 mills and taking over 4,000 head of livestock. Will got angry. "Some feat! Stealing and destroying from innocent women and children with all their men off in the army. Bully bastards!"

"Will," admonished Mrs. Mitchell. "That's enough. It is what it is and we must remain strong." Then she leaned over to him and whispered, "You're right, of course."

"Will," cried out Benjamin, "Look at all those legs."

It was a gross sight. Off to the side of the road was a large collection of legs.

"There must have been a field hospital around here," Jane said. "We had stacks of limbs outside our hospitals, too."

"Do you think those soldiers are alive now," Benjamin asked.

"Hard to know," Will answered and, then, to everyone's surprise, most of all his, he began to sing.

"Where have all the soldiers gone,
Long time passing
Where have all the soldiers gone?
Long time ago.

"Where have all the soldiers gone?
Gone to graveyards, everyone
Oh, when will they ever learn?
Oh, when will they ever learn?"

"Will, how do you know that song," Mrs. Mitchell asked. "I never heard it. Was it written by Stephen Foster? I thought I knew all his songs."

"No, it was written by a man named Pete Seeger. He always wanted the world to be at peace. My grandfather used to sing it to us when we were children."

"Sounds like we could use your Mr. Seeger around here right now," she said.

"We sure could."

"Will," Mrs. Mitchell continued gently, "You never speak much about your family. You must miss them."

Will choked up and couldn't answer. He wasn't sure whether it was the sadness he felt when he looked around the broken Valley, or the rhythm of the slow-moving wagon, or simply Mrs. Mitchell's kindness. He swallowed, took a deep breath and said, "Yes, I do."

"Do you think, perhaps, you should go back home now?"

"In the middle of all this? How can I?"

"I like to think one can always go home."

"Not to disagree, Mrs. Mitchell, but I don't know if you will ever be able to go back home again. After the war, other people may take over and who knows what they will do."

"That is true, Will," agreed Mrs. Mitchell, "but home is also in your heart and that no one can ever take from you."

"But my heart is in two different places. It's here and it's home."

"The heart does not tear. It expands. Just as you can love more than one person, you can love more than one place. Why don't you tell me about your home?"

Will started to talk and Jane and Benjamin quieted and began to listen.

"My home is in Litchfield, Connecticut, but it wasn't always in Litchfield. We used to live in New York, not New York City, but in Harrison, a small town. I was happy there. Then my father left us and my mother got a job teaching in Litchfield so we had to move. I don't think it was so bad for my sister, but for me . . . it was terrible. So I came here and, in a funny way, I grew up. At least I think I did. Edward taught me a lot."

"Edward?" Jane sounded surprised.

"Yes. He taught me to stand up for myself. It's funny, but when you know how to stand up for yourself, you usually don't have to."

"So, Will, what about your family?" Mrs. Mitchell would not be sidetracked.

"I miss them, but I kind of stopped missing my father a while ago. He moved all the way to New Hampshire and wasn't part of my life anymore. Later, he wanted to see me, but then I didn't want to see him."

"Did you, though?"

"Yes, Mrs. Mitchell, I did."

"And . . ."

"And it was all right, but not like it was before he left."

"You know, William," began Mrs. Mitchell, "and I am using your full name because you are a man now, you know that people do all sorts of things that we cannot possibly understand." She looked at Will's confused face. "Can you forgive your father? It will be better for your family and, most of all, it will be better for you."

"I already did. He came to see me at the stable where I was working and he saw me do something brave. I rescued a little girl from an out-of-control horse, and that made him proud of me. He apologized and said he was sorry that he hurt me. But, he can't undo leaving us."

"No, that he cannot do. What he can do, dear, is begin to be your father once again."

Will raised his arm and waved it around. "Can you ever forgive the Yankees for all this?"

"The Yankees are not trying to make amends. Your father is. He is trying to see you now. You know, Will, when it will be our time to be judged, we will hope for mercy and forgiveness. If we cannot forgive others, how can we expect forgiveness for ourselves?"

"I think that's too complicated for me, Mrs. Mitchell, but, after my father came to see me, things got better between us."

They rode on for a little while and suddenly Benjamin said angrily, "You are nothing but a Yankee, Will. And I hate Yankees."

Will was quiet, then answered, "I hate these Yankees, too. I hate the men who burned the barns and killed the sheep. But I don't hate all Yankees. And I don't hate all Confederates. I just hate the bad ones."

Day slipped into evening and it got chilly as nights in autumn do. When they reached Aunt Cornelia's house, Benjamin was half asleep and Jane had thrown a blanket on top of him. They stopped the wagon and Will turned to his friends. "I won't come inside. I'm not sure that your relatives would welcome a Yankee."

Jane rolled her eyes in exasperation. "Stop being dramatic and come on in with us. You are family — our Northern family, God help us."

"Jane," her mother said.

"Sorry."

"Will," asked Benjamin sleepily, "Who do you want to win this war? Them or us?"

"Well, that's a hard question. You know what I really want? I want everyone to just go on home. Let's all say we won, and call it a draw."

"A draw?"

"Oh, never mind."

Mrs. Mitchell and Jane visited with their relatives, while Benjamin and Will went to bed. Everyone was up early and breakfast was served, so the Mitchells and Will would be able to get on the road quickly. Mrs. Mitchell was impatient to find Edward, and Will just wanted to get where they were going.

At the same time as the Mitchells and Will were having their breakfast, Union General Philip Sheridan was in Winchester, having his breakfast. He had just returned from a strategy meeting in Washington and was planning to join his troops camped near Cedar Creek. What Sheridan did not know was that Confederate General Jubal Early was also camped close to Cedar Creek, but even if he had known, he would not have imagined that Early had any fight left in him, not after losing that last battle in Winchester.

Sheridan underestimated Early. While General Sheridan was having his breakfast, Jubal Early was leading his men on a little-known path toward the Union soldiers. It was five o'clock in the morning when the Confederates silently positioned themselves and suddenly charged, catching the Army of the Shenandoah totally by surprise. The fog was so thick that it looked as if phantom soldiers were coming out of the mist to attack. But these were no ghosts. These were hungry men out for victory.

When General Sheridan finished his breakfast, he went outside and saddled his black horse, Rienzi. He thought he may have heard the sounds of artillery somewhere south, but believed that was unlikely.

After thanking the family for their hospitality, the Mitchells and Will got back into the wagon and continued their journey on the Valley Pike. They also thought that they heard the sound of firing, but shrugged it off since, as Jane said, "There are guns everywhere these days."

"You know, Mamma, it really sounds like another battle," Benjamin said as the wagon rolled on, slowly traveling up the Valley Pike. "Should we keep going?"

"Of course we should. It's probably a little skirmish somewhere. After all, General Early left when the Yankees took over Winchester again so who could be fighting?"

Suddenly they saw wagons, ambulances, soldiers, and even horses, running toward them. "There are hundreds of Union soldiers coming and they're all running north. What should we do," cried out Jane.

"Keep going," answered Will.

They watched the infantry run while more horses came galloping wildly. Will wondered what could have happened. Soon they came upon men who had stopped running and were almost strolling. Will even thought some of them were just hanging out.

He suddenly remembered reading that Early's small band of Confederates drove the Army of the Shenandoah away. Thousands of Union men ran toward Winchester while Early's men captured their camps and feasted on their food. Now Will was watching them run right in front of his eyes!

Meanwhile, Sheridan was riding toward Cedar Creek. He quickened his pace when he saw clusters of soldiers ambling along, heading back toward him. The General was aghast. Could this be his army, these disorganized cowards who were leaving Cedar Creek? Never. But it was his army and they were retreating!

General Sheridan took off his hat and pointed it toward his men and shouted. "If you love your country, come up to the front! . . . There's lots of fight in you men yet! Come up, God damn you! Come up!"

All over the Pike, he rode Rienzi and cheered on his men. When they saw their own General Sheridan galloping on his tireless horse, shouting for them to turn around, these men did just that; they turned around and went back to Cedar Creek. And they cheered their General.

Will watched dumbstruck. It was quite a sight! To see General Sheridan, his dark face contorted with anger and exasperation and something else that Will recognized: Fight. The General was able to get all these men to turn around and go back to fight. That was awesome!

Suddenly, one of Sheridan's staff officers came over to them. "What are you doing here?"

"We are heading up the Pike to Staunton," answered Will.

"No, you're not. Do you think we are going to let a bunch of Rebels come that close to Cedar Creek? Maybe you're spies for Jubal Early. I could arrest you all."

"We are not spies," Will answered stoutly, remembering when one of General Sedgwick's men asked him that very same question.

"Oh, yeah? Prove it."

Will reached down into his boot and took out his pass. "Here, look at this." The Mitchells all stayed quiet.

The soldier examined the pass. "General Pellam is no longer here. He left the Valley months ago. And how do I know this is his signature anyway?"

"It is his signature."

"Why would a Union general give a pass to a Rebel boy?"

"First of all, I am not a child! Second of all, I am from Litchfield, Connecticut and I marched with General John Sedgwick to Gettysburg."

"He's dead."

"What? Uncle John is dead? No, he can't be. You are just saying that and I won't let you." Will rose as if to fight, when the soldier, more kindly now, said, "I'm sorry, lad. I did not know you were with him. Whoever fought with Uncle John loved him and his death was a great loss — not only for his men, but also for the entire Union. His Sixth Corp is now right here at Cedar Creek."

"They ran? I don't believe it."

"No, they didn't run. No one who served with Uncle John would run. If they did, they would be afraid that he'd come back down from Heaven and yell at them. The Sixth Corps is still here and they'll fight hard, don't you worry."

"How did Uncle John die?"

"He was hit by a Confederate sharpshooter at a skirmish at Spotsylvania Court House."

"When?"

"May 9th."

The same day I became a cadet. "I always thought I would see him again. He promised me that we would talk."

"If it's any consolation, he died closely supervising his troops. He was warned to stay away, but he refused. I guess he thought his men needed him."

"Sounds like Uncle John."

"We are turning all our men back to Cedar Creek and we'll get rid of Early and his men this time for sure. You know, it really is not safe to be traveling up the Pike right now, especially with two ladies and a little boy."

"I know, but we'll be careful."

"Suit yourself. Here is another pass, this one from me which may carry a little more weight than the pass from General Pellam, since he's not here anymore. Don't throw out General Pellam's pass, though. In this war, you never know what you'll need."

"Thank you."

"Any friend of Uncle John is a friend of mine. Take care and Godspeed."

As he rode off, Jane turned to Will. "Well, you did it again."

"Did what?"

"Saved the day."

Will couldn't tell if Jane was being sarcastic or not.

"Is Will a hero," asked Benjamin.

Jane rolled her eyes.

"Hey, I'm only doing what anyone would do if they had a pass. Let's just get going," Will answered.

"Well, I think he's a hero," whispered Benjamin.

"That's a good thing to think," answered his mother.

They continued on the Valley Pike, going more slowly as Will tried to avoid both the Union troop activity and the potholes. It was a close question which was more dangerous.

"I remember what the Pike was like years ago," reminisced Jane. "It was the best road in the Valley, if not the whole of Virginia. Just look at it now."

Will looked and saw a road that was all broken up. Too many armies had worn it down and now there was little left to show that it had once been a paved road that wagons and carriages easily traveled on. "A big rut like that can take off a wheel," he said, pointing to what looked more like a pit in the road. Nobody disagreed.

They watched and listened as the soldiers swarmed around them. "I think they're running faster back to Cedar Creek than they ran away from Cedar Creek," called out Benjamin. "Why?"

"Because they caught Sheridan's fire," answered Will.

"Are they going to win?"

"Yes, Benjamin. Cedar Creek will be a Union victory. It would have been a Confederate victory if it wasn't for Sheridan's ride." Will pulled off the Pike and started driving the wagon toward Mrs. Pritchard's house. They pulled into the yard and Will was surprised to see no one there. In the past, Yankees lounged in the garden and there was always a Yankee or two close to the house.

"Where is everybody?"

"Well, I am here," said Mrs. Pritchard as she walked toward them. "I was at the back of the house, in the kitchen garden. I am so pleased to see you all. Please, forgive my attire and come inside."

Will looked around. "But, Mrs. Pritchard, where are the soldiers?"

"Those Yankees, you mean? They left a while ago, and I cannot say I miss them. Although, General Pellam was rather nice, even if he was a Yankee."

"Will's a Yankee," said Benjamin, "and we still like him."

Mrs. Pritchard smiled. "We do not talk about that, do we, dear?"

Benjamin looked confused. Mrs. Mitchell explained to him, "It might be dangerous for Will if Southerners know that he is a Yankee."

Mrs. Pritchard continued, "I am so happy to have you stay with us. I think you will enjoy my guests. Come on in."

As Will entered the house, he look around appreciatively. It was good to be back.

Mrs. Pritchard was talking, "Now I believe you know these gentlemen . . . "

"Edward," cried out Mrs. Mitchell, as Jane and Benjamin ran toward him.

"Hello, Will."

As he turned toward the voice, Will saw Big Red standing in front of him.

"What are you doing here," Will stammered.

"Visiting my mother."

"Your mother? Mrs. Pritchard is your mother?"

"That she is." Big Red smiled. "I am Jonathan Pritchard. My friends call me Jon."

"But . . . you never told us. "

"Of course not. I certainly did not want to put my mother in jeopardy. Remember when I told you that the names we went by were not our real names? It was a necessary fiction."

"But what about the Camp? Why aren't you and Edward there?"

"It was no longer safe," said Edward as he came over. "Thank you, Will, for taking care of my family."

"So, where are the rest of the men," stuttered Will. This was so confusing.

"We live with trusted friends and family now and we move around throughout Virginia. We all live separately so if something does happen to one of us, the rest of us are safe."

"We thought the Yankees were going to hang you," shouted Benjamin.

"They did hang some of our men, but Big Red negotiated a peace and now the hangings have stopped," Edward answered.

Everyone looked at Big Red with respect.

"What are you going to do now," asked Will.

"Besides eat supper?"

"Yes, besides that."

"We're going to do pretty much the same things we have been doing throughout the War. The real question, Will, is what are you going to do now?"

Chapter 20

"Look at all this food," cried out Benjamin as he approached the table at suppertime. "This is going to be the greatest supper I've had in . . . in . . . a hundred years! Where did you get it all?"

Jon smiled. "Little Brother, that's one question we cannot answer."

Benjamin's mouth dropped. "You mean you stole it?"

"No, Benjamin," said Edward. "We didn't steal it. We appropriated it as the spoils of war."

"I'm going to apopiate it too."

Everyone laughed.

"I'm going to have seconds of everything," Benjamin said with a big smile.

After supper, Edward stood up. "Will, come. You and Benjamin will share a room with me just like we did in the old days."

"I hope you aren't planning to sneak out of the house and kill any Yankees." As soon as he said the words, Will immediately regretted them.

"Not tonight. I hope to get some sleep in a nice bed with clean sheets and walls all around me."

"Are you complaining again," Big Red teased.

"Why would I complain? We just ate a roast and there's nothing better than that."

As everyone went to bed, Will found he couldn't sleep. He was worried. What was going to happen to him now?

I can go to Staunton with the Mitchells and wait for the war to end. But then what? The Confederacy lost. If Tom makes it home from the war, he'll run the farm again at Willows. But what about me? I'm not a farmer. What can I do?

Robs will . . . Here Will's imagination failed him. Robs cannot go back to West Point, because he fought against the U.S. government and they would consider him a traitor. He cannot be an officer in the Confederate Army, because there will be no Confederate Army after the war. Maybe he will work on the farm, too. That is, if the Mitchells are even allowed to return to Willows.

Edward could be arrested, I guess, and maybe Big Red too.

But what about me? What is going to happen to me?

The night got longer and longer and Will still couldn't sleep. Every noise disturbed him as he kept thinking about his problems. Suddenly Will heard the sound of a fiddle way off in the distance. It was playing "Dixie" but instead of the spirited fife and drum or regimental band version, this one was slow and haunting.

"I wish I was in Dixie, Hooray! Hooray!
In Dixie's Land I'll take my stand
To live and die in Dixie
Away, away, away down south in Dixie
Away, away, away down south in Dixie."

Will could almost hear the fiddle cry and he imagined the fiddler's yearning to be back home. But Will knew the fiddler wanted to go back home to the time when there was no war, no hunger and no killing fields. Will recognized that feeling. He, too, wanted to go back to another time. He didn't want Gettysburg. He didn't want New Market or Cedar Creek. And he didn't want to be here in the desolate Shenandoah Valley in 1864.

"I want to go home," he thought. "Edward can take care of Mrs. Mitchell and the children until Robs and Tom come home. I need to go back to Litchfield and my own family."

But he still couldn't sleep. The fiddle seemed to be getting louder so Will stood up, dressed and quietly crept out of the house. "Must be someone else who can't sleep. I'm going to see who that fiddler is and why he is playing "'Dixie'" in the middle of the night."

As Will followed the sound, he heard a group of voices somewhere a little off to the left behind the fiddler. They were softly singing "The Battle Cry of Freedom" but, again, like "Dixie," this version was sad and mournful. The men sang very slowly and with great feeling. There was a cry in their voices and Will couldn't tell how many men were singing together.

"The Union forever! Hurrah, boys, hurrah!
Down with the traitor, and up with the star;
While we rally round the flag, boys, rally
once again,
Shouting the Battle Cry of Freedom!"

"What can this mean," Will wondered. "How can they both be singing their songs while they are standing so close to one another? Why aren't they fighting?"

As Will moved forward, the voices started to move further away. He followed their sound and then, suddenly, the songs got louder and louder as men, Confederate and

457

Union, sang together. He saw waves of gray and blue uniforms standing and singing each other's songs.

"They crossed the River! I remember those letters William Bradford and the Union soldier wrote about crossing the Rappahannock River and shaking hands. These men must have crossed the River!"

Will watched in awe, then shook himself. "Wait a minute. Now where am I? There is no Rappahannock River here and this is not 1862."

He walked over to a soldier. "Excuse me," he began.

"Will, what are you doing here? Is my Mother all right?"

It was Tom Mitchell. "Yes, last time I saw her she was fine, and so were Edward, Jane and Benjamin. What are you doing here? What's going on?"

"I don't think I'm the one to ask. Robs will know. I'm just a lowly soldier, remember?"

"But . . . "

"Things are bad here, Will, very bad. We have no food. We were supposed to get rations but there was a mix-up or else the Federals captured the supplies, I don't know. We are close to starving and we've lost so many men that I don't remember who is alive and who is dead. I don't know why I'm still here, but I am."

"All these soldiers standing around . . . are they waiting for something?"

"There is a truce."

"A truce?"

"That's when . . . "

"I know what a truce is. That means the end is near."

"Is it?"

"Tom, what year is it?"

Tom looked at Will curiously. "It's 1865."

"April, right?"

Tom nodded.

Will walked through the lines of Confederate men, hungry, tired and ragged. He caught a glimpse of Robs through the crowd and was amazed to find him laughing with a Union soldier.

"Robs," he called out.

"Will," Robs answered, "What are you doing here?"

"I have no idea."

"Will, meet my old classmate, Franklin Hayes, from our West Point days. We roomed together."

Will took the man's hand in a daze. "You are friends?"

"Well, we were friends," laughed Robs. "Then we were enemies. Now, because of the truce, we are friends again."

"And when the truce is over," chimed in Franklin, "we will be enemies again."

Will looked at both of them. "I don't understand . . . . "

"That's war."

Will walked on. He found himself in the Union lines and there, almost in front of him was Charles. Will wondered what work he had found to do, since he was missing an arm.

"Will, it's good to see you. Heard Sheridan destroyed Winchester and the Valley. I'm sorry for Mrs. Mitchell, but that did help to end the war faster."

"It's not over yet."

"All but the signing," said Charles. "Remember how I mourned the loss of my arm? Now, I barely notice it. You can get used to anything, I think."

"Even this war?"

"There were days when I kind of thought we would be fighting forever, but now I see that even Robert E. Lee can't fight without men and resources. Stick around and you'll see this bloody war end."

"I can't. I have to go home."

"Don't we all?"

Will continued walking.

He came to a Confederate line and heard one of General Lee's subordinates advise the

General, "Don't surrender. Let's fight the Union Army guerrilla style."

General Lee's answer was strong and clear. He said no. He didn't want the country torn apart by guerrilla warfare.

"He wants what is best for his men ," thought Will in admiration. "Even now, when everything he fought for has been lost, he still doesn't want vengeance. He wants his men to be able to go home, plant their fields and start their lives all over again."

Will continued walking. It was midday now and Will looked around at the sea of soldiers waiting. Will knew what they were all waiting for, so he hurried on toward the small village that was called by the strange name, "Appomattox Court House."

The two generals, a tall man in gray and a shorter man in blue, met in the parlor of Wilmer McLean's home. It was April 9th, 1865.

General Robert E. Lee surrendered to General Ulysses S. Grant and the War ended.

Chapter 21

Now that the Army of Northern Virginia had surrendered, the soldiers wanted nothing more than to go home. It took a few days, but bands of tired and hungry men headed home through the April rains. Those who had horses rode; those who didn't, walked, and those who couldn't walk, tottered along as best as they could. All Will wanted was to go home, too, but he didn't know how, so he just followed along.

"Where is Tom," Will shouted. "And Robs? Joseph didn't make it, but they did. I saw them, but now I can't find them anywhere. And Charles, where is he? Maybe I'll meet him when I get back to Connecticut. And where is Mrs. Mitchell? Who is going to take care of her if her sons aren't around here? And Joanna and . . . "

His mother came running into Will's room as Rebecca cried out, "Mom, Dad, Will is speaking."

He opened his eyes, and there were both his parents leaning over him.

"Thank God," his mother said as she began to cry.

"Will, Will, please be all right," said his father and he, too, began to cry.

"Why are you here? Where is everyone? What happened to Robert E. Lee after he surrendered? Where did he go? And where are Tom and Robs?"

He looked around. He was lying on a bed in a small room.

"I knew it," shouted his mother. "It's that nasty Civil War again."

"It was nasty, Mom, very nasty."

A doctor leaned over to look at Will.

"I wish you were there in Gettysburg, Doctor. We needed you so much. I didn't know enough, and the doctors there knew even less. Do you know that one doctor wiped his knife on some kind of bloody apron and then went right to another patient?"

"Did he? Well, they didn't know anything about germs then," said the doctor.

"I know. When I first saw Charles, I used alcohol to clean his wound."

"You did the right thing. Where was that?"

"On the Valley Turnpike."

"I see. Well, why don't you rest now? We are going to step outside so you can sleep."

"Okay. I am very tired. I think the Surrender was harder than I realized."

Will fell asleep immediately and the doctor took his parents aside. "He seems to be hallucinating now. The blood tests we took showed nothing and that's a good thing. We have to wait for the MRI to be read."

"Doctor," Will's mother said urgently, "Will has been working in a stable for quite a while now. I don't know where he learned to ride, but Mrs. Johnson said he rode very well. She always insisted he wear a helmet, but I don't know if he was wearing one when he fell."

"He may or may not remember. Did anyone see him fall?"

"No. Apparently, he took one of the horses out on his break. Mrs. Johnson found him, called the ambulance, and they brought him here to this hospital."

"That was the right thing to do."

"Then there's the Civil War and some people called the Mitchells. He talks a lot about them. That's really all he's interested in."

"It's more than an interest," interrupted Rebecca. "He's like a crazy person when he gets going on the War. Remember when he told us he was at someplace called Willows in Virginia?"

"We could call a psychiatry consult now that he is awake. I'll talk to Dr. Phillips and send him in to see Will. For the moment, though, I suggest we just listen to what he has to say. Concussions can create odd states and the chances are that he will come out of it."

"When?"

"I wish I could tell you that, Mrs. Bradford."

The family took turns sitting by Will's bedside. "Go and eat, Rebecca."

"I'm not hungry. I don't want to lose Will. He's my brother, after all." Tears filled her eyes.

"Come on," said her mother. "I'll go with you."

Her father stood up. "We'll both go with you. Will needs his sleep right now."

An African-American doctor walked into the room just as Will woke up. "Hi, I'm Dr. Phillips."

Will looked at the man and smiled. "You made it! I'm so glad you're free. I remember you from the Pike."

"Do you?"

"Yes, I guess that was the good that came out of this war. You and your family were freed."

"That certainly was a good thing. I don't think my ancestors enjoyed being slaves."

"Did you get to see Lincoln?"

The doctor was quiet. "No, Will, I have never seen Abraham Lincoln. He died a long time ago."

"But you and your family were heading to Washington back in . . . " Will thought for a moment. "I think that was in 1862, but I'm not sure."

"Do you know what year it is now?"

"I think it's 1865 because Robert E. Lee just surrendered, but, if it's 1865, why are my parents and Rebecca here?" Will started to get agitated. "What's going on? What happened to me?"

"You hit your head when you fell off a horse."

"That must have happened on the trip back from Appomattox."

"Who is the President now, Will?"

"Well, if it was before the Surrender, I would say either Abraham Lincoln or Jefferson Davis, depending whether you lived in the North or in the South. After the Surrender, it was Abraham Lincoln."

"And now? Who is the President now?"

"That's a tough question. It's probably Abraham Lincoln, but I'm not sure. What year is this anyway?"

"What do you think?"

"I don't know. Why is that? Is something wrong with me?"

"You are probably feeling the effects of the concussion you sustained from your fall. Don't worry, you will be fine, but now you need to rest."

Will agreed and promptly fell asleep again.

When Will awoke next, he found Rebecca in his room. "Hey, what are you doing here?"

"I'm visiting you."

"Where exactly am I?"

"This is a hospital. You . . . "

"Oh, yeah, the doctor said I fell off a horse. Wonder if it was Peaches?"

"Who is Peaches?"

"He's the horse I found on the Valley Pike when I rescued Charles."

Rebecca started to ask who Charles was, but then remembered that the doctor told them to let Will do the talking and not excite him. She guessed that the rescue of Charles might be too exciting for him, so she said nothing.

"Do you know Charles," Will asked.

"No."

"He was very nice. He's from Connecticut, too . . . Danbury. Did you know that General Sedgwick was from Cornwall, Connecticut?"

Rebecca shook her head.

"His men called him Uncle John. I did too."

There was a knock on the door. A petite girl wearing a beige skirt and a green tee shirt stood at the entrance to the room. "I'm Maya," she told Rebecca. "I was in Will's class and I heard about his fall so I thought I would come to cheer him up."

Will said nothing.

"Are you forgetting your manners, Will," reminded his sister.

"Since you are here," Will grumbled, "I guess you better come in."

"I brought you a present."

"Thank you," he said grudgingly as she gave him a wrapped package. He put it aside.

"Aren't you going to open it?"

"Later," Will answered. "I'm kind of tired right now."

Rebecca took charge. "Will needs a lot of sleep. Let's go and you can come back another time."

Will yawned ostentatiously.

"Bye, Will," Maya said, "I hope you feel better soon."

Rebecca winked at him. Will frowned. Now that Maya had left, he didn't feel so tired. Dr. Phillips came in and motioned for Rebecca to leave, too. "Why don't doctors or nurses ever knock," Will wondered.

"So, Will, how are you feeling today?"

"Tired."

That answer worked better with Maya. The doctor didn't take the hint that Will wanted to be alone and showed no signs of leaving. In fact, he sat down and leaned back in the chair. "Beautiful day outside today. Do you know what day it is?"

"How could I? I am stuck here in this hospital."

"How about guessing? Let's start with the year. Do you know the year?"

"I told you it was 1865 because Robert E. Lee surrendered yesterday." Will stopped. Maya had just come to visit him. She wasn't at the Surrender.

"Will? You look as if you just thought of something. Would you like to share it with me?"

"I was just . . . . Someone from school came here to visit me. She was in my Social Studies class and I know she wasn't at the Surrender. Now, how can that be?"

"What do you think?"

"I don't know. I wish the Mitchells came instead. Or Joanna."

"Who are they?"

"The Mitchells, of course, were the family I stayed with in the Shenandoah Valley."

"And Joanna? Who was she?"

"She was a friend at Gettysburg. I always thought we could have become really good friends, but I had to leave."

469

"Why?"

"I needed to help out on the battlefield. You of all people should know about that."

"Really? Why me?"

"Well, you're a doctor and you know how important it is to save lives and help people get better. I put tourniquets on and stopped bleeding at Gettysburg and I think at New Market, but I'm not sure. I fought there, you know," he added conversationally.

"Where?"

"New Market. I was always afraid that I was a coward. Mean kids used to pick on me. But then there was New Market and I fought and I didn't run."

"How did New Market make you feel?"

"Proud of myself. But I also felt sad. A lot of cadets died and some of them were my friends. Say, why are you here? I thought you were going to see Abraham Lincoln?"

"We'll talk again, Will. Go and rest now."

The doctor left the room and Will closed his eyes.

"Doctor Phillips, how is he," asked Will's parents as soon as he came out of the room.

"First of all, the MRI was normal so that's very good news. Secondly, Maya's visit brought a touch of reality to Will so that's also good."

"When can he come home, Doctor?"

Dr. Phillips smiled. "I don't think we can release him until he stops talking about the Civil War. Even though what he says is very interesting, I think I will be happier when he orients to the present time."

"When will that be," asked Will's father.

"Soon, I hope. We have to wait and see."

That evening Will couldn't sleep. He tossed and turned and kept thinking about the War and all he had witnessed. Suddenly he realized that all these doctors and nurses and even his parents and Rebecca just wanted him to forget the War. They might even be keeping him here because of the War. "Doesn't seem as if it's over," he said aloud.

"What's not over," asked Dr. Phillips who had stopped by Will's room before going home.

"The Civil War."

"What do you mean?"

"Everyone wants me to stop talking about the Civil War. Be honest. Admit that you, too, want me to shut up."

"Well, I wouldn't put it like that, but I will admit that I would like you to live here and now instead of in the 1860s."

"Why? Give me one good reason."

"It's reality. You do live here."

Will was quiet. This is it . . . the moment that decides whether I go home or stay here in the hospital. "And if I say I live here, what do I think about the Shenandoah Valley in the War? And what do I think about the Mitchells and Big Red and all the other people I met?"

"I can't answer that. What you think about them is up to you."

"Well, then, I'll say goodnight."

"Goodnight, Will."

Will slept soundly and woke up when a nurse came into his room.

"Good morning. How are you feeling today?"

"Fine, but I wish you would come a little later so I could sleep."

Later, when Dr. Phillips walked in, Will immediately complained. "If I ran a hospital I would let patients sleep late so they would get better faster. Didn't you ever hear that patients need their rest?"

The doctor smiled. "I always like to hear my patients complain."

"Why?"

"That usually means they are getting better. So, Will, where are you right now?"

Will was ready. "Litchfield, Connecticut."

"And what century is this?"

"That's easy. It's the 21st century."

"Well, well, well . . . I don't think I need to ask you anything else except what do you think about the Civil War?"

"I think people are still fighting." Will saw the frown on the doctor's forehead and quickly added, "No, I don't mean they are really fighting now. I just mean they are still angry. As awful as things are, still, you have to learn to forgive."

"Why," asked the doctor.

"Two people I once knew told me that if we can't forgive others, then we can't expect God or anyone else to forgive us. But there's another reason, too."

"What's that?"

"So that we can move on."

"Well, I believe we can now safely say that you will be moving on."

"When?"

"Just as soon as we can get you ready."

"I'm ready now."

"Good. Let's call your parents in and tell them the good news."

Will quickly put on his shirt and pants, hoping his parents and Rebecca would remember to knock. "What's that bulge in your pocket," Rebecca asked as soon as she entered the room.

Will reached into his pants pocket.

Folded neatly was a small Confederate flag. He opened it and looked at it very closely. He found the tiny initials Mrs. Pritchard had carefully sewn.

Something else fell out. It was a dusty and faded Union pass, once signed by General Pellam. He put the flag and the pass together.

"It's time to leave," he said to his family. And he smiled.

The End